The Buddha's Bone

First published in 2021 by Leilanie Stewart

The Buddha's Bone Copyright © 2021 Leilanie Stewart

ISBN: 9781739952303

Thank you for supporting independent publishing.

Website: www.leilaniestewart.com
F: facebook.com/leilaniestewartauthor
Twitter: @leilaniestewart
Instagram: @leilaniestewartauthor

The Buddha's Bone

Leilanie Stewart

CYCLE 1: DEATH

1

cs

Twenty-four hour Nirvana

We were four *gaijins, aliens,* lost in Dotonbori. Osaka
spread out in front of us, a neon network in the black
of night. I yawned, out of tiredness and a need to pop
my ear; it had been crackling since the thirteen hour
flight from Heathrow. It didn't pop. I still had my
flight socks on. I needed a shower. I needed to feel
human, but didn't; I was in a zombie-state.

Was this culture shock? I had no basis for
comparison. This was a new adventure. I had signed a
teaching contract for a language school, Voyce, in
Japan; a foreign country. No; it was me, who was the
foreigner here, not Japan. The stamp in my passport
and blank form of alien registration proved it. Maybe
it was a moment of madness when I had applied for
the post, but as the saying went, a puppy wasn't just
for Christmas. I wouldn't be one of those teachers,
like the rep at the airport had warned me, who was on
the first flight home once reality had sunk in that I
had committed myself to a year in a country where I
didn't speak the language.

I wasn't even a teacher; I had never taught
anything in my life. What about my companions?
They were absorbing the evening sights in Osaka in
wonder as I was, none of us talking. I didn't even
know them; we had been stashed in the same hotel
for the night and would be leaving for different parts

of Japan in the morning. Four strangers forced into temporary companionship through mutual bewilderment. I could feel a poem coming on:

Four lost souls,
Forced into friendship
For a night, comradery,
Under the cloak of darkness,
Only to become strangers again
Come daylight.

If only I'd brought my green book, my poetry journal out with me. A writer should never be caught out without paper and pen. I caught myself; I wasn't a writer. Nor a teacher. Nope, just Kimberly Thatcher, a wannabe adventurer.

"Is anyone else ravenous?" said James, the Australian bloke.

"We could get street food. I know this great takoyaki stand in America-mura that I found backpacking last year," said Brodie, the long-haired American guy.

"Mm, I'd prefer somewhere we can sit," said Hong, the London-born Chinese girl.

"I'm with Hong. Honestly I'm more parched than hungry, but sitting sounds good," I said.

Brodie steered us out of Dotonbori onto the main drag of Namba. I was grateful to have a guide; someone who knew even a bit about Japan. I had no ideas. Small groups of young Japanese people passed us; friends ready for a night out in Dotonbori. They didn't pay much heed to us four travellers; whether because of the blanket of darkness, or because they were used to foreigners, wasn't clear. We must have looked an odd quartet: James was of average height, stocky and looked of Maori-descent – his name was an incongruous fit for his appearance. Brodie on the other hand fit what I imagined a 'Brodie' to be: tall and lean with a California-tan and shoulder-length blonde hair swept back in a ponytail – he was more surfer than teacher to my eyes. Hong was petite with long, black hair and glasses, ethnically Chinese but entirely a Londoner. Hong had been on the same flight as me from Heathrow. And me? Gangly and blonde, a Londoner too.

As we turned off the main road, modern glass-fronted buildings gave way to traditional wooden-panelled ones. Rows of red lanterns with Chinese letters painted on them hung from their rooftops. An image of old-world Japan came to mind, with graceful geishas on the arms of dashing gentlemen in top hats, a bygone era of glamour and zen-like repose.

"What does the writing say?" I directed my question at Brodie, our expert.

Brodie shrugged. "Advertisements for Asahi beer, apparently. These are Izakayas, traditional Japanese pubs."

My romanticised image of glamourous Edwardian Japan had evaporated. I was kidding myself anyway; I'd formed it from watching *Memoirs of a Geisha*. What did I know about Japan?

I returned Brodie's shrug. "Pub grub is pub grub. I could go for a beer, if anyone else is up for it?"

"Lead the way," said Hong, ushering me in.

The interior of the Izakaya was wooden too. There was a large table in the middle of the room with eight chairs around it and along the sides of the room were private booths with curtains drawn to each side. The booths had raised platforms and *tatami* flooring, Japanese grass carpeting. Each booth had low-set tables with no seats; clearly this was for more traditional dining where the customers kneeled or sat cross-legged. I didn't fancy it, not with my lactic-acid-filled-flight-sock-entombed legs.

We sat at the big middle table, James facing me with Hong next to him, and Brodie beside me. A waitress came over, with three menus. She bowed and said a short greeting in Japanese that I didn't understand. James passed the menus around as the waitress left.

"Oh, you've got to be kidding me," said Hong, her menu spread before her.

I looked at my own menu. The entire thing had Chinese characters; no English at all, or even any pictures.

"Any of you guys speak Japanese?" said James.

I shook my head. "I took weekly night classes once I found out I had this job," I said. "But I'd only gotten through introductions, numbers and some emergency phrases in the six weeks before I had to leave."

"I know a few travel phrases, but that's all," said Brodie.

Hong shrugged. "Well, that was the whole angle of Voyce as a company though, wasn't it? They specifically wanted to hire teachers who couldn't speak Japanese to create an English bubble in each school for the students."

I thought back to the advertisement I'd applied for in the local newspaper: a white male English teacher, a Japanese man and Japanese woman in business attire sitting around a desk with English textbooks on the table. Bullet-points underneath: *Teach English in Japan for a year; groups of friends can apply together; no*

Japanese required in our home-from-home schools; we'll sponsor your visa; we'll arrange your flight; we'll pair you with a like-minded flat-mate in our pre-arranged accommodation; we'll pay you an excellent monthly salary; and the catch? All you need to have is a degree in any subject, a willingness to commit to a one-year contract and a readiness to undertake our intensive teacher-training course. Ready to apply? Contact our Head Office at Voyce, London today!

The waitress came back. She spoke in a flurry of Japanese.

"I'm sorry, I wish I could speak more Japanese," I said. "I hate to ask this, but do you know any English?"

The waitress waved her hands in an apologetic gesture and bowed again.

"Well, deductive reasoning," said James, "She must be asking us what we want to drink, right?"

"Yeah, I guess so. I didn't catch a word of that," said Hong.

I looked at the waitress, eager to take our order. "I'll have a glass of water, please."

The waitress gave another Japanese speech, even faster, even more flustered with another bow and an embarrassed giggle.

"Erm, waw-terr, you know? Waw-terr," I said. I brought my right hand to my lips and cupped it around an invisible glass. I held my left hand below the invisible glass and pretended to sip, making a slurping sound. "Come on, Brodie, help me out – do you know restaurant phrases?"

Brodie flushed. "Er…water-oh-yawn-could-ah-sigh." He held up four fingers.

The waitress bowed, smiled and left. Hong slapped her hand against her forehead. James closed his eyes and massaged his face.

"I'm getting myself a Japanese teacher once I'm in Nagoya, that's it," said Hong. The waitress returned with four small tumblers of a brownish liquid. I looked at the others; Brodie took a swig and smacked his lips with satisfaction.

What was it? I sniffed, then sipped from my own glass. A bitter taste met my lips; cold tea. Not green tea, as I might have expected, but a strong woody flavour, to my unrefined palate. I gulped it all down in one go then winced.

"Does water mean tea in Japanese?" Hopefully my face didn't betray my displeasure; I really didn't want to look like an uncultured barbarian on my first night in Japan.

"Water means water," Brodie said, his face flushed. "Sorry dudes. I didn't know the word in Japanese."

"Well, it won't kill us. Thanks for trying," I said, hoping it would appease him. Poor Brodie; at least he'd made an effort. "I think I'll be getting myself a Japanese tutor too, once I get settled in. I know Voyce wanted teachers who don't speak Japanese, but I really wish I'd crammed in more night classes in London before I'd come here."

Heat crept into my face as I realised the waitress was still standing there, waiting with a smile to take our order. How rude must she have thought me? I was an ignorant foreigner who should have made more effort to learn the language. But hold on; the waitress couldn't understand English. Thank goodness; I had been absolved of my ignorance, just this once.

"What should we order?" said James, an uncertainty to his voice.

Hong laid her menu down in the manner of someone about to pore over a detailed set of instructions. "Let's see here. Some of the characters are similar to Chinese, so maybe I can try ordering. This one looks like soup. Shall we try that?"

"That sounds great. Anything but tea," Brodie joked. He pointed to the Chinese character that Hong indicated on his own menu and said, "Yawn."

Yon, meaning four in Japanese. I smiled to myself, happy that I knew something.

The waitress said, in English, "Fish?"

Hong shook her head. "No, not fish, we want soup."

"Fry?" said the waitress. "Fish?"

What was the waitress on about? I cupped my hand and gestured with two fingers to suggest a spoon scooping soup. "Can we have soup, please?"

"Fry?" asked the waitress. "Four?"

"Wait a minute, is fry the word for soup?" James asked the waitress. "Yes, fry please. Four of them. Er...fry oh yawn could ah sigh."

The waitress smiled and bowed. Then she went through a hanging curtain into the kitchen.

"What does yawn could ah sigh, mean?" I asked Brodie.

"Yon is the number four. Kudasai means please," he explained.

A fresh new heatwave assaulted my face. "I really should have known kudasai from my Japanese night classes in London."

"Don't worry about it. You'll be an expert before the year is over," he said, giving my shoulder a reassuring pat.

"A year in Japan, can you imagine?" said James, a glazed look in his eyes.

"So, why did you all decide to come and be teachers here?" said Brodie.

Hong smiled. "I'm a huge Manga and Anime fan, so I thought I'd learn more about my favourite comics while I'm out here. Have you heard about *Otaku*? Anime geeks, that's me."

"That's cool," said Brodie, though he didn't sound particularly interested as he rounded on me. "What about you, Kimberly?"

I paused, gathering my thoughts. Where to start? Normally I wasn't one to share my feelings, but these were three strangers, who I probably wouldn't see again after the following day. The Clinical Psychologist in me saw a golden opportunity: use my three new-found companions as an evening of free therapy. Or, at the very least, to get the truth off my chest.

"To be honest, it was a last minute decision." I looked at Hong. "I'm not a Manga Otaku, nor did I backpack around Japan for a few months like you did, Brodie. I hadn't thought of Japan until I saw the ad in the local paper looking for teachers. Last year I finished my Masters Degree in Clinical Psychology and I'd just started working as a trainee in a private practice, but I wasn't sure I wanted to stay there – I really want to work in a hospital, but there were no job openings at the time."

I lifted my glass and tried to take a sip before realising I'd drank all my tea when the empty rim hit my lips. My throat was dry; I was entering painful territory in my anecdote.

"I need time to think about my career direction and then to top it off, things haven't been going well with my boyfriend. We've been together for about seven years, and we shared a flat in Camden, but he has quite a negative outlook on things – it's just the way he is – but lately it's been getting me down." I shrugged.

"So, you came out here to escape from him?" said Brodie.

I studied Brodie's face. He didn't know me, but he knew so much about me.

I shrugged again. "I guess you could say that. Japan is as far away from London as you can get, isn't it? It's the fresh start I need to think about things."

"That's cool," said Brodie again; the same phrase he had used as a response to Hong, though this time his tone showed me the sentiment was true. "What about you, James?"

James cocked his head in an off-handed way. "Bit similar to Kimberly really, to get my head straight after my relationship went sour. My ex-fiancée back in Tasmania is Japanese. Even though we split, I got interested enough in the culture by then. So here I am." He cast his eyes down at his empty glass, the hint obvious that he didn't want to keep talking.

"Sorry to hear that, man." Brodie's mouth turned downwards in sympathy. "But there are plenty of fish in the sea. And speaking of – looks like the waitress brought us all battered cod!"

The waitress came back with a tray. She gave us all a hot towel each. Hong wiped her hands and set it on the table. Brodie wiped his face and neck with it and I did the same. The hot, wet flannel was a sufficient substitute for a shower; the recycled air on the flight had done my skin no favours. I set the flannel down in an untamed heap only to see the waitress fighting to suppress her bemusement as she served our food. Instead of soup, there were four plates of battered fish in front of each of us, with head, tail and eyes intact and a set of wooden chopsticks for each person, in a paper sleeve.

When the waitress left, I turned to Brodie. "Did I do something wrong with the flannel?"

"Not necessarily wrong, it's just an unwritten rule that only men in Japan wipe their faces with oshiboris. Women are considered too dainty and polite for such things."

"What about uncultured cavewomen?" My joke hid my real feelings; I didn't want to stand out like a sore thumb. How had I missed the part about *oshiboris* in my culinary etiquette guide to Japan? As if being a lanky, pale blonde didn't make me stand out badly enough as it was. I slid a sideways glance at Hong's *oshibori*, which was neatly folded in half and laid in front of her. I folded my own into a quarter and placed it delicately in front of me. "I'll pass for Princess Sen one of these days."

I slid my wooden chopsticks out of the paper sleeve. "Brodie, can you call the waitress back? My chopsticks are faulty – they're still stuck together."

Brodie snapped his chopsticks apart and held them out to me. "You're supposed to break them apart. They're disposable."

I squeezed mine between index finger and thumb and pulled them apart as though snapping a wishbone. The wood broke unevenly; I peeled away a large splinter and set it next to my folded oshibori. I held both chopsticks in my right hand as I would hold a pencil and looked at the battered fish in front of me.

"How do I cut with these?" I regretted speaking straightaway; the more I talked, the stupider I made myself look to my companions. Probably everyone else was *thinking* what I was saying, but nobody was foolish enough to voice it.

Nope, wrong again; Hong apparently knew what to do. She manoeuvred her chopsticks deftly between index finger and thumb, working the fish into bite-sized chunks. "Fish is one of the harder foods, like rice and eggs, but you'll get the hang of it with practise. My parents are originally from Hong Kong, so we eat with chopsticks back home, but Chinese ones are longer."

I had eaten sushi before at Wagamama in London, but California rolls were already in small, bitesize chunks. This was a whole fish, one intact, inaccessible meal. I took one chopstick in my left hand and one in the right like a knife and fork. My cheeks burned as I held the fish with the left chopstick and sawed with the right chopstick.

James wasn't doing much better than me. He tried to lift a chunk of fish in a pincer grasp between the tips of his chopsticks and dropped half his fish on the floor.

Before I could control myself a giggle burst out of my mouth. "Oh my gosh, I'm so sorry." I grabbed my oshibori and covered my mouth.

I always laughed when I was nervous, or insecure. It was almost like a defence mechanism, a form of self-protection. I had to hide the real, culturally inept person under the savvy Londoner-exterior. Inside though, I wanted to melt. I didn't know the language, or culture, or even how to eat with chopsticks. Bet a Japanese four year old could eat with chopsticks. There I sat, a great, big, stupid toddler learning everything fresh.

So be it: I was a fully grown toddler. I put both chopsticks back in my right hand and scooped like a spoon, using my left index finger to push a piece of fish onto them. It worked. Thank goodness I wasn't the worst in our party to manoeuvre chopsticks: after casting a sheepish glance to check that the waitress was gone, James set his chopsticks down and ate with his fingers. Brodie was only a notch more skilled than I was, his fingers battling over the chopsticks like spiders on an ice-rink. Only Hong manoeuvred hers with dainty expertise.

The fish was crispy on the outside and tender inside with a deep, flavoursome flesh. It was a wonderful meal, the intimacy of our inadequacy at Japanese culinary etiquette compounded by our solitude in the middle of the izakaya.

***

Late night Osaka on a Thursday night was thriving. We walked through a lively arcade in Shinsaibashi, full of casinos with row upon row of slot machines. Young people rode through the mall on bicycles. Groups of teenagers loitered listening to Japanese rock, the boys wearing helmets to practise spinning on their heads. They were no different than kids chilling in Camden, yet back in London, there was an edge. Here, everything seemed safe and inviting, not intimidating. Even the men in dark suits standing in entranceways gave off a friendly air. All of them had their hair dyed either blonde or red and had their eyebrows immaculately plucked. As we approached them, the men smiled and called out to us in Japanese.

"They want you, Kimberly," Brodie laughed.

"Me?" I looked again; the men *did* seem to be fixated on me. "I hardly look like I'm ready for a bender, clubbing is the *last* thing on my mind, trust me. I'm ready for my scratcher."

"They aren't club promoters," said Brodie.

Come to think of it, there wasn't any pumping dance music resonating out. "Then what are they, gangsters?" Could they be Yakuza? I'd heard about the Japanese mafia, but had always pictured muscular, tattooed men. These guys were all young and slender, shaved metrosexuals; delicate mimbos.

"They're hosts," Brodie went on. "Basically entertainers. They'll sing karaoke to you, sit with you and laugh at your jokes, tell you you're the most fantastic woman in the world."

"Only women?" I said.

"Yeah, mostly lonely women who want company, or to be flattered. Maybe even a smooch if the host is up for it." Brodie gave a boyish smirk. "There are hostesses too at bars for men, and even a few ladyboy hostess ones for gay men."

"Good to know Japan is so liberal, I had no idea."

"Liberal is one way of putting it. If the price is right, and the company good, some hosts or hostesses will even go home for the night with a customer."

Prostitutes. One of the hosts stepped out in my path and made an inviting sweep of his arm as though to usher me towards his bar.

"I suppose I should be offended, but actually I'm glad you're getting all the attention." Hong forced a laugh.

I didn't answer; my thoughts made me uncomfortable. Was it because of my blonde hair? My mum had warned me about the Japanese fascination with white women, especially with blonde or ginger hair. Did Hong look Japanese to them, and therefore not a curiosity like I was? No, my mind wouldn't let me entertain such a thought. Japan was Buddhist for crying out loud, enlightened. Japanese people surely didn't objectify a person over looks or ethnicity. I cast an eye over Hong; she looked a stereotypical nerd with her glasses and mini leather backpack. Could it be that Hong looked too erudite to venture into a host bar, whereas I, in my denim casuals, looked 'up for it'? Yes. That had to be it.

I had to be Zen. My goal was to have no expectations, to bypass culture shock by reaching a meditative state, to truly absorb myself in Japanese culture. This would be the only way to perceive the true nature of daily life in Japan.

Had I made a good start? Yes. In twenty-four hours, I had braved my new Asian adventure alone, battled insomnia, unburdened myself of my rush to leave London, brushed aside jetlag and for now, beckoned forth a Nirvana of sorts. I was at peace.

2

 C8

Bentos and Buses

It was the last leg of my journey from plane to hotel and now to coach. Voyce, my new employer, had sponsored my visa, provided my discounted one-way ticket on Japan Airlines and had paid for my transport from Osaka to the town where I would spend the next year: Tottori. I twirled the ticket over and over between my fingers as I waited at Namba bus station.

The coach arrived five minutes before it was due to leave. The driver helped load my suitcase into the baggage compartment, checked my ticket and ushered me on board with a smile. The seats were spacious, each one covered by what looked like a white doily. As the second person to get on board, I had my pick of places to sit. I sat at the front behind the driver and opened the breakfast that I'd picked up from a *konbini* convenience store after I'd checked out of the Dotonbori Hotel. It was a bento box; a plastic container divided into four parts. One had rice, one had pickled vegetables, one had what looked like a hash brown, and the last one had green beans. I popped one of the green beans in my mouth, chewed it and spat it out in my hand. It was tough and fibrous, not soft like green beans back home.

A middle-aged Japanese businessman stopped in the aisle next to my seat and spoke to me in slow, curt Japanese. It was obvious he was speaking clearly for my benefit as his manner was friendly, yet the words were lost on me.

I looked at the chewed beans in my hand. "Sorry, I didn't mean to be so rude. I'm not used to Japanese food."

The man showed me his ticket with the number 3a and pointed above me to the seat numbers indicated on the baggage compartment overhead: 3a and b.

"Oh, I see. I didn't know it was a reserved seat."

I grabbed my handbag and bento box. The man stepped aside to let me squeeze into the aisle. He gestured to seats further back and gave an accompanying explanation in politely-spoken Japanese. It fell on ignorant ears. I would have to figure out which seats were reserved or non-reserved all by my disconcerted self.

There were only three other people on the coach and all were seated from middle to front. Guessing it was a safe bet to sit near the back, I grabbed a seat and resumed my breakfast. The hash brown looked more appetising than the beans and the rice at least offered much needed stodge, but it was too early in the morning for disposable chopsticks after the fiasco of last night's fish. Besides, I didn't want to risk another faux pas; putting chopsticks vertically into a bowl of rice was a Buddhist symbol of death. What about a ready meal bento box? I snuck a glance along the aisle towards the front of the bus. Nobody paid me any heed. So be it: fingers it was.

As I ate, tall buildings with billboard ads for beer and hotels changed to motorways leading into suburban spreads and winding roads taking me past small villages. The houses looked like the traditional wooden ones in *The Last Samurai*. I had my first glimpse of rice fields scattered in between, worked by hunched, elderly men and women. Urban grey gave way to green woodland as the coach climbed winding roads into the mountains. My hash brown turned out to be fish. Fish for dinner, fish for breakfast. A diet of fish and rice; no wonder Japanese people were all so slim. I was familiar with sushi from the many conveyor belt restaurants in London, but battered, sweetened, cold fish cakes were new to my unseasoned palate. Still, hunger was the best medicine; I devoured it with good appetite. Would such traditional food be my only option in Tottori? I had never been a fan of McDonald's but I had a sudden craving for a McMuffin and coke.

Fish. Cold fish, more like it. Truth be told, I was nervous with anticipation. How long would it take to reach Tottori? Thankfully it was the last stop for the coach, so I didn't have to worry about getting off too early or late. They'd told me back in Namba that I'd be picked up when I got to the bus station in Tottori. I wasn't worried about not being recognised. I was pretty sure I'd be the only blonde, white girl at the station, considering it was a rural town.

The mountains closed out the sun. The clouds obscured the mountain. There were green rice fields in between. The only thing missing from my imagination was mist skirting the tops of the distant mountains like in a Hokusai painting.

I pressed my face against the window and cupped my hands around my forehead to close out the bus and its passengers. I had captured my own private corner of the world now, a perfect solitude for me alone to enjoy. The clouds obscured the mountain and jetlag obscured my head. My head was foggy.

Fish and fry and fish and fog and fish. Sleep and a good McDonalds breakfast would fix it. Did Tottori have a McDonalds? I'd be screwed if there wasn't any Western food at all. A year on a diet of fish and rice would whittle my size ten frame away to nothing.

The bus passed through a valley and in the distance I saw sea. The Sea of Japan, vast and serene, an azure expanse and Tottori lay along its coastline. Maybe being sent to a town by the beach was a blessing in disguise; my first preference had been Osaka, but as a sun worshipper, living by the coast had its perks. The thought of being landlocked by mountains had started to get a bit claustrophobic, but a coastal escape restored my sense of zen-like equilibrium. After darkness came light.

I watched Tottori grow closer, the cluster of grey dots on a flat plain by the sea becoming visible roads and buildings. Civilisation. Even if they didn't speak English, I needed to know humanity lay ahead after three hours of fields, forests and mountains on the journey from Osaka. The road signs had Chinese symbols and English letters. Bilingual notices gave me comfort; familiarity in the face of the unknown.

On the outskirts of Tottori, scattered houses in between rice fields and the odd petrol station gave way to hotels, office blocks and a supermarket that looked much like Tesco back in England. Jusco. The name even sounded Western. Maybe I could settle in a place like this after all.

The traffic began to build as the bus turned into a large terminal in front of Tottori train station. I got off the bus last to find that the driver had already unloaded my suitcase. The other passengers walked with purpose this way and that way. An urge to scream: come back, don't leave me, struck me. I was afraid to be alone, naked without a phone, dumb without words, cowering behind my suitcase and bag on the walkway.

Where was I even supposed to be picked up? I looked again at my orientation sheet, given by the Voyce rep at Kansai Airport. Tottori station. Did that mean bus or train?

"Hello there - Kimberly?"

English. I spun round to see a thirty-something white man with a black, bushy beard, bald head and glasses. He spoke with an American accent. Or Canadian; I wasn't the best at accents.

"Hi, I'm Ben. My car's over there."

I let go of my suitcase handle and shook his hand. "Good to meet you, Ben."

He took my suitcase and wheeled it over to a white car with Chinese symbols and numbers on its license plate. All the cars had Chinese symbols. Of course they did; it was Japan.

I was in Japan and this was my new life.

"Thank you – it's been hard lugging this all the way from Osaka," I said. "It was hard trying to decide what to bring for a year, so I emptied my wardrobe."

"If you think this is bad, you should see what your roommate brought – Americans are allowed sixty kilos. I think she brought everything but the kitchen sink." Ben loaded my suitcase and bag into the boot of his car, one side of his mouth raised in a half-smile.

"Sixty kilos? I thought twenty-five was bad enough. They almost didn't let me on at Heathrow – I had to tell them I was going for a year."

I got into Ben's car; the passenger side was on the left, same as in the UK. We pulled away from the station and into the throng of Tottori.

"How was your flight, anyway?"

"Not too bad. Bit of a nosebleed from the pressure but otherwise fine."

"Did they put you in the Dotonbori last night?"

I nodded. "It was lovely. I'll never get over the heated toilet seat and bidet, so civilised."

"Just wait until you come across the ones that activate with birdsong when you sit down, to hide the sound of you peeing."

"Hah! That's great. Japan certainly has everything covered, proper space-age."

Yet Tottori didn't look space-age; the restaurants and department stores were all normal concrete and glass buildings. Grey buildings, grey mountains, grey sky...grey mind. I was drowning with jetlag, too brain-frazzled to take it all in. I forced senility from my head: first impressions of differences between England and Japan? Tottori had lots of overhead telephone cables, much more than London. A further analysis? Not needed. This was my hometown now, I had a year to figure it all out.

"How long have you been out here, Ben?"

"Coming up to two years. I'd been thinking about going back to Alberta, but then I got married."

"Oh, that's nice. Is your wife Canadian too?"

"No, she's a local. She used to work at reception in our school. She's keen to live in Canada, but we're settled here."

"Aww, how romantic. Though I don't think the boss would be too happy if you not only quit, but take one of the Japanese staff with you."

Ben smiled. "Actually, I *am* the boss."

My cheeks burned. "Oh my gosh, sorry, just a joke."

"It's okay. We're pretty informal out here. It's a small school, you'll enjoy it."

Faux pas. What a first impression; inadvertently insulting the boss before I had even started the job. I saw my glowing cheeks in the passenger mirror: burning red cheeks shining out through the grey of Tottori like a beacon of embarrassment. I almost laughed at my own sleep-deprived musings. Did Ben mean what he said? Were they informal at the Tottori branch of Voyce? I hoped so; I really could put my foot right in it at times.

"You tired?" he said.

"Fuzzy-headed, but I'll be okay. It all feels surreal. I don't know if it's just the lack of sleep or that it's all been so fast, but it feels kind of like a dream in a way. Do you know what I mean?"

Ben nodded. "Yep. The jetlag will last a week but, trust me, the culture shock takes at least six months to get over."

"Six months?" I shook my head. "I suppose everything is so different, it's like starting from scratch. I thought I was getting sent to Osaka – I mean, I picked Osaka as my first choice cause I thought it would be similar to London. I guess it probably is, at least in size."

"One of our teachers went back to New Zealand early to get married, so we had an opening. I'm just glad we got you. We were waiting for six weeks. Your new roommate was getting stir crazy without anyone to talk to."

"Tottori looks a manageable size though. I'm sure it won't take that long to get used to."

"It's great if you like winter sports. The snow gets thigh deep in January and February."

"Is there much nightlife?"

"There are some decent restaurants and a few snack bars in Yayoicho, the nightlife district near Tottori station."

"Are snack bars those host clubs? I saw a few hosts in Shinsaibashi."

"Not always, though Tottori does have one or two hostess bars with mainly Filipino and Thai workers."

We passed a residential area, where the traditional wooden houses had sloping rooftops like pagodas. "It's hard to imagine hostess bars in somewhere as quaint as Tottori."

"They're not all sleazy," said Ben. "You get some really upmarket ones in Tokyo or Osaka where they hire Western women, mainly with blonde hair like yours. Those women are treated more like models than hostesses."

A fresh heatwave assaulted my face. Was Ben referring to the colour of my hair, or making a statement about my relative attractiveness? An image of myself in a satin mini-dress and faux-fur wrap standing in front of a club trying to entice men in, like the hosts in Shinsaibashi, popped into my mind. I pictured myself laughing at a random, fat Japanese buisnessman's jokes, feeding him cake, making him feel he was a king. Could I do that?

"Do they get paid more than language teachers?"

"Probably our monthly salary in a week," said Ben.

"No amount of money is worth doing that sort of work though."

"One of the teachers at our branch, Nadia, used to work as a hostess in Tokyo. She's a trained ballet dancer," said Ben, matter-of-factly. "She did it for a few months and went back to Australia loaded."

I looked up at a passing billboard. A beautiful Japanese model advertised make-up, the brand, Kanebo, written in large English letters. "Well, the way I see it is, if Japanese women aren't keen on being hostesses, then it must be risky work. Being an English teacher is much more respectable."

"Japanese women work as hostesses too, but there are just more foreign women in that kind of work in Tottori than Japanese."

We passed a bowling alley with a huge pin on top before turning off the main drag. I was about to steer the conversation onto a less awkward one; after all, what sort of first impression was I giving my new boss, when Ben changed the topic. "See that convenience store on the corner? Remember where that is, because your flat is just behind it," he said. I noted the store with its blue neon sign reading 'Lawson' in English letters. "It has an international pay phone, in case you want to call your family. You can get calling cards there too."

We pulled up in front of a grey duplex with a rice field behind and vegetable gardens growing tomatoes and persimmons to either side. Ben parked and we got out. The building had a silver logo towards the top right.

"Villa Libido? Is that really the address?"

Ben gave a tight-lipped smile. "Yes. Japanese names can get," he paused, "A little strange at times."

"My mum will have a hernia when I tell her – she won't want to post anything to an address with that in the title," I laughed. Did Voyce approve of this building for its teachers?"

Ben reddened. "Actually, it was me who picked it. The name didn't occur to me until afterwards. I only thought of the close proximity to work at the time."

Second faux pas; I wanted to clap my hands over my face. "Of course, the distance is far more important. Good choice."

Ben carried my suitcase up a flight of stairs and I followed behind with my bag. He opened the door at the top of the stairs – flat two-oh-one – and nudged the door open with his foot.

"Here's your key." Ben handed a silver, oblong-shaped fob to me. "You have to turn it clockwise until the lock clicks open and counter-clockwise to lock it."

I put the key in the circular lock, pushed down until it clicked and turned the bolt to practise locking and unlocking it. Japan really did have the best technology, it wasn't just a stereotype. A complicated lock but a smooth action; at the very least it would save me from fumbling if I came home after a bender.

Ben led the way inside. A pair of large women's shoes, at least a size eight, were lined up next to a pair of pink cotton slippers near the front door.

"Did you know you have to take your shoes off inside Japanese houses?" Ben asked.

"But isn't my roommate a foreigner?"

Ben kicked his shoes off. "J.P likes to follow the rules – she's into all the Japanese customs."

I slipped my shoes off. "J.P? I thought her name was Joanna, or something?"

"Yeah, Joanna Patricia." Ben smirked. "But she spells it, J.e.i.p.i - Jei Pi. Your roommate's really *something else.*"

Something else. Something meant good, but *something else?* Didn't that mean bad? And what of Ben's knowing smirk? Jei Pi. Was she half Japanese? Why else would she spell her name in a Japanese-sounding way?

Ben set my suitcase down by the door and stepped inside in his socks. I set my bag down next to it and followed him inside, remembering to kick my trainers off next to his. The wooden floor was cold through my socks. "So, don't you take off your shoes at home? I mean, I thought your wife was Japanese?" I said.

"I take them off when she's around. But when she's out shopping, I put my feet up on the coffee table, shoes and all."

I smiled. Ben seemed nice, but she wondered about Jei Pi. I couldn't ignore the subtle, but sarcastic tone Ben used when he talked about my new flatmate. Was she a weirdo?

"That's Jei Pi's bedroom through the sliding door — it's Japanese style with tatami mats."

I peered in. The door was only half-shut, as though purposely meant for people to look in. The still-life snapshot through the gap showed Japanese word charts on the far wall and a poster of a Japanese boy-band. "What age is Joanna?"

"Twenty-five, same as you." Ben jerked a thumb towards the boy-band poster, following my gaze. "Smap are pretty popular over here — with the *girls.*"

Girls: again with the sarcasm. That was it. I was soon to be living with a half-Japanese, teenage giant with man-sized feet.

The living room was western style with a small, blue faux-leather two-seater sofa and TV. I noted the Japanese tub in the bathroom: about a metre long, but deep enough to submerge a person neck deep. I turned to the last door to be opened, right by the entrance way: my bedroom. It had a western style wooden door, not a sliding Japanese one. Good. It felt more private, a place I could retreat to. Inside I saw a western style wardrobe, a chest of drawers and in the corner, a folded-up mattress.

"Where's my bed?"

Ben pointed to the mattress. "That's your futon. You fold it out and sleep on the floor."

I opened my mouth, but didn't say anything.

"It's actually comfier than you'd think. The company sent you sheets and a duvet cover too – don't look so worried, you'll get used to it." He walked towards the door. "Jei Pi's on the early shift today, so she'll be home around six. Have you had anything to eat?"

"No, not since breakfast."

"Well, it's a bit early for dinner yet, but Lawson do some great hot food if you want a late lunch." Ben put his shoes on near the door. "Jei Pi said she'll take you out later to meet the rest of the teachers and have something to eat. I won't be able to come as I have to take care of my little girl while Jackie's at her mum's."

"Jackie? That's not Japanese-?"

"Chiaki, not Jackie. Don't worry, all the new teachers anglicise Japanese names – at first. Japanese people are even starting to do it themselves, for fun. But listen, chill out for a bit before Jei Pi comes home, she'll keep you busy enough later. I'll pick you up tomorrow at ten to show you around the school, alright?"

Ben winked and went out. My mind raced. This Jei Pi sounded a bit overbearing; hopefully I was wrong. But that aside, how could a Westerner come to Japan, to a totally different culture, and immerse himself so well that he was married and settled within two years? Could Ben's wife speak English? I hadn't got round to asking him if he spoke Japanese. And what about their little girl; did she speak English or Japanese?

What would it be like to marry a Japanese man? I imagined myself wearing a white kimono, like Lucy Liu in *Kill Bill*, inside a Buddhist temple on my wedding day next to – who? I didn't know any Japanese men. The businessman from the bus popped into my head and I wrinkled my nose: too old. One of the bleach-blonde hosts from Osaka filled his place. I snorted aloud at the thought: too effeminate. Jei Pi's poster of the Japanese boy-band, Smap, flitted into my mind. The tall, good-looking one, he would do. I pictured him standing next to me wearing a traditional kimono for men, a *hakama*, in black silk as a counterpart to my white *shiromuku* traditional kimono. Blonde and dark, white and black, yin and yang.

But then there was Carl. Carl snapped my musings back to reality.

I felt a pang of guilt. I hadn't given my boyfriend much thought since I'd arrived; apart from admitting to my companions in Osaka that our relationship had gone south. The lack of mobile phone didn't help. I pushed the thought of the attractive J-pop boy-band member out of my head and slotted Carl in next to me, in the temple, wearing the black silk hakama. Tall and pale with his brown hair and green eyes, the image in my head seemed incongruous; two gaijin had no place in at a Shinto shrine wearing traditional Japanese wedding clothes. My fantasy was ruined.

I unfolded my pristine futon and ripped the accompanying white fitted sheet out of its plastic wrapping. I would see Carl in eight weeks' time, for Christmas. We would go travelling to Tokyo together. Eight weeks wasn't long; fifty-six days.

What would Carl get up to in London for fifty-six days?

Wank, had been his curt answer, which he had later said was a joke.

Facts were facts; even men in relationships masturbated to relieve themselves. When that got boring, then what? I imagined Carl watching porn on the sofa in our flat back in Camden, or worse; going into a strip club in Soho. I looked around at my bare room with its white walls, white wardrobe and white futon and felt empty. No Carl, no home, no identity, no job. No. Wrong. I was a teacher and my apartment, in Villa Libido, with Jei Pi, was my address for the next year. My life wasn't so empty. It was a blank canvas, yes, but empty, no. Instead of relaxing, I would spend a few hours unpacking and making my room more lived-in and less clinical. A home to shelter me from the unknown.

Why was I there, on the other side of the world, in a little-known corner of Japan, where I had run to for some soul-searching, alone? I dragged my suitcase into my room, opened it and got down on my knees.

3

ᎧᏃ

Lava

Lava
Darkness and light
From distant poles
Morphed together
Only in a dream
Frozen in fear; my demons realised
Dehydrated lids closing over protein-washed stone
Heart stops – dare not exhale
Surely it's not true?
A tortured fantasy that only exists
Much deeper than epidermis would reveal
Subconscious writhing
In the twisting bonds of shadows of past
Time heals all, they say
For me, when beauty has gone;
Ash over flesh

I stopped writing. Poetry seemed a natural outlet for twenty-four hours of confusion stemming from my west to east travails. I hadn't written poems since finishing A-Level English seven years ago, but it seemed to come back naturally enough. The mind was willing, but the body was out of sync; damn pins and needles. Sitting cross-legged on a futon on the floor didn't come naturally. The living room sofa probably would have offered a more comfortable physical space but the thought of writing there left me emotionally impotent. I couldn't have a creative outlet among a stranger's personal effects; it made me feel like an intruder. This was my address, but not yet my home. I had decorated my room with photos of family and friends, had left my wardrobe door open so that I could see all my possessions, and had sprayed perfume on my unfamiliar bedding, but it wasn't home yet. Home was a space in my mind that would take time to seep into my surroundings.

Could I psychoanalyse my own poem? Probably better not to. Therapists and other similar professionals were never supposed to treat their own patients. What about oneself? Course, I wasn't yet a registered Psychologist. I had my Master's Degree in Clinical Psychology, with six months of trainee experience before quitting and leaving my boyfriend, and my home, and my old life behind.

Lava. It burned through my soul. Darkness and light: London and Tottori? Tottori and London? My mind and body, body and soul?

The swoosh of the front door opening jolted me from my musings. Shuffling and the sound of dropping shoes preceded a woman's voice, deep and unctuous.

"Ta-die-mah."

Japanese? I stood up and stumbled to the door, waking my numb legs.

Jei Pi had two inches on me in height at around five eight. Even under her oversized grey duffel coat and coils of purple woollen scarf, I could see that she was a large woman, a UK size sixteen, or eighteen at least. Tufts of wavy ginger hair stuck out from under her bobble hat, violet to match her eyes. Jei Pi greeted me with a huge grin, showing two rows of very even, bleached teeth.

"Tadaima means I'm home," said Jei Pi, managing to talk and keep her huge grin intact. "You have to say okaeri, for welcome back. That's the answer."

"Have to?" My derogatory tone made it a harder H than intended.

Her smile ebbed. "It's what people here say. It's just polite."

I almost mentioned that we weren't Japanese, but stopped myself from being rude before it slipped out.

Jei Pi flapped her hands. "Never mind, you'll get the hang of it." She stepped into her pink towelling slippers and traipsed past me. At the living room door, she turned back and jerked her thumb over her shoulder. "You coming, roomie? We got loads to catch-up on!"

I bristled; what was I, a dog being called by its master? The thought dissipated as Jei Pi jerked her head, a goofy grin on her face. Now she was the dog, eager and playful. Irritation became sympathy. How long had Ben said she had been waiting for a flat mate?

Jei Pi dumped her work bag on the kitchen table and uncoiled her purple scarf. I leaned against the kitchen doorway, my arms folded.

"Kimberly Thatcher," said Jei Pi. "When I got your information, I thought you sounded English before I even knew you were. I guessed you'd either look like Princess Diana, or a butch dyke librarian type. Donno why though. Go figure."

My mouth dropped open. I shut it without saying anything.

Jei Pi peeled her coat off and hurled it across at the sofa. "Have a seat. I don't bite." Jei Pi snorted. "Well, not always, anyways."

I plopped myself opposite Jei Pi at the kitchen table. Was Jei Pi for real? An image of a bouncing orange clown popped into my head, wide red smile and flashing white teeth, larger than life. I forced it out of my head and refocused myself to listen to my new flat mate.

"There's eight teachers at our branch. Nadia and Zoe are the other two chicas. Nadia's from Christ Church and Zoe's from Brisbane and then there's the guys: Ben, who you met, Vince from Arizona, Adrian from Sydney and Carter from Toronto. You'll meet them all tomorrow - I've invited them over. Did Ben tell you about your welcome party?"

"Em, he might have." I honestly couldn't recall.

"Well, I was gonna have them come round tonight, but I changed the plans."

Jei Pi was more considerate than she seemed. "That was nice of you."

Jei Pi didn't catch the sarcasm and smirked. "I know you're grateful, don't worry."

Hmph. Or maybe not.

"I haven't had a roomie for almost two months, I want you to myself for a while. I thought we could go for yakitori at Tsutaya, one of my favourite places, or we could get dinner from Lawson's and, like, watch a bunch of movies all night."

"Yakitori?"

"Grilled chicken on sticks. It's the nearest thing to western food anyways. You do have chicken on sticks in England, don't you?" Another snort.

I gave a deliberate smirk. "Of course, but you know us barbarians, we have to hunt it with the sticks first."

Jei Pi threw her head back, her uvula wobbling as she laughed. A glob of spit landed on my hand. I wiped it off with my sleeve.

"I like you Kimberly, I think I've got you worked out. You know, I was going stir-crazy out here with no roomie for two months, but now I can go back to being just plain crazy. I think we're gonna get along just fine."

I didn't answer; I was too tired to even muster a polite smile.

Jei Pi's frog-mouthed grin dropped. "Sometimes people don't like me though, can you imagine? I didn't get along with anyone in high school – they just didn't like me. Supposing that happened – suppose I lived with someone I didn't get along with, someone who didn't like laughing. I'm a humourist you see, I like to see the fun in life and I like my life to be full of people who laugh along with me, not at me, you get me?"

"Em, what?"

"You know what I did once to this chica I lived with, who didn't like me?"

I opened my mouth, but no words came out.

"I left a used tampon in the middle of her bedroom floor."

Threats. Jei Pi was giving me a veiled threat.

"If someone did that to me, I'd shit on their pillow and wipe my bum with their blanket." The words rushed out of my mouth, a torrent that surprised me, was uncharacteristic for me.

Jei Pi hesitated, her eyes darting back and forth between mine. Then she burst into raucous laughter. "Bum! You English are so quaint!"

A poem sprang into my head as I watched Jei Pi doubled over.

The ginger clown laughed
A crude cackle, a horrible laugh
A disgusting display of wobbling jowls,
And stringy saliva, with
Quivering uvula, and
All of it, amidst
A halitosis gale

I held my breath as I stood up. "I think I'll go and get changed for dinner."

"Sure thing, roomie. Whenever you're ready."

As I turned, my elbow knocked a white bottle off the edge of the kitchen counter. I stooped and picked it up. Prozac prescription for Joanna Patricia Watt. So, my flat mate was depressed? Bi-polar? Manic depressive? Regardless of the diagnosis, the prognosis was obvious: the pills were on display intentionally. They positively screamed, 'look at me, I've got issues, feel sorry for me.'

Joanna Patricia's get-out-of-jail-free-card.

Princess Diana versus the Ginger narcissist.

What the hell was I getting myself into?

4

಄

Potlatch

"Tadaima!"

I closed my Japanese language book and stood up from the kitchen table. "Okaeri," I answered.

"Good girl." Jei Pi's syrupy voice coagulated as bitter wax in my ear. "You've been paying attention to what I taught you."

Good girl, indeed; like I was a dog. I brandished my Business Japanese textbook, not to give Jei Pi the satisfaction. "Actually, I've been studying."

"I've got everyone with me. We're here for the Pot Luck."

"Pot Luck? Luck for what?"

"Latch, Potlatch. Oy vey, you Brits really are uncultured. Native American custom to you, loads of food."

A niggle of irritation. "Oh of course, I should've known. I must be ignorant if I don't know American traditions."

Pot Luck. Luck was exactly what I'd need to survive living with Jei Pi. I made a mental note not to eat anything that my new flat monster cooked, just for spite. Spite was petty, certainly not Zen or Buddhist, but I would allow myself a few token petty foibles on my journey to enlightenment. After all, Jei Pi was a blockade on my road to inner peace. How could I reach my true higher nature if I couldn't centre myself?

Jei Pi came in first, leading the other teachers. "Go-shokai shimasho!"

"Oh-kay." I censored myself before saying 'whatever.'

A brunette with an Australian accent elbowed Jei Pi in her ribs. "Cut the Japanese, she's English, come on!"

Fantastic; another person aside from Ben happy to deride Jei Pi. We exchanged smiles. I hadn't a clue what Jei Pi had said and didn't care, other than to know it was something completely pretentious.

Jei Pi ignored the brunette and instead, flapped her hands around as she pointed to everyone in turn. "This is Zoe."

Poker straight pale brunette, check.

"That's Nadia behind."

Tall, sharp-featured honey blonde, check.

"You already know Ben, and these two are Ade and Vince."

Ade: gym-honed, white-blonde, crewcut-headed. Vince: black gel-haired, sunbed-tanned.

"At the back there is Carter and that's Akemi, one of the reception staff at our branch."

Round-faced Carter with red hair and a red moustache and rosy-cheeked, wide-eyed Akemi, with sleek hair and a heavy fringe. I pinned a mental name-tag onto each person and noted their images to help recall them all later.

"Everyone, this is Kimberly."

"Nice to meet you all, should be fun." My voice escaped a little too high-pitched and a notch too singsong to give a casual impression. Aware I was twisting my hands, I dropped them by my sides.

We flooded into the living room, each carrying food or drinks for the Potlatch. As Akemi reached me, she bowed. "Welcome. To. Japanese. Ando welcome to. Tottori. School. Voyce," she said, in slow, heavily-accented English. She turned to Ben and spoke in her native language. Ben answered back in slow, but fluid, Japanese.

"Don't worry, you did a good job," Ben said in English, then turned to me. "Akemi also studies at Voyce, though at a different branch."

I extended my hand to Akemi. "Nice to meet you, Akemi. Your English is very good."

Akemi hesitated, her brow furrowed as she looked at my hand. I withdrew it and bowed instead, making Akemi smile. "My. Name. Eez. Akemi. I. Am. Barry. Preezed. To. Meeto. You. Keembaree. San."

Carter, last to enter handed me a blue plush cat. Its eyes were shut and in place of a mouth it had a yellow bird's beak. A large yellow V for the school, Voyce, was emblazoned on its stomach.

"The Voyce Neko, a present just for you. Neko means cat. He's a hit on Japanese TV. Even has his own cartoon."

"Cute," I said, taking the cat, although creepy was more like it. "What's with the beak?"

"So that it can talk. Neat, huh?" he said.

Jei Pi sat at the kitchen table with me, leaving Zoe and Ben to grab plates and cutlery from the cupboards. Jei Pi watched me with a glazed look, one hand under her chin, a wide, toothy grin on her face. Did she want an opinion on the food? It made me even more reluctant to taste it. I looked away from Jei

Pi towards my other soon-to-be colleagues. Nadia did a pirouette in the middle of the living room before dropping into a graceful lotus position on one of the floor cushions. She tossed her honey-blonde mane back and narrowed her eyes at me, a hint of a sneer playing around her mouth.

What the hell had I done to merit such a venomous look?

I peeled my eyes away from Nadia to Akemi, comically perched at one end of the two-seater sofa, leaning away from Carter, who took up the main bulk of the couch as he edged closer to her and tried to engage her in small-talk. Ade and Vince leaned, hands in pockets, against the living room wall trying to look cool.

Ben handed me a plate and I slopped a tablespoon full from each bowl onto it, to be sure I wouldn't offend anyone. Despite me being the new girl, I wasn't the centre of attention, to my relief. Ben and Zoe, having finished handing out plates were engaged in some boring work chat. Nadia relished attention from Ade and Vince. Carter had finally ensnared Akemi with oversimplified idioms that he was surely saying just to help her practise English.

That left me with Jei Pi and her cat-got-the-cream grin.

"What do you think of everyone then?" said the ginger monster.

I glanced around the room, aware that everyone was within earshot, if they so wished to hear. "They seem nice."

Jei Pi shrugged. "They're a decent bunch, I guess. Four gals and four guys. Shame Ben is taken or it would've been perfect."

I shifted in my seat, wondering if anyone was eavesdropping.

"You and Ade would go well. You're both so blonde and gorgeous, you'd be like two mannequins getting it on. He probably takes steroids, am I right? Who has those muscles naturally?"

I almost gagged on my fork, pushing the bite of chicken vol au vent too far into my throat.

"Nadia and Vince would work well together. He's all brawn and no brains, to use one of your English expressions and she loves no one more than herself. I'll bet she hates you. You're younger, blonder, and smarter, a sexy psychologist. She's a sun-dried Kiwi, a dancer who was probably good-looking once, but now she looks like if you dipped a pedigree horse in an acid bath."

That time, I actually gagged on my food and spluttered into my hand.

"Then there's Zoe. She's a poker-stiff Aussie, so rigid she looks like she's got a coat hanger stuffed up her back. She'd go well with Carter, the two of them are polar opposites. She has a jaw so square you could sharpen knives on it and he is so round and misshapen, he looks like a laundry bag stuffed with foam peanuts."

"Jei Pi, they'll hear you..."

"I'd be a good match with Ben. We're both smart, both wear glasses and, well. Thing is, he's not my type. I'm not into bald men with big beards. Go figure."

Jei Pi smirked at her own musings and looked at me for a reaction. I scooped the rest of what was on my plate into my mouth and swallowed it after three chews, the lump catching in my gullet. Oh my gosh, what was I in for with the red devil as my flatmate?

"Hey, roomie, you wanna know something real juicy?"

Oh no. What now? I forced my eyes up off my plate and looked at Jei Pi.

"I just saw Vince checking you out. You know what's amazing about that? I had him figured as gay. Seriously, a fitness fanatic like that is either gay, or overcompensating for having small equipment in the produce area, if you get me." She snorted, tossing her ginger mop as she laughed.

That was enough. I stood up. "Just gonna get a drink."

Ignoring Jei Pi's offer of an empty glass, I grabbed another and slid into the kitchenette to fill it from the tap. A couple of sips of water did nothing to sober my Jei Pi-intoxicated head. Unnoticed, I slipped into the safe haven of my bedroom.

I pushed the door behind me, but before it snapped shut, a hand caught it. The owner of said hand curled four blocky fingers into a fist and wrapped the door lightly: knock, knock, knock, knock-knock, pause, knock, knock.

Vince's face peered inside before she could even respond. "How's tricks?"

Not sure of what else to say, I answered, "Fine."

He held out a red and white can with dark blue letters reading, *Asahi*. "Wanna beer?"

I didn't, but took it anyway. Maybe the alcohol would flush away my anxiety over Jei Pi's harsh and selfish critique of people I didn't yet – hadn't even had a chance to – get to know.

His eyes swept my room, taking in the green checked duvet set and bamboo blinds I had bought that morning at Jusco, my photo boards of friends from London and my family, and spotted my green travel journal on top of my chest of drawers. He smiled, "Are you journalling?"

I snatched it away and curled it against my chest. "Not really. I was just trying out a few poems."

"Care to show?" He cocked his head in too-haughty a manner for my liking.

"I'll pass. They're pretty rough anyway."

His eyes slid upwards from the journal over my chest, then lingered on my eyes. Smooth. Had to be a practised move. I tried to formulate my thoughts. I didn't get a sense that he was attracted to me; simply curious, taking in both my room and my space, as a whole. I should have felt uncomfortable, exposed, but I didn't. Wasn't it Zen to take in one's surroundings and be completely immersed in the here and now? Wasn't that what I sought to do myself? I admired Vince, at that moment. He wasn't all brawn and no brains as Jei Pi's character assessment – no, assassination – had indicated. Vince had a tranquil aura. He smiled at me. I returned his smile before raising the beer can to my lips and taking a sip.

5

 og

On the job

I straightened my cream-coloured suit trousers and jacket, tussled as they were from the ride to work, and grabbed my briefcase out of the bicycle basket. My vagina hurt, and no wonder: it had been a decade since I'd last ridden a bike. No tube in Tottori, for sure, but no matter. Cycling would keep me fit. I fixed a wedgie with a surreptitious glance around; thankfully it was far too early for shoppers at Jusco yet. A deep breath to centre myself and then I walked into the large department store.

Up the escalator beside a trendy women's shop, *Classy Girl*, then past the opticians to my new workplace, Voyce, tucked in the corner.

At first glance, Voyce looked like a travel-agents rather than a school. Behind the reception, with its smiling Japanese admin staff were wooden booths where English-speaking teachers gave one to one demo lessons to potential students, trying to sell them expensive language contract packages, or students wearing headphones took online lessons with teachers elsewhere in Japan.

Ben appeared from a door behind reception and threw his arms wide in a theatrical gesture. "Welcome to the McDonalds of the private teaching world."

"What, really?"

He dropped the sarcasm. "Apparently so. Latest meeting I had to go to in Namba said we hold sixty percent of the market. Must be how they justified keeping us there til ten at night."

"McDonalds sounds great. Maybe I'll treat myself after my first day."

Ben smiled. "You've got a nice one, only two classes and I've given you some of the better students to ease you in."

Maslow's hierarchy of human requirements: easy students and comfort food, in place of food, oxygen and water. I followed Ben into the staffroom behind reception and took the student files that he handed me to plan my lessons. Easy-peasy: the Voyce textbook laid out a choice of activities to do anyway. I could pick a topic and wing it. I looked at the colour-coded sticker on my first student's file then picked the appropriately coloured textbook. I opened it to the first topic: vacations. American textbook, American vocabulary. Would my students understand my London accent? Would I have to enunciate instead of blending words? Would all my students end up with homogenised Amero-pean accents? I flipped to another topic: making a reservation. Sorted.

One hour to go. Thirty minutes to go. Ten minutes to go. Countdown. Nine to one. On five, I went via the toilet, killing a few painful minutes. A series of beeps sounded lesson time as I walked along a short corridor, as though walking the plank. Would I sink, or swim? Dry land swimming. Where was my lifejacket?

Oh my gosh, it was excruciating. I had no idea how frightened I would be. My hand shook as I walked into the class. Nothing scary about the two students who sat there: a woman of about fifty and a businessman in his forties.

I set the student files and textbook on the desk and swallowed a dry lump in my throat as I sat. "Hi. How's it going?"

"Hello. Is you mean, how are you?" said the woman. "I am fine thank you, and you?"

Her speech was clear, although stilted and rehearsed. I thought back to my Business Japanese book: Mister Tanaka meets Mister Smith. Standard greetings, textbook perfect. But this was the real world.

"I'm fine, thanks. My name's Kimberly and I'm from London. Have you ever been to England?"

"Igirisu? I mean, In-goo-ran-doh, no. I has been to Eee-gip-toe ando I see pah-mids," she said.

"Oh, that's nice," I said. So far, so smooth. "Did you have a nice time?"

"I hab bery nice-ooh time, sank you. I ride on-" The woman looked upwards, searching the ceiling. "Rakuda, nandaro-"

"No Japanese, please, Kimiko." The Japanese businessman grinned and waggled his finger at her. "You mean sand horse?"

Sand horse. "Was it a camel? A kind of yellow animal with a hump on its back?"

"Ah, so ka," said Kimiko. "Eto ne, yes, eet was camel. I ride on camel."

"Thank you, Daichi that was a very helpful explanation," I said. "Sand horse, I like that."

My students smiled at me, both happy, both eager. It felt good. First lesson and we had breezed through the small talk with a bit of circumlocution over camels, student initiated, no less. I was getting the hang of it. Time for the main course.

"Okay then, so today we'll be doing a lesson about making a reservation. Alright, so I want you to imagine that you've made a booking in a hotel, but when you get there, you realise they've given you the wrong room. Er, can everyone picture that alright?"

"What picture is it?" said Daichi, flipping through the textbook.

"Um, there's no picture. I meant, you need to picture the scene in your head," I went on.

Kimiko frowned. "What does booking mean? Do you mean, the hotel manager gives me a book?"

My hairline prickled as heat flooded my face. "Well, no. It's like a reservation, you know, when you book something in advance."

"Advance?" asked Kimiko.

My hands were cold, clammy. "Um, yeah, it means like – so imagine, before you want to do something, right? Er, like you want to plan something so it doesn't go wrong, or something. You know, you have to secure it, so you make a booking."

Crap. Bollocks. Shit. My students were no longer smiling. They stared at me with vacant expressions. I had panicked, had become flustered and babbled. Kimiko and Daichi were confident only with stock phrases. I had lost them. I had lost control of the lesson.

I had lost myself.

I wanted to cry. There was still half an hour of the lesson to go. I would have given anything to hear the end of lesson beeps, that death-knell from only fifteen minutes before that had sounded my long walk off a short plank.

Nothing for it; I had to dig myself out of the hole I had made. "Erm, a reservation is when, say you want a hotel room for tomorrow. You make a phone call today and tell them what time you want to check in, and how many people there'll be."

Phew, saved! I didn't know I had it in me. My explanation was simple, but not simple. The complications of simplicity. I had taken the proverbial bull by the horns, untangled the metaphorical ball of string, fuck, whatever idiom suited the moment. In my head, I threw up my hands.

Booking wasn't so hard to understand, was it? Fair enough, book had two meanings in English, but nothing overly complex.

I needed a drink, a strong one. I'd never been much of a drinker back home, but now I could see the appeal. Half an hour then lunch, and tune-out time. Something stronger than a Smirnoff Ice, my usual in London, maybe a vodka martini would set me straight. Burn through the jetlag, the language barrier. The loneliness.

Now that my students understood the lesson objective, I set them a role-play task and sat back in my chair to listen, off the hook. As Kimiko and Daichi talked, I glanced behind them through the window into the next classroom. Vince sat conducting a one to one lesson with a young, attractive woman in business attire. He leaned across the desk, his hands extended towards hers within an inch of touching, almost as though they were a couple on a cosy restaurant date, not a teacher and student. Intimacy from teacher was unrequited though, as student sat oblivious, her head buried in her textbook, practising customer complaint phrases when returning a mobile phone.

I must have tickled his spider sense, for at that moment, Vince peeled his eyes away from his attractive student and locked his gaze onto me. I should've looked away, guilty as charged, but I kept staring back. His cheek muscles twitched as a flattered smile spread, butter-smooth across his face. He winked, cheeky and benevolent. Butter wouldn't melt.

"That was great, guys," I said, still looking past Kimiko and Daichi to Vince. "I'm very impressed."

Vince, mistaking my intention, mouthed. "Right back at you."

6

ೞ

Tottori

Villa Libido, Akisato. The taxi driver had made me repeat it three times. At first I had thought it was the fact that Japanese people struggled with V's and L's and that he hadn't understood my pronunciation, but by the third time, I was convinced he knew the English meaning and was gratified by my mortification. If it wasn't for the embarrassing name, I would've enjoyed the poetic syntax of my new home from home. Whoever thought up the title must've done it for kicks. Probably some bored Western businessman married to a local, having a laugh at the Japanese peoples' expense. What would Carl have to say when he came to stay? Once I'd figured out the international payphone at Lawson's round the corner, we'd had a long chat. Carl was going to sell his beloved Honda to pay for his three month visit, the maximum a tourist visa would allow. He'd probably laugh at my new apartment building name. Either that or rant about how it was crude. It could go one of those two ways, depending on his mood. Carl was unpredictable. He liked to call it *keeping you on your toes*. Maybe that was what I liked about him. *Did* I like that about him? I sniffed. At the very least, he certainly wasn't boring.

I had been out longer than planned. After getting my alien registration card at the town office, I had been enticed by Kyushu mountain and had decided on a climb. Reaching the top took forty-five minutes and from there I had whiled away three hours idly taking in the spectacular view across Tottori, from the distant rice fields and mountains beyond the urban centre to the blue expanse of the Sea of Japan where South Korea lay on the horizon.

I unlocked the door and stepped in, forgetting to remove my shoes, then swearing, then calling out an apology to Jei Pi. Remembering that Jei Pi was at work, I reprimanded myself for talking to no-one, kicked aside a particularly plain and scruffy pair of her shoes and lined up my own ones neatly in their place. Jei Pi had taped a hand-drawn note in Japanese to my bedroom door, executed in marker in crude writing by a clumsy hand. Unintelligible, I was sure, if a Japanese person were to try reading it. My flat-monster really was pretentious, and definitely not an artist. I left it hanging and went into my bedroom, stopping to perform a quick eye-sweep of the room; hangover habit from my student-living days. Curtains drawn, as I'd left them that morning. Futon folded-up and piled in the corner with my blanket and pillow on top. Fold-up holdall stuffed with casual wear, necessary for a tiny Japanese apartment. Clothes rail with business wear ready for work. Chest of drawers near the door, completing the three hundred and sixty-five degree check.

My eyes jumped back to the chest of drawers. The top drawer was open half an inch. It had been shut when I had left. A lifetime of obsessive compulsive disorder was tantamount to a PhD in forensics: no subtle change in my private, safe space could escape my eye. It meant only one thing. Jei Pi had been in my room.

But for what? I pulled the top drawer open and rummaged around. New pens, stationery, passport, British coins, green poetry journal. I picked up my writing buddy and flipped it open. My poem on the first page remained untitled. Maybe I'd call it, *An Escapade*, or *On the Flight*.

I thumbed ahead through the blank pages. My bookmark was missing. I had wedged the receipt from my bento on the bus from Osaka in order to keep my place and now it was gone. No mistake; my poetry journal had been tampered with. Jei Pi had not only been in my room, but had snooped through my things. My eyes slid from the chest of drawers across to the waste paper bin behind it. Inside was a crumpled up ball. I picked it up and unfolded it. Sunkus convenience store receipt, seven hundred and fifty yen, from the bus station in Namba. On the floor near it lay a single ginger hair.

I rolled my head back and stared at my bedroom ceiling, my mind flooded. What a nosy, snooping, control-freak bitch. Why had Jei Pi been through my things? What business was it of hers to look through other people's possessions? The open drawer, the bookmark in the bin, the obvious strand of hair left behind; they had to be intentional clues to show her spying. Jei Pi didn't seem the type to be careless. Someone who could line up all their bloody shoes by the door in perfect order had to do everything on purpose. And what of Jei Pi's half-opened bedroom door? Was the crazy bitch trying to lure me into her own dark lair to do the same, to poke and pry?

What now? I would seem the crazy one if I blatantly accused Jei Pi of invading my privacy. '*Oh, by the way, did you read my journal and leave your filthy ginger hair in my room?* The nosy cow would deny it. Should I snoop in Jei Pi's room and find some dirt on her in return? Two wrongs didn't make a right. In any case, I was sure any dirt on Jei Pi was bound to nauseate me.

What to do? This was new territory for me. Maybe mulling it over in the bath would be best. I had never tried a Japanese *o-furo*, but Zoe and Nadia insisted that they were to die for.

The bathroom door was a sliding type, more of a fogged, perspex folding shutter than a door, really. There was no lock like in a western bathroom, but no concern either; Jei Pi was on the late shift, thank goodness.

I stepped into the tiny compartment-like room. No toilet. The Japanese valued cleanliness and wouldn't have sewage near a clean space; the loo was in a separate room next door. There was a drain in the middle of the bathroom floor and a shower head with a tap on a hook. The bath was a small, deep box-shaped space. O-furo. Bath. Looked cramped, but I would take my colleagues' word that it was more relaxing than a western bath. I liked being able to stretch my legs out, but was willing to give it a go. I put the stopper in, emptied a sachet of bath salts that I'd picked up at the one hundred yen shop and started the tap.

While the bath filled up, I had a shower. *When in Rome*: I would follow the Japanese custom to wash first, then have a bath already clean. Baths were for relaxation only. Wonder what Japanese people thought of westerners bathing in their own dirt? I would have to remember to ask the students at work tomorrow.

The bath salts filled the air with spicy-scented steam. Intriguing. Maybe South-east Asians knew something about health that Caucasians didn't. Made sense; they all looked so young. Their skin didn't wrinkle as fast as Westerner's skin did. Couldn't all be down to a good diet, though I supposed eating fish did help, with all the omega oil. And those beans I'd had on the bus; Carter had revealed the secret of how to eat them. Edamame. They had to be popped from their pod, not eaten whole. I had actually found them tastier than green beans or sugar snap peas back home, once I'd tasted them properly.

With my body a sufficient shade of prawn-pink, I stepped into the o-furo. The water lapped up over my chest, reaching my neck. So the guidebook was right; sitting with my arms wrapped around my legs in a foetal ball was comfier than it looked and didn't feel cramped as I had feared. I lay my head back against the rim and inhaled the aromatic mist. Hedonistic heaven. For the first time since my Eastern journey had begun just over a week ago, I felt relaxed. I closed my eyes and let the water lap around me, adrift in a decadent dream.

At an unspecified time later, the bathroom shutter scraped back and I jolted upright from my slumber with a gasp. Jei Pi's unruly ginger mane appeared and her blinding, cat-got-the-cream grin. I crossed my arms over my chest and spluttered on the spicy steam.

"Hey roomie," said Jei Pi. "The o-furo's awesome, isn't it?"

"What are you doing? I'm naked-"

Jei Pi held up a blue shower curtain, still in its cellophane wrapper. "Oh, yeah, about that. I picked up a curtain for privacy, see? It'll fit across the glass screen. I figured you Brits were modest. I'll hang it now."

"Don't bother. I'll finish my bath first." I sank up to my chin in a tight ball.

"M'kay, but just FYI, I didn't see your nakedness. Still, if you're that sensitive, I'll get out of my work stuff first. I picked up a rental DVD for us too. Slumber party, what do you say?"

I wiped hair out of my face. "Great. Fine. Could you shut the door please, I'm losing my heat."

"Gotcha. Catch you in a minute, roomie." Jei Pi slid the door shut and clicked it. I clapped my hands over my face and ran them back through my hair. Who the hell was this person and what planet did she come from?

I balanced one hand on the rim to climb out of the bath, and let the other linger over my private parts as a pre-emptive measure, though there was no sign of the ginger monster. I snatched a towel and swept it over my body one-handed, while simultaneously holding the door shut. Never in all my life had anyone violated my personal boundaries in such a disrespectful manner. And now I had the sorry misfortune of living with such a person.

I pulled my house clothes on; an old T-shirt and jogging trousers. I lifted my comb and noticed what it had been next to: a pair of violet contact lenses in a see-through case. So Jei Pi wore coloured lenses? What else was fake about her?

Jei Pi was spread across the sofa when I went into the living room, a great lump infesting a pair of beige pyjamas decorated with pink cartoon pigs. Apt. She had glasses on, and her eyes were magnified behind the lenses. Brown, not violet. She patted the cushion next to her. "Come sit."

Quick grab for a kitchen chair instead. "I'll sit here, thanks."

Jei Pi wrinkled her nose. "How did I know you were going to sit in that chair? That chair, Thatcher, get it? Kimberly Thatcher!"

I forced a smile. "Oh, right, ha ha."

"Did you get your alien registration sorted?"

"Yep, and I went for a hike up Kyushu mountain. I really should have brought my travel journal with me though, you never know what you might see when you go out."

"Oh, so you keep a diary? Me too. Well, kind of. I write home every week about my adventures out here - my family are putting them together as a manuscript for me. I'm planning to sell it when I get back to Maine next year."

The lying bitch. So she was pretending not to know about my green journal. Got to find some way of getting it out of her.

"Say, maybe we could collaborate on something, wouldn't that be fun?" Jei Pi stretched her arm across the back of the sofa, an open gesture that failed to make her more trustworthy. "I mean, I've never been good at poetry, but if you did some poems to go at the start of each chapter of my book, I think that'd be neat, huh?"

Ha. The moron had ensnared herself. "How did you know I wrote poems?"

Jei Pi blinked. "Didn't you say it?"

I shook my head, revelling in the deliciousness of confrontation. So satisfying to see Jei Pi squirm.

"Oh." Jei Pi's face was all jowls and no chin in the absence of her manic smile. "Well, I looked through your book when you were away."

"Eh, come again?" Mouth before mind, but for once it was necessary; given any more time and my higher functions would have choke-chained my lizard brain, and I needed my aggressive base instincts to fight my corner. Honestly, how was I supposed to react to that? I had expected a defensive retaliation, not an upfront confession. Got to have a good retort, quick.

"So that's what you do then, is it? Go around snooping through people's private possessions and walk in on them in awkward situations? Is that the kind of person you are, huh? Do you get some satisfaction out of that?"

Jei Pi stared at me for a long time, like her mind was working as her eyes narrowed. Then her face broke into its usual stupid grin.

"Gotcha for a minute, didn't I? Oy vey, you Brits are so touchy! I didn't look through your diary, whaddaya take me for? I figured you'd be the type to write poems, that's all. You know - serious. Sensitive."

Ding dong.

Jei Pi threw her blanket off and darted for the door. Saved by the bell, the coward. I gave the table a light thump, my clenched fist a Faraday cage dissipating negative energy. Liar. Jei Pi was a lying, rotten, intrusive cow. The ginger monster came back into the room with a petite Japanese woman. She had a deep suntan and a cropped, bowl-style haircut. Tomboyish looking, in baggy jeans and a polo shirt over a long-sleeved vest.

"Kim, this is Yuri. Yuri, this is Kim. Yuri's my Japanese teacher."

Self-satisfied lump. Jei Pi stood with her hands on her hips and her chest stuck out, waiting for a response.

"Hi Yuri." I turned to Jei Pi. "Let's get something straight. First of all, I'm called Kimberly, not Kim. And also, what's this? You just invite someone over without telling me?"

Jei Pi's eyes widened. "Am I getting you right, you want me to ask permission?"

"No, of course not. But we are sharing a flat. If I was going to invite someone over, I'd be considerate and ask my flatmate."

"Flatmate? You Brits can't even speak English." Jei Pi snorted. "You people aren't designed to travel. You come all the way to Japan and you don't even want to meet anyone new."

Yuri shuffled backwards, her face red. "Sorry, I think, perhaps I mastu go."

"Don't leave because of her, I brought a DVD." Jei Pi grabbed Yuri's arm.

I stood up. "Don't mind me, Yuri. I'm going into my room, I'm not going to stay here and be insulted by this roommate of mine. Satisifed, Jei Pi? Am I using the correct American-English for your delicate ears?"

Jei Pi smirked and cocked her head, playing coy, but said nothing. Yuri gave an embarrassed bow and handed me a bottle of soft drink and a small cellophane packet of sweets.

"This is present for welcome you in Japan," said Yuri. "Sweets is anko, mosto tradition sweets you try.

Sweets is make in rice and inside is put red bean paste. Drink is healthy taste cowpiss."

"Cowpiss?!" I set the bottle on the table.

Jei Pi cackled. "Cowpiss!"

Yuri looked from me to Jei Pi. "Eh? Nandatte?"

"It's Calpis, dummy." Jei Pi's throat wobbled as she laughed. "Cowpiss, that's so funny!"

"Well how was I supposed to know? I heard cowpiss, not Calpis. What is it anyway?"

"It's a probiotic yogurt drink. Japanese are health conscious, you know, but not enough to drink cowpiss. Cowpiss!" Jei Pi strapped her arm across her bulging midriff and bent double, heaving.

"Get over it, it's not that funny." I rolled my eyes across to Yuri and forced a smile. "Thanks for the present."

Jei Pi sniggered. I pursed my lips. Best leave it. There'd be other battles worth fighting. I bowed to Yuri and turned my back on Jei Pi as she headed for her bedroom. Feeling the need to exorcise Jei Pi's negative residue and restore my safe sanctuary, I opened the window and lit my aromatherapy burner. Soothing Jasmine would heal all. I leaned both elbows on the window sill and inhaled the fragrant smoke from the burner. I was barely starting to relax when I heard Yuri outside my door.

"...It says irrashaimase..."

I pressed my eyes tightly shut, trying to ignore them, trying to focus on the wafting Jasmine smoke.

"This message is, eto ne, chotto chigau," said Yuri.

Jei Pi sounded miffed. "Yeah, how so? It says welcome in Japanese. I've been practising my hiragana every day."

Good. A definite note of sulkiness in the ginger dragon's voice. The higher pitch, the distinct whine; satisfaction to listen to, indeed. Worthwhile being distracted to hear Jei Pi flail.

"Word is said welcome, but meaning is what people in shop can say, not house. You mastu say yokoso. Yokoso is correct Japanese word you can write."

Silence. Had to indicate that Jei Pi was well and truly put in her place. I held my breath and listened. Shuffling feet and mumbled voices from the living room. Let them watch their DVD as long as they left me in peace. I took a deep, soothing breath of scented smoke. Now to cleanse my poetry journal that Jei Pi had defiled. I would write a warning poem, in case she ever felt the need to invade my privacy again.

With a great big mouth, stretched into a manic smile,
Horsey tooth hussey comes a hollerin'
Curly red tufts of clownish hair billowing
Shapeless and saggy, cutting a figure more akin
To a bin bag stuffed with foam peanuts than a woman's body,
Flapping her podgy hands, she's a great lump,
infesting whatever clothes that have the misfortune
To be stretched over her awful podge, a sand dune stomach.
Hollerin', snooping, and poking,
Among others' possessions, where her big neb is unwanted.

There. That ought to do it. Harsh, callous, petty and using Jei Pi's own words; her description of Carter's foam peanut body. I would not reach enlightenment from such a puerile poem, and indeed it was a cruelly exaggerated description of Jei Pi, but the purpose was to rile her up, to provoke her into admitting her guilt in snooping. Let Jei Pi dare invade my space ever again.

7

ॐ

Tricks in translation

Zoe led us across the restaurant to a long table with ten chairs around it, five on either side. A round barbecue grill was set into the middle of the table with a pan of unlit charcoal. Zoe took the innermost seat by the wall on one side and I sat facing her.

"Don't you hate being the first to arrive?" said Zoe.

"Why, is it a cultural faux pas in Japan?"

Zoe shook her head. "It's just awkward. Like, are we meant to order drinks now, or wait for everyone else to get here first?"

I shrugged. "I wouldn't know. This is my first time eating at a yakiniku restaurant. I ate at an izakaya in Osaka on my first night, but it was a normal table."

"You mean, a Western style table," said Zoe, pulling a face.

I paused. "No, I meant, not a barbecue table."

Zoe broke into a grin. "Sorry, devil's advocate. I was just being a dick."

I smiled, relieved. "Oh, good. I was worried for a minute that you were another pedant. I've had enough of those types to last me a lifetime."

Zoe leaned forward, her elbows on the table. "By those types, I'm guessing you mean Jei Pi?"

"Erm, what made you think that?"

"How're you getting on living with Jei Pi anyway?"

I stared at Zoe. Was there an ulterior motive behind the question? "She's okay. I don't really know her."

"Don't you find her weird?"

Blunt. And unexpected. I wanted to say, yes, and thank Zoe for making me feel less alone, but I bit my tongue.

"I mean, she wears Disney cartoon socks and what's with the violet contact lenses?" Zoe went on, wrinkling her nose.

I plopped my chin in my hand. "To be honest, we don't get on so well. But if she keeps to herself, I'm happy to mind my own business."

"I don't like my housemate either, Nadia. Her name's Ivanovitch, but I like to call her Ivanobitch. She has heaps of insane rules about the apartment. Like, do you know she randomly put up a sheet with chores that she allocated to me, without even consulting me first, of course."

"What sort of chores?"

"Like, I would have to keep the kitchen and toilet clean and she would vacuum the living room and clean the bathroom. As if that's a fair division of labour. The sheet was stuck on my bedroom door when I got home from work one day."

"What a total cow! I take it you ignored it?"

"We had a big row about it and I ripped the sheet off my door and threw it right in her face."

I laughed. "Wouldn't it be nice if we could move in together and let Nadia and Jei Pi have each other?"

"I'd love that, four months living with Ivanobitch has been hell. But actually, I'm thinking of moving in with my boyfriend Ryuji. If it wasn't for that, I might've taken you up on the offer."

"Oh, that's nice. How long have you been with Ryuji?"

"Three months." Zoe leaned close and whispered. "He's a Voyce student, so you'll meet him soon, no doubt. Some of the other teachers know, you know, like Carter and Vince and Ade. But don't tell Ben, hey?"

I sat upright, affronted. "I wouldn't do that, not that Ben would mind anyway. He's married to someone who's ex-Voyce, you know?"

"She's former staff though. There's nothing against liaisons with staff in the contract, but socialising with students in any way is forbidden."

"Banging someone isn't socialising though, technically," I said.

We both burst out laughing at that. Anyone who found Jei Pi weird and Nadia a bitch had to have a well-tuned radar in my opinion. Akemi arrived in the midst of our laughter with a tall, pretty Japanese girl. Zoe and I simmered down our laughter at the arrival, lest we explain it to our company, and exchanged secretive smiles as Akemi sat next to me and her tall friend next to Zoe.

"Haro Keem-ba-ree. Is you met Tomomi yet?" said Akemi.

"Hi Tomomi. Nice to meet you. I'm Kimberly," I said, the polite but rehearsed greeting now second nature.

"Hey," she answered. "How's it going?"

Have to admit, I was taken aback. Not only did Tomomi have perfect enunciation, but even an American accent.

"Are you – from the States, Tomomi?"

Tomomi cocked her head, playfully. "Aww, I'm flattered you think so, that must mean my English is good? But no, I'm from Nagoya originally, although I studied English abroad in Georgia, Atlanta. That must be why you thought I was American."

While we talked, Akemi watched our lips: first mine, then Tomomi's. Akemi's eyes widened as she turned to Tomomi. "Sugoi, Tomomi San," she said slowly, followed by a quick succession of Japanese that I didn't catch. Tomomi answered in Japanese, occasionally pointing at me and I knew Tomomi was translating for Akemi.

"So, Kimberly, how do you like Tottori?" said Tomomi.

"Great, so far, from what I know of it in a week."

"Have you got your gaijin card sorted yet, you know, your alien registration?"

"Yeah, I did that a few days ago. I still need to get set up with a bank account though."

"I'll take you to Tottori bank tomorrow. We can get you a cell phone and a bicycle afterwards too," she said.

"That'll be great. I'll be glad to not have to call my boyfriend Carl from the payphone at Lawsons and to give Ben his bicycle back, it's really uncomfortable."

"Did your Voyce rep at Osaka give you an *enkan*, you know, a wooden stamp?"

I pulled my flat key out of my bag and showed Tomomi the keyring attached. Inside what looked like a lipstick box was a small, wooden cylinder, the size of a crayon. Apparently it was a stamp with my name written in katakana, phonetically as 'keem-bah-ree-sah-cha'.

"Good, because in Japan, we don't use signatures. You'll need to give your *hanko*, a stamp of your name in red ink."

"It's all so new to me," I said.

"You'll get used to it," said Tomomi. "How's your Japanese?"

"Actually I don't know any, really. I'm learning a few phrases from a Business Japanese book, but honestly, it hasn't been that helpful. I can't read any labels in the supermarket, I've basically been living off boiled eggs, fruit and McDonalds. I bought some stuff that I thought was cooking oil and I think it was vinegar, it basically evaporated on the frying pan."

"Sounds like it was probably *mirin*, Japanese rice-wine vinegar," said Tomomi. "You should apply for a Japanese tutor at the International Centre."

The sound of loud male voices speaking English announced the arrival of Ade, Vince, Ben and Carter, completing our party. Zoe hadn't mentioned who was coming when she had invited me, but I was glad it wasn't Jei Pi.

"Hey gang," said Carter, sitting next to Akemi."

"How's tricks," said Vince, sliding in next to Tomomi. He caught my eye across the table and winked.

"About time you lot got here, we're starving," said Zoe.

Interesting that everyone was out for dinner, except Jei Pi, who was obnoxious, and Nadia, who according to Zoe was unbearable too. The table had only ten places with no more room for extras. I felt safe to enquire. "Were Jei Pi and Nadia not invited?"

"They were, but Jei Pi is on the middle shift and Nadia's covering the late shift," said Ben.

That made me feel placated. As much as I disliked Jei Pi, I didn't like cliques generally. Some workplaces had a tendency to exclude others. My experience of working part-time in retail on Oxford street during Uni had put me on the receiving end of such bitchy nastiness; I had been excluded from girly nights out by skanks who openly discussed plans around me, but not with me. I later found out that one of their boyfriends had taken a liking to me when he had popped in to the shop one day and ever since then, I'd been given the cold shoulder.

"Irrashaimase," said one of the waiting staff, a middle-aged lady wearing a blue *jimbe* with the restaurant logo emblazoned in red Japanese kanji letters on her left breast. She leaned down and turned a switch on the end of the table to fire up the grill, then stoked the charcoal, turning them from black to orange.

Irrashaimase: it meant welcome. I knew that much from Yuri's satisfying humiliation of Jei Pi.

The waitress looked at each of us in turn, then locked eyes with me. She gave a bemused smile and said a short phrase in Japanese.

"She wants to know if you will need a knife and fork," Tomomi translated.

"No, I'm okay, I can manage chopsticks." Time to practise some Japanese from my lesson that morning; Mister Tanaka and Mister Smith had exchanged business cards and had introduced their secretaries to one another while having a business lunch.

"Hisho o hitotsu onegaishimasu." I held up one finger to indicate that I wanted one pair of chopsticks.

The waitress gave a longer Japanese response this time, ending in something, something masho. Masu was a present tense ending; I knew that much from my textbook, and mashita was past tense, but I didn't know masho. Whatever I had said though, the woman looked confused. Maybe it was my pronunciation.

"Erm, hisho o hitotsu, you know? Hisho?" I made a snipping gesture with my index and forefinger and touched my lips to imply eating.

"Ah, wakarimashita." The waitress giggled and bowed, but she took a pair of disposable wooden chopsticks off her tray and set them beside my plate of pickles, so clearly she understood my gesture, if not my Japanese. She gave everyone else chopsticks too, took Akemi's order for the table then bowed and left.

"Don't worry, she knows you're a new teacher, as we come here a lot," said Tomomi.

I snapped my chopsticks apart, my mind on the dialogue exchange with the waitress and at Tomomi's inexplicable comment. What had the waitress found so funny? My pronunciation couldn't be that bad, could it? At any rate, Japanese was a phonetic language, easier than I'd imagined it would be to speak, albeit harder than anything to read. Hisho o hitotsu onegaishimasu... can I have a pair of chopsticks please? Onegaishimasu meant please, and I was pretty sure I'd said it right too, silent 'u' on the end and all. Hitotsu was definitely one; I'd learned the numbers first. And hisho was chopsticks, wasn't it? Tomomi saying 'don't worry' ensured that I definitely did.

"Eez you learning Japanese, Keembaree san?" said Akemi.

"Mm-hmm."

"You eez learn about secretary?"

"What?" I looked from Akemi to Tomomi; maybe Akemi was struggling with English. What was she on about secretaries for?

Wait. Hashi meant chopsticks. So what was hisho? Business Japanese lesson, I wracked my brain, mentally going through my recent lessons. Think, think.

Hisho meant secretary.

I clapped my hand over my mouth. "Oh my gosh, I just asked that waitress, 'can I have a secretary, please?' No wonder she laughed!"

Zoe chuckled. "It could've been worse."

"Hashi o hitotsu onegaishimasu, hashi o hitotsu onegaishimasu." I muttered it aloud, like a mantra, the repetition driving the words into my brain.

"At least you didn't ask for something really bad, like condoms," Vince laughed.

Tomomi slapped his knee. "Why would she do that?"

"I don't know," he shrugged. "Ask her."

I opened my mouth to defend myself; such jokes at my expense could lead to trouble if not nipped in the bud, but the waitress returned with a silver platter of raw meat slices on ice. She set the platter in the middle of the table next to the grill.

"Has you eaten yakiniku before?" said Akemi.

"No, never."

"Ah, this is fast-o time?"

Huh? "Fast time? Oh! First time, yes."

"I'm glad you like Japanese food. Most-o abroad people likes a sushi and-o cup noodle or sea chicken sando-o."

"Erm, what's sea chicken?"

"It's tuna," said Tomomi, cutting in. She snapped her disposable chopsticks apart and laid strips of raw meat on the grill with skilled precision, then turned them the chopsticks around and used the other end to lift the thin slivers of curled, browned beef off the grill. "We should have a toast to honour Kimberly joining the Voyce family."

Vince smiled. "If we're doing it formally, then she needs a good phrase, like you made me say."

"Vince started about a month before you," said Zoe.

"What phrase?" Did they want me to say a religious phrase like Grace? Or a drinking phrase, like Cheers?

"I've got the best phrase," said Tomomi, stiffening her back in a purposefully regal manner. She cleared her throat. "Watashi wa Kimberly tomoushimasu, itsumo mura mura."

Akemi giggled and muttered in Japanese to Tomomi behind her hand.

"What does it mean?" I watched Akemi for any clues. "You're not playing a joke on me?"

"She's laughing because it's really formal. You'll sound like the Queen of England," said Zoe.

Formal was okay. I would rather be too polite than too casual. "Alright then, say it again for me?"

Tomomi cleared her throat to suppress a smile. "You should stand when you say it too." She repeated the phrase.

I stood. "Watashi wa Kimberly tomoushimasu, itsumo mura mura."

Everyone at our table, Japanese and *Gaijin* alike rolled around laughing.

I gawped. "What did you just make me say?"

"My name's Kimberly and I'm always horny," Tomomi spluttered.

I sat down with a thump and fixed Tomomi with a disapproving stare, then the other orchestrators, Zoe, and Vince. Nobody was innocent; everyone had laughed. "You lot are so nasty," I said, shaking my head.

"If it's any consolation, what I had to say was even worse," said Vince.

"It's true, we were so cruel to Vince when he came in September. Akemi, tell her the joke we played on Vince." Tomomi snorted. "Kawai sou, ne?"

Akemi nodded, a tight-lipped smile on her face. "We had-o welcome party for Veen-su san een Gusto. Eto ne, we teached him a good phrase in Japanese: 'Watashi no chin chin wa chisai desu ne' and we tell him to stand up and say it in the restaurant as a nice introduce phrase."

"What does it mean?"

"I have a small willy, don't I?" Tomomi burst into a fresh wave of laughter. I forced a laugh. I was starting to get the sense of humour among my colleagues at last, even if the joke was on me.

I gave Tomomi a sly smirk, "Chin chin means cheers where I'm from. So, your joke would backfire if you were in England. People would think you were just making a little toast."

Carter gave an exaggerated chortle. Zoe gave a polite guffaw and Ade lowered his head to hide an awkward smile. Vince had his usual smirk, as he tried to catch my attention. I wasn't even sure if that was true, but at least I had the upper-hand; Tomomi looked confused. I could imagine that Tomomi was trying to translate the Japanese phrase into English with the new meaning of 'chin chin' in mind.

My new colleagues seemed a close knit group, even if practical jokes was their thing. It wasn't my thing, but I could learn to give – and take – one for the team. Flow with the river of life, adapt to one's environment; this would be my new mantra on my journey of self-exploration. Toilet humour lowered my spiritual energy, but it was balanced by the need to find a new community so far from home. A little effort to fit in would go far in raising my soul to a higher plane of psychic energy. That way, I would begin to attract new, positive experiences and like-minded, good-hearted souls into my life.

My new mantra had opened a channel in my mind. Everything I experienced was a test to improve my inner, spiritual character. I devoured the strips of beef, ox tongue, octopus tentacles, squid and prawns passed to me with good appetite, savouring the subtle flavours. I let the first strip of beef melt on my tongue, tasting the full flavour of the Kobe beef, savouring the fat. I worked hard to master the wooden chopsticks, even though my fingers had cramp and I longed for a fork. All of it built character, improved my spirit.

The yakiniku main course ended and Akemi ordered desserts for our table. I looked at the plate of six small, white balls set before me. They reminded me of my childhood favourite dessert, snowballs, but without the coconut flakes. The white balls appeared to be made of icing sugar. I picked one up with a new set of disposable chopsticks and bit into it. The outer casing was soft and sticky with a sugary, but otherwise bland flavour and the brown filling had the texture of a sweet-mince pie, but the gritty residue of mushy peas.

"Mmm." Time to show my Japanese culinary knowledge. "These are unko, aren't they? Yum."

Tomomi sniggered. "Pardon me?"

"Aren't they unko? Jei Pi's friend Yuri brought some round the other night."

Akemi concealed an obvious grin behind her hand and spoke in Japanese with Tomomi, her speech punctuated by giggles.

I felt my face prickle. "Oh, great. What have I said now? What is it?"

"Tell Akemi what these are," said Tomomi, choking back laughter.

I hesitated. "I'm not saying it, cause clearly it means something else."

"What do you think they're called?" Tomomi looked across at Akemi and sniggered.

"Well, I thought they were called something like unko," I ventured.

Akemi and Tomomi screamed with laughter.

"They aren't unko, they're mochi filled with anko." Akemi giggled behind her hand. "Anko is sweet red bean paste. Unko means…it means…"

"Shit!" Tomomi's eyes streamed with tears. "Poo!"

Great. My plan to impress had backfired, and not only that, but I had inadvertently lowered the toilet humour tone even more. Everyone was laughing – at my expense. I sighed. What was that about a new mantra, building character, improving my spirit? Right then, I struggled to convince myself. If there was a greater life lesson to be learned, then it would be a steep learning curve, huge tribulations of the human condition for me to overcome. Whatever. I reached for the sake bottle in the middle of the table and snatched a cup. I poured a generous amount and necked it in one, aware of Tomomi's raised eyebrows. Cultural faux pas most likely, but who gave a crap? Enlightenment was for another day.

8

 C3

Eentanetto café

Sunday. Pretty lucky really that one of my days off fell on the weekend. Most Voyce teachers complained about putting in request after request for weekends, to no avail. Sunday, Monday wasn't too bad as far as days off went. My first day at the branch yesterday had been busy, because it was a Saturday, so I was glad for the rest.

I sat in my internet booth looking at a laminated menu with loads of pictures, which I was grateful for, even if most of them had rice. Rice and egg. Rice and seaweed. Rice with what looked like sesame seeds sprinkled on top. Rice and more rice. Was there anything without rice? Yes, soup.

I pushed the buzzer next to my computer and a teenage girl came over with a notepad to take my order. I pointed to a photo of yellow soup and held up one finger. Couldn't go wrong with cream of mushroom.

This was the life; Japanese internet cafes had it right. Comfy, all night booths for weary travellers to have a sleep in with massage chairs. Wooden partitions for privacy, and food to go with it. Sure put England to shame.

I logged into my email. Carl's name showed first in the inbox. Subject: Tickets. Email body: *Hi honey. Got the tickets for my trip so im all set to go. Work weren't too happy about me taking three months off so i packed it in.*

Didn't like the place anyway. Chezza put it on her credit card for me so i sold the bike to pay her back. See what i do for u? Hope ur grateful, you little brat! The trouble you put me through Manny, can't take you nowhere. From, ur gorgeous mug.

So, he'd quit work? I'd known for ages that Carl didn't like the sorting office, but they wouldn't put him on rounds. The Nine Elms Royal Mail centre gave him full time hours, but he didn't see much opportunity for promotion. He felt stuck. Still, it was no reason to resign. How would he pay the last month's rent? He was planning to move into a shared house with four other blokes in Croydon to be near his parents after he got back from Japan, but that was three months away. The deposit on our current flat, the one we had shared back in Camden, was thirteen hundred pounds of my savings, not his, and I wanted the money back. But if he skipped out on the final month's rent, we'd lose it.

I sold the bike. It gave me a pang of guilt. He loved his Honda, rode that old one-twenty-five cc everywhere. He must've loved me more than I thought to sell it for plane tickets. And Chezza had coughed up the cash? I was surprised that Carl's bitch of a sister had even bothered to help us out. Cheryl had hated me ever since she'd taken my Adlerian psychological assessment as part of my undergraduate thesis. Wasn't my fault it had uncovered Chezza's pessimistic resignation. Made sense; larger than life usually equated to an inferiority complex. Of course in hindsight, saying it bluntly to a five foot nine, twenty-two stone woman maybe wasn't the most tactful thing to do. Still, whatever. Chezza was an adult, she needed to deal with it.

Gorgeous mug. Carl was proud of the fact that he once got mistaken for Stephen Gerrard. In my opinion, it wasn't a good thing. We had been eating dinner in Knightsbridge when some bimbos had banged the window, wanting to come in for autographs. Sigh of relief that the doormen had intervened. Course, it was more of a compliment that the girls thought I looked like Gerrard's wife, Alex, but in terms of footballers, there were far better lookers. Carl had walked with more swagger in his step ever since, joking that I was his WAG, and was lucky to have him. His newly established bravado had brought some close shaves. Like queueing in VIP nightclubs lines, only to be embarrassed at the last minute. I didn't have the heart to tell him that he was much too stringy to really pass for the muscular Gerrard, and in any case, his hubris was too deep-set to believe me, even if I tried.

The Japanese girl brought my soup. Looked good. I stirred and blew, before spooning a mouthful. Tasted sweet; not like soup, but with more of a custard flavour. Once the sweetness faded, it had a distinct garlic aftertaste. I gulped it down and smacked my lips, savouring it. Taste bud overload. In terms of places to try culinary curiosities, an internet cafe with partitioned walls was the best choice: I wondered what faces I was pulling. Another spoonful, a mission which I embraced with trepidation. As the liquid swirled over my tongue, I felt solid pieces. Corn. Sensory confusion at maximum power. What sort of soup was this?

My teeth crunched. Croutons. Garlic-corn-custard soup. Weird. The creamy texture started to grow on me. A bizarre, yet satisfying experience. By the last spoonful, I loved it.

Back to Carl. What to reply to his email? Title: Garlic-corn-custard soup. Email: Served by a cutesy woman with a high pitched 'anime' voice. I stopped writing. It had never occurred to me before, but what would Carl think of Japanese women? They were all so petite and cute next to my comparatively lanky five six frame. I was pretty sure they wouldn't know who Stephen Gerrard was, but there weren't too many foreign men in Tottori, so he might as well have been a celebrity. A pang of jealousy overcame me. Those little tarts in mini skirts and fuck-me boots had better keep their mitts off. I leaned back in my chair and exhaled. No need to over-react. Japanese women were a completely different type than me. Carl liked blondes; I had no competition.

"Hey there Chica, no idear you'd be here."

Idear, indeed. Jei Pi. I didn't even have to look up to know the nasally whine and irritating pronunciation.

"Yeah, well my laptop packed in before I left London, so I'm here til I get a new one."

"You need to get your ass down to Yamada denki, the electronics store. I can take you if you want?"

Seemed the ginger cow was back to being civil after their tiff. "It's okay. I have plans with Zoe and Tomomi after this."

"Oh." Jei Pi rested her flabby chin on the wooden partition, looking deflated. "You three are lucky to have Sundays off. My days are Tuesday, Wednesday. I wanted a weekend day myself, but they wouldn't give me any."

"I know." Thank goodness.

Jei Pi's eyes flicked across to my computer. "Who're you writing to, roomie?"

I minimised the screen. "No one, just my boyfriend back in Camden."

"I split up with my boyfriend back in Maine before I came. He couldn't handle me being gone for a year."

Like I cared. I didn't even try to disguise my yawn.

Jei Pi shrugged. "It's better that way, I figure. Now I can see any Japanese guy I want."

The Japanese guy who got Jei Pi would be an unlucky bugger, indeed.

"Long distance relationships rarely work out," Jei Pi prattled on. "Why don't you dump yours and save yourself the bother?"

The bloody cheek! "Carl and I have been together for seven years. We have a really strong relationship, for your information."

Jei Pi gave a derisive snort. "That's what you think. The creep's probably cheating on you now you've gone."

"No offense, Jei Pi, but I find that really rude. I don't appreciate you making insinuations about my boyfriend." I wheeled my chair around to face my computer. "My relationship is nothing to do with you. If you must know, we're happy enough that he's coming to visit me in a few weeks."

"For how long?" Jei Pi's eyes bulged.

I couldn't resist smiling. "Three months."

"That'll cost a fortune in hotel bills."

"I was wondering if you wouldn't mind letting him stay with us – at least for a few weeks."

"Yeah, like heck it'll be a few weeks." Jei Pi's face turned beetroot. "Oy vey, you'd a cheek to get at me for not asking permission."

I folded my arms. "I *am* asking permission – or at least trying to. Anyway, he would be staying in my room, he wouldn't be in the living room, or in the way at all."

"We'll see." Jei Pi's orange mane disappeared behind the partition. "He'll probably wear out his welcome pretty soon, and then he'll be off to a hotel. Got it?"

"Well, I'm hoping you two will get along. Carl is pretty easy going."

"I'm off. I gotta go to work, and digest this news. Jeepers." Jei Pi spat every word.

Jeepers indeed, she was unbearable. Why did I have to live with Jei Pi, why couldn't Zoe be my flatmate? Why couldn't Carl be with me now? I needed comfort. Zoe and Tomomi were a sufficient substitute, but I barely knew them. What solace did I have?

My poetry. Yes, immerse myself in writing. Japan had made an idle hobby into a fully-fledged project. I finished my email to Carl, adding a note about my awful flatmate. Now, time to disappear into my writing for an hour or so. I shut down the computer, and opened my poetry journal. The scent of fresh paper on a new, blank page was comforting. I savoured the smell momentarily, my pen hovering over the empty lines, ready to write. Ready to write, any minute now. Write what?

My mind was blank, not the page. What would my online tutor at *Writers Write* say? Nothing that would give me creative inspiration at that moment, anyhow. I was too annoyed at Jei Pi and the irritation had stymied my muse.

"...Yeah, my room-mate's from London. I went there once, horrible place. The weather was awful and the food even worse, eugh! I mean, the mayonnaise was like jello-lard, and-"

Bloody distraction. I shot to my feet and looked over the wooden partition. Jei Pi was standing near the internet cafe door, talking on the phone and gesticulating like an orangutan on acid.

Don't rise to the bait, don't rise to the bait...

"Southampton, actually." I called across the cafe to where the ginger monster stood, blocking the door. "So I'm not from London, for your information. Get your facts right before you start laying into my country."

Jei Pi fixed me with a spooky, purple-lensed gaze. "Southampton? Like anyone's ever heard of that. What's so good about a place that's only famous for having a ship that sank halfway across the Atlantic."

This was war. "Better than Maine. Who's ever heard of that?"

The pucker-mouthed cow snapped her mobile phone shut. "There's loads of famous things about Maine, as a matter of fact. Stephen King's from my hometown."

"Stephen King?" I huffed. Before I could stop myself, the words rolled out of my mouth. "Well, now I know where he got the inspiration for Pennywise the Clown."

Jei Pi gawped at me, like a bloated orange carp on steroids, gasping for oxygen. I half expected her to charge, to land a punch right, smack on my nose.

Instead, Jei Pi's face broke into a wide-mouthed grin and she gave a loud, wicked-witch cackle that surely roused the whole internet cafe.

"You're such a bitch, Kimberly Thatcher." Jei Pi waggled a finger at me and watched me through narrowed eyes. "I'll get you back for that, just you see."

"I'm really scared." My voice came out a monotone.

Jei Pi turned to the door, her coat a whirling maelstrom behind her. She had to do everything with the utmost drama. I wheeled my chair back into my cosy booth. Jei Pi was three and a half months into her contract and I had been there two weeks; that meant we had eight and a half months more as flatmates. Oh my bloody gosh! If Carl didn't come soon to intervene, one of us would end up dead.

9

☙

The complications of simplicity

"Hello. I am meet you fasto time. My name is Nishima Nodoka."

The Japanese girl looked about twenty. She had a wide, silver-braced smile and her eyes were magnified behind pink, plastic glasses. I looked down at the student file with Nishima Nodoka written on it. Was Nishima her first or second name? I didn't want to make a faux pas.

"Hi Nodoka." I looked at the thirty-something man next to Nodoka. "And what's your name?"

"Harada Takayuki. Nice to meet you."

"Nice to meet you too, Harada. Er, Takayuki." Mental note that the Japanese way to introduce oneself was by family name first: Takayuki was his first name, not Harada. I shuffled the student files and set them to one side. "So, what do you both do for a living?"

"I am Pachinko girl," said Nodoka. She blinked benignly behind her specs.

"What's Pachinko?"

Takayuki smiled, reducing his eyes to slits. "Slot machines." His voice was blunt, monotonous. I wasn't sure if he was upset or not. But then he cracked a grin. "Pachinkos are run by Yakuza. She's a mafia girl."

"Mafia girl, you is too funny, Harada-san."
Nodoka brayed; a long, sheep's bleat of laughter,
making both Takayuki and I jump. This was going to
be a fun lesson.

I opened my teacher copy of the English language
textbook to the lesson I had planned. At the top, a
picture showing a man and a woman, naked except
for strategically placed fig leaves dominated half the
page. The woman held an apple in one hand and the
man gazed longingly at it. A snake dangled down
from a tree, above their heads. "Tell me about this
picture," I started.

"It is Adam and Eve," said Takayuki.

"I want you to take turns to tell me a story about
Adam and Eve, one sentence at a time. Got it?"

Nodoka and Takayuki nodded. Great. Three weeks
into the job and I was already getting better at
simplifying my language to set up activities. I was
starting to see what my trainer in Himeji, Ray, had
meant; it wasn't so complicated after all.

Information gap time; I leaned close to Nodoka
and whispered. "You're going to tell a tragedy." I
leaned close to Takayuki. "You're going to tell a
comedy."

I leaned back in my seat. "You are both going to
react to what the other person has said, so that you
can continue the conversation. You both know what
you have to do?"

Nodoka winked one hugely magnified eye.
Takayuki gave a solemn nod.

"Good. Nodoka, you can start and Takayuki, you
can continue. Remember to take turns until the end,
and to use hesitation devices if you're stuck. Can you
think of some that might come in handy?"

"Er, um, ah, eh." Takayuki rattled them off in a robotic manner, his austere expression fixed in place.

"Nice one, Takayuki." I cleared my throat; better lay off the patronising tone a bit. "And I'm glad you didn't slip in an 'eto' or 'ano' with that. Okay, fire away, Nodoka."

"Eh? Nani? What do you mean, fire away?"

I grimaced. "Let's try not to use any Japanese, please. Fire away is an expression that means, start."

"Ah, so ka. Sorry... One day there was a man and a ooman and they was talking in za garden. Bato, sadenly snake eez come down een a tree and eeto bit Adam on heezo foot."

"Okay, that was a good start." Apart from the katakana enunciation of every last incorrect syllable. Not that I'd say it though, positive reinforcement only. "And what happened next, Takayuki?"

"But Adam was a robot and he couldn't feel any pain." Takayuki's speech was slow and precise. I smiled. "Good comeback. And then?"

Nodoka hesitated, staring at the picture. "The poison was so strong that eeto burned a hole een Adam's rubber boot ando got on heezo metal foot, so he was sad."

"Nice tragedy, Nodoka."

Takayuki rubbed his chin. "Then, Eve helped him. She was a konpuuta programmer and she fixed him."

I concealed my giggle with a cough. Hilarious story, but I had to stay composed; a serious teacher. "Very good, Takayuki, well done."

Simplicity. These people were great storytellers, if not the best English speakers. Was it a Zen thing to be able to deconstruct the story of Adam and Eve, strip it to its bare essentials? Or an Eastern thing? The balance of Yin and Yang, masculine and feminine, and all that. Eve was the herione in the story, instead of the villain as in the Judeo-Christian version. Did the Japanese see women as equal, perhaps?

The complications of simplicity. Beneath the butchered English was the spark of higher understanding; a link to a complex society and its assumptions of gender. I watched the two students waiting for their next move. The corruption of innocence. Eve was no longer the baddie; she was the epitome of purity, a more enlightened being than Adam. Without woman, man would be lost.

Carl. Carl was lost. Lost his job, lost his motorbike, lost his Manny.

"Kimberly sensei," said Takayuki.

I abandoned my thoughts. "Er, yes, Takayuki?"

"I like your lessons. I think you are a good teacher. Your classes are my favourite of all Voyce teachers."

My chest swelled. "Thank you Takayuki. That's very kind of you to say."

"Me too," said Nodoka. The cute, pink, Pachinko girl nodded; with her magnified eyes, she looked like an excitable owl. "Your teaching is best. Bato, Jei Pi is worst. His lessons is very strange."

His. I fought a giggle.

"Yes, Jei Pi's teaching style confuses me too." He looked at Nodoka. "Mezurashii, ne?"

The pair nodded, and whispered in Japanese. I savoured the words they had used to describe Jei Pi's lessons: strange, confusing. Sweet revenge to hear that Jei Pi was a rubbish teacher.

Nodoka handed a small package to me, with 'Tottori' written in English letters on the front. "Here is present for you. Eto ne... you are my mosto favourite Voyce teacher. You have a small face and a tall nose."

"She means you hasn't got a wide, round face like Japanese," Takayuki explained. "And you have a straight, pointed nose, not small and flat."

I opened the package. Tottori tourist information and two free tickets for Kawahara castle. Save those for when Carl came in one week's time. "Thank you so much, Nodoka. I'm touched, really I am. It means a lot to me that my lessons help you so much."

Nodoka started talking about sightseeing places, waving her hand over the Tottori information. I filled in the words Nodoka had missed, making her English sentences complete in my head as she spoke. Teaching gave me a new appreciation of my own language. English was *hard*; I was grateful to be a native speaker. Most of the Japanese people I had met so far struggled to recall even the most basic sentences from their five years of high school English; much like how I had forgotten my French since GCSEs ended nine years ago. Spliced phrases, strings of words thrown together in random order, and not for want of trying. *Are you have an enjoy sightseeing day, please.* It made sense, but only to a native speaker who could arrange the word puzzle and create the finished jigsaw. English was the international language of Business, or so Ben had told me. I listened to Nodoka restart a sentence three times, playing verbal hop-scotch with the words. It made me thankful that I had absorbed English grammar naturally by osmosis as a baby, rather than having to pay an exorbitant fee to learn it in adulthood.

Takayuki interrupted Nodoka, jolting me from my thoughts. "Sometime I want to go to England," he said. "I want to see Big Ben. Are all English oomen so beautiful, like you?"

An unexpected turn in the conversation. I shuffled in my seat, embarrassed. "Aw, that's so sweet, thank you."

"You have a good... how can I say it? Physique."

"Figure," said Nodoka. Error correction, or so Ray had called it, when one student helped another. "For a ooman, you masto say figure."

Ooman. Woman. I let it slide. I wanted to encourage Nodoka to talk; the more she spoke, the more fluent she would be.

"Yes, but it's not what I mean." Takayuki trailed off, thinking. "Kimberly sensei has a nice hip."

"Huh?" I shook my head. "Hip? You mean, hips?"

Nodoka's face turned beetroot. "It's not nice meaning. It's chotto... eto ne. Rude. He means you have a nice shape."

"No I don't, nadaro, how can I say it?" Takyuki rolled his eyes upwards, searching the ceiling as if it would bestow the correct words upon him. "Nadatake... bom tee bom. How do I say that in English?"

"Bom tee bom? Surely you don't mean bum?" I spat the last word, unintentionally. I was offended, but couldn't conceal it.

Takayuki nodded vigorously, putting me in mind of a toy dashboard dog. "Yes, that's it. English oomen have a bom-te-bom shape." He moved his hands to demonstrate an hourglass shape.

I folded my arms across my chest. "Oh I see. So that's why you come to learn English at Voyce?"

"Yes, beautiful teachers and most fascinating talk.
Are you self-proclaimed?"

What the hell did that even mean? I didn't bother
to correct his jibberish. What was the point in
answering? The bloke might as well have been
spouting off words straight from a dictionary with no
prior thought. Dirty pervert, coming to Voyce
language school over a fetish for foreign women.

"My family don't know I study English. I come
from a Samurai family. My father thinks English is the
language of animals and Japanese is more superior.
But I have freedom in English. I can say things to
English women that I can't say to Japanese women."

I put my hands up as an invisible barrier of
protection and shook my head. "No, you're getting
English women wrong. Saying unwanted and frankly
inappropriate things to anyone, no matter where
they're from, is downright rude. Learning English
should be done with respect. It's the international
language of business, so tell that to your father and
maybe that will help broaden his insular mind."
Narrow mind, not insular, though I dared not say it.

Death of Eve. I had underestimated simplicity. I
had relaxed my guard too much with my Japanese
students, oversimplifying their needs. Learning
English was much more than learning another
language. Just as I was learning about the Japanese
language and culture, I needed to educate my students
about the English culture as much as the language
itself.

Takayuki had insulted Nodoka with his gibe about
being a Mafia-girl, and had crossed the line with his
remark about English women. I made a mental note
to tell Tomomi at reception that I'd never teach

Takayuki again. He might be accustomed to disrespecting women, but I didn't have to take it.

"What is it mean, insular?" said Takyuki, blinking blandly at me.

"Look it up in a dictionary," I said, as the beeps sounded the end of the lesson. I stood up. "See you next time, Nodoka. Goodbye, Takayuki."

Bom tee bom indeed. Bum, huh? The only arse in the room was on Takyuki's shoulders. I walked out, letting the door slam shut behind me.

10

༁

Kyoto

Sa-ra-da. Sarada. Of course: salad. I felt good. Six weeks in Japan and I had learned all of the hiragana script and most of the katakana chart. I was still slow to read, but it was nice to be able to read one of the dishes in katakana on the menu. No more needing McDonald's, or having to drag waitresses out to the window of their restaurant to point at wax moulds.

Had it really been six weeks? Yes. Because Carl was coming today. I'd been looking forward to this day since I came. And now? Nervous. Excited. Not only was it his holiday, it was mine. Two weeks off for Christmas in Kyoto and New Year in Tokyo.

I still had 'I'm in Japan' moments most days, six weeks or not. As I cycled to work through rice fields, past farmers in conical hats. As I sat in class with four baffled students, trying to explain what Guy Fawkes night meant. As I saw the distinctive red torii gate of a shrine in a natural beauty spot, or looked at road-signs written in kanji. I doubted my culture shock would ever fade. Life was surreal. I was in my own little Ja-pinglish bubble.

Should I order food before Carl arrived? I looked at my watch. Ten minutes late. A bit early to be anxious. I couldn't help it: it had been hard enough for me to find my way to Kyoto and I lived in the bloody country. How would Carl do it within his first hour? Maybe I should have met him at Kansai airport instead?

Pointless crying over spilt milk. I would get a salad and a drink. Carl never ate starters anyway; we could order a main when he got there. And I could practise my Japanese with the waiter, put some polish on it to impress Carl.

The waiter came to greet me at the door. "Irrashaimase."

I knew what that meant. Welcome. All good so far. "Nanmei sama desu ka."

Oh no. Hopes dashed. "Er, two people, please?" I held up two fingers.

"Kashkomarimashita. Kochira e dozo."

Huh? I followed him, since he seemed to get the gist. Thank goodness two fingers meant two, whether in Japanese or English. I sat at a table.

"O nomi mono wa ikaga desu ka," he said.

Shit. Think. Nomi mono meant drink, right? "Er, coke, please. Oh, and... sarada o hitotsu onegaishimasu."

He bowed and left. Nomi mono. O nomi mono. My Business Japanese book said 'o' was honorific. So sticking an 'o' in front of a word made it more polite. Useful to know. O sushi: raw fish. O hashi: chopsticks. O furo: Japanese-style bath.

The waiter returned and set my coke down. "Amerika jin desu ka," he asked.

"No, I'm English." I shook my head. "Iie, igirisu jin desu."

"O yasumi desu ka."

What the heck did that mean? I stared at him and felt my face grow hot. Wait; yasumi meant holiday, didn't it? And 'o' was honorific.

"Ah, I see. Hai, watashi wa... er, sorry. Watashi no yasumi desu. Yes, it's my holiday."

Wow, all so easy, even a bit fun. My Business Japanese book was turning out to be a good last minute buy before leaving London. Time to show off. What was this morning's rushed lesson on the train to Kyoto? *What do you do on weekends, Mister Yamada? I play tennis.* Got to stretch it out, longer sentences to impress.

I went over it in my head. *In Kyoto, what do you do on weekends? Shumatsu, Kyoto de, nani o shimasu ka.* But I would make it more formal, with an honorific thrown in. Show him that I was culturally aware.

I cleared my throat. "Shumatsu, Kyoto de, o nani o shimasu ka." Perfect. The words flowed off my tongue, like native Japanese to fellow Japanese.

The waiter didn't answer. He stared at me, the faintest tint of pink in his cheeks.

Maybe I didn't say it loud enough. "Er, you know - shumatsu, Kyoto de, o nani o shimasu ka."

No mistake; his face was flushed. He launched into a burst of flustered-sounding words, in a quiet voice, then turned and rushed into the kitchen.

Cripes. I bit my lip. It had gone wrong, but I didn't know how. Shumatsu was definitely weekend. Nani was what. Shimasu was do. O nani made it extra polite. Hmm. Better check that. I rummaged in my bag and pulled out a travel dictionary, that one of my students had given me as a present. O nani, O nani...

Onani. Masturbate. Do you masturbate at the weekend in Kyoto.

Shit!

He came out of the kitchen with my salad, his head hanging low. No wonder; I had embarrassed the poor bloke. What would he think of foreigners? Crass was one of the nicer things that came to mind. Masturbate. I looked at the opaque dressing on my salad. After what I'd just asked the guy, I dreaded to think what it was. Special sauce. Enough to torpedo my appetite.

"Manny!"

I turned. Carl. He stood in the doorway, arms outstretched, his suitcase blocking the way.

"Did you miss me? How's my little slutty geisha?"

"That's so rude, you're such a knob." I rolled my eyes.

"You know it's true. My little tart."

He swooped upon me before I had time to protest. "Eating rabbit food too I see, you'll be iron-board flat like all these Japs in no time."

"Good. It'll serve you right if I have no boobs for you to paw, you bell-end."

Carl peered at my salad. "Let's go and get some proper food, there's an English pub near the bus station. I passed it on my way."

I stood up. "I won't argue. You wouldn't believe what I just said to the waiter in Japanese before you got here."

"Nothing good, I'll bet. You chav."

I tutted at him and stood up. The waiter looked sullen as he came to meet me at the counter. He said nothing as I paid for her salad, and gave me a short, awkward bow, before muttering a few words in Japanese as we left. Hopefully not an insult.

"Our hotel's across the street. I booked it at the travel agent near my workplace, Voyce. I wouldn't have found it without their directions — did you know there's no street signs in Japan?"

"Yeah, weird place, innit? Dunno how you can live out here."

Close shave. Gotta try to dodge another uncomfortable chat. It had taken Carl ages to come round to the idea of me being away for a year in the first place, and I didn't want the mood being dampened on our holiday. Luckily Kyoto was enough of a distraction. We dumped off his luggage in reception, to take up to the room later, and went straight out to find the sights.

Grey street, crossing. Another grey street and crossing. Opulent temples, serene shrines floating in a sea of concrete as brief flashes of red and gold. Hard to find, tucked behind modern buildings, if you didn't know they were there. As we wandered into the shopping area of Shijo and Kawaramachi, the overcast sky gave way to rain. Blatant and unashamed pathetic fallacy. It was a pity how the day had transpired. Too much tiredness, hunger and stress to properly enjoy the elegance of the ancient capital. And to top it off, rain.

"These Japs all look the same. All black hair and yellow skin. At least people back home have blonde hair, ginger hair, blue eyes, green eyes. You can't tell one from another. I'll bet it's cause they're all inbred."

Shut up Carl. I blinked raindrops off my eyelashes and powered ahead, leaving him trailing behind. Always social commentary, no matter where we went. On holiday in Italy, and the people were greasy wops. In Spain and the paella was 'disgusting'. Moan, moan, moan. And the culture in Europe was similar, most people even spoke English. But this was different; virgin territory for us both. I was enjoying it, why couldn't he? Uncultured, uncouth, He could be so annoying at times.

Japan was interesting, completely different from anything familiar. Being out of my comfort zone suited me. All of my experiences were food for the soul: Japanese language, customs, weather, the landscape. My brain continually worked, my mind over-processed.

But Carl was sticking a spanner in the works of my excitement. This was no good. I didn't want to talk with Carl when he was in one of his moods. He was tired, probably jet-lagged. If we were to go sightseeing properly, it needed to be quick and solitary. Bikes.

I searched the map the travel agency had given me. Tourist information was marked with an 'I' and the map indicated a bicycle rental place next to it. I navigated us towards the location. Time to impress Carl with my Japanese.

"Jitensha... er, two, um. Futatsu onegaishimasu." I held up two fingers and pointed to myself and Carl.

Two bikes coming up. The little old lady shuffled away and came back wheeling a bike, her husband pushing the other behind her. Who said Japanese was hard? Simple. Zen country, Zen system. Just had to know how. The woman spoke Japanese in a cackling voice, her smile a gummy, toothless one. I let her finish talking, then stamped forms the woman handed me with my hanko. Six thousand yen for the day: thirty quid. Easy peasy. Now we had transport to go further afield and find Ninnaji temple and the most famous sightseeing place in Kyoto, Kinkakuji, the golden pavillion.

Smile and nod seemed to be the ticket in Japan. Pretend you knew what people said when they gave their polite, rehearsed speeches. People in shops, restaurants, businesses. Passers-by on the street. People were so friendly. They complimented my Japanese, and I responded correctly according to the culture.

Japanese person: "Ah, Nihongo wa jyozu, desu ne?" *Your Japanese is good, isn't it?*

Me: "Iie, iie, jyozu ja arimasen." *No, my Japanese isn't good.* That along with a shake of the head and an apologetic bow. Accepting compliments in Japan was arrogant; to fit in, I had to politely decline well-intentioned words. How well I fitted in. Even I was impressed at myself. A pro after only six weeks.

Ninnaji had to be around there somewhere. I looked at the temple symbol on the map. Like the other temples so far, it was most likely tucked behind a building, or up a flight of stairs, disguised by some trees. I kept my eyes peeled for a dash of red within the grey. The rain drummed on the ground. Slow and steady was the trick. I was rusty after a decade of not cycling, and it was harder in the wet weather. Deep breath. Got to be Buddhist about it all.

Carl wiped his face with his sleeve. "What did you bring me out here for? If I'd wanted rain, I would've stayed in London."

Whine, whine, whine. "You're not helping."

Ninnaji. Brown and grey, a wooden let-down; I needed a big, colourful, impressive temple to win Carl over, or at the very least, stop his whingeing. Where were the bald-headed monks I'd heard tell of? The incense I'd read about in my tourist guide? The misty mountain backdrop from my imagination? How was I supposed to tap into the Eastern mystic calm in the grey environs with carcinogenic exhaust pouring over me and Carl stifling the chi with his incessant complaints? Not to mention I had wet feet.

Carl cycled away. "Take a photo and let's go," he said over his shoulder.

"Don't worry – Kinkakuji's bound to be better than this." I shielded my camera with one hand and pressed the button.

Onwards. We weaved among the rain-soaked pedestrians. Carl kept ringing his bell, revelling in making people jump. On any other day, it might've been funny. But today, the tinny noise irritated my ears.

The golden pavilion came at a distance. This was more like it. Kinkakuji sat, serene, across a lake. The bright temple was reflected on the still water. We parked our bikes and walked to the lake edge.

What would Carl have to say now? "This more than makes up for things, don't you think?"

He stared at the golden temple. "It's alright. The Albert memorial is nicer."

"Oh come on – we're in Asia! How many people get to do what we do?"

He shrugged. "Shit loads. That's all those stupid fucking students do these days – take a gap year and go back packing. They're not original, none of them."

I exhaled hard and looked the other way. Xenophobic bastard. Take him out of England and everything was 'better in London this' and 'better in London that'. Never mind London, take him out of Croydon and nothing was good enough. He moaned about Camden, our flat, my friends.

Be the bigger person; be Zen. We were cranky because we were wet and hungry; lunch at the English pub forgotten amidst the excitement at Carl's arrival.

I took in a deep breath and sighed, feeling a touch of the divine reach me. "You know, one of my students told me that this temple was burned down about a hundred years ago by a famous Japanese writer. Apparently he wanted to see the effects of fire on gold."

"Hmph. Sounds like something you'd do just to get a poem out of it." Carl smirked. "Only, you'd do it by accident cause you're a clumsy oaf, not cause you meant to."

I nudged him with my elbow. "You're so rude. You always say such horrible things to me, I don't know why I put up with you."

"Cause you love me too much." He pulled me in for a tight hug. "And no one else would put up with you."

I rolled my eyes. "I was telling you an interesting story and you had to ruin it."

"Sorry, your highness, you were saying?"

"Never mind. You're so unromantic."

"It's an unromantic story. Go on then, tell me. Was the whole place burned down?"

I pushed out my lip. "You really want to know?"

He kissed my head. "I do. No kidding, I'm listening."

"Yes, the temple went up in flames, like sparks flying everywhere. It had to be totally rebuilt. I mean, loads of Japanese people were shocked that something like that was allowed to happen to a National treasure. I don't think the guy even got arrested."

"Why don't we do it then?"

"We're foreigners. We'd be thrown straight in jail." I watched the reflection on the lake, broken because of the raindrops rippling the surface. "It's a Buddhist nation, so you can imagine, the temple wasn't even popular in the first place by a country that values simplicity, not opulence. It goes to show you, doesn't it? Japan's weird, isn't it?"

"Told you, unromantic. You should've listened when I said the Albert Memorial is better. Good 'ol Queen Vic built that cause she was pining for her hubby after he died. You wouldn't do that for me, you'd hook up with someone right away."

I let my mouth drop. "I can't believe you'd say that – not right away, what do you take me for? I'd marry at some stage I'm sure, would you want me to be miserable and celibate the rest of my life?"

"Yes."

"Now *that's* what I call unromantic."

Another squall, as the Japanese liked to call it. Awful day, awful chat. I walked away from him, trailing my hand along the fence. Keeping my eyes on the tranquil temple kept me grounded. Serene and golden like me; it had seen its fair share of worse-weather days, as I had. Funny, it was the first day of terrible rain since I'd been in Japan and no coincidence, perhaps, that it was on Carl's visit. Symbolic, or one of those higher universal wonders that I'd yet to understand.

I stopped and looked around. The bikes. They were gone.

"Oh shit. Carl – the bikes have been nicked!"

Chaos, not tranquillity. Carl's fault. Our argument was causing bad karma in such a beauty spot. I needed to bring them back into alignment, keep the harmony in balance. Start some visualisations: we were coming together in the healing light of a purple crystal. Purple, my favourite colour. Releasing the toxins of bad energy, unblocking the chi flow. Sod's law: why had I forgotten my book on inner peace when I needed it?

Because I was in the heartland of spiritual rebalance, I didn't need it. If a journey to Asia wasn't to help my spirit grow, then what was it for?

11

❧

Daily Yomiuri

Short days. Rain lashing the windows. Space heater on full blast. Chocolate on one side, vodka on the other. Gilbeys. The only import that Jusco had, better than nothing. Drinking was becoming a habit lately. Gone were the days of occasional Smirnoff Ices. I needed Gilbeys every weekend to warm the January days.

The weeks went by in a haze. A blur of snow. Carl had been over for three weeks. We'd spent New Year's in Tokyo at Sensoji Temple in Asakusa. I had gotten one rushed photo of him amidst all the wafting incense. Looking at the developed print now made me sad; it was a fading memory, sliding into the annals of yesteryear. Could I manage the first draft of a poem to capture the moment? Maybe a quick one before Carl got back from Lawson's with his Asahi. I had a poem brewing, Carl was simply on the brew.

Probation wage. Two more weeks until my observation to decide whether I would get a pay rise. In the meantime, money was tight. Carl had brought three hundred quid, which had barely lasted through Kyoto and Tokyo. I sighed before opening my poetry journal and touching pen to paper.

Ode to Sensoji
Folding back on itself
four times over
a magnificent snake

of worshippers, fused;
one entity,
under the giant lantern,
I stood, an intruder
a foreigner; gaijin
watching the ritual
of clapping and bowing,
cleansed in incense
while I, a lone yellow soul
in a wave of black
floated lost in a sea
of words unknown to me.

"What's that crap you're writing?"

Carl. He leaned over my shoulder, sneering down his nose at my poetry journal. I shielded it with my hand, then shut it.

"You waste more time on that boring shit than you do spending time with me," he said.

I slipped my book under the futon. "It's not boring shit – and anyway you were at the shop."

He tossed his six pack next to me, squashing my chocolate. "It doesn't even make sense. How can a snake be the sea?"

"It's a metaphor, for your information. What are you now, literary critic of the year? You're so annoying, Mr. Erudite."

"Big words from a small, stupid girl. You think you're so fancy." He flopped down beside me on the futon and cracked open a can of beer.

"I'm not stupid. Would someone stupid get a Masters in Clinical Psychology from UCL?"

He tutted. "Go ahead, lord it over me. Whoopy fucking do, so you have an education. You're the same as all these other rich toff dopey students who get their degree with Daddy's money and fuck off to Asia for some spiritual growth."

The corners of my eyes stung. "I can't believe you said that."

He paused, staring at me. Then he leaned close and kissed my forehead. "You know I love you really. I'm in full support of your profession – didn't I tell you, you shouldn't give up the day job."

"You're making fun of me." I shoved him and he toppled over. All a joke, no harm done.

Crunching sound. Carl grinned up at me. "You just squashed dinner."

"I'm sure it's still edible. What culinary delight did you bring home then, dear?"

He pulled a packet out of his hoodie. Spaghetti Bolognese from the One Hundred Yen shop: the equivalent of fifty pence. I wrinkled my nose. "Gourmet. Bargain bin food again, I see?"

He shrugged. "The beer cost a thousand yen, wasn't my fault it was a fiver. You should've given me more money, you cheapskate."

"Hey, I'm feeding us, don't forget. I could turf you out on your ear and what would you do then?" I scowled at him. Good. One up.

Carl smirked. "Big neb would want it that way. That cow of a flat mate of yours should do this diet too. She could do with losing a tonne of weight."

"Diet? Starvation more like it. I'm glad I've got chocolate and vodka left over. Empty calories is better than nothing."

"Ah, stop your yapping." Carl stood up. He grabbed his beer and walked out.

What's that crap you're writing. My poem wasn't crap, his meagre dinner was. So beer was more important than food? Yes, if it was his beer. I poured vodka into what was left of my coke and took a swig. Stiff. Just what I needed.

The sound of Japanese TV from the living room droned on. I rested my cheek in my hand. It was turning out to be a long winter. Not much to do in Tottori, considering I hated winter sports. Things with Jei Pi were still at an impasse and as for Carl and me, we were pretty much in hibernation until the following weekend when we would be off on our next venture to Matsue. I was glad for Carl's company, a reminder of home in a foreign land. Maybe the meagre dinners were worth it; Buddhist monks starved themselves to climb through the hole of enlightenment at Todaiji temple in Nara, after all. I'd find out soon enough if Nirvana was in my fate when we went to Nara, after Matsue.

Sightseeing. Temples. Inner peace. Starvation. All to gain higher knowledge and wisdom for the next life. Carl was right about my poem. It was shit. It didn't do Sensoji temple any justice at all. I needed to be a better writer. No, I needed to *master* my craft.

I scratched out *Ode to Sensoji* and wrote a new title: *Sensoji Temple.*

As I stood, watching
the line of patient worshippers
inching towards the giant lantern,
I stood, motionless,
electrified by incessant chatter,
smells of soba and tempura
lingering in the air,
and knew,
that it wasn't my religion
my ritual, or my place,

and so I went back
to the arms of my love.

Better. More humanity, fitting with the touch of Eastern promise. Carl would like it. I reached for today's copy of The Daily Yomiuri. A bit of higher wisdom was in order to purge the soul of the winter blues.

Horoscopes. Aquarius.

You must face up to someone if you are to get your own way. Right now, you need to be more forceful and use a more self-interested approach. Often you go along with the plans of others, simply to keep them happy.

Hmm. Not so good. I looked down at Cancer, Carl's sign.

Now is a good time to do some thinking about your personal life. You seem to be making a strenuous effort to find out what somebody else feels about you on a romantic level; after all, the crab doesn't like to walk alone. However, you must avoid any kind of possessiveness.

Interesting. Could be coincidence, or could be a greater power giving me some much needed thinking material to mull over, but I couldn't help recalling Carl's words on our first date:

"Do you mind possessive men?"
"Not really. In a boyfriend, it shows he cares about me."
"Good. Because I'm possessive."

Carl. He was so sweet. Always looking out for me, always pushing me to do my best. He knew I wanted to be a poet, so he kept me on my toes, making sure I did my best work.

My stomach rumbled. Time for some Buddhist food; minimal and essential. I brought the spaghetti packet into the kitchen and tore it open on the counter.

"Are you in a better mood now?" He didn't look up, his eyes on the tacky gameshow.

"I was never in a bad mood to start with, oh my gosh, you can't take a joke!"

He jerked his thumb towards me. "Did you see those hooks?"

"What hooks?"

"Fatty put hooks along the wall to hang your pots."

"So?" I took a pot off a hook and dumped the spaghetti in it.

"She's changing things without asking you."

I shrugged. "I don't care, as long as it's for the better."

"She's controlling you. She thinks she owns you."

I lit the burner. "That's rubbish. How could she control me - we don't even talk?"

"And did you see on the table? I left all her shit from her Japanese lesson with that Yuri girl this morning."

"Yeah, and?" I stirred the spaghetti. What was he getting at now?

"She can't have her lessons on your day off – it interrupts our time together. It really pisses me off to be woken by that fanny-eyed mate of hers coming in at half nine." Carl took a swig of beer. "You'll have to talk to her about it."

"Carl, don't say things like that about Japanese people." I stirred too hard and sauce slopped onto the counter. "And what am I supposed to say to Jei Pi? I don't have a problem with it. Do you want me to say, 'oh by the way, can you have your Japanese lessons on your own day off instead of mine, cause my boyfriend who's staying here rent free for three months hates being woken up too early?'"

"Yeah, that about sums it up."

"Forget it – there's enough bad blood between me and Jei Pi as it is."

"All I'm saying is, it's not fair. It's not like you have a fanny-eyed mate round waking that fat bitch up at fuck knows what hour."

"Carl, stop saying that – it's a horrible way to talk about Asian people."

"What, fanny-eyes? But it's true, innit?" He pointed at the TV. "Look at this shit, this guy is called Hard Gay. They're not exactly P.C. out here themselves, are they?"

I looked at the dumpy man clad in leather, prancing about on the screen with his nipples circled in permanent marker. "Still, it doesn't mean you have to be racist."

"I'm not racist, I'm honest." He set his empty can down and cracked open another. "Come on, do you find this sort of thing appealing? Some fucking nancy boy like that?"

"Well, no – but what do you mean, appealing?"

"As in, if you weren't seeing me, would you go out with a Japanese bloke?"

I stopped stirring and folded my arms. "That's a weird question to ask?"

"In other words, no." Carl leaned back, looking smug. "Whereas I, on the other hand, have seen one or two Japanese women who're rather passable, for fanny-eyed girls of course."

An acrid whiff. I snapped from my thoughts. Burning. A moment's distraction and the spaghetti in sauce was stuck like a lump of shit on the bottom of the pan.

"Carl, please. Just cool it a bit, yeah? Things are tough enough without causing more friction around here."

He looked brooding. "What's that meant to mean?"

"I just want to focus on studying grammar for my test to get off teacher probation, okay?"

Carl turned up the TV volume. "Fine. Have it your way as usual. You care more about that shit job than you do about our relationship."

"What? Oh come off it, that's not fair. I've done loads of shift swaps so we can go to Nara and Matsue and God knows where else. I'm trying my best, please honey."

"Please honey nothing. You're so selfish, Manny. You don't ever think about me, do you? I don't have a degree, I can't work out here with you. I'm in the middle of a career change myself and do I have your support? No! You piss off to some country across the world because you don't think of us, you only ever think of you."

I swallowed a dry lump in my throat. "That's not true, don't say that. What's good for me is good for us both. I need to do this – I'll be a better person for it."

"You and your New Age spiritual growth crap. You know what I think about all this Buddhist bullshit? You clearly hate it here and this job stresses you out. I don't know why you can't see sense and pack it all in. You had a good job as a trainee psychotherapist with an opportunity for career progression and you left it for this dead-end post. I can't for the life of me think why you won't come home with me. You must be completely radio fucking rental."

He sank low on the sofa. A single tear ran down my cheek.

"I just want to make you happy." My voice shook. I swallowed. "But I don't know how."

"I've told you how and I won't say no more. Maybe you'll listen when you grow up a bit."

"That's not fair and you know it. I thought we'd agreed all this before I left London. You said you were okay with me going to Japan for a year, if it meant I'd come back and marry you at the end of it."

"Yeah, that was back in Camden," he spat. "The reality is not exactly hunky dory now, is it? Out here, it's just all about you, you, you. You're a selfish bitch."

My appetite was gone. I went into my room, letting the tears flow. What did the Daily Yomiuri say? Face up to someone if you were to get your own way. But there was no pleasing Carl. I thought we'd reached a compromise before I'd left England. Apparently not. Not a compromise, an impasse.

Face up to someone if you are to get your own way. Was the Daily Yomiuri right?

Fine. Have it your way as usual. Or Carl?

Was Carl right? Was I selfish?

How could my whole journey be for higher knowledge and spiritual understanding if it hurt others? Clearly Carl was in pain. Emotional turbulence blocked the path to inner happiness. I took a bite of chocolate and washed it down with a swig of vodka. Food for the spirit.

How long had I been lying in bed? Hopefully Carl had cooled off a bit. Better see if he was stewing, simmering, or over it altogether.

Gone. Must've went out for a fag and not come back. I felt a twinge of hurt. So, he wasn't even going to tell me? The spaghetti pot had been scraped out and sat empty in the sink. Carl had either been considerate by binning it, or selfish by eating it all. I checked the rubbish. Nothing. Fine. He was the selfish bastard then, not me. Didn't even bother to soak it, plain thoughtless.

Jei Pi's Japanese books were shoved into a dog-eared pile on the kitchen table. I tidied them. No point aggravating the ginger monster any further. On the cleared patch of table, Carl had left a note, ripped from Jei Pi's notebook. I picked it up.

There was a young girl called Manny
Who had a smelly fanny
She opens her heart
and lets out a fart
and I find it all so funny

Awful attempt at a limerick; badly rhyming and mixed tenses. The cheeky imp was trying to one-up me. He should've used 'uncanny' instead of 'funny'. Nevertheless, job done. I couldn't stay mad at Carl. I folded the note and smiled.

12

☙

Material Needs

"Wow, how did you get so many students in your *Chat* class today? I've never seen the room so crowded." Ade flashed an impressed smile.

I couldn't help giving a sly grin. "Talent. I did my topic on superstitions and themed it around Friday the thirteenth. People go for scares every time. Piece of cake. I gave them British coins for prizes if they guessed right. They'd never seen UK coins before."

"Did they tell you about the numbers four and nine?"

"Yeah, death or something. But they told me better ones too, some Buddhist stuff."

Ade frowned. "Like what?"

"Well, like you know how most bodies are cremated in Japan? Shinobu said that when a body is prepared for cremation, it has to face south. Something about good luck for the spirit or other. She didn't really know the significance with facing south though."

"Shinobu's my favourite student, I always try to get Tomomi to book me for her lessons on days when I know she's in." Ade looked deflated. "Wonder why she didn't tell me? How do you get so much information out of the students?"

I gave a dismissive wave. "Maybe she likes me."

"You must've bribed Shinobu with the money, didn't you? I'll bet that's what you did. And you probably offered the guys kisses – or more!"

I bristled. "I don't have to do any such thing to get the students talking, I'm just popular. You're jealous cause you fancy Shinobu and she won't have any of it."

Vince walked into the staffroom. "What's that? Who's popular? Who fancies who?"

Ade jerked his thumb at me. "Kimberly gives the students money in exchange for kisses."

"Oh come on, lying now? Really mature." I stood up.

"Hey, I've got an idea," said Vince. "You should come into my fitness *Chat* class next week - I could do with more students coming. Maybe you could wear a bikini."

Ade and Vince guffawed, morons that they were. I rolled my eyes. Enough of the ribbing. "Ha, ha. You're both hilarious, any more of your exhilarating quips and I'll die of laughter."

Idiots. I shook my head, smiling to myself as I walked to reception. Conscious of my grin I sobered my expression and exhaled, loud enough for Ade and Vince to hear the dramatic gesture, which I'd done for their benefit. Was I flattered? Being honest with myself, yes. To joke about my looks like that meant they had to find me attractive. Why did that matter to me? It certainly wasn't spiritual to objectify another person. I would have to reflect on why base flattery mattered, when normally it didn't.

As I turned into reception, I almost crashed into Ben. "Hey there, everything alright?" he said.

"What? Uh – oh, yeah, fine. I was away there for a minute, didn't mean to block your way."

"You just looked so serious, I thought I'd ask what's the matter."

"Nothing, I'm fine." I fixed a smile.

"Settling in okay? You aren't worried about your teacher probation observation coming up?"

I shook my head. "It's not that. Though the money will help."

"Mm, I heard you were having a hard time money-wise. Listen, if you need to borrow the odd ten thousand yen here and there, you just let me know, 'kay?"

Fifty quid. Generous. "Thanks Ben. I might have to at some point."

He squeezed my shoulder and walked past. "Not a problem. I like to think I'm not such a stuffy boss, eh?"

Hard times. Tottori was turning out to be a major tribulation of the human spirit. I waved goodbye to the Japanese staff on the front desk and took the escalator down.

Down. Down and out? My feet carried me onwards. I let them take charge, walking on automatic pilot as I fell victim to my musings once again. Why was it always fights? Fights with my flat mate, fights with my boyfriend, fights with my colleagues. Did I bring it on? Maybe I had accrued too much negative energy, bad karma?

I walked out of Jusco and got on my bike. What I needed was a good girly night out. But Carl protested every time. I hadn't had so much as a coffee with Zoe and Tomomi since he came. And even if he didn't stop me, I barely had the money. Yes, this was down and out. Carl had three weeks before leaving Japan, and so I wanted to spend all my free time with him, in any event. Still, all we did was argue these days. I wiped a tear off my cheek and cycled into the bitter night wind.

Onto the bridge over Sendai river; an uphill struggle. When Carl left, I'd have no free time to go out with the girls either. I'd be working all the shift swaps I'd taken to go sightseeing with him at Nara and Matsue. At least it had been worth it. The rows of Samurai armour at old wooden Matsue castle had been impressive, and Nara was stunning. The original ancient capital of Japan hadn't disappointed my Buddhist notions; the sheer size of Todaiji temple alone was mind-blowing, never mind the breath-taking giant golden Buddha inside. Thankfully I had been thin enough to fit through the hole of enlightenment, what with all the meagre meals Carl and I had been having to accommodate our increasing habit of self-medication. Asahi mornings for Carl washed away his winter blues. Then Sapporo afternoons, onto Shochu evenings. And for me? Vodka night after work to fight the monsters in my sleep.

Downhill and through the underpass by the river into Akisato. How ironic that living in Villa Libido had turned out to be an anti-climax. How many times had we fornicated in nearly a month? One let down of a time. I turned into my street and parked in front of my grey duplex.

The burden of the steps tired my legs as I climbed to my flat. What was for dinner tonight? A one hundred yen pot noodle each, half a left-over pizza-baguette from yesterday to split and a bag of nuts to share for tonight's dessert and tomorrow morning's breakfast. A Royal feast fit for a Queen of the Blues. I forced my key in the lock and turned it with a sigh. A tough day at work and now home to be moaned at by Carl, after his daily routine of drinking beer at Karo beach and reflecting on his stalled career. What a shit end to the evening.

I stepped inside. This was really the pits.

"Hello? Carl?"

No answer. Light on, then into the living room. No Jei Pi, mercifully. From my peripheral vision, I caught sight of the bathroom screen in the corner, slid shut. Full of condensation too. I walked across and knocked. Still no answer. Carl's boxers lay below the sink. I opened the door.

"Carl? Why didn't you answer when I called?"

He sat chest-deep in the water, stony-faced, his skin red from the heat. "Take a look in the bedroom and you'll find out."

He glared at me, forcing me to break eye contact. Mystified, I went to my room.

Photos were laid out on my futon; pictures of a night out I'd had with my friends at Piccadilly Institute, two weeks before I had left for Japan. They had been pulled from one of my photo albums.

I went back into the bathroom. "Huh? I'm confused. What is it?"

"If you don't know, that's even worse." Carl said no more, his jaw clenched.

I put my hands up in a gesture of defeat. "Clearly I don't know. Would you enlighten me please?"

"You. Sitting on Ronnie's knee."

"Yeah, and? He's my friend. I sat on Aaron's knee too."

"Aaron's gay. It's different."

"It is *not* different. I sat on Sasha's knee too, big deal, they're my friends. It's just drunken silliness."

"It's more serious than that. Why didn't you tell me about these goings on before?"

I let my head bang against the sliding door. "What goings on? I really think you're over-reacting to all this."

Carl clenched his jaw. "Aaron's gay, Sasha's a girl — but Ronnie's straight."

"Ronnie's engaged — you've met Clara, you know how into her he is." I pulled the sliding door across until it was almost shut. "I don't believe we're even having this argument. I'm going to make dinner."

"You're not going nowhere till you get rid of those photos. If you want to act like a stupid fucking kid, then you'll learn to deal with the consequences."

"What's that supposed to mean?" I scowled. He needed to know he was being irrational. "I'll hide them away, so your delicate eyes won't have to see them ever again."

"Not good enough. You'll have to rip them up. If you can't do that, then Ronnie means more to you than you're letting on."

I let his words digest. "I don't believe what I'm hearing. After nearly seven years, you don't trust me. Ronnie's not even my type, even if I *was* single."

"Do it. I'll say no more."

"Fine. Have it your way." I slammed the sliding door fully shut. Carl was exasperating at times. I stamped into the bedroom, snatched up the photos and flew back to the bathroom in a hurricane of anger.

"Here, Carl – watch." I tore the photos and threw them into his bath water. "Are you happy now? That's how much Ronnie means to me."

Out. Out of the room, out of the flat, into the cold early evening air. This was rock bottom alright. Too many insults, not enough money. As spiritual as I wanted to be, material needs were always on my mind. I should've taken Ben's ten thousand yen and drank all of it at the local izakaya. But for now, hunger. Empty stomach, empty night, full mind. Full of detritus. Something would have to give, soon. Hopefully not any more food. Compliments on my figure came more frequently the thinner I got – flattery was material needs for the brain. Japanese people were obsessed with *thin* and I revelled in the attention, but as I lapped up the praise, it blocked up my psyche. Clogged, like cholesterol for the soul. Deep breath. Be centred. Be zen. Keep walking. I turned the corner towards Lawson and the main road. Stay balanced; I had to ignore both compliments and insults.

Ah, the sacrifices.

13

ଏଓ

Dark room

I opened my eyes in the darkness. Carl was sitting up in the hotel bed, staring at the TV. But the TV wasn't switched on.

"Carl, what is it?"

He turned and looked over his shoulder at me. "I can't sleep. They keep going at it next door."

"Put the TV on, I don't mind. Better to drown out the sound than listen to it all night."

I rolled over. Carl was fast asleep next to me. Wait: two Carls. One on his side, eyes shut, the other upright, disturbed. My head, disturbed.

Watashi no sei de, atama ga okashiku naru yo... I'm out of my mind... I'm out of my mind...

"Carl, what's going on?"

The TV was on fire. The red dot, signal of no signal was glowing, throwing burning light across the blank screen. I jolted upright and rubbed my eyes. No fire; tricks of the early hours, tricks of my mind. Mind playing tricks. Mind games. Damn. English my first language and yet I was translating it, rearranging the sentence structure of my own thoughts. Crazy country, attacking my sanity.

Carl had gone. I looked around. The hotel room door lay open. The corridor beyond was poorly lit. Why didn't the lights come on automatically? Who was running the bloody place?

Carl's face appeared in the doorway. "I went to find out what's making the noise. The room next to us is haunted."

"What? What do you mean?"

"I mean there's a ghost."

Wow. Sounds of the thrashing deceased. I pulled the blanket close to my chest.

"I'm going to complain at reception," said Carl. "They knew this place was haunted when they booked us in."

He turned on the TV and cranked the volume up. I clapped my hands over my ears and sat, waiting for him to come back.

No return. The TV droned on. The headboard vibrated with the reverberations from the wall behind. Beyond it, a corpse, tormenting me. I walked to the window.

In the street below, a crowd had gathered around a three-tiered wooden structure that looked to be an unlit bonfire. It was crudely fashioned, like a tree-house pagoda. The people threw books, clothes, possessions onto the heap. I walked downstairs and joined the throng in the street.

As I got nearer, I noticed that the people were all dressed in Elizabethan-era English clothing, apart from a ring of what looked like Polynesian people in traditional grass skirts closest to the fire. The items on the pile were paraphernalia belonging to a witch. I took my place among the semi-circle of Hawaiian people. I was out of place, still in my pyjamas, but I blended among the circle as if I were one of them. At my feet lay a gold watch, similar to the one Carl had given me on our first date. His had been a family heirloom, passed down to him from his grandfather:

he had said that he wanted me to have it because I was special. But the watch at my feet had stopped, frozen five minutes into the witching hour. I swung it into the air and it landed on top of the wooden structure.

One of the Polynesian people had a torch. I held it for him to light, then threw it onto the structure. The wood caught light and fire spread from the middle upwards and down towards the bottom. The golden watch shone in the glow before it was consumed.

A hideous roar announced the coming of the witch. She was gruesome and odious, with yellow-grey sagging skin and grey-streaked hair that hung in limp strands all over her plain, white nightdress. An air of menace clouded her aura; she was the epitome of evil. I stood back as the witch lashed out in protest at the burning of her belongings.

"Get the witch," yelled one of the English men. "Chuck her on too!"

The crowd grabbed the witch and threw her onto the bonfire. I didn't help; a witch was still a person, and I would have no part in burning a human. Yet the human in me couldn't tear my eyes from the carnage. The witch shrieked as sparks attacked her clothes and hair. The fire burned high, bright. When there was no more to burn, it died away until a few embers remained.

No more witch. Dead. Death of evil.

I looked around. The people had scattered, the English leaving without a word. The Hawaiians had already gone. I looked up to my hotel window. Carl's face appeared against the dark pane and for a brief instant, she saw the dead witch's face over his shoulder.

"Carl!"

I raced back inside and ran upstairs. The hotel room was empty. No Carl, no witch and our possessions had gone. No money, no clothes.

A horrible thought crossed my mind. What if *I* was the witch?

I clutched my chest and staggered to the window. I turned around. The hotel room door had gone. I was in a sealed room with silver-blue metallic walls. There was no door, only a window.

In the street below, I could see houses, parked cars, vegetable gardens and rice fields; my street in Akisato. No more hotel room, no more bonfire. I was looking out from my bedroom in Villa Libido.

I was awake.

What a horrible, terrible nightmare. I stood at my bedroom window with both palms on the glass, my breath condensing on the frosted pane. A wave of embarrassment overcame me. Had I been sleep-walking? But I'd never been prone to somnambulating before. Had I woken Carl? Jei Pi?

I looked around. Carl was asleep, the covers tucked tight around him on the futon. I walked back to my futon and lay down.

***

"Carl, seriously, I had the freakiest series of nightmares last night." I rubbed my eyes and smoothed back my hair, chasing any residue of night terrors away.

Carl spooned his cereal. "You know why? You give too much credit to that radio-rental dream interpretation rubbish you do. If you didn't take it so seriously, it wouldn't fill your head with shit."

"Dream analysis – and it's serious. That was the basis of my thesis at Uni that I spent a whole year working on, only for you to sit there and slag it off." I took a bite of toast and chewed, watching him. "But really, did you hear me shouting out last night? I mean, I swear I was loud enough to wake the dead."

"No I didn't. And I heard you asking Jei Pi earlier too. You know what I think? This place – Tottori – is driving you mad. When you get snowed in like this with sod all to do, you get cabin fever. I think you should come home with me next week. Otherwise, give it a month and they'll be sending you home anyway to check into a funny farm."

I reached into my pocket. I had grabbed Carl's gold watch as soon as I had woken up. It was like an amulet in my pocket, warding off bad omens from the night. I rubbed it with my thumb. The gold watch in my dream had burned, along with the witch. The Shakespearean English people and native Polynesians harked back to a more ignorant, innocent and uncorrupted state in my mind. The witch and evil paraphernalia was self-explanatory. But the dream-watch? Was Carl's watch evil too?

He had given it to me because he said I was special. How many women had been special before I had? In the seven-odd years I had known him, I had never doubted Carl's love for me – until now.

I let go of the watch and felt its weight as it hit the bottom of my pocket.

14

ɞ

Winds of spring from China

Satisfaction/ happiness working at Voyce = 5/10.
Overall happiness in Japan, including sightseeing = 7/10.
Enough incentive to stay?

I stopped writing. I hoped so. Today was my teaching off-probation observation: make or break at work. If probation got extended, should I quit?

If. What type of question was that? Conditional. Good practise for my grammar test. Turn the negatives into a positive.

My student would be along any minute and Ben too, to observe my lesson. Gotta get all extraneous thoughts out of my head. No Carl, no fights. No nasty colleagues. Only work. Only English.

All work. Was I selfish? *You care more about that fucking job than you do our relationship.* Should I blow it on purpose, do a bad job to sabotage my career as an English teacher? Go home with Carl as he wanted. Maybe he was right after all. I was only thinking of my own needs when I had made the decision to come to Japan.

But no. Everything happened for a reason. Yes, it had started as a self-growing-learning-fulfilling desire, but now fate had intervened. This was part of my pre-planned destiny.

A destiny that didn't include Carl? He was unhappy for sure. And he had waited on me long enough. Through my A-levels, through Uni and now as I embarked on a new career. Should I pay him back for his patience by going home to help him sort out his own path in turn? Or should I nurture my own desires in a place where I knew I'd neither settle nor make a career. Did I really owe Carl, and even if I did, was that how relationships worked? He'd hindered me as much as helped me during my A-levels, when he'd cheated on me with his ex.

I don't love her, I never did.

Then why did you go back to her house?

We stayed friends. I was drunk. It was an accident.

What, so you took off your clothes by accident? Your dick got hard by accident?

Alright, it was a mistake, not an accident. I thought I wanted it, but I was wrong.

You thought you wanted her?

Not her, just sex, the idea of it.

Just sex, the idea of it. I sighed. If only it were that simple. I was torturing myself. It wasn't very Buddhist of me to keep score. Let go of Carl's past indiscretions; scars on the psyche only served to block the passage to enlightenment. Stay focussed on the issues at hand. Would I regret it if I stayed in Japan? Sure, I was enjoying the ride, but was that all it could ever be, a ride? Would I be a better, more worldly-wise person if I stayed the full year?

Distractions! I was becoming a bit too self-preoccupied lately. Too much drifting off, less staying grounded in the moment. The issue at hand was my teaching off-probation observation. Got to stay centred, be balanced. No more mind and body going their separate ways.

The door of the glass booth opened and in walked Koichiro Saito, my student. A quick processing of his name and I was ready for the handshake.

"Hello Koichiro, I'm Kimberly."

"Haro Keembaree, nice-ooh to meet you," said Koichiro.

"How are you today?"

"I'm very well, and you?"

The exchange of pleasantries was robotic and perfunctory, more so because I could see Ben from the corner of her eye, scribbling away. How I longed for English; proper colloquial English, none of this falsely enunciated crap I had to speak in a stilted tone for the sole purpose of making my students understand me. A Queen's English accent put on just to make Japanese people studying English feel like they could communicate, while I clapped and praised their rubbish attempts in a sanitised bubble of no-swearing, no-slang, faux-posh English tosh. I wasn't a qualified teacher, I couldn't give any real feedback other than positive reinforcement; constructive criticism could cost Voyce Language School their paying customers, so my employer had a vested interest in my ability to speak like a toffee-nose. Really, I was no better than a hostess in a Tokyo bar, paid to sing and laugh and praise guests and act like an all-singing, all-dancing clown. What a joke it was; what a joke I was.

Vent those feelings. How I was tempted to prattle on in London slang, watch Mr. Saito's head spin. Let's speak proper fucking English, innit, bruv?

Alcohol. I needed a drink. The lesson was awful; my timing off, my explanations poor and a moron for a student on top of it. I wanted to throw the textbook, walk out and never come back.

"What does it mean, she-ah-chin?"

I felt my face burn. Shut up! Stop asking questions. Stop getting me in trouble. Stop scribbling, please, Ben!

"Em – a sea urchin is a funny looking creature with spiky bits all over and it's usually red."

"Eh? Nani?"

I drew a hasty picture; a circle with sharp lines protruding from it in all directions.

"Ah, you mean, uni. It's green in Japan, not red, and we can eat it in sushi."

Green. Red. See red. Argh. When was the lesson over? It was killing me slowly, lulling me into a stupor. No, that was green. This was red. Rage. Yes, this was bright red; a power colour. Ah, shit, I'd drawn a picture of an anemone, not a sea urchin. What did a bloody sea urchin look like anyway?

Oh my gosh. Take control.

"So what's the strangest food you've ever eaten?" I asked.

"I have eaten she-ah-chin and I have eaten tattle."

"Turtle," I corrected. "Good work Koichiro, nice job!"

Lesson done, student gone. Ben gone, head down. It was over. Whatever happened now was out of my hands. If Ben gave me a fail, so be it. I liked not having to make the decision whether to stay or go, it would be down to my work.

Enjoying the ride. But was I really, or was I lying to myself? I honestly didn't know. I really needed someone to tell me the answer, even give me a little guidance. At twenty-five, I felt not yet mature, not wise, yet not naive. And if I was honest, if I was honest...

I couldn't be bloody-well arsed.

Last lesson of the early shift, out of work, sayo-fucking-nara. Carl waited at the bottom of the escalator. I could see him before he saw me. Looked like he was preoccupied. He stared ahead into the women's clothes shop opposite: *Classy Girl*. Dance music blared out from the store and a pretty Japanese girl bustled about putting club-wear on dummies. Carl tapped his foot along to the music.

I stepped off the escalator. "You're early for a change."

"And you look nice – for a change. A first for everything."

"Ha, ha, cheeky sod." I clipped him round his ear. "Well, it's over. I'm out of my limbo. Amazing how in the space of twenty-four hours I'm finally free. No more grammar test, no more weight on my shoulders."

"Except me," said Carl, his eyes behind me, drifting aimlessly in *Classy Girl*.

"No, you're my rock, not my weight." I started towards the door. "Let's go. Where do you fancy? Wanna go for lunch to celebrate?"

Carl held up a Lawson bag. "I already got us a liquid lunch and some sandwiches to split."

"Great. Let's go to the beach."

I led the way around *Classy Girl*. The Japanese shop assistant putting club-wear on dummies looked over as we got near. She walked towards us, making a beeline for Carl and stood in front of him, forcing him to stop.

The girl looked right up at him. "It's a new dress. How do I look? Sexy?" she asked.

Carl's face flushed. "Er — yes," he said.

Bold! How dare the tart catch him off-guard, just to wheedle a cheap compliment out of him in faltering English. I put both hands up in front of the girl's face.

"Excuse me, you're in the way." I looked down my nose at the petite, pretty girl, who held her chin high as she glared back.

"Leave it, just ignore her." Carl prodded me between my shoulder blades with his knuckles, goading me to walk on. Was it my imagination, or was it more like he was telling *the girl* to ignore *me* rather than the other way round? No; only me being stupid, and paranoid.

"See ya round," he said, in a chirpier tone to the girl; dare I say it, almost a flirty tone.

I shook my head. "Can you believe the audacity of that girl? She was practically throwing herself at you, just because you were interested in the music in her shop."

"She probably thought we were colleagues at Voyce — I'll bet she didn't realise we were a couple." He tugged my sleeve. "Come on, forget it."

I huffed. "What did you have to say yes for, encouraging her?"

"Slip of the tongue." Carl looked over his shoulder at the girl's retreating back as she disappeared into her shop. I noticed a smile flash across his face for a mere second.

"Alright, when you've finished drooling."

We exited and rounded the corner of Jusco. Wind hit me hard in my face, cooling my body, refreshing my mind. Let go. Gotta let go.

First winds of spring. Apparently they blew from China, or so Hiroki, one of my students said in *Chat* class. True or not, it was a romantic thought. Winds from the desert in China, bringing with them a fine dusting of sand to coat the houses and cars of Tottori. The smell of spring was certainly in the air. I felt happier. Was there any need to turn Anti-Christ on the poor shop worker in *Classy Girl*? The woman didn't deserve the brunt of my bad mood. She was simply a backwards country girl who'd probably never been to Osaka, never mind abroad. And here I was, a world traveller, the bigger person. Literally and figuratively speaking. To top it off, I had Carl, we'd soon be married and that girl was single and sad. I pitied the poor, pathetic girl.

We got on our bikes and started towards the river. The wind from China was so strong, it blew us along the path. I lifted my legs off the pedals and let it carry me forth, faster than I could cycle. Enjoy the ride? Yes.

Yes, I'd had my ups and downs so far, but I could see light at the end of the tunnel. In the long run, I would forget the dark days of snow and remember the politeness of the people in Japan and the fun I'd had sightseeing. Spring brought with it spiritual awakening. I was on an adventure that most people weren't fortunate enough to ever have. Maybe as spring blossomed, my blinkered sight of winter would be given a new perspective. Save it for a poem:

The birth of new feelings
Oh mountain high! Oh river deep!

Awaken me from this sleep
The winter has taken its toll
It's nearing spring and I'm on a roll
The breeze is new, I smell a fresh scent
Some days are truly heaven sent

Jot it down in my poetry journal later. For now it could swirl amidst all the other thoughts, edging out the colourful choice of words from earlier that could put a dampener on even the brightest spring sky.

We parked our bikes at Tottori harbour and walked along the sand. Too cold yet for wading, yet it would've relaxed me; my calm was broken. Rubbish was strewn everywhere, all along the water line. Hiroki had told me about this too. Though according to him, it was all washed up from Korea. The kanji on the discarded food packets and bottles looked Japanese, not Korean. Another excuse for denial and on top of it, racism. All those hours of separating rubbish into different recycling bins, all for it to be dumped to waste away on lonely winter beaches to blame on another country.

I stooped and picked up a broken bucket. Might as well make the most of my day at the seaside and do my bit for the environment too. Some nice shells had washed ashore from the Sea of Japan. I picked some nice ones for my bucket. Could come in handy as decorations for the bathroom, even a soap dish.

Close to the water's edge lay a small pufferfish on its back. At first, the rotund creature appeared to be dead. I was about to walk away when it twitched. Pitiful thing, all washed up. I picked it up and hurled it at the waves. The backwash carried it straight towards my feet.

Carl cackled. I turned to see him stretched out on the sand, can of beer at the ready, rolling about with horrible laughter.

"What're you like? Florence Nightingale to the rescue!"

"Shut up – the poor thing'll die."

"Then let it. They're poisonous. Bring it here and I'll stamp on it."

I snatched it up and cradled it. The tiny body writhed in my hands. "You're such a monster. I'm going to save it."

I set it in my bucket and took off towards the pier. The bucket swung and my breath condensed. Cold hands, sore chest... critical fish. The Buddhist in me had to save it, one way or another.

Onto the pier. I shot-put the pathetic gasping fish far into the Sendai River. The dark waters swallowed it. I waited.

It swam; it was safe. Carl's taunts followed close behind on the breeze.

"I think you killed it – did you see the little bastard plonk right in there? Brilliant!"

"It lived – I watched it swim away. It's probably on its way home now to its wife and kids thanks to me."

"Yes Ghandi, whatever you say." He spluttered beer and wiped the froth off his chin with his sleeve.

"Just cause you're a brute doesn't mean the rest of us are." I spun on the spot and looked away from him, out to sea. The wind whipped my hair and stung my face. A spot of blue and a dash of light showed between the clouds. *Always look towards the sun, then the shadows will fall behind you.*

15

❧

The South Terminal

I struggled back across the bridge into Akisato, pedalling against the wind, but the basketful of snacks for the three hour trip to Osaka was worth it. What a day to be going to Kansai airport. And yet, I couldn't deny it: excitement welled. I felt as though I too would be going back to London with Carl. Though in reality, my Asian adventure would continue.

How would I cope once Carl left? In all honesty I was filled with fear. Would I end up depressed? Although the first spring winds gave hope, the bitter chill reminded me that winter never seemed to end. My own personal winter; winter of the soul. Work would be jam-packed with making up shift swaps that I'd taken to spend all my time with Carl. Thirteen days in a row, before only one day off. Unlucky for some. On the plus side, overwork would quench the loneliness of Carl being gone, and make sure I saw as little of Jei Pi as possible. All good. Scar tissue for the spirit. Was I succumbing to the itch of boredom at work after a mere four months, or simply dreading the extra hours? Was I trying to make excuses to pave the path for going home with Carl? It could be so easy to buy a ticket, jump on a plane, fly home and come back for my stuff later. But, on the other hand, not so easy. I had passed probation with flying colours, achieved ninety-two percent in my grammar test. Second highest in the branch after Zoe. In addition, I'd made a commitment, a promise to stay for a year when I'd signed my teaching contract.

What did Camden have that Tottori didn't? Nothing had changed back home, or ever would. Same drunken nights out at the same pubs with the same conversation. Watching, sober from the sidelines, as Ronnie threw up in alleyways and Sasha moaned about the call centre job she hated, but was stuck in. Better to be working in Asia, out of the rat race.

I parked my bike in front of Villa Libido and jogged up the steps to my apartment. Carl would've finished packing by now; I had been gone for half an hour. My fingers fumbled with the lock and pushed the door open.

"Hey honey, I'm back."

No response. Carl had stashed his suitcase in the hallway. I peered into my bedroom and saw that it was empty. Romantic music emanated from the living room. Curious, I creaked the door handle open slowly.

Carl lay sprawled on the sofa, a can of beer in his left hand and his right hand inside the opened fly of his jeans. On the TV were two men in their thirties and a petite young blonde, no older than eighteen, all three naked. The two men stood while the woman, on her knees, performed fellatio on each in turn. She looked Eastern European and she didn't look comfortable as the men each thrust their ten inch penises into her mouth. One man flipped her over and grabbed her hair, roughly, as he plunged his giant member into her. The girl winced in discomfort. The other man pleasured himself all over her face and rubbed it in her hair. I wanted to look away, but was frozen with shock. Carl's face was twisted with devious ecstasy as he watched the exploitation on screen. The man who ejaculated on the girl now got behind the camera while the girl lay on her back, legs splayed and the other man rammed into her. Finished, he pulled out and his fluid poured out of her; he mopped it up with the girl's own white, lace knickers, before pushing them inside her red-raw vagina. The cameraman zoomed in to a close-up of her chopped-liver private parts with a tiny sliver of lace trim poking out. I watched horrified and Carl climaxed, unaware I stood in the doorway. The video had an exploitative feel, as though the woman had either been trafficked and forced into it, or was doing it as she needed money for drugs. Her fearful eyes had almost pleaded with the camera, as though hoping someone, anyone out there would help her.

"Are you ready to go?" My voice, several octaves lower, was cold.

"Manny? Oh fuck." He jumped to his feet and turned his back to me, fumbling with his fly. In a fluid, skilled move that had to be practised, he swooped across to the TV, ejected the dirty movie and switched off the DVD player. I caught sight of the box: the cover was a poorly photocopied job. Must have been a wannabe porn filmmaker that had been sharing his movie around, or worse; someone Carl knew.

"Where did you get the smut flick? Hope it wasn't rented with my card," I said, hurt.

"I brought it with me," he said, quickly.

"Oh, so this is what you get up to while I'm away? You know, if you wanted sex, why didn't you let me know?"

"I didn't really, though. Just fun."

My brow tightened as if it had a life of its own. I rubbed my forehead. "I'm not fun then, huh? Well, at least that makes sense. You realise we've only done it twice in the three months you've been here?"

Carl said nothing. He stood, his head tilted to the left, scratching his hair. He was at a loss for words and so was I.

We walked out in silence. A few, fat flakes of snow pelted me in my face. Winter definitely had no intention of shifting, but at least it matched my mood. The taxi I had ordered earlier pulled up below. I let Carl pass, carrying his luggage, then locked up. Numbness set in as I watched the jovial taxi driver help him load the suitcase into the boot. Numb from cold, numb from shock. Did I really know this man at all?

Taxi to Tottori station, on the bus, on our way. The bus crawled through a tunnel under a wide mountain. When we came out on the other side, the snow flurry had stopped. No snow on the ground and a weak, but welcome sun in the clear sky. Bizarre. The weather was as schizo as my moods. Flitting between misery and elation, sun and snow; enough to make the head spin. For now, I would try to learn something from it: Carl would be going soon and then I would have time to think.

The long journey south. The mountains had given way to the wider world beyond Tottori. My stomach rumbled, but I felt too motion sick and nauseous from the exploitation porn to eat. Carl was subdued too; I was grateful, as I didn't want to talk to him. The bag of snacks jostling on my lap as the bus rumbled on, lay unopened, uninviting. I had gone out in the bitter cold to get food for our trip while Carl had watched filth; bitter saliva swirled in my mouth. Food was merely subsistence anyway; not good to fixate on pleasures of the flesh whether food or sex. Indulgence wasn't Buddhist. What would Ghandi do? Die of starvation if he hadn't been killed.

Oh enough, enough! Desist. I had to stamp out the negativity. To err was human, yes, but I wanted to rise above it, control my earthly capabilities. Rest, relax, these would be the last few hours I would see Carl for the next eight months. Hoo-bloody-ray.

Just fun. What a bastard. He'd rather watch a young blonde barely-legal woman on screen who resembled a younger version of me, who was being exploited, than make love with the real thing? What kind of a pervert was he anyway?

Off the bus at Namba, onto another bus, off at Kansai airport. Still, not a word spoken.

Carl checked in and got his ticket. I watched his suitcase slide away on the conveyor belt. Soon he would slide away too.

"I won't be able to go with you once you pass through security," I said.

Carl pulled a face. "You could come with me. You would if you were a good girlfriend."

"Maybe I'm not a good girlfriend, but I'm certainly a good teacher." I pulled a face back. "I'll see you in eight months."

"Maybe sooner, with a present for me?" He patted my tummy. "That would keep you from wandering off on any more travels."

I pushed his hand away. "You wish. After only two goes, I doubt it."

"Two times is the charm, my boys can swim." He squeezed my bum. I tutted and swiped at his hand.

Carl cuffed my cheek in his usual playful way of hiding his real feelings and pulled me into a tight hug, yet I felt numb. Or maybe not; his face swam behind a waterfall of tears that fell from a part of my subconscious that I didn't understand and I did nothing to stem the flow. He walked towards security. He passed through. I wanted to look away, but couldn't. As painful as it was, I needed to see that it was real. He was really going, he was leaving today. No point waking up tomorrow pretending he was there; it would hurt much more that way. Carl turned, waved and disappeared behind the opaque screen.

Up a flight of steps next to security into a glass-fronted lounge overlooking duty free; my feet propelled me without thought. I watched Carl make his way past the shops towards his gate. He didn't see me, as he didn't look back. I stood and watched until he turned a corner and was gone.

South journey to Osaka. South Terminal Building. Facing South. I followed directions to the observation hall and watched the people board their planes. Carl was one of those many dots; a colour in the crowd.

Once outside for fresh air, my feet kept going taking me the length of the perimeter fence. It felt less claustrophobic than being inside. I was empty. Empty and desperate. I didn't know what to do other than walk. The plane taxied on the runway. The plane took off. I watched it rise and disappear into the clouds.

The plane flew south. It would change course over the sea, but for now, like everything else, it was headed south. South. In Japan, cremated bodies faced south. Death. Cremation. Emptiness. Desperation. Loneliness. My fingers gripped the last metal railing at the end of the airport fence, at the end of an era. I wanted the fence to go on forever; I wanted to run my hands along it to the end of the world. But it stopped; an abrupt cut-off; concrete wall and grass. What would I have to fill the void in my life now? What would block out the fear?

Music. I fumbled in my bag and pulled out my old smartphone from London. Carl had given it to me as a present two years ago. The contract had ended and it was disconnected as a phone, but it still played music. It was an amulet to protect me; a piece of Carl to take back to Tottori and comfort me. Headphones in, power on—

And—

It dropped, a slip of the fingers and smashed on the concrete ground. Filaments and microchips; if only the contents of my head could be so easily viewed. My body faced south, ready for cremation.

How would I cope? Here, alone, at the end of the biggest chapter of my life?

CYCLE 2: CREMATION

16

☙

Abyss of Loneliness

Climbing out of the abyss, slowly,
Carefully, she pondered,
Whether the lonely journey was worth it,
If it always gave her calloused hands
And a painfully bleeding heart.

My pen ran out of ink. Sod's law, indeed. Not to worry, as it was an excuse to lob the damn biro across the bus aisle with enough force to cause a decent thud. Two Japanese businessmen in front inclined their heads enough to watch me in the reflection of their glasses, but didn't turn around. Still, their gesture made me feel bad. Bloody Japanese giving me a guilt-trip, as if my barbaric foreign actions sullied their damn country, a brazen hussy. What sort of businessmen were they anyway, going out into the arsehole of nowhere, Tottori? Bell-ends! No, not them; me. What an idiot decision not to have gone home with Carl; it sucked feeling lost now that he was gone. A lanky, awkward, white girl didn't fit in here in Japan at any rate. Weird customs, weird people made me feel alien, hostile.

Another read through my untitled poem showed the obvious: too many adverbs. My Writer's Write course said to show, not tell. Easier said than done for a novice. Time to think on my poem was time well spent, next best thing to writing. Carl didn't appreciate my writing. He'd said my New Year poem,

Ode to Sensoji was shit. Then again, anything that diverted attention away from him was shit, in his opinion. Best to immerse myself in the moment: eyes closed, leaning back against my seat, rubbing my back against the velour. No point thinking negative things about Carl when he wasn't here to defend himself and more to the point when it distracted me from my work.

The Namba bus pulled in to Tottori station, on a now-familiar journey. This time there was no Ben to collect me. There would be no Carl either. This is what it was to be truly alone. And yet? Despite the fear and loneliness, it was hard for me to ignore a trace of an unknown feeling. Giddiness? Excitement at the unknown?

Off the bus, then over to a row of waiting black taxis, where the back door of the first in line opened automatically. The doily-covered back seat was comfy and in front, the taxi driver wore a suit, complete with black cap and white-gloved hands. Nice change from rough London cabbies; felt like being chauffeured.

"Konbanwa." The greeting rolled off my tongue. "Villa Libido, onegaishimasu." *To Villa Libido, please.*

"Eh? Doko desu ka," he said, forcing me to translate in my head; *where's that?*

"Akisato. Villa Libido."

"Akisato?"

"Yes, it's near Lawson's in Akisato. Hai, Akisato no Lawson no chikaku ni arimasu." Oh my gosh. Was this guy stupid? Couldn't the idiot hick understand perfectly clear Japanese?

"Ah, Akisato no Raw-son. Wakarimashita."

This was great; directing a taxi in Japanese. My Japanese was so good. "Villa Libido wa Ro-son no chikaku ni arimasu."

"Eh?" The taxi driver shook his head to himself. "Wakaranai. Dou shiyo kana?"

Oh no; maybe my pronunciation was rubbish. The bloke was confused. He radioed through for help, babbling in Japanese too fast for me to catch. So he'd been dumbing down his speech for me, had he? My confidence ebbed. Must've been my bad pronunciation. "Um, Bwee-rah ree-bee-doh." Maybe my best katakana pronunciation would do the trick. Damn Japanese with all its substituting the letter l for r and swapping v for b; turning simple words into legitimate tongue-twisters. If they allowed their own apartment buildings to be given foreign names, then they should have bloody well learned how to say the words properly in English, not katakana pronunication.

Miaow, saucer of cream for one. Deep breath, slow exhalation. What the hell was wrong with me; the words coming out of my mouth sounded more like Carl, not me. Being nasty wasn't in my nature, even internal thoughts, which were best to keep under control, lest they spiralled.

Time to be objective. Tomomi could speak fluently; many Japanese people could speak English perfectly fine. When nasty thoughts overrode my sensibilities, it was helpful to let the two R's come into play: reflect, then show respect, even to a country-bumpkin driver with no English ability.

"Eigo no sensei desu ka," he asked.

"That means are you an English teacher? Yes. Hai, Voyce no sensei desu."

"Doko no shushin desu ka."

"Huh? Doko means where, but shushin? Erm –
wakarimasen." A shake of my head showed my lack
of understanding.

He rephrased. "O kuni wa?"

"Kuni – yes, that means country." A moment to
translate the question he asked. "Igirisu desu. Erm –
from England."

"Sou ka. Samui ne?"

"Samui? No, England's not any colder than Japan.
Er, iie." Another vigorous shake of my head
emphasised the point.

"Nihon wa motto samui?"

"What? Sorry, don't know what you're asking –
something about Japan?"

"Nihon ga suki desu ka."

"Huh? That means do you like Japan?" A nod of
confirmation. "Er – hai, suki desu."

"Nihonjin otoko mou?"

Questions and more questions. "Um, what? My
Japanese isn't so good, sorry. Ah, you're asking if I
like Japanese people? Hai, suki desu."

The taxi driver smiled at me in the mirror.
"Koibito imasu ka."

Enough of the pretence; where was my dictionary?
My fingers fumbled in the bottom of my bag, found
it, then... Koibito. What was that? A topic to do with
the weather, or England? Koibito – k in my romaji
script dictionary. Quick scan down the page and
found it. Koibito: lover.

What? The bloody cheek! How foolish it had been
giving the bloke the benefit of the doubt through guilt
at my judgemental thoughts, and what had he done?
Taken liberties. Do you have a lover, indeed! "Kankei

nai desho!" *None of your business.* The words burst from my mouth, the intonation of each word raised for effect. None of his bloody business indeed.

The guy didn't apologise. Lucky for me, Tomomi had taught me some useful pervert Japanese one lunch time. Telling the *hentai* to mind their own business had come in handy. If Carl had been here, he would have warded off the weirdos; no country bumpkin taxi driver would've dared ask me such a disrespectful question. The taxi pulled up in front of Villa Libido; thank goodness the creep of a taxi driver didn't know the meaning of the building name or else he'd be cracking jokes to me about that too, no doubt. Villa Libido: no point having a libido anymore. Kimberly Thatcher was one chick who'd be celibate as a frigging nun for the next eight months. Maybe being pregnant would've been good to fill my time. A derisive snort; only myself to amuse.

Loneliness set in. Lonely for company, an oxymoron if ever there was one. Scratch the oxy, only pure unadulterated moron for throwing my seven year relationship down the drain. My feet thunked up each cold, grey metal step into the cold, grey apartment of my life. Worse still, into the fire-dragon's den. But as the door clicked open, the lack of man-sized shoes indicated that Jei Pi was out.

Hurray! It was late, but the flat was all mine. There were a few choices: comfort eat, snuggle up on the couch to watch DVDs while wrapped in a quilt, do exercise, write, or...

Or dwell in self-pity. Wallow in misery.

Control, alt, delete, reset. No thanks; distraction, not depression was the goal. Shoes off, pyjamas on, then a quick rummage for the hoover; time for a spring clean. One hand whizzed the hoover across my bedroom floor and the other did the living room; both sides balanced for exercise and to counter Yin with Yang. Feng shui mattered, now more than ever. Jei Pi's unwashed lunch plate lay on the kitchen table along with half a tin of tuna in brine, fork still stuck in it. Dirty cow. Time to get at the mucky pup later for her crimes. After the hoover had been stowed away, it was time to rearrange my room. Stripping the futon, blanket and pillow took seconds, then once all the bed-linen was in the washing machine, it was off to the balcony to beat the hell out of my futon. Surprisingly therapeutic to whack the large mattress with a bamboo beater, as if it was a door-sized piñata. The smell of Carl's aftershave on the futon was unbearable. An image of his face popped onto my piñata-futon. My hand beat harder, the wing coming from my hips and along my arm, unleashing seven years of frustration.

My phone rang inside my pocket, snapping me from my self-therapy. The lit screen read 'Jei Pi'.

"Hello?"

"Moshi-moshi, roomie! Hey, whatcha doing?"

Lucky she couldn't see my derisive smirk. So, the past month hadn't happened? Our simmering resentment at each other, the snide remarks in passing? All of that was gone, now that Carl was out of the picture?

"Hitting the sack. It's been a long day."

"At nine thirty on your day off? Come on, you need to live a little. The night is young."

"For what?"

"Come join me and Zoe." Excitement filled Jei Pi's voice. "We're at Mo's sports bar over in Minamiyasunaga."

My overtired brain struggled to process this switch in Jei Pi's tone towards me. The temptation to refuse her was over-ruled by the idea of being alone with my thoughts in the flat; no way. My feet were one step ahead of my feelings, inching towards the door.

"Okay then, gimme half an hour."

"Great. See you then."

Manic. Jei Pi's moods changed, quick as the weather. Still, Zoe was there, so it couldn't be all that bad. My stripped duvet and pillow would have to tolerate a night on the sofa devoid of bed-linen; and Jei Pi would have to put up with my choice to sleep in the living room. My bedroom felt more Carl than me; after all, he had spent more time in it in the past three months than me. Being reminded of him was the last thing a lonely girl so far from home needed. Tomorrow a bedroom makeover was top of my list. Tonight, getting hammered would suffice to block out the world.

17

ᘓ

Tottori Castle ruins

Igusa: A Japanese Summer Rug made of Tatami.

Was it best to write the word in Romaji, English letters, or in hiragana? Japanese characters, why not? Ee-goo-sah. Saying it phonetically helped dictate the characters to my obliging hand. Job done, green travel journal closed, my legs propelled me to my feet to admire my new igusa. Kusa: grass. Igusa: grass mat. The new bamboo blinds looked great too, giving my bedroom more light and life than the heavy curtains. New life, new start. Winter was over and spring was the birth of new adventures; even a new beginning with Jei Pi. After all our differences since my arrival in Japan the previous November, it really had been a surprise how well we could actually get along. In the two weeks since Carl had left, we'd been out for yakiniku Japanese meat-grill, or yakitori chicken-on-sticks every night after work; Jei Pi, Zoe, Tomomi and myself. Loneliness had helped us bond and for once, Jei Pi's need for companionship didn't seem so alien to me. People needed other souls around them to live, and love, and thrive.

A cursory glance at my watch showed it was quarter to five. Jei Pi, Tomomi and Zoe would be meeting at Kyushu Park for their Hanami cherry-blossom party at six. Cherry blossom season lasted for about a week during the first week of April. A week of beauty in the world for Japanese people to celebrate before the pink petals faded. It felt symbolic to me, significant in a different sense of the Japanese meaning; important because it resembled the transition in my life. Beauty before what? Calm before the storm? Maybe life was all futile. What was with me, feeling so desperate?

Maybe some early alone-time in Kyushu Park was necessary medicine; the bike ride took twenty minutes. Sunset and detox; my system felt sluggish. Too much alcohol and excess lately had seen to that. All day long, drinking nothing but a plum-based tonic to cleanse my body had left me feeling suitably Zen. And now, the climb towards Tottori Castle's ruins halfway up Kyushu mountain left me feeling energised yet calm. Maybe my chakras were in balance for the first time since arriving in Japan. The rows of cherry blossoms lining the steps to the castle helped too; the pink petals falling on me like confetti; the lanterns hanging from them adorned with Chinese characters holding mystical messages of Eastern wisdom, all for me.

Tottori lay spread out before me; a sea of white and grey homes, offices, shops and schools bathed in the pink glow of sunset. Down there before me, two hundred thousand people breathed as one entity under the serene watch of the cherry blossoms that they so celebrated. Beyond, towards the south were the distant mountains keeping Tottori separate from Okayama in its own secluded niche. North West was Karo kaigan; Karo beach, and far across the Sea of Japan was Korea. Tottori was growing on me. With winter behind, it was becoming a warm, welcoming place. Ben had talked of Tottori's great nightlife; Japanese bars called Izakayas, karaoke clubs and sports bars, but when Carl was visiting, he didn't want to go out. Apart from sightseeing endless temples and castles that he complained about as much as visited, he wanted to stay in and watch DVDs. It almost seemed like Carl wanted me to resent Tottori, to bore me so much it would drive me to quitting the job and returning to London. Tottori Shi, the whole of the prefecture laid on a silver platter before my eyes, was my home, my place in the world to stay. It called to me, soothing words to say it needed me as much as heart, head and very essence needed it. No quitting, no running away. If Carl loved me, he would wait. *Come home with a present for me - that would keep you from going off on any more travels.* Carl called me selfish, but he was the selfish one for pressurising me to come home after we'd agreed on my year long contract.

"Hey Chica!"

Five past six; time sure flew while sitting alone, absorbed in my thoughts. Jei Pi, Zoe and Tomomi walked over the ruins of Tottori castle towards me.

"Whacha doing?" Jei Pi asked.

"Nothing much." A quick, nonchalant shrug. "Thinking about things. Tottori and stuff, you know, Carl."

The girls flopped down on the grass beside me. Jei Pi puckered her mouth. "I didn't like him much."

"Me neither," Zoe added.

It was the first time anything had annoyed me since Carl had left.

"He acted like you were his possession, like he owned you," said Jei Pi.

"Funny, he said the same about you." My face grew hotter. "The way you put all those hooks up in the kitchen without asking me – he thought it was disrespectful. Even controlling."

Jei Pi pulled a face. "That is such bullshit! And anyway, if we're talking disrespectful, let's be fair – I'm not the one with my bedding all over the living room. I didn't mind you sleeping on the living room floor for the first couple of nights, but then you moved your futon out too."

Zoe waved her hands between them. "Come on guys, let's not argue, hey?"

Best to ignore Jei Pi. "It was only a temporary thing while my room was in the middle of a spring clean. The new igusa and blinds are in today, so that'll be me moved back in tonight."

"Oh, you got an igusa," said Tomomi, in a high voice. "Sugoi pronunciation too, your Japanese is so good."

Shallow, but this made me feel much happier. Fighting with Jei Pi would serve only to ruin our hanami. Tomomi's compliment came at a good time, lifting my mood. Neuro-linguistic programming; change your mental state.

Zoe took out a bottle of ume-shu plum wine from a plastic carrier bag along with sakura mochi sweets; cherry blossom rice balls filled with anko bean paste. Anko, not unko. So culturally adept now that my Japanese vocabulary had expanded. The sugar fix was welcome. It was news to me that Carl was so disliked. Wonder what Zoe thought of him? "Why didn't you like Carl?"

Zoe sniffed. "He kept you to himself too much. I mean, you're in Japan to meet people and have fun and he stopped you doing that."

My eyes skirted across the city, now glowing in twilight. "Well, maybe you have a point. Guess the same thing had crossed my mind. When we were in London, we were always together. He didn't really like me seeing my friends in Camden either. But now that he's gone, there's been loads of time to reflect."

"The problem is, you two weren't two people, you were one half of a couple," said Jei Pi, in an offhand way. "There was no 'I' in the equation. You couldn't function on your own, you were both so co-dependent. That's why you're so screwed up now – you don't know who you really are."

My mind was cauterised, listening to Jei Pi speak. Did what she said make me feel angry? No. Getting cross was impossible. Being anything other than emotionally impotent was impossible. It was true. She was right. Seven years with Carl on a spiritual journey to nowhere. Together through A-levels and Uni. Three holidays together. A flat rented together. A change of job for him. A new job after graduation for me. A move to Japan. Three months of hardship, getting adjusted to Asia during the longest winter of my life. And now? Lost, both spiritually and emotionally.

"Guess he made me feel sorry for him." My eyes were on the grass, not Jei Pi, as the words poured from my mouth, and a couple of sneaky tears slid from my eyes, unnoticed. Curse that Carl. "He'd lost his job, then sold his bike to come and keep me company, even though he knew he needed the money. Dunno – the sacrifice of material possessions just to see me meant something, you know, like he knows about my interest in Buddhism and he was making an effort."

Tomomi choked on her sakura mochi. "Oh boy," she said.

Irritation stabbed me. "What?"

"It's just, well, how do I say it – he wasn't sacrificing *that* much."

"Get to the point. What are you trying to say?" Hard to speak my mind through gritted teeth.

"I don't want you to get upset."

Jei Pi nudged Tomomi with her elbow. "Sheesh! Just rip off the band aid already. Oy vey!"

"Yeah, yeah, alright." said Tomomi.

"Just tell me already, oh my gosh." What was with all the pussy-footing around? "I'm sure it's gonna hurt anyway, whatever it is."

"Okay then." Tomomi tried to look concerned, but there was an annoying trace of a smile about her mouth. "It's just that I saw Carl having lunch with Shiori san from *Classy Girl* once after you went to work, and another time I saw them leave Jusco together."

Strange, but it didn't hurt as would be expected; more numbness really. Above, the full, pink, seductive cherry blossom petals dangled their insults, the lanterns swaying in the wind full of mirth, at my expense. The Chinese writing was no longer mystical; it taunted me, teased about Eastern promise that could never be part of me. Carl had had it. Three months in Japan and all his talk of 'fanny-eyes', yet all this time... my jaw clenched. All this time.

It's a new dress. How do I look? Sexy? The words popped into my head. Shiori, the petite, pretty Japanese worker from *Classy Girl* had stepped into the aisle between shops, blocking Carl's path. Sexy; her lips as pink and seductive as the sakura petals. *She must think we're colleagues.* Carl's words haunted me. She hadn't been a silly girl, out of his league next to his leggy blonde girlfriend; she'd been a rival.

"It might've been innocent," said Zoe. Her voice sounded far away.

A defeated shake of my head. "He would've told me about her if they were only friends."

"I always knew he wasn't good enough for you." Jei Pi put a hand on my leg and squeezed. It didn't make me feel any better.

"All those times he said he was at the beach, just drinking beer and watching the sea – he was probably with her. It makes me feel sullied."

No, not sullied; nothing. Empty. Lost. Desperate. Beneath the beautiful cherry blossoms lingered darkness and danger.

"Sorry to tell you bad news." Tomomi put her arm around my shoulders and hugged me. For a split second, my hand jerked towards her arm, ready to swipe. She was Japanese; she was the enemy. Tomomi was prettier than Shiori from *Classy Girl*. It made me seethe with jealousy. Tomomi wasn't a friend; she was a competitor too. Blonde and white wasn't Carl's type, Tomomi was pale and Asian and apparently more Carl's cup of tea.

My anger ebbed. It wasn't fair to blame Tomomi because of her racial heritage. Carl obviously liked cute demure Japanese girls, not tall, sexy Japanese women.

"It's fine. Really, it's okay."

Tomomi poured all of us a plastic cup of ume-shu plum wine. She pointed to the lantern swinging above us. "The sign wants us to drink, so let's drink."

"What does it say?" asked Zoe.

"Drink Asahi beer," said Tomomi. "They're all advertisements. That one over there says 'Jusco'."

Mysticism gone; my bubble of Eastern promise had popped. So the lanterns were nothing more than glorified billboards. How unromantic. My relationship with Carl was unromantic. The sleek, pink blossoms, like Shiori's lips were unromantic.

Tomomi raised her glass. "Gan gan nomo."

"Gan gan nomo." They clinked glasses.

"Does that means 'cheers'?" Probably guessing the obvious, but knowing Tomomi's crude mind...

"It means, let's get pissed!" Tomomi laughed. "This is our night – forget men!"

"I'm with you on the let's get pissed part, but not the men," said Jei Pi. "Almost a year of no sex is tough."

Double the reason to drain my glass; not to mention the image of Jei Pi sleeping with anyone was distasteful, to say the least.

"Oh come on, so you're telling me that you haven't had the odd one nighter now and then?" Zoe stretched out on the grass, leaning on one elbow.

"No." Jei Pi sat rigid, her legs crossed in lotus position. "And you have?"

"Yeah." Zoe gave a sly grin. "I've kinda been seeing one of our Voyce students, this guy Ryuji who works at Bar Nightfall – you know that place over in Yayoi-cho?"

Tomomi and Jei Pi nodded. Yayoi-cho might as well have been in China; spending all winter cooped up had left me senile in Tottori.

"Japanese men are alright. They're a bit small down there, but I'm not fussy." Zoe pointed to her crotch and smirked.

Everyone laughed, but Tomomi looked awkward. "What difference does size make?" she said.

"Better for your G-spot." Crass, perhaps, but it slipped out of my head and rolled off the tongue quicker than you could say, drop your knickers. "Are you saying small guys can reach up there, you know, to make you come?"

"Come where?" Tomomi's face looked blank.

Was she for real? This was a new side to Tomomi that hadn't reared its head before. The suave, sophisticated Japanese business-woman in her neatly pressed suits was gone. Here was an innocent, uncultured girl. "It means orgasm." Straight face to clear the smirk, no point being patronising.

"I've never had one," said Tomomi, matter-of-factly.

No laughter this time. Jei Pi's eyes widened. "Wait a sec… you're twenty-three and you've never came?"

"See, the thing is, Japanese men tend to do their thing and that's that. My friends have said the same thing," said Tomomi, with a small shrug.

"Maybe you've just been shagging the wrong men – Ryuji is Japanese and he can really get me off," said Zoe. "Sex is a two-way thing. Women need pleasure too. Besides, if you can't service yourself, how can you expect a man to figure it out?"

Poor Tomomi. In the silence that followed while we poured more drinks, my eyes rested on her while my head processed her words. No orgasms, ever. Alone, or as a couple. Good sex was an important part of any relationship. Tomomi said the problem was Japanese men – or at least the ones she had slept with. My mind strayed to Shiori. Was that why she had enticed Carl, to try a Western man instead?

Best not to stay on that last thought too long; my mouth switched the topic away for me. "Well, getting back to the whole size-thing, don't know about the rest of you, but a bloke can't get me off no matter how hard he tries if he isn't well equipped. My men have got to be well-hung."

"Ahem."

We looked around. Jei Pi spluttered her drink and Zoe sat bolt upright. Vince and Ade stood behind us, carrying a plastic bag with drinks.

"Didn't mean to interrupt your interesting chat, but we saw you sitting up here and thought we'd invite ourselves along," said Vince.

"We were having a girly party, but we ended up talking about men anyway, so you might as well join us," said Jei Pi.

"Well, not men exactly," said Zoe, giggling. Her face was flushed. "But about men's stuff."

Zoe rolled backwards on the grass and Tomomi keeled over on her stomach, both of them laughing. Drunk. So much for me; not even tipsy. The green-eyed monster reared its head.

"So I heard," said Vince.

"Oh no – you heard us?" Zoe slurred her words. "So you'll know that size doesn't matter to me... but it matters to Kimberly!"

Vince and Ade looked pleased.

"Thanks for sharing that with the world." Humiliation wasn't my idea of a fun afterthought to an already awkward conversation. A moment away from the party helped me to centre myself, and the view from the edge of the Tottori castle ruins, where they gave way to a sharp drop onto the terrace below certainly helped keep me grounded. Below, vendors sold food to the cherry-blossom festival goers. The throng down there knew nothing of my worries. The world went on without a care. It helped put my troubles in perspective.

"Kimberly," Jei Pi called. "Let's go. We're taking the party back to our place."

***

Empty bottles of ume-shu, shochu and cans of Asahi littered my new living room igusa. Boxes of pocky-chocolates and wrappers from appetising sweets with unappetising names such as *Colon* lay across the floor. The incessant drone of Japanese TV combined with the chatter of seven voices gave me a headache. The party had grown to eight people when Akemi from reception had arrived after work, and Yuri, Jei Pi's Japanese teacher had dropped by after her lecture at Tottori University. How much more socialising could my poor, tired brain handle, especially when half of it was in Japanese. My body was drowning in alcohol, in dire need of food to absorb the excess. Lucky for me there was a spare Lawson chicken bento in the fridge.

Vince's face appeared around the fridge door, and he leaned low over my shoulder. "Jei Pi says you have another igusa in your bedroom. Can I have a look?"

His hushed voice tickled my ear. Nobody else apart from Jei Pi, who lived with me in any event, had noticed or cared at my recent feng-shui efforts in the flat. Would Carl have cared? Certainly bloody not. "Sure. There's new bamboo blinds up too."

Bento in one hand, chopsticks in the other with Vince in tow behind me we made our way, albeit staggering, to my bedroom. Chasing the ghosts of winter away helped with someone else who appreciated my hard work. Anger at Carl had fuelled my need to wipe all traces of him from my room. We walked into my room and Vince shut the door behind us, muffling the sounds of conversation from the living room.

"What do you think?" My arms were wide, encompassing all the joys of my new decor.

He looked at me, not the igusa. "Nice room, very natural-looking."

"Thanks." A bite of chicken-katsu. Yum.

He looked at my chest of drawers and caught sight of my green journal. "Still not going to let me read any of those poems, hmm?"

My hand was quicker than his, snatching it away. "They're personal, they're only for me."

"You should try to get them published, I'm sure they're good." He raised his eyebrows in approval. "Voyce has an English language magazine for the students, there was a teacher from Kyushu's poetry in one of the issues. Why don't you send off yours?"

"Maybe. It's just, well, you know how some people can get shy about their work." My face grew hotter. Another bite of food; tsukemono, Japanese pickled vegetables. A bit tart, chased down with a chopstick-load of rice.

He came closer. "I didn't get to know you much cause you were never around when your boyfriend was over. But if you ever want to hang out, you know, me and Ade don't live that far. We're just over the bridge in Minamiyasunaga."

Strange that Vince had never seemed to want to be friends before. If anything, he seemed more like a gym buff, too preoccupied with himself and how he looked than making friends with anyone. But then he was right about me never being around. How could anyone get to know someone who kept herself isolated? Now that Carl was gone, this was my chance to get to know my colleagues properly.

"I know it must be hard for you with your boyfriend gone, so all I'm saying is, you have more friends than you think out here – people who'll look out for you if you need it."

Another bite of chicken katsu rolled around my mouth, though there was far more than food for me to digest; Vince's words resonated. Lately life had served me a big slice of humble pie: Jei Pi had become a friend and now Vince too was different than he had seemed at first. My family and friends were all back home – Carl was back home. A whole new network of people cared for me out here; like a surrogate family. People weren't as they'd seemed. Hadn't my view about Carl been wrong? Seven years with him and it had never crossed my mind that he could be cheating on me. And now? Now what?

"Thanks. It's good to know. It really means a lot." We fell into a momentary silence, punctuated only by my munching. My jaws were still busy masticating chicken and rice when Vince's mouth closed over mine in a sloppy, passionate frenzy. His tongue pushed its way into my mouth, making my lips part wider to allow it in. It skirted my teeth, roved the insides of my cheeks, giving little time for the food to roll down my gullet. Not exactly romantic, not exactly consented to, but being honest it was a good feeling. How long had it been since someone had kissed me like that? Too many months devoid of passion, even when Carl had been in Tottori. Months? More like years. In seven years my relationship with Carl had whittled down to barely more than pecks on the lips, never mind sex, that came once a month unless he was drunk. Not to mention the burden of Tomomi's news about Carl and Shiori that my mind was still processing. Was that where the sliver of enjoyment slipped in: two wrongs making a right? Regardless, Vince was a colleague: we shouldn't have done it besides the fact he wasn't desirable in that way. Honestly, it was about my need for something more visceral; physically touching a person, smelling his skin, tasting his warm mouth and holding him, feeling his breath in my ear or on my cheek. Tomorrow, sober at work, Vince and me, well. Well indeed. We would be back to simply friends and colleagues and nothing more.

18

ᘓ

Club Passion

"So, Vince – about last night."

"Yeah? What's up?"

Hugging my coat against my chest provided comfort, an instinctive reflex. If only Nadia hadn't been sitting there, pretending to be marking work. Damn the small staff room.

"It would be a shame if it affected things between us, you know, here at work."

Vince leaned against the notice board in a casual manner, with one hand in his pocket. "Don't worry about it – we're friends, that's all."

My body relaxed as a sigh escaped; this was too much worry over nothing. He understood. We could forget the whole thing. What was a kiss between friends? The pips sounded the end of my early shift and a smile broke across my face; it was a perfect wrap-up to an otherwise tense day in anticipation of a confrontation with Vince that thankfully, had ended up a fizzle rather than a bang.

"Hey – yo, Kimberly, another thing."

"What's up?"

"There's a hip-hop night over at Club Passion in Yasunaga tonight. Jei Pi and Zoe are coming. You up for it?"

"Sure, sounds good. Whereabouts is it?"

"You know where the karaoke place is, on the road heading towards Koyama? Turn right before you get to that, and follow the music." He winked at me. "See you there, then."

A deep breath and an exhalation. It was settled. There was no need to feel bad about Carl either since there was nothing between me and Vince. He was another friend, same as Ronnie, Aaron and Sasha back home. Probably better not to mention Vince to Carl though; no point getting him jealous all the way over in England. We'd talk on the phone later. It had been nearly two weeks. He was settled in back with his parents in Croydon while he looked for work. The call would be about how the job search was going, but better to be honest with myself; it was more to ask about Shiori.

On the way down the escalator, my eyes gravitated towards *Classy Girl*. Shiori stood talking to a customer at the counter. She had a black, punk-style dress on with a pink lace trim to match her shiny pink shoes and shiny pink smile. To be honest, this made me seethe. Wannabe goth-bitch-slut-whore. How could she take Carl? Shiori had seen me with Carl, she must've known we weren't simply Voyce colleagues; it was clear we were a couple. The urge to throttle her was hard to resist; it wouldn't take much to march into the shop, overturn the racks of clothes and throw the little slag on the floor.

My commendable willpower surprised even me; once off the escalator, my feet propelled me the other way, each step easier the more distance covered. Deep breath. Not worth it. Going to jail in Japan would be hell. Apparently you were only allowed to speak Japanese so that the guards knew what you were saying. They beat the hell out of you too, someone had said. Women as well? Not going to be me to find out.

Homeward bound. The smell of spring in the air was the smell of excitement. My bicycle made easy work of the short ride across the bridge into Akisato, but instead of turning into the underpass, it was straight on towards the main road and along to the Lawson convenience store. The international phone outside was always free. Who in Tottori other than the few foreign teachers had a use for it?

My fingers punched the number into the international payphone in time to my hammering heart heartbeat.

"Hello?" Carl's voice had a touch of aggression about it.

Shit, was this a bad idea? "Hi, it's me."

"Hmph." His tone was cold. "Left it a while, didn't you?"

"Sorry honey, the past couple of weeks have been busy. They gave me more training to teach classes to kindergarden children."

"Oh, so you're too busy for your relationship, is that right? What's more important than that?"

My muscles relaxed in defeat, my back slumping against the phone box. Not good to start regretting the call. "Listen, it's been really hard since you left. You think this is easy for me?"

"If it was that hard, you'd come home. But you're such a dumb blonde, you wouldn't think of that."

The temptation to hang up was strong, but he was under stress; we both were. "Don't be like that, honey. It's been a really rough day. My first kids class was really hard, they didn't understand a thing and there were some tears. Maybe it was a bad idea to call you for a bit of support, obviously it wasn't a good time for you."

"Too right it was. You know, I've been doing some thinking and it came to me that the longer you stay out there, the quicker we're going to drift apart."

"What's that supposed to mean?"

"I'm saying that if you're not back within ten weeks, I don't know if I can wait for you."

Was he saying he intended to dump me? "You know, that's so unfair, Carl. That's almost like you're giving me an ultimatum."

"So you're not as stupid as you look then?"

"Stop calling me stupid." A dramatic sigh into the receiver for effect. "Things have been difficult, that's all. The others haven't had very nice things to say about you."

"Oh, so you'll let those conniving single women you hang about with brainwash you against me that quick?"

My mind worked quickly, formulating a retort. Why did he have to make it a war? "They're not conniving. And what's being single got to do with it?"

"Everything. They want to go out and get men. They're a bad influence on you. Spit it out then, what've they been saying about me?"

He was asking for it. If only he hadn't been so rude, it wouldn't have crossed my mind to mention anything. "They said they saw you having lunch with that worker from *Classy Girl*, Shiori. And that another time, you left Jusco with her."

Silence. That had got his head spinning.

"Those gossipy-bitches fill your head with shit and you're so fucking gullible, Manny, that you believe everything they say. I'll bet it was Jei Pi, wasn't it?

You're quick to make friends with her now that I'm gone."

"Stop straying from the issue, Carl. Is it true, or isn't it? About Shiori."

He tutted. "I don't get you, seriously. I don't know why you've given up on your friends back home so fast, for these users who don't even like you."

"They're not users, or bitches. You don't even know them. And as for Ronnie and Aaron and Sasha – you've sure changed your tune. You used to hate them. But anyway, you're not answering my question. Did you, or didn't you meet up with that girl Shiori?"

A pause. "Look, I had lunch one time in that udon-noodle place and she was there. She sat at my table cause there weren't enough seats. We didn't even talk. How could I, she can't speak English."

"Well that's funny, because she spoke English perfectly fine that day we both saw her when she asked you if she looked sexy in her new dress."

Carl gave a forced laugh. "You're a funny-cunt, aren't you? You're trying to catch me out, but you can't. Seems you've already made up your mind about the whole thing. Think what you want. After seven years, I shouldn't have to prove myself."

A wave of guilt assaulted me. Was it my paranoid mind? "Fine then. You promise you're telling me the honest truth?"

"Swear down, love. You know I can't stand those fanny-eyed women, alright? I can't even speak Japanese." His voice sounded weary without the hard edge.

"What about leaving Jusco with her? If it wasn't you, who was it?"

"It was me. I went outside for a smoke, like, and she might've been there too, on the phone, or something." His voice sounded animated again, even a touch defensive. "I dunno, I never noticed her. All those Japs look the same to me – you know, black hair, black eyes, like they're all inbred. You know I like your blonde hair and blue eyes best, there's more variety in Western women. I don't know why you're making a big deal about some girl I don't even really remember."

My finger was white from twisting the phone cord round it. "Don't lie to me – you know the girl. The one from that club-wear shop, *Classy Girl*? She always wears punk clothes."

"Oh, her? She's a bog-beast. What was she, like ten years old? No tits, no ass, not my type. You're the only one who's beautiful babe, all the other women in the world are pigs."

How the naive, trusting side of my mind wanted to believe him, but a part of me couldn't. Was he protesting too much? His eyes had always strayed in restaurants or shops, so why not his dick too? Not to mention the fact that Tomomi had seen them and she was more believable than Carl.

"It better be true Carl, that's all."

"If you're so worried about me, why don't you come home to keep a better check on me?"

Damn his quick retort. "Because it shouldn't be my responsibility. Listen, other people need to use the phone. We'll speak again soon."

One click and the receiver was back in place, saving me from Carl's irascible mood. No 'love you', no 'goodbye'. The numbness was back. Shame it couldn't be alcohol-numbness. It would be; soon.

My feet navigated the way back home while my mind, on automatic pilot, was a robot: a Japanese-programmed robot. Back home my jaw chomped lunch in a mechanical rhythm. Thirty chews, swallow, thirty chews, swallow. My skin barely registered the water in the shower. The soap didn't sting my eyes. My hand applied makeup in a sloppy, perfunctory way. What to wear? First top out of the drawer. Perfect; low cut and spangly to show off my thirty-four C's. Tight jeans, great. Jei Pi was on her day off, Zoe too. They'd probably already be over at Club Passion with Vince and Ade. Phone, wallet and umbrella tossed into my hand bag; time to let my hair down. It took half an hour on foot to get to Yasunaga, but it was a pleasant walk along the path between the rice paddies towards Sendai River, then across the White Rabbit Bridge into Minamiyasunaga. No one had ever told me the real name of the blue bridge decorated by white rabbits in running poses; still, White Rabbit bridge was catchier, and the story even more so. A student, Karin, had told it to me in *Chat* class: a crafty rabbit trapped on an island, had lured sharks to help it escape. When the sharks came to the surface of the water, the rabbit had bounced across them safely to land. The white rabbit was me. But who were the sharks, and would my crafty skills save my skin?

It was a fun idea to muse while crossing the bridge. On past the yellow neon light of an amusement arcade, then a burger restaurant that was surprisingly empty for a Saturday night, and a right turn before the karaoke place. Hip-hop music blared in the still air, just like Vince had said, leading me to a street full of warehouses. Club Passion was on the left. Strange place for a nightclub. A couple of Japanese blokes stood smoking outside and moved away from the door for me to enter.

"Bijin da!" said the nearer one.

What did that mean? Gaijin meant foreigner. Was this an even more derogatory way of insulting my alien status? One stood in front of me and beat his chest. "I-am-Sa-mu-rai!"

His friend reached towards me and touched my bare, white arm, which made me flinch, reflexively. "Sawaranai de... don't touch, creep!"

Samurai, my ass. Tomomi's hentai-Japanese was really coming in handy. A dismissive wave of my hand brushed them off for good. The entranceway of Club Passion was dimly lit; black painted walls were covered in neon graffiti that glowed under an ultra-violet light and a Japanese woman with dread-locked hair sat at a desk with a cash tin. Sen en: five quid door charge, then she stamped my hand. A tall Japanese man wearing low slung jeans, a white hoodie and skate shoes stood at the inner door to the club. Was he a bouncer? Didn't seem like there was any need in a rural town like Tottori, but then it was all new to me.

People were still arriving; it was easy to spot my friends in the half-empty club. Surprising really, how many foreigners there were. Was it a gaijin night? Couldn't be; there were Japanese as well. Still, it was a congregation of the most non-Japanese people, surely in Tottori; probably English teachers from all over the prefecture in one room. A quick eye sweep of the room showed Jei Pi and Zoe dancing in the middle of the half-full floor. Ade was over at the side, chatting up a giggling Japanese girl with a dyed blonde bouffant. Vince was at the bar talking to a Japanese bloke while they waited for their drinks. He spotted me and waved me over.

"Yo, Kimberly – you met Ryuji before?"

Ryuji stuck out his hand in a Western manner that surprised me. We shook instead of bowing.

"So you're Zoe's boyfriend? I've heard all about you."

"Good things I hope," he teased. His English was natural, better than any of my Voyce students.

Vince nodded towards the bar. "You want a drink?"

A moment's hesitation to process this: was it a come-on? Wasn't it only on dates that a man bought a woman a drink?

"You can buy me the next one," he added.

So he'd picked up on my thoughts? Very attentive. "Alright then, vodka and orange."

"I'll see you both over there – I'd better not keep a lady waiting," said Ryuji. He took his drinks and squeezed between Vince and myself, making his way across to Zoe.

It was a tight squeeze into the space that Ryuji left as the club filled up quickly behind me. "Ryuji speaks good English, doesn't he?"

"He lived in Sydney for a year when he was in college." Vince handed me the vodka orange and we made our way towards our friends. Jei Pi and a Japanese guy cleared a space in the middle of the dance floor, wildly throwing their arms in the air. Zoe and Ryuji gyrated together, locked in an embrace. Time to let my hair down: drink necked in one, empty plastic cup abandoned on a sticky table at the side. Winter had repressed me long enough.

Vince followed me onto the dance floor, dancing close, but not touching me. We grabbed hands and he twirled me around. He was my friend; we were allowed to touch within reason, no more awkward distance. As the night progressed, the dance floor filled. Club Bridge was hot, sweaty and cramped. Vince slipped away and returned from the bar with two more drinks.

My hand closed around the plastic cup he handed me. "You forgot, it was my round."

"What's a drink between friends?" Vince shouted above the music.

My ears rang with the pounding hip-hop, but who cared. Hip-hop wasn't even my thing, though it didn't matter. All that mattered was to keep drinking and keep dancing. Zoe came over with more drinks; down the hatch while dancing. Jei Pi bought more; necked that in one and more dancing. My head spun with all the vodka, heat and noise, but it never crossed my mind to stop dancing. Maybe it killed the pain; endorphins, a flood of oxytocin. Who knew.

Jei Pi danced closer to me. Her face was red from dancing and her hair was plastered to her head with sweat. "Zoe's outside throwing up," she said, with a wicked grin.

"Should we go check on her?"

"Don't worry about it, Ryuji's taking her home. He's coming back later," said Vince, cutting in. He pulled me closer and gave me a sweaty hug. Jei Pi threw her arms around us both and my head was squashed against Vince's shoulder as we were all squeezed in a tight bear-hug.

"This is the most fun I've had in ages." It was true, not a word exaggerated.

"Me too, roomie." Jei Pi bounced from foot to foot in her usual boisterous manner. "Let's dance!"

"In a minute, gotta use the loo."

"I'll come with you," said Vince.

We staggered through the crowd, Vince weaving behind me through the throng. The single unisex toilet was occupied. As we waited, my head lolled against the wall.

"Hey, you okay there?" Vince caught me as my vodka-numbed body slipped sideways.

My tongue struggled to form the words. "All good, just woozy."

The door opened and a petite Japanese girl came out. It took a moment for me to realise it was Shiori. She wore a white, ripped, off-the-shoulder T-shirt and a black and white kilt. Her punk look was rather out of place at a hip-hop night. Vince gave her an approving glance as she slid past, slippery smooth and sleek; a snake in the grass and she batted her false eyelashes in response. His eyes lingered on her ass. A pang of jealousy stabbed me. Why? Vince was a colleague and a friend, nothing more. He wasn't my type; it was a platonic friendship, nothing more. What was my type? Carl? A man who cheated on me, treated me like crap?

Frustration welled. If it wasn't jealousy, then why did Vince checking out Shiori bother me? The vodka had soaked my brain, loosened it, and the answer bubbled to the surface easily: because clearly Shiori, with her petite, exotic appeal had a charismatic magic that absolutely ordinary, blonde, gaijin Kimberly Thatcher simply couldn't match. That magic had tempted Carl to stray after seven years of coupledom.

Seven for a secret. Unlucky seven. Eastern mysticism
had won.

Vince held the door wide and made a sweeping
gesture with his other hand, ushering me into the
small cubicle. My shoulder dragged against the wall;
too much alcohol equalled lack of coordination. One
wrong footing and my arse landed on the loo with a
thump. Vince came in behind me and helped steady
me back onto my feet. The door swung shut behind
us.

"Woah, don't hurt yourself. Let me give you a
hand."

The room was claustrophobic enough without
Vince fumbling to prop me up. The single, dingy blue
lightbulb shining down made me feel nauseous too;
the kind of light straight out of a B-movie horror.

Vince pulled at my belt, undoing it and tugged at
the buttons on my jeans. He tried to slide my jeans
down, though a couple of swipes and he'd backed-off.

"It's okay Vince, really, you don't need to give me
a hand to use the loo."

His arm slipped around my lower back, his hand
grabbing me around my waist. He leaned in for a kiss,
but a crafty turn of my head deflected his
unwarranted advances, causing his lips to smear
across my cheek. His other hand slipped up my top; a
quick sweep of my breasts, under the bra. All too
quick; all too much of a surprise. A practised move?
Too drunk to think straight. Vince kissed my neck
and in the process of escaping his marauding lips, my
head smacked backwards against the cubicle wall. The
offending boob-grabbing hand skittered downwards
and slid inside my trousers, inside my underwear, fast
and skilled while he still had me lassoed with his arm.

He skimmed over my pubic hair, almost as though checking what was down there, then whipped his hand back out in an instant. Nothing more, but all in his control. Too quick, too fast, my body tarnished by greedy, perverted fingers on a mission of their own.

The unlocked toilet door opened. Ryuji's face appeared around it.

Vince shut it hard, banging Ryuji's forehead. "Yo, we're occupied in here, what's your problem?"

"It's me," Ryuji protested. "I came to help, what's the deal, man?"

A rush of heat flooded my face. "Aren't you with Zoe? Thought you'd gone to take her home."

"She's getting some air outside. I came back for our coats, then I'm getting her into bed. Come outside with me, Kimberly."

Vince was surprisingly easy to shove aside when caught off-guard; a well-placed palm in the centre of his chest granted me a nanosecond to duck under his arm. It was only two staggering steps to the door for my limp, vodka-drowned body to collapse into Ryuji's arms. He wrapped a supportive arm around my shoulder.

"That was good timing." My words were slurred, barely coherent.

"Will you be alright? You can come along for the car ride while I drop Zoe off, I'll be coming back here after."

"S'alright. Lemme grab water at the bar. Jei Pi's around, she'll look after me."

Ryuji steered me towards the bar. "Okay then. Watch out for yourself. Vince is a nice guy, but he's a bit of an idiot when he's drunk."

"You can say that again." My head reeled, from
alcohol and Vince. Jei Pi weaved through the crowd
and hooked an arm around my back. Behind us,
Vince skulked out of the toilet and padded across the
dancefloor to a dark corner, a prowling panther. He
bobbed in time to the music; awkward, lumbering, as
though his body wasn't accustomed to dancing, as
though it were made of too many balloons stuffed
inside a sock, as though one sharp pin would pop the
lot. My fist could have popped that lot, one deft aim
at his jaw would be all it would take.

"Hey chica, whatcha looking at?" said Jei Pi. "Oh!
My, my, my."

My head spun in the direction of Jei Pi's gaze. The
panther had found its prey: Vince leaned over Shiori,
one hand propping him against the wall as he
cornered her in a shadowy nook. Yet she didn't look
like a damsel in distress; her body language was bold,
brazen as she lured him into her web. Panther was
feasting on a black widow.

A powerful urge to march across and rescue Vince
from the she-demon struck me. He was my friend,
and she was a man-trap. Thankfully the alcohol
stopped me. My emotions were haywire; it was
beyond me how to even reign them in. For starters,
Vince wasn't a friend: a friend wouldn't have touched
me up when drunk for his own kicks. Secondly, Shiori
and Vince were both single and free to do as they
pleased. And third. Well, third. My booze-bogged
brain wouldn't work. Thirdly, maybe they both
deserved each other. They were both sleazy. What
mattered more was me. Or perhaps, more aptly, the
lack of me. My mind, the inner me, incinerate me.

Yes. That was it; the problem. Me didn't exist. A remnant of me had been burned up.

"Is it just me, or are you burning up?" The words tumbled out of my mouth, haphazard. That was exactly it; words and no sense. "Gimme some water. Oh-me-zoo-on-knee-guy-she-mass."

19

ೞ

Face in the mirror

Three AM. My head hammered. Thank goodness
Sunday was my day off. Poor Jei Pi; she'd probably
have a banging headache on the early shift. What had
happened after she had left? It hadn't been as much
fun dancing with Ryuji since both Jei Pi and Zoe had
gone, not to mention watching Vince and Shiori like a
couple of tentacle-monsters all over each other on the
dancefloor. Ryuji had plied me with water and soft
drinks, undoing the damage from the vodka. Ryuji
was a good guy; Zoe was lucky. Vince on the other
hand; what a creep. False pretences of friendship only
for him to cop a feel in the toilet in the sleaziest
possible manner. No more nicey-nice with him; my
ten foot barge pole would have metal spikes at the
end of it in future. Course, if it wasn't for me getting
so drunk, he wouldn't have tried his luck in the first
place.

What was wrong with me, getting so drunk? Carl
was right about me being stupid, acting in a
disgusting, drunken, despicable manner. No, that was
unfair; using his words to beat myself up didn't solve
anything. It only made things worse. Too much
alcohol, plus too little sleep, plus not enough food
was a recipe for disaster. My detox had been working
and then? Well, it was all ruined now. Overindulgence
wasn't what Buddhist monks would do to reach inner
peace.

Then again, my life was as far from Buddhist monk as you could get. You had to be Buddhist for a start. What was my pitiful existence? Just a joke.

My life was a smear on the arsehole of existence. What a pathetic article: my shoulders were slumped, deflated; my hair hung straggly over my shoulders; my eye make-up was smeared with sweat from the drunken night of dancing. The reflection in the mirror was an eyesore, indeed. Who was the real Kimberly Thatcher under all the caked-on powder? Who the hell knew: it wasn't like my true self had been seen for seven years. And even then, that Kimberly had been a naive, eighteen year old girl, immature and unwise to the ways of the world. Since then, Manny had emerged, absorbing Kimberly, consuming her until she became a co-dependent girl, one-half-of-a-couple who couldn't think for herself. How long had Carl been making my mind up for me? It was as though my mouth opened and his words came out. Is that what it came down to, Manny the mynabird, mimicking her moronic boyfriend?

It was a wonder my wretched mind had even been capable of making the decision to come to Japan, considering that it had been my and not Carl's choice. Then again, it wasn't so much a choice, as a chance to escape.

My life was a mess, my mind. Me. Even on a basic, fundamental level, my ability to take care of myself was lacking. The night before, Ryuji had needed to walk me home, as he had been too drunk to drive; though not as drunk as me. At some point, both of my shoes had gotten lost. One shoe had fallen off the White Rabbit Bridge. The sharks from the story had it now. The other had fallen into one of Tottori's deep, open storm drains. Poor Ryuji had struggled to carry me up the stairs to my flat and unlock the door, with me over his shoulder in a fireman's lift.

My reflection blurred, then re-focused as my nose came closer to the mirror, stopping several inches away. Who was the gaunt person staring back; mid-twenties, but naive, vulnerable as an adolescent. Manny was a savvy Londoner, who wore baggy jumpers and comfortable trousers. My mind struggled to identify with this Euro-trash resemblance of me in the mirror: tight clothes, almost heroin-chic. Eighteen to twenty-five was seven years of no soul-searching that had left me staring at a blank face. Would the real me under it all ever surface? Who was the real me? What were her likes and dislikes, her desires? It was a start, to know my fears. Fear of being alone. Fear of not having anyone to share the world with. Fear of myself.

A couple of handfuls over cold water sobered me a tad; black mascara-tinged water poured down the plughole. Where to begin on my inner journey? If only it were as easy as having a flow chart with arrows to follow; different options leading to various outcomes.

Step one: do you like yourself?

No.

Step two: do you trust your decisions?

No.

Oh my gosh, is that what it came down to; a psychological assessment of myself? Four years of university training all to be applied to my own inner journey?

Carl was worried that single women with only themselves to think about were influencing me; but was it *him* who was influencing me, even dominating me. For how long? How long had Manny existed?

Manny had to die.

If Carl couldn't wait for me, for eight more months, was he right for me? Was he worth it? My bare, makeup-stripped face in the mirror stared back, obvious fear in my eyes. It was hard to look at that expression.

If that person in the mirror wasn't Kimberly and wasn't Manny, then who the hell was she?

Carl had given me an ultimatum. Was it really love if someone could force you to make a choice you didn't want to? No. Did that mean Jei Pi was right; that Carl saw me as a possession, a thing to control?

Why were my feelings so confused?

Such a whirlwind; a vicious circle. What to do when you were caught in a cycle? My training came to mind. The Kolb Cycle; the four components of experiential learning. Which one best fit my current circumstances? Concrete experience: learn from everyday experiences.

What to do? Maybe getting back to basics would be a start. My feelings for Carl were strong, but was it worth it to give into his demands and come home early? Heart over head; my heart yearned to be with him, it longed to support him – but at twenty-five, so young yet, my mind wanted fun and freedom not to be stifled and judged and condemned. Spontaneity, travel, adventures; not desperation, loneliness, fear. Mind before heart. Maybe my life goals and his were too different.

He wanted me home.

Home wasn't for me.

He'd never be happy.

So how could we be happy?

Was it best to let go now?

Three thirty AM. My feet itched to go round to the international phone at Lawson and call him. London was eight hours behind. It was tempting to tell him straight about my decision to stay in Japan for the whole year, for him not to put words in my mouth, to force him to listen for a change.

It was futile. He could make a mountain out of a molehill. He'd call me a stupid little girl, out at all hours of the night. We'd fight. It would end in tears: my tears. All it would achieve would be me brooding for the whole day and then getting pissed come nightfall.

So much for my bravado; nothing but a useless coward.

Hating on myself was the easier option, rather than face telling him the truth. A lot of pain and for what? For all Carl cared, he was probably sleeping with some Asian girl from Chinatown, back home in London.

Nothing more to do for the time being except get my mind off it. Vodka and poetry. No, poetry first, then Glens. Alcohol would stem the flow of words.

Alcohol and excess
Medicine for the soul
A tormented life, directionless,
Unable to love, incapable of being loved.
Wallowing in self-pity.

Writing was a good move; my energy was spent from creativity. It felt good to be distracted from the disjointed reality of my life. My bedroom felt friendly again, reclaimed. My mind was fragmented, my relationship was fragmented, the whole damn world was fragmented, but a fragment was a starting place.

Goodbye Manny.

Where was Kimberly?

Was the person in the mirror Kim, an interim person, an avatar? Kim could be tough, suave, sophisticated, sexy...everything that gullible Kimberly and down-trodden Manny weren't. Every little step on the soul-searching journey made it better. Carl treating me badly in the physical world was to teach him a lesson in the spiritual world. My suffering in this world meant a bit of extra soul-poultice in the next world. My job now was to forgive others, starting with Carl, and to forgive myself.

20

ଓଃ

Hamamura

"You have to go in naked."

Jei Pi had got to be kidding. "Come again?"

"Naked. It's the custom. You have to obey the rules. It's not optional, *Kim*."

My new nickname felt strange in my ears; it would take getting used to, for sure. Even my students at Voyce had adopted it, willingly too, since Kimberly was a mouthful. *Kim-ooh*, they said.

Jei Pi led us along the main street through the sleepy village of Hamamura. We were about to go into an onsen, a Japanese public bath, in the nude. The notion was strange to me, but as the saying went, *When in Rome...*

"Okay, sure, it's not optional. But it's all female, right?"

Jei Pi cranked her face into a sarcastic smirk. "Course it is. All public baths are, except if you hire a private one in mixed company."

A fleeting image of me in a private onsen with Zoe, Jei Pi, Tomomi, Vince and Ade popped into my mind. Did Japanese have no inhibitions? Maybe they were used to it. Mind you, most Japanese women were flat up, flat down; easy for them. Would they stare at my round ass and ample chest in the onsen? Shiori had no tits and no ass. Though, what about Tomomi? She was tall for a Japanese woman at five six, and busty as far as Japanese women went, with a curvy arse too. Got to be honest with myself: it wasn't that *all* Japanese women were ironing boards, only Shiori. Lashing out at my nemesis was no reason to spite all Japanese women.

That bitch Shiori. How could Carl cheat on me with a pancake-flat tart who looked like she was twelve, especially when pitted against a tall, curvy blonde. Most people thought of me as conventionally beautiful, even if my mind rejected that notion most days. Could that be the problem? Did Carl find me too insecure? How could he do it; how could he embarrass me like that; everyone knew but me? My mind reeled. Because it wasn't about looks. It was about games. It was about control.

"I hope you haven't shaved. You know — your bits." Jei Pi gestured to my crotch and my cheeks burned.

"Why, what's wrong with that?"

"They'll think you're hentai. Only brazen women do that in Japan, like porn stars."

A deflective, no, defensive shrug. "Well, normally Carl liked it that way, but it's grown back since he left."

Jei Pi's eyes widened. "He *makes* you shave?"

"He doesn't *make* me, exactly. Carl wanted it all off so he could see everything, but it was my choice to leave a landing strip."

We said no more. Jei Pi led us into a traditional-looking wooden building with a sign written in Chinese characters. Five hundred yen at reception; about two pounds fifty. The wooden interior made the place look like a spa. We bought cellophane-wrapped towels from a vending machine. A quick tear made short work of the wrapping; it was a tea-towel sized cotton cloth with Kanji writing and a picture of a cat holding up one paw along the edge.

Holding it up, it was obvious it wouldn't cover both chest and crotch. "What's the point of this? It's tiny."

"It's a scrubbing cloth. I hope you brought a bath towel to dry?"

"Of course. Brought my bikini along too."

Jei Pi smirked. "You won't need that. C'mon."

A steeply sloping corridor led us up Hamamura mountain. We climbed for a couple of minutes to the top. Quite the stretch on my calves; nothing a good soak in chloride-sulphate water, naked or not, couldn't fix.

Two sets of sliding doors at the top separated the men and women. Curtains hung in front of the doors, one with a male symbol and the other with a female symbol, written in Kanji. It gave me a boost of confidence being able to read the characters. Throwing myself into studying from my Business Japanese book had been good for two reasons: distraction from my relationship troubles and safety in the knowledge of never having to inadvertently walk into the men's toilet by mistake from illiteracy.

We walked into the female changing room and each took a locker to one side. Naked women walked to and fro. Awkward. A fresh wave of self-consciousness overcame me at getting undressed in public. Jei Pi dropped her clothes on the ground as if she hadn't a care in the world. My wide open locker door served as meagre shelter to strip off behind. Funny how only moments before, confidence in my body was high, but now was almost nil. It felt strange to drape the wash cloth over my modesty since my body was bare to the world. The tea towel-sized cloth barely covered my chest and crotch; Jei Pi in front became my human shield of shame. Jei Pi, despite her wobbly thighs and stomach rolls walked with confidence. How nice to be her: not ladylike, but not a care. Still, the superficial part of my brain summed her up: no wonder Jei Pi didn't get laid as much as she would like. Japanese men were terrified of domineering western women and western men were only interested in easy Japanese barflys. Although the past few weeks had seen me overindulge in more than my fair share of alcohol and junk food through comfort eating, thanks to good genes, my size eight skinny jeans were a loose fit. Genes, jeans; a new poem formed in my head, bringing a welcome distraction from thoughts of insecurity and nudity.

The shower room was adjacent to the changing room behind an opaque sliding screen. Jei Pi picked up a plastic stool and wash basin from a pile, which prompted me to follow suit. Taps were lined around the sides of the tiled room, at crotch height. Japanese women sat at a tap each on their stools and scrubbed, using their basins to pour water over themselves. No shower cubicles, no curtains, no privacy. Looked more like a school shower room than a luxurious spa. We found two taps side by side and set our stools down, careful not to slip on the wet floor.

"I'd advise you to wash your stool first," said Jei Pi. My poor, unassuming stool no longer looked so innocent. Who knew how many bare bums had sat on the plastic stools before me. My first action, courtesy of Jei Pi was to pour shower gel on my stool and rinse it, holding my towel in place with the other hand.

"You don't need to be so shy, we're all naked," said Jei Pi, her ginger triangle stark against her flabby white body. My eyes were drawn to the untamed bush. Bleurgh. Thank goodness for my own taut physique. A few stolen snatches of sun in between typhoons and the Spring Winds from china had marinated my body in a light bronze glow. Deep breath; Jei Pi was right. No need to be shy, we were all women. My protective hand released slowly and let the wash cloth fall.

"Woah!" said Jei Pi. "Alrighty-mighty Aphrodite!"

Awkward. One arm shielded my chest and the other clutched my groin while my bum dropped quickly onto the stool. My peripheral vision showed Jei Pi's eyes lingering on my naked body before she looked away and started rinsing. What the hell was that all about? Girl on girl comments usually reeked of an underlying jealousy, yet this was more like admiration; like how a man would marvel at my body. Weird.

Liberal amounts of shower gel and a basin full of water over my head served to wash away Jei Pi's greasy gaze on my bare skin. Around the room, Japanese women dipped their wash cloths in their basins and used them to scrub their skin until they were raw red. Were any of them looking at the red and gold heads that stood out from the rest of the black-haired women? Nope. No one cared. Knowing this helped me to relax. So long as no one looked, it felt liberating to be naked.

In the corner of the wash room, was a small, deep plunge pool of cold water and next to it, a wooden sauna. Beyond that a set of sliding doors led outside. Jei Pi led us out into what looked to be a zen garden.

A bamboo fence around the perimeter gave the mountain top garden privacy. Around the edges were piled stones, bonsai trees and a miniature waterfall. In the middle, was a wide, deep volcanic stone pool. The view across Hamamura showed rice paddies and beyond, a glimpse of the Japan Sea. Spectacular view. This truly was bliss.

We waded through the comfortably warm water to the far side of the pool. It was deeper than it looked; the thigh deep water reached to my chin when seated. Jei Pi dipped her towel under the waterfall, folded it and put it on her head. Mine sufficed around my shoulders.

The sliding doors opened and two Japanese women joined us. Fighting the urge to stare was tough. It was rude to stare, but my curiosity was too strong; here was a chance to see what Carl was attracted to. What did Japanese women have over me? My eyes were locked on their lithe naked bodies; this definitely constituted staring. Not my fault; my sheltered British sensibilities were unaccustomed to public nudity. Were Japanese women different from Western women in the buff? Yes. Taut stomachs, small boobs no bigger than A-cups. My own 34 C's floated upwards on the water and my chest swelled with superiority. The two women also had short legs in proportion to their longer upper torsos. My long, bicycle-honed legs were stretched out in the pool. Towels folded on their heads like Jei Pi, hands hanging openly by their sides; my eyes travelled downwards. The one in front was certainly no hentai with her untamed black bush, as Jei Pi had explained. If the Japanese were so into hygiene, how could they keep such thick carpeting down below clean? But wait; the one behind, with the small, nicely shaped boobs, had shaved everything down below except for a landing strip. Very un-Japanese. My gaze travelled upwards to her face and a horrible jolt in my stomach woke me to reality. An unfortunate coincidence: Shiori.

Shiori and her companion waded across the pool and sat opposite us. As Shiori's pert boobs sank below the waterline, an image of Carl touching them popped into my head. Tarty little slut. It would've been so easy to launch myself across the onsen and tear out her hair, but my restraint was commendable. Did Carl like Japanese bodies instead of English? Did he prefer brown nipples, not pink? It was obvious he liked Asian women, not Caucasian. The thought forced me to swallow a lump in my throat and turn to watch the view through the bamboo fence instead. From the corner of my eye, it was clear Shiori was watching me.

Knowing this helped me will my head around to face her. Shiori stared.

"Kao oboeteta," said Shiori in a voice higher and sweeter than she had sounded during our last encounter in Jusco, when she had spoken to Carl. The 'How do I look? Sexy?' was ingrained in my mind. Spiteful cow. Was this war? My sadistic mind imagined the sugary-sweet voice whispering dirty words in Carl's ear, gasping in the throes of an orgasm. Why torture myself with such devilish imagination?

"What?" My answer came out cold and direct in English; that would spite the bitch. "I don't know what you're on about."

"She said she remembers your face," said Jei Pi. She addressed Shiori. "Kanojo wa doko de aimashita ka."

My amazement at Jei Pi's Japanese momentarily halted my anger at Shiori. All those times my flat mate's immersion in Japanese culture had been easy to dismiss as annoying and pretentious, but now it was most useful indeed. Without Jei Pi, the Japanese would've been beyond me.

"Kita Jusco," said Shiori. "Voyce no sensei desho ka."

"I asked her where you guys met and she said in Jusco. Do you know her?" Jei Pi didn't wait for the answer; she turned to Shiori. "Hai, watashi tachi wa Voyce no sensei desu."

"Too right we know each other – she's the one Tomomi mentioned at the cherry blossom party, remember?" It was a struggle to contain my anger. "Ask her if she was seeing Carl and you'll get my drift."

"I'm not sure if I know how, my Japanese is pretty basic, but I'll try." Jei Pi cleared her throat. "Eto, Igirisu kara kareshi wa imashita ka. Kare no namae wa Carl desu."

"So da you." Shiori's voice had taken on the deeper, more threatening tone that was all too familiar from when the cow had forced her unwanted presence upon Carl and me in Jusco. Still, it had lost none of its femininity. Conniving little witch. "Anta ni kankei aru?" Shiori added.

Jei Pi looked puzzled. "I don't know what she said."

"Isn't it obvious?" My teeth were gritted. "Let me guess. Kankei nai desho means none of your business

– Tomomi taught me. So, anta ni kankei aru must mean something along those lines, something rude like that. The little slag is insulting me to my face. She can speak English perfectly well too, she's speaking Japanese to be insulting."

Shiori and her companion blabbered in animated Japanese. It was humiliating to need Jei Pi to translate our confrontation, and annoying on top of things that my supposed friend seemed to be enjoying the chance to speak Japanese rather than take my side in the emotional conflict. Jei Pi doing all the talking made the situation less dignified, somehow. Frustration welled; indulging myself in a daydream about punching Shiori right in her smug face relieved my tension.

A quick, deep breath to centre myself. "You can speak English, so don't pretend you can't. You know exactly what we've been saying."

"Ee. Yoku kiita yo." Shiori said the words in a sarcastic, singsong way. The snarl playing about her mouth let me know it was all for added effect. Shiori knew everything that had been said. How nice it would have been to throw her off Hamamura mountain.

"You can understand me perfectly well, so stop with the games." Spitting the words back at Shiori in the same sarcastic manner she had assumed felt satisfying. The sentiment needed to be clear so the meaning wouldn't be lost. "Carl is my boyfriend. You had no right to steal him behind my back. But since you did, you should know this. You had him on borrowed time, but that's all you could ever have. You're not worth him. A man like Carl would never want someone like you."

Adrenaline propelled me to my feet; getting out of Shiori's presence was my number one priority, both for my mental health and emotional dignity. It would've made everything a million times worse to give Shiori the pleasure of seeing me cry.

"Carl liked me better, and she can't take that," said Shiori. A chorus of giggles followed, assaulting my retreating back. "Even worse, I had her new man last week too. I kissed him in Club Passion."

She meant Vince. That revelation almost made me laugh, but got me dangerously close to retaliating. The little bitch was good at her game. Deep breath, zen meditation, stay calm. Be the bigger person. It was hard to have my dignity intact wading stark naked past Shiori through the onsen, but once my hands had slid the doors closed firmly behind me, anger consumed me.

Into the cold plunge pool, without a second thought. Only then did the tears flow, dropping into the frigid water. Why couldn't hypothermia set in to numb the pain? No such luck. Intrusive thoughts wormed their way through my tepid brain. Shiori was shaved, a landing strip, like how my private bits had been until recently. Did Carl suggest it? The vindictive other woman in his life had been toying with me, adding insult to injury.

Where was Jei Pi? She hadn't followed. Why did she stay outside in the onsen with the enemy? So much for loyalty. Was she a traitor? No; just because Carl had betrayed me didn't mean everyone else was a traitor too. It was a good thing Jei Pi stayed behind. Later, she could fill me in on what, if anything, Shiori said about me, or Carl.

Getting dried and dressed took a fleeting, perfunctory moment, my mind elsewhere. How ironic that only now, away from the cold plunge pool, my body felt chilled; clothes did nothing to warm me. It took less than a minute to traipse down the sloping corridor of Hammamura mountain, alone, and fuelled by anger: twice as quick as it had taken to climb it beforehand. Once outside, with my back rested against the wall at the entrance to the onsen, a long intake of air to my lungs cleared the poison breath of air that had been shared with Shiori. It helped to visualise her toxic aura leaving my soul, like a slimy residue washing off. It was a shame that my body, and soul didn't feel cleansed, but quite the opposite: tarnished. Shiori and me, we were two *hentai*, the only shaved 'perverts' in the onsen, thanks to Carl. My pubic hair had grown to a short fuzz in the month since Carl had gone back to London, but now, it would forever become untamed. No wonder lesbians and feminists kept an unruly bush. For once the appeal was clear; rebelling against men.

Time for a self check-in. Shiori, had hurt me. No; Carl had hurt me. Shiori had got together with him under false pretences, thinking we were Voyce colleagues. My angry exchange of words with Shiori in the onsen was because Shiori felt defensive. How could she not? She saw me as a competitor for Carl as much as she seemed one to me.

"Sumimasen." A Japanese man interrupted my thoughts. Got to save face; a quick wipe removed a wave of fresh tears from my eyes. Our eyes met, then the gaze broke. He'd better not ask about me crying. In my current mood talking to a stranger about my feelings, never mind having to use over-simplified, staccato English, seemed a slow death.

"You eez bery boot-ee-ful lady... no, wait." He gave a small bow. "You has bery kindo face and you is gentle body."

A fleeting thought to tell him to piss off crossed my mind; za-ken-na-yo, as Tomomi had put it simply when she was teaching me anti-hentai-Japanese. But why bother? He found me attractive and maybe this pleased me. Why not? It was no crime; and the pick me up came at a welcome time. But how to react? This bloke was a perfect stranger. What did the real me think about anything? Manny would've answered rudely; Carl's words speaking through his puppet. Kimberly might've walked away. But this limbo-me, Kim or whatever her name was, she was neither of those two. Kim chose to smile.

He was forty-something, with grey-streaked hair and clearly no inhibitions. Could he be trying it on because all he saw was a foreigner in front of him? No time to analyse the situation now; the bloke carried on in his stilted English. "Can I ask you favour, please?"

Mustering my best sugar-sweet smile made me feel good, especially to see his face crack a grin in response.

"Can you buy me... no, can you sell me please, one of pubic hairs? I has not seen golden pubic hair before. Eez you pubic hair same colour as hair on head and eyebrow?"

It took serious willpower not to laugh at his poor grammar. "Course it is. How much do you want it for?"

He pulled a ten thousand yen note from his wallet. Ichi-man en: fifty quid. Wow. Money in one hand while the other delved inside the waistband of my trousers. Right there on the street, in broad daylight, my deft fingers yanked out one of my recently regrown blonde pubes and handed it to him. He put it inside the plastic cover of his mobile phone, next to his bank card.

"Nice doing business with you." The words rolled off my tongue with the same greasy ooze that had made me participate in the whole sleazy endeavour in the first place.

He gave a small bow. "You eez make me bary happy mens."

Hmph. His clipped English was sufficient to hit on foreign women, but not enough to understand subtle nuances. Maybe all men were the same; tossers who wanted to take women for all they could get. Well, not me. This situation was under my power, my control. It was Kim, not Manny or Kimberly, but Kim my alter ego, who stuffed the money in her pocket and walked along the empty street towards Hamamura train station.

21

○3

Tottori kaigan

May. A brand new month. It was also another day to score off on my wall calendar and the realisation, with a sudden pang of sadness, that my year in Japan was half over. Tottori had grown on me. After the rough winter, the town had opened itself up. Everything that had happened: my friends, my social life; all of it had happened after Carl left. In six months, there were still many things for me to accomplish; my tick list had barely begun. My leaving date was the third of November. My flight home remained to be booked yet, but still...

But what? My desire to go home was lacking. My heart wanted to see Carl; but did my mind? Heart and mind, body and soul; all too confusing. Staring at the blank spaces on the calendar resolved nothing. Yes, maybe my heart was winning. This thought depressed me, but yes. Yes. The vengeful part of me wanted to rant at him, to lay down the law to his face and make him hang his head in shame. Phone calls weren't the same. The bust-up with Shiori in Hamamura the previous week had blown out most of my anger. Now all that fuelled me was pain.

On that note, my mind took over, safely shutting my heart back in its box. Shoes on and out into the sunshine with my beach bag. May brought with it gorgeous weather that would've been a shame not to take advantage off before my Japanese adventure was over. Another pang of sadness.

Why all the sadness? Maybe extending my one year visa, renewing it for another year was the way forward. It seemed my sadness at the thought of leaving Tottori was stronger than excitement at seeing Carl. Could it really be love if that was the case? Carl or Tottori. Is that what it came down to; a choice? Did it have to be a decision between the two?

The bicycle ride to Tottori Kaigan, Tottori beach, made me feel free; the brisk wind cleared my thoughts. My head was a storm that had blown itself out, spent its energy on Shiori. Much as it irked me to admit though, Shiori was the wrong target.

Carl deserved the brunt of my anger, not Shiori. Shiori was a stranger; the girl didn't owe me any loyalty. Shiori had been the scapegoat for my anger, which should have been directed at Carl. Shiori detracted from the real issue; my relationship with Carl. *Kim's* relationship with Carl, face it. Kim was who Manny and Kimberly had become. Why did *Kim* love Carl?

Did Kim love Carl?

The question, when posed to me, felt strange. It had always been my assumption that our relationship had been based on love. Carl had been five years older than me when we had got together; a fresh-faced eighteen year old, starting my final year of A-levels wowed by a man who made her feel grown-up. It had seemed cool at the time, but now? Naive. Perhaps, but he'd seemed so fascinating; a working man, not a schoolboy. He'd taken me out, bought me expensive gifts. It didn't matter when it came out later that he'd had to borrow the money from his sister,

Chezza, to buy the presents; in fact it made him even more appealing that he was so enraptured with me, that he would get himself into debt all for me. The infatuation was equal between us – at the start. Soon our relationship had settled into a comfortable routine and we'd moved in together. Well, not comfortable, exactly.

He had been a self-employed painter and decorator when we had met, in a business that he ran with a friend. The romantic in me had thought of him as an *artiste*. But when the work had dried up, he'd been forced to close the business and sell the van. He'd hit the booze hard for a while, then picked himself up and got a new job as a janitor at Luton airport. Still, we'd managed to get a cheap flat in Croydon, near his parents at his request, while my daily commute into central London to study Psychology at UCL had lengthened; a necessary sacrifice to help us stay strong. There had been tension in our relationship then, since Carl was resentful of me studying, while he had to work.

Why was my cruel brain dredging all this up now? The bicycle weaved along by Sendai River towards Tottori Beach, the journey distilling my thoughts. Because now was as good a time as any for some soul searching.

Carl had exerted a control over me since when we'd moved in together. *I have to pay the rent while you go off and have fun with your mates. I want you back by one o'clock at the latest. I don't like you hanging about with those people, they're a bad influence. All I do is work, and all you do is have fun.* It was always a complaint, never a compliment. Why hadn't it occurred to me before? Maybe because it was hard to see a situation

objectively when you were in it. Being away from Carl
gave me an outside perspective.

The beach was empty. After parking the bike, my
first thought was to wade into the sea for a soul-
soothing dip. But there was no rush. The whole beach
belonged to me. Moments like that one really made
me glad to be living in Tottori, to be grounded,
centred and living in the present. It was lovely to feel
the warm sand beneath my toes, to feel the fresh
breeze on my face and revel at the blue expanse of
sea. It helped to flush away the detritus that Carl had
caused, blocking up my head; a cholesterol clog of my
chakras.

My last visit to Tottori Kaigan had been with Carl
when he had chided me for rescuing a pufferfish, a
potentially dangerous act. But this time there would
be no poison; and the only rescue would be of myself.
This was me-time, a purging experience for my soul.
My bedroom had been spring-cleaned of all physical
traces of Carl and now the time had come to spring-
clean my memories of places we'd been together too.
The perfect medicine for the job was in my bag to aid
the journey towards new happy memories: a bottle of
Pimms, some Lemonade along with cucumber,
strawberries and mint leaves. Yum. Thank heavens
for that specialist liquor shop in downtown Yayoi-
cho. Even a small town place like Tottori had good
taste, clearly. Everything was in order inside my beach
bag; with it slung it over my shoulder, my mission to
cleanse my memories began. On that last trip to
Tottori beach, the sand had been strewn with rubbish.
This time, the rubbish had been burned. Charred
remains lay in neat piles. Maybe it had been cleared
ahead of the summer months after the rainy season; a

torrential downpour would make short work of the cremated food packaging. Nevertheless, the physical cleansing of the beach helped the metaphysical cleansing of my mind.

Moeru gomi and moenai gomi: burnable and non-burnable rubbish. Japan was pedantic about cleanliness and order, even for its rubbish disposal system. Some of the moeru gomi had been burned on Tottori beach. What was the moeru gomi in my head? What could be burned and what could be recycled? Maybe the charred remains were a metaphor for some kind of inner doom; or worse, a psychic failure on my part. But no, burned rubbish in my mind would not dash my hopes. My short trek along the beach soon became an epic adventure towards the Tottori sand dunes, famous for their gigantic size, as my head rather than feet guided my inner journey.

Blue skies. Bag down. No clouds. Vest-top off. No rubbish. Shorts off. No people. Shoes off. No people... A quick look both ways to be sure, peering over the top of a large dune towards the shoreline revealed that the beach was still empty. Japanese people didn't sunbathe until July; a truly Type A society. My bikini top was the last item to whip off, thong safely on in case the need to dress quickly arose. It was no hindrance; skimpy enough for me to get an even tan despite keeping it on.

Stretched out on my back, enjoying the freedom of near-nakedness behind the large dune was a wonderful, liberating experience. What were the laws about public nudity in Japan anyway? Were women allowed to sunbathe topless? If someone caught me, would they call the police to come and arrest me?

The sun beat down on my stomach. My breasts tingled, unaccustomed to the sun. Wiping off my sweaty brow caused a sand-smeared streak across my forehead. A quick dusting got rid of the sand on my bum and legs, then a flip-over onto my belly to settle down with a contented sigh, a brown sausage on the barbecue of life.

Behind the dune, time seemed to be at a standstill. It was lovely to be lost in my own personal world, where even the sound of the wind and rush of waves couldn't reach. Once or twice my hedonistic repose almost had me doze off, when a sting on the back of my right butt cheek jerked me upright. An insect? Couldn't be; it felt bigger. A stone that had rolled from the top of the dune maybe? Three feet away, a golf ball was lodged in a clump of marram grass. A golf ball meant people had to be nearby. Where was my bikini top? One arm through the loop, one cup wedged into place, but not quick enough–

"Konnichiwa."

An old man in a polo-shirt with a golf-cap on stood over me, his shadow consuming my near-naked body. His grin was so wide his eyes were reduced to slits; hard to tell if his greedy gaze was roving my body, or staying fixed on my face. My right hand shielded the bare right breast while the skimpy bikini provided meagre cover of my left breast. The old man had appeared so fast, it was a safe bet he'd caught a dirty old glimpse of my girls.

"Ah, Kimberly San, it's you!"

Who? Crap; a hurried fumble allowed me to snatch the beach towel hastily across my front. My sand-encrusted hand shielded the sun from my eyes, allowing time to study his face. A name came to mind: Yoshitoshi, a Mid-level Voyce student who came to lessons infrequently. He was always away on business trips to the States. My face burned. Yoshitoshi didn't look embarrassed at all. He kept grinning, waiting for my response.

"Hello. Er, didn't see you there. Wasn't expecting anyone to be here, in fact." It was an awkward reply that spilled out of my mouth; awkward gaijin, not suave English teacher.

Yoshitoshi pointed across the dunes away from the beach. "I has been playing golf over there with Noriyuki," he said in stilted, but comprehensible English.

Noriyuki... fleeting images of Voyce students crossed my mind. Noriyuki. Grey-streaked hair, round face, mid-level. Shit. Had he seen me too? "Er – were you both playing for long?"

He nodded. "Two hours, around."

This unpleasant revelation made me cringe, knowing the inevitable. "Oh right, all that time?"

"We saw you walking along the beach. We knew you is person because you are the only teacher with bright yellow hair."

So they'd seen everything. They'd watched me strip off. They'd seen me topless in a thong. Why couldn't the ground swallow me up?

"Yamamoto San, kochi kochi."

Yoshitoshi made a waving gesture across the dunes and the sound of feet padding across the sand announced another person drawing near. "Kimberly San is here," said Yoshitoshi. "We are lucky – not often we is get to practise English outside of Voyce."

They had *got* to be joking. The beach towel cocooned me, every available area of skin covered, with the exception of my fingers holding it over my foetal pose. Even my feet, legs and arms felt sullied as they watched me, making normality of the uncomfortable situation. Noriyuki gave a little bow, not in the least bit embarrassed by my state of semi-undress. "We was playing the golf at over there," said Noriyuki, his English a little less proficient than Yoshitoshi's. "We can't find a ball, and we saw you was a sitting up, and I wonder is perhaps you was looking for something."

One of my brave fingers un-clutched itself from the beach towel and pointed at the golf ball, still lodged in the marram grass, hoping they would go away.

"Do you often come to the beach to get sun-burned?" asked Noriyuki.

"Sun-tanned." Damn my tongue and damn the ingrained English teacher within me. Correcting his English meant perpetuating the conversation, but responding quickly had been instilled through my teacher training. "Sun-burned means when your skin is red. Sun-tanned means getting brown."

"You have a nice sun-tan, Kimberly San. All over," Yoshitoshi added, with a sly smile. Funny there was no problem with his English that time.

Bleugh. This was more than pleasantries, or English practise, for that matter. The prick was making his sleazy point with no subtlety, or nuance, or grace... or respect. If they didn't know when to get the message, time for action. "Listen, it was nice to see you both, and maybe the custom is different here, but if you see a lone western woman sunbathing it's a pretty sure bet she doesn't want to talk. So if you wouldn't mind?" Just in case they didn't understand my English, while one hand held the beach towel in place, the other flapped to shoo them away. Who cared if it was rude.

The two men shuffled closer. "You is need help to privacy with beach towel? We can hold beach towel and-o you is get dress?"

Enough was enough. "No, please go. Thank you."

"Bat-o, this hand sign with finger you is give to us." Noriyuki demonstrated my gesture to go away. "Means 'come here' in Japan."

"Well, in English it means go away." Get lost had been on the tip of my tongue; lucky it hadn't slipped out.

The two men started back across the dunes. "Well, goodbye Kimberly San. I will see you at Voyce on Wednesday when I have my next lesson booked," said Yoshitoshi.

"See you again next time we is meet," Noriyuki called.

Gone. My beach towel over me like a tent provided a much needed refuge. This was the worst. *The worst.* Could anything more humiliating, more undignified possibly happen to me after this? What now? Were Japanese men the type to gossip? Would they tell everyone about the encounter? What about Vince and Ade; they'd never let it go if they found out. This was worse than dying. How would it be possible to get over the shame? Students needed to have respect for their teachers. Now that they had seen me naked, there was no hope of that.

Or was there? Didn't Japanese people go freely into onsens and walk around naked, without staring? Of course, public baths were separate for men and women, but despite this, there weren't the social

taboos around nudity like in Britain. This was the
East. It was more enlightened, wasn't it? They cared
more about matters of the spirit than matters of the
flesh, didn't they? Bodies were simply for daily
functions; eating, sleeping, living. The mind was more
important. Japanese didn't care about aesthetics. Deep
breath; permission to relax. That would explain why
Yoshitoshi and Noriyuki had been so comfortable
around me and why they joked about it; they didn't
care. It was a big deal to me, not them.

Shorts and vest-top on, towel in my bag, Pimms
and Lemonade out. It didn't seem fitting to have my
celebration behind the sand dune; beside the sea
seemed more zen. Away from the shelter of my
sunbathing nook, the wind assaulted my face. Bum on
the sand, my face inclined towards the sea, and a stiff
drink in a plastic cup. Strawberry in, slice of cucumber
in and a few mint leaves. Yum.

As the rim of the plastic cup met my lips, a
nagging doubt struck me: maybe matters of the flesh
weren't trivial to Japanese people. Didn't that
businessman at Hamamura pay me fifty quid for a
pube? That experience wouldn't be quickly erased
from my subconscious. This was time to drink down
the shame. No cleansing ceremony on a charred
beach where my body had been burned by the sun
and cremated by impure eyes. No such celebration of
new memories. Death of the old me, cremation of
what? The image of me? What was that, anyway?

22

℘

Limelight

The large float full of hanging lanterns passed by along Tottori's main street. Men wearing white jimbes, traditional Japanese shirts, walked behind it. The kanji on their headbands was lost on me. A man in front of the float carried a large banner with a message in flamingo pink Japanese characters.

"What does that say?"

Zoe answered, as Jei Pi looked just as mystified as me. "Matsuri," said Zoe, "It means festival."

Thank heavens for having Zoe around. When Tomomi couldn't be there because of her time-consuming admin work for Voyce, Zoe was the next best thing. Not only did she have a Japanese teacher, but she seemed to have a photographic memory for kanji. Jei Pi was most keen to communicate, even if she tended to gesticulate wildly rather than speak, but at least she tried. My own ability lacked a knack for reading or speaking Japanese. Studying from my Business Japanese book had to suffice while my application for a Japanese tutor probably still sat on a bureaucrat's desk at the Tottori International Centre. In the meantime, the universe looked after me. Zoe and Jei Pi did the talking when it was needed, and my meagre ability now coped with reading menus when we dined out. Would a tutor be assigned to me in my remaining six months? Hopefully.

Six damn months. Not much time to do anything. It was bloody Carl's fault, wasting three months during winter and now demanding that for me to come home early. Fuck him! Even the incident at Tottori beach with Noriyuki and Yoshitoshi was a funny memory, now that two weeks had passed and the men didn't appear to have mentioned the encounter. Life was fun now that Carl had left.

Fun. There; it had finally slipped out. Life was fun without Carl. Japan was a fun adventure now that he was gone. No boring winter nights in watching dull movies. No isolation from friends because he wanted me to himself. The misery-guts was gone. Hurray! My happiness at freedom from Carl translated into a wave at a group of festival-dancers passing by. They waved back.

Zoe raised an eyebrow. "What's got you so happy?"

"Nothing. Just having one of those 'This is really my life in Japan' moments."

"I get those all the time," she said.

The dancing women wore traditional yukata, summer counterparts to the heavy kimonos. My feet always slowed when passing the kimono store a few doors along from Voyce school in Jusco shopping centre. The kimonos were made of silk whereas the yukatas were made of cotton. It was tempting to buy a kimono, but they looked too complicated to put on by myself. Younger women tended to wear yukatas more anyway, it seemed. And in Jusco, they were only ten thousand yen. That was like, fifty quid. Or the price of a blonde pube... this gave me a grin. Better not let Zoe see; a 'life in Japan' moment wouldn't suffice as an explanation for such a sly smile. What would Carl say? Fuck Carl; who cared what he would say? If my nether-region had been shaved as he liked, there wouldn't have been a pube to sell. It was a fitting punishment as an insult to a crap memory.

"Haro."

A Japanese man with a professional camera slung around his neck approached us. He stuck out his hand for me to shake. His smile was aimed at me too, although Jei Pi and Zoe clearly stood by, waiting for a handshake as well. A Western handshake; no Japanese bow. This bloke was either a cultured-traveller, or a smooth-operator.

"I'm Kensuke. I'm a photographer for the Asahi Shimbun," he said, in fluent English. "Would it be okay if I take your photo for the newspaper?"

He had directed his question at me too, though Jei Pi pushed forward and forced a handshake upon him. "Of course it would, we'd love to help."

Kensuke stared at her, then recovered his composure. "Oh, great. Are you girls on vacation?"

The vain part of me was flattered, but the rational side of me agreed with Jei Pi that her pushiness, in this instance, was well served; three of us would look better in a festival photo than only me. "No, we're Voyce school teachers." My straightforward response filled the awkward silence.

"Where do you want us to stand for the photos?" said Jei Pi, motioning with her hands in a desperate display. She really needn't have bothered with her continued attention-seeking; Kensuke's face showed that he was sold on the gaijin-girls-posing notion.

"Why don't you sit at the side of the road? There's a kid's parade coming up and it'll make a lovely photo

with you girls watching it." Kensuke's voice had
confidence, as if to show that he was in control.

Jei Pi hovered near him until she was sure where
he planned to line up his shot, then plonked her bum
down closest to his camera, pushing in front of Zoe
and me. It didn't feel right to stop her; no point
spoiling her fun. Zoe sank onto the footpath as far as
possible from the camera and hunched over, almost
ducking out of view. That left me to fill the gap in
between, perched at the edge of the kerb. A women's
parade passed by while Kensuke talked to a man at a
nearby vendor. The kimono-clad women, doing a sort
of kabuki-style dance with fans held my attention
until Kensuke returned with three red and white cans
of beer in his hand.

"Okay, the kid's parade is coming up." He handed
a can of beer to each of us. "Could you sip the beer
please? I thought it might be fun to have you all
drinking Asahi beer in the Asahi shimbun - kind of
appropriate, really."

Not only was beer not my thing, but it was Carl's
favourite Japanese drink. Still, it was all for fun. The
alcohol would wash him out of my body, however
bitter, no matter the taste.

Kensuke took a few shots at different angles. "You
girls look great – beautiful – I love it. Blonde,
brunette and red head. It's too bad the newspaper
prints in black and white. Hold the cans near your
mouths." He clicked again. "Not such a big smile
though, red head – a bit more natural. Yeah, that's it."

Click. The kid's parade approached. Cute little
boys in jimbes and girls in hapis danced closer. Jei Pi
sat forward, jutting out her jaw to pull her double
chin taut. Part of me felt amused at how desperate

she was to be seen, though part of me also felt a stab of annoyance. She was forcing me to have to shuffle my bum forward to the very edge of the kerb so her ginger mane wouldn't block me entirely from view.

"Hey, could I have blondie in front please? You look so… what's the word? Mysterious. Yellow hair is so attractive to us Japanese. Beautiful, just lovely."

Jei Pi reluctantly switched places with me, standing up with a look on her face like a dog turd had been smeared under her nose. How had Kensuke described me? *Beautiful.* His eyes were on me and it was clear he directed his praise at me, not my friends. A fleeting sideways glance showed me that Jei Pi was pissed off. It was hard not to feel smug. Beauty was in the eye of the beholder and Kensuke was the holder of the professional camera.

Kensuke's camera clicked in time with my winning smile as the kid's parade passed by. A little boy caught my smile and grinned back as he danced in front of me, clapping his hands. Kim, plus boy, plus Asahi beer, plus camera clicking. One of the shots would surely make it into the paper; this thought prompted me to flash my white teeth in a wider smile yet. Jei Pi wallowed in the shadow of my limelight; a sorry end for publicity whore. Poor her.

"Alright girls, we're all done," said Kensuke.

"When will the newspaper be out?" Jei Pi asked.

"Tomorrow." Kensuke shook their hands again. "Thank you for participating. It'll make a lovely addition to the annual Tottori Matsuri write-up this year."

***

More hip-hop. Club Passion's repetitive music was starting to wear thin. Better not to fuel my boredom with booze; a detour away from the bar to the dancefloor helped. Taking my bike had been a good idea as it reminded me to stay sober. Ben had told me about a previous Voyce teacher who'd cycled right into one of Tottori's storm drains – a deep open ditch. After only two weeks in Japan, the poor woman had needed to fly back to the States for emergency orthodontic treatment: she'd broken all of her front teeth.

Once on the dance floor, the music travelled osmotically into all of my pores. Jei Pi and Zoe hadn't arrived yet; whereas most clubbers would feel insecure about dancing without their friends, it was liberating to me. My body swayed, my arms waved and my head filled with a euphoria that had been sadly lacking in my life.

Tonight, nothing plagued me, not a worry in the world. No cheating bastard for a boyfriend, no need for alcohol; just the chance to close my eyes and lose myself in the music. My whole body spun. My legs swayed. My hips gyrated. An admiring crowd of Japanese men and a few unknown gaijin blokes watched me from a safe distance. All eyes one me, not any other woman in the room. What made me such hot property; my confidence? They were intimidated by me, by my power, or the power in the music that had unleashed something in me. They were mine, for me to take my pick of. Not that such a notion appealed. What did appeal? Who the hell knew?

The power ebbed, my confidence waned. What was left when confidence dissipated into the ether?

A feeling of emptiness?

A sense of being so lost?

And jealousy. Why when the men wanted me did the green-eyed monster want to eliminate any other woman in sight? Why did they all have to be a threat; why did my ego have a need to compare myself to them? Why did my inner child so need to direct all the attention in the room towards herself? And if that ego really felt that she was the hottest woman in the room, why did it feel so self-conscious, so competitive on the lowest most base level?

Animal brain, reptile mind, limbic system. Didn't this constitute fight or flight? Where was the fight? With Carl? But he was on the other side of the planet?

Why couldn't my mind give straight answers, why didn't it know? If only my brain had a switch that could be flicked off to let me lose myself in the music with no ulterior motive for dancing. But there was always a hidden agenda and there always would be. The serotonin made me feel good, the eyes of the watching men even more so. Why was there always, *always*, a desperate external need for love and approval.

Tears flowed down my cheeks. Eyes closed, head raised to the ceiling and they still poured silently down my face. Still, my legs kept dancing as though the world would explode, my body implode. Mega-ego Kim was the centre of the universe and life itself hung in the balance.

At some point, Tomomi had arrived with Vince. They stood near the bar, deep in conversation. Looked like they'd been there some time. In all honesty, this left me momentarily hurt; Tomomi hadn't even bothered to come and say hello. Vince leaned over Tomomi and whispered in her ear. Tomomi threw her head back as she laughed,

thrusting her cleavage forward for Vince to get an
eyeful.

Hmm. Could it be; were they a couple? But
Tomomi would've told me, wouldn't she? She hadn't
said that much about her sex life, apart from her lack
of orgasms. Would Vince settle for someone who
wasn't sexually sophisticated? If his amorous
proclivity was anything to go by, most likely not.
Tomomi was making quite the effort: tits forward,
check, hair-flick, check, glossy-lipped smile, check.
Sloshing her drink around in a bimbo-manner, check.
She was certainly hot. Too hot for Vince. Come to
think of it, Vince wasn't that good-looking at all. He
was a sweaty, lumbering oaf and at only twenty-seven,
he had a receding hairline. It had to be the desperate
Asian-girl-Western-man appeal. But wait; we had
shared a kiss, me and Vince. Even more in fact; an
unwanted drunken fumble. That made me a
hypocrite. Bleugh.

Ryuji made his way towards me with a friend who
cut a striking figure; at six foot, tall for a Japanese guy.

"Hi Kim," said Ryuji. "I thought you were coming
with Zoe?"

A pause from dancing to catch my breath. "No –
weren't you?"

"This is my friend Naoki. Naoki, this is Kim."

On closer inspection, Naoki was attractive, with a
natural athletic build, not a gym-pumped physique
like Ade and Vince. His look appealed too; he wore
an army surplus style jacket with pinstripe trousers
that gave a grungy edge to his smart-casual look.

"Are you a Voyce teacher too, Kim?" Naoki asked.
His fluent English was softly spoken. Intriguing.

"Yeah. Been here six months."

Ryuji backed into the crowd. "I'm going to say hi to Vince. I'll catch up with you two in a bit."

A clubber bumped against Naoki, pushing him against me. Heat flooded my cheeks. Was this a set-up of Ryuji's doing so the four of us; Zoe, Ryuji, Naoki and me, could double-date? Ryuji vanished into the throng and a moment later stood talking to Vince, leaving Tomomi to scowl over her drink. It was hard to catch Tomomi's eye, as she didn't look my way. Naoki was good-looking, but there was Carl to think of; the unresolved situation. It was all too soon.

Warm, sweaty palms on my waist made me flinch, but as Jei Pi's face appeared over my shoulder, any tension released; thank goodness it was Jei Pi and not some random perve. Jei Pi pressed her cheek against my neck. "Hey roomie, who's this?"

"Jei Pi, this is Naoki. Naoki, this is Jei Pi. Naoki is a friend of Ryuji's. Jei Pi is my flat mate."

Jei Pi grabbed Naoki's hands. "You wanna dance?"

Naoki looked embarrassed. "I'm not much of a dancer. I'll leave you two to it."

"M-kay, suit yourself." Jei Pi shrugged. Instead she grabbed both my hands. "But *you* don't get away so easily – let's dance."

Not so; apparently this was simply a ruse to entice Naoki. Jei Pi left me alone in the middle of the dance floor; she stayed where she was, gyrating against Naoki. Naoki looked uncomfortable, though he held his ground.

"Hey, Kim! Kimmy!"

Zoe's voice reached me across the dancefloor before she did. She sidled up behind me and wrapped me in a bear hug. We grooved, in sync, to the pounding music.

"Sugoi!" said a man's voice. "Asobinins!"

A man; another photographer. What a coincidence. He snapped a few pictures of the crowd, then trained his camera on Zoe and me, dancing back to back.

"Our photos are gonna be plastered all over Tottori at this rate, we'll be proper famous." My voice barely carried over the music.

"Yeah – Ryuji said the photographer is here taking pictures for promo flyers for Club Passion."

"What does asobinin mean anyway?"

"Players," Zoe translated. She twirled in front of me and pressed her body against mine, dancing with her arms around my waist, fingers linked in the crook of my back. The whole lesbian-show that girls liked to do for attention in nightclubs wasn't really my thing, but then again, what the hell. This was Japan. Different rules, different show. Music, lights, action. Not that there were any illusions of me being a natural in front of the camera, yet still being photographed twice in one day. The Asahi newspaper and the Club Passion promoter should've been paying me. The camera flashed, and again. Buffeted by the sweaty bodies around me, feeling the pounding hip-hop through the floor, my body shimmied on the euphoria in the room. Big fish in the little pond of Tottori, or little fish in the big pond of Japan; it didn't matter. Either way, this was my limelight. My unique charisma drew the camera towards me, all for me. Only one thing mattered: attention.

Naoki sidled up beside me. "You're very photogenic," he whispered in my ear.

"Thanks." A sexy smile for the photographer, looking back over my shoulder. Naoki backed away and stood with Ryuji by the bar. Both of them watched Zoe and me dancing.

The photographer handed us shot glasses with an unknown clear liquid inside. "Gan gan nomo, girls!"

"It means, let's get pissed," Zoe shouted. She danced behind me, our bodies spooning on the dance floor. Zoe looped her arm around me and offered her drink; my arm slipped under her chin and offered mine in exchange.

"Can I get in on the action?" said Jei Pi. She sidled up, in front of me, sandwiching me in the middle with Zoe behind.

The photographer took a few snaps, but in a perfunctory manner, seemingly not to offend Jei Pi. Poor Jei Pi; not aesthetically pleasing, bless her little cotton socks.

"Only these two, please, very sexy now." The photographer pulled Jei Pi aside and pushed me and Zoe into the spotlight shining in the middle of the dance floor. "Why don't you two kiss, it would look great."

Zoe looked serious for a split second before we both burst into tipsy giggles. Zoe leaned over my shoulder. Her face came closer, her eyes closing. My eyes drifted shut too as my body veered closer to Zoe, two magnets unable to repel each other. It was a soft, wet kiss, no different than kissing a guy, especially with my eyes closed. Zoe's tongue roved my mouth. It was weird, kissing my friend, but what the hell. It would make a great promotional flyer. The music boomed, the lights flashed on the dancefloor and around us, the whoops of the clubbers watching our show. Jei Pi's retreating back disappeared into the throng, Ryuji had an embarrassed smile and Vince might as well have stood drooling.

23

ɔʒ

Mafia chick

The sun beat down. The weather had more mood-swings than me. Last week, rain. A few days ago, gale-force winds. My bronzed body stretched out on the sand at Tottori Kaigan enjoyed the heat. Let it burn. Let it fry me to a crisp while it lasted, anyway.

Two Japanese girls ran along the shore, splashing each other in the waves. Bored of watching them, my eyelids drifted closed to resume tanning. No sooner than my eyes had closed, a ping on the front of my bikini jerked me upright, as intrusive fingers snatched the band between the cups.

"Ooh, no padding," said one of the girls in heavily accented English.

The other girl, curious, peeled back one of my cups and looked inside. "Oh, soo-goy! Big oh-pie!" The girl cupped her hand under my left breast and bounced it. "Bom, bom!"

A quick smack on her hand put her in her place. "Oi, what do you think you're doing?"

"You is wear no padding in bikini." The girl peeled back her own bikini top and showed a thick wad of material stuffing it.

"No, there's no need for padding." My arm shielded my chest from prying eyes.

The two girls ran away; end of conversation. What audacity. Eight months in Japan was enough to feel a veteran immersed in Japanese culture, yet the country still had its surprises.

What was the obsession with big boobs? Western women were generally curvy and larger than petite Japanese ladies; this was common knowledge, yet having full breasts made me a curiosity, a zoo animal on parade anywhere on my travels. My blonde hair didn't help. Japanese people were so touchy-feely, they helped themselves to my body as if it were public property. If it wasn't an inquisitive finger poking my white skin, it was an intrusive hand stroking my hair, or someone making an opportunistic grab for my chest, under the pretence of touching my clothes. There'd been schoolboys pretending to fall asleep, slowly keeling over sideways towards my chest and business men daring a cheeky squeeze of my bottom on the train.

Whew! What a hassle; *mendokusai* as the Japanese would say. A damn nuisance when the sole appeal to me was peace and quiet, alone time on the beach.

Two Japanese girls were gone and one Japanese guy replaced them, seemingly out of nowhere, and making a beeline for me.

"Ah, kah-co-ee!" said the guy. He held his phone up, pushing a button with his thumb, clearly taking photos. "Bee-jean-dah."

Kakoii: cool. *Bijin*: beautiful. Back to Tomomi's good old hentai Japanese, with enough knowledge now to understand sleazy come-ons. A ninja grab of my towel, draping it across my chest. "Get that bloody thing away from me unless you want it broken!"

Quick as the man came he disappeared, with a quick thumbs-up as though to thank me for the unwarranted snapshots. No apology, no respect. What was *with* everyone today; it was as though they sensed my boyfriend trouble, as if they sensed me as a bucket of insecurity. Not good to radiate fragility, to send pheromones to the hungry wolves waiting to devour me.

Enough already. With no more distractions, it was finally time to spread my towel out and lay down, determined to enjoy my morning at the beach before the late shift at Voyce. The world on the inside of my eyelids was yellow. Yellow: calm, soothing, serene, non-judgemental, refreshing. Listing the words in my head helped lull myself into a zen-like repose.

A shadow fell across me; the inner world of my eyelids went from mellow-yellow to khaki-cloud in a micro-second.

"Hello. Sorry to interrupt you."

A young female voice in softly spoken, but perfectly fluent English caused me to open my eyes and sit up; quite different from the annoying girls and the irksome man.

"We are having a barbecue over there and we wondered if you would like to join us." The woman pointed along the beach to a large, white marquee with closed sides that resembled the kind set up for official events, next to a long, blue-canopied tent propped up on metal poles. A middle-aged Japanese man chain-smoked as he cooked burgers and a woman, presumably his wife, wearing a white kerchief over her hair, ferried the burgers on a tray into the white marquee. A group of seven women, all ranging in age from mid-twenties to late fifties, sat talking and eating in a loose group around a large, fold-down picnic table. Two small children chased each other on the sand while several older boys and girls tossed a beach ball around. It was probably biased of me, but the presence of women and children reassured me that no funny business would happen. Still, my defences were up. A reasonable query formed on my lips. "Why?"

The woman dipped her head in a polite bow. "We have never met a *gaikokujin* before and we would love to talk to you in English about your culture. You are *Amerikajin*?"

It seemed benign enough; the critical part of my mind detected no ulterior motive for the woman's invitation. Not to mention my curiosity had gotten the better of me: if she hadn't spoken to foreigners before, how was her English so good? It hadn't escaped my attention that she had called me a *gaikokujin*, the polite word for a foreigner, rather than *gaijin*, a derogatory word, an alien.

"No, not American, English. Alright then, why not." The woman waited for me to scoop my beach towel into my bag and tie a sarong over my bikini bottoms. "If you've never met a foreigner before, how come your English is so good?"

"Eh, nani?" The woman said. She shook her head. "Sorry, I'm still learning. I take lessons at *Voyce* class, but through their online lessons, *Lingonet*."

That explained it: *Lingonet*, *Voyce* school lessons where a student came into the branch and took a language class at a private booth wearing headphones in front of a computer screen, with a teacher at any branch across Japan. In my own experience, Ben had never booked me to do a *Lingonet* lesson, for scheduling reasons rather than my experience, or lack of it, in teaching at the Tottori *Voyce* branch. So, my new companion hadn't lied: she had technically never *met* a foreigner, even though she had talked to foreigners through her online lessons.

We approached the blue tent. The sleaziness of my earlier, disruptive encounters at the beach had coloured my thoughts unfavourably, so it was refreshing to be invited to a social event for legitimate reasons, for a change. The man cooking looked up and jerked his hand in a half-wave, half-salute, a puff of smoke rising from the cigarette at the right corner of his mouth, the left corner twitching as he spoke: "Good-oh even-ning."

"Good morning." My response was performance-review perfect: subtle correction without overt criticism. Boss man Ben would've been pleased that my training had paid off.

"Ha-ro," said one of the older children. The others waved. The women waved too. How lovely. Certainly made me feel welcome and appreciated.

My companion led me past the blue tent and inside the large, white marquee. There were about twelve men standing chatting in small groups of two or three and casually eating hamburgers. Only one man sat. He looked to be in his late fifties or early sixties and was dressed in a black long-sleeved top and red knee-length shorts with beach flip-flops. When he saw me he stood up and approached me with his hand outstretched for a western-style handshake. He was tall for a Japanese man, about six feet tall, sinewy and muscular like a boxer. As he neared me, a second glance showed that he didn't wear a long-sleeved top: he wore a black vest, but his arms and chest were heavily tattooed with black ink, giving the appearance of clothing. What looked like a black dragon covered his right arm, the scales highlighted in a thin line of green and the top of what looked like an *oni*, a demon, in black and red ink peered out from above his vest-top. A koi fish decorated his left arm, its body in black and fins in green and red. The tattoos on his arms ended abruptly at his wrists and the *oni* on his chest stopped at his neck; easy to cover with business suit, or ordinary clothing, if necessary.

"Welcome," he said, in English. "Why don't you sit down?"

What was that accent? Didn't have the usual American twang that most Japanese people who spoke English with any degree of fluency seemed to have. He almost had a European lilt, like a Japanese person who had learned English in Germany, or Austria, not in the States or a Commonwealth country. In any event, it caught me unaware: the accent and the rhetorical question saw me distracted enough to be guided into the chair by one of the man's associates, who steered me by the shoulders and applied gentle pressure to make me sit.

"Have something to drink. Do you drink beer?"

A can of Kirin beer was pressed into my hand before my mouth even had a chance to let loose an acceptance.

"We would be honoured if you would join our barbecue. You do eat meat, don't you?" he said. His eyes pierced me, almost as though his intense gaze could read my thoughts.

"Er, yes. Of course—"

The man smiled. "I'm glad you aren't vegetarian. Sometimes Europeans, English in particular, can be more conscious of the environment than us Japanese. We're delighted to have you with us."

"Er, me too." *Oh my gosh*, did it make me feel put on the spot. Very perceptive. He had spotted my English accent even though we had exchanged few words. A plate with a burger was handed to me; my fingers almost opened the bun to see what was inside, but my brain chortled into action quick enough to save me from a culinary, possibly cultural, faux pas. The man watched me for my reaction. Under the spotlight of his gaze, my only option was to take a bite of burger and wash it down with a sip of beer.

The men stood around while my meal was slowly devoured, dry swallow by dry swallow. Why wasn't anyone else eating? Where had the demure woman who had brought me into the marquee gone? Eating alone, with all eyes on me felt awkward, even a tad uncomfortable.

"So, are you all colleagues? Is this, like, a company outing or something?"

The man looked pensive. "You could say that. We're associates of a sort. But I think of everyone as more of a family."

My head inclined a notch in the direction of the blue tent outside, full of women and children. That made sense.

"What part of England are you from?"

"London." Another bite of burger; it was actually quite good.

"Funny, you don't have a London accent. I would have placed you more from somewhere like Portsmouth."

My stomach must have bottomed out; a jolt like dropping suddenly in a rollercoaster flipped it right over. "Actually, you're not far wrong. My family are originally from Southampton, though for the last few years, Camden was my home. Have you spent much time in London? You seem to know England well."

"I studied at a private school in Switzerland for a time," he said. He didn't answer my question, nor did he elaborate and as much as it niggled me to ask more, it didn't seem a good idea. There was a finality to his tone. Better leave the mystery hanging. A few things were clear, and that was enough: he was well educated and most likely rich. The sandy flip-flops and surfer-style shorts didn't give the appearance of a person with money, but maybe that was part of his intrigue.

He moved behind me and placed his hands on my shoulders. "Are you enjoying yourself?"

A sip of beer cleared my mouth. "Yes, it's been a lovely time. Thanks for inviting me."

He began to squeeze my shoulders, pressing his thumbs into my shoulder blades and rubbing his fingers into my neck muscles. He had skill at massage; his hands were firm, but delicate. Once or twice, his fingers skidded over my collarbone, but not a fraction lower. Skill indeed. "Now that you've had something to eat and drink, perhaps it's time for you to make your choice."

"Choice?" As my head tilted upwards to look at him, his eyes peered down his nose at me, letting me fall under the shadow of his jutting chin.

"You can choose one of these three. They're the most fitting." He gestured towards three of the youngest Japanese men, each in their early to late thirties. The men stood in a row, watching me, their expressions neutral, each a blank canvas on display.

They held their hands behind their backs and stood with their feet shoulder-width apart. It reminded me of contestants on a dating show, waiting to be matched with a blind date, expecting to be sized-up. A tsunami of stupidity swept over me; how obvious it was. He had groomed me for sex with one of his sons, colleagues; whatever the hell they were.

My body jumped into action propelling me to my feet, the chair skidding backwards. "Listen, sorry. You've got me wrong. It was my impression you wanted me here as a chance to speak English."

He smiled. "Surely you must have realised that my English is already good enough." He relieved me of my plate. "If you don't want one of the younger men, that's fine. I had picked you out for myself, but you see, as an old man I decided to be generous and let someone closer to your own age have a chance first for once."

Indignation bubbled inside me. The audacity of him, old enough to be my grandfather, and expecting to buy my body in exchange for a burger and beer. "Sorry you got the wrong impression, but nobody here interests me in that way. Thank you for the food and drink, but it's time for me to get going."

"That's a shame. You honoured us with your presence."

Out of the marquee without a backward glance; my feet kicked sand up over the backs of my calves in my hurry to leave. Further along the beach, three black vans waited alone in the car park. Black vans, with black-tinted windows. Who the hell were they? The question troubled me, and the security of my lone bicycle ahead, my means of escape, offered comfort. Thank goodness they didn't know my name, or anything else about me.

***

"Did you hear who was at the beach today?"

Vince's question broke my concentration, making me look up from marking my student files. "What, Tottori Kaigan? You know, something funny happened to me there this morning. So there was me, minding my own business sunbathing on the beach. This woman comes over, and invites me to a barbecue. She takes me into a big marquee where there are all these guys and then she disappears, so it's just me and them. And it's really awkward, of course, sitting there in my bikini with all these men around me. They give me food and beer and this one guy, the boss most likely, is the only one who can speak English. He starts to massage my shoulders, but you know, his hands are *dangerously* low on my chest, if you get my drift. Then he asks me to *choose* one of them, like, as a boyfriend or something."

Vince burst out laughing and slapped his hand against the desk. "You're fucking kidding me, right?"

"Ssh, Vince." Zoe had her fingers to her lips. "There might be students at reception. They'll hear you."

He kept laughing. "No way, this is too fucking funny. Do you know who they were? Didn't you see the vans?"

Vans. Black vans with black-tinted windows. "Yeah?"

"I'll bet they were tattooed, right?" said Vince.

Ben walked into the staffroom and set his student files on the desk. "Who was tattooed?"

Vince pointed at me as he looked towards Ben. "Kimberly had lunch with the Yakuza today, can you believe that?"

Ben's brow furrowed. "Say, what?"

"The mafia were having a barbecue at Tottori beach today and Kimberly let the head honcho grope her tits in exchange for beer," Vince spat.

Anger welled. "That is such a lie!"

"Watch the language, Vince." Ben looked simultaneously appalled at Vince and confused at the story. "What went on today, Kim?"

Zoe spared me the recap, as she summarised my story. Ben listened intently, along with Ade, who walked into the staffroom and sat next to Vince to mark his files.

Vince stood up, followed by Ade. "We're going downstairs to get something to eat. Anyone want anything? Kim, sure you don't wanna beer? I'll give you a list of what I want in exchange when I get back."

Jei Pi's academic diary, next to me on the table, sufficed as a missile to lob at the moron's head. Vince and Ade smirked and left.

With the buffoon and his mate gone, a deafening silence fell between Ben, Zoe and me, almost as though they were surveying me in a new light. "Did you know they were the Yakuza when you said you'd have lunch with them?" said Ben.

"Well, of course not!" Ben and Zoe stared at me as though they didn't believe me. "Someone told me Yakuza had tattoos, and the men at the beach did, but it just didn't click. To me, Yakuza were gangsters who didn't bother normal people, they ran their criminal business, drugs or whatever, at night time. Who the hell would've expected them to be at the beach in broad daylight, talking to a foreigner. They're the mafia, you would think they would keep to themselves."

"Well, you would think that, but they play by their own rules." Ben looked worried. "Listen, stay safe, alright? Tottori might seem like a sleepy town, but watch out. I've been here long enough to see guys zoom in on the girls, especially when they're vulnerable."

"What do you mean, zoom in?"

His face was serious. "I don't mean to be blunt or anything, but be careful of Japanese guys. They have this thing for Western women, especially pretty blondes like you. You'd be shocked if I told you the number of rapes that go on in Tottori – unreported, of course."

It wasn't lost on me that he called me pretty, but there were bigger fish to fry with what he was saying. "What, rapes of foreign women?"

"Mostly Japanese women, but some Westerners too. A few Filipinos or Thais as well, you know, the ones who work in the exotic dancing bars. They kidnap them in vans, drive them out to the mountains, rape them and leave them stranded. All I'm saying is, watch out, alright? I've seen how much you and Zoe and Jei Pi can drink."

Kidnap them in vans. "Don't worry, if anyone can hold their liquor, it's me. No Japanese man'll try anything with me. I'm bigger than most of them anyway, they'd have a hard time getting me into any van."

Ben cracked a polite smile at my joke. "Just be careful, pay attention round here and you'll be fine.

I'm only saying it because I care about you. Not just because I'm your boss, but as a friend."

Vans. Black vans with tinted windows. A chill took hold of me. Had it been a close escape? Would the situation at the beach have degenerated into me being raped? It didn't bear thinking about. Yet, it made me defiant. Ben was wrong; about me being vulnerable, whether through distraction at my relationship with Carl breaking down, or at my increasing tolerance for alcohol. No man would kidnap me into a van and rape me. No man would ever make me do something against my will.

24

 С3

Rainy season

"Check it out, I found it, our Japanese tabloid debut!"
Jei Pi had barely knocked on my bedroom door
before it burst open and an orange hurricane blew
into the room. She waved the open paper under my
nose. After a yawn and stretch, my body was ready to
sit up. Jei Pi tossed the *Asahi Shimbun* onto my lap.

The black and white photo covered half the page,
with a small write-up in kanji letters in right to left
columns down the page. Most of the right side of the
photo was filled by me, in profile. Jei Pi in the middle
jutted forward behind me, trying to maximise her
visibility. But Zoe was almost entirely blocked by the
two of us.

"You photograph so well, chica," said Jei Pi, the
envy clear in her voice. "Not only that, but I got a
text from Zoe this morning. Ryuji was saying that
you're famous in Tottori."

"Really? In what way? The paper only came out
this morning."

"Not that. From Club Passion. Everyone's calling
you the cute blonde-haired gaijin dancer."

Jei Pi took the paper back from me. *Cute blonde-
haired gaijin dancer.* A part of me relished the attention.
Over here, men wanted me; they craved my attention.
Not that it got me the attention from the one man
who mattered: Carl. Another part of me wanted to say
that was because he respected me too much, that he

loved me for more than my body, that he desired me for my mind. Though we both knew that wasn't true either. He wanted to control me, nothing more.

"Listen chica, I gotta run. I'm on the early shift today. But I'll see you after. Zoe and Ryuji said they'll meet you at Zen for drinks first." Jei Pi kissed the top of my head and dashed out of my bedroom.

Shit, almost forgotten: plans to go drinking at Bar Zen before trying out the new club, Three-Six-Five. The only catch was that we'd made those plans before Zoe and me had made utter bell-ends out of ourselves by kissing in the dance floor at Club Passion for the photographer. At work, Zoe had acted as if nothing had happened. But how would we avoid it in front of Ryuji? Surely Zoe's boyfriend would have something to say about me kissing his girlfriend.

My mind drifted to that night, dancing at Club Passion. On the dancefloor with Zoe. A photographer, spotlight shining and? Cringe. Zoe and me had kissed making arses of ourselves, right there, in the middle of the dance floor. No wonder Ryuji had said *famous*. Famous for making a tit of myself for all to see.

Back to the same old feeling of being lost. No direction in my life, no direction for my poetry. My last decent poem had been as long ago as my last decent shag: months ago. My mind had been sucked into an abyss, a limbo between worlds, body and soul now derailing. Because of Carl? Because of my fear of him. He had become a phantom; a ghoul in my subconscious. Yes, that had to be it, otherwise there'd be no reason for the gamut of excuses that came to mind, delaying me calling him or emailing him. Last time we'd spoken had been at the start of April, right after the cherry blossom party when everything about Shiori had come out. He had given me a ten week ultimatum: get home or else. A brief count of the weeks on my fingers showed that today marked ten weeks. Shame really that the news about Carl's affair had transpired on night of the sakura hanami; hopefully it wouldn't tarnish my memories of cherry blossom festivals forevermore. Deep breath, get centred, refocus. Time to bite the bullet, albeit the cowardly way in writing, and break the ridiculous ultimatum. My head led the way, hauling my sleep-fatigued body into the living room, dragging my duvet behind for comfort. Jei Pi's laptop was still open on the kitchen counter.

Even though it was a hot, humid June morning, typical for the rainy season in Japan, my body remained cloaked in the duvet. To cloak: chlamydia in Ancient Greek. A shiver ran through me; best get checked for STIs in case Carl had tarnished me with his dirty dick. Duvet pulled tighter; definitely needed the padding as shock absorption in anticipation of what would surely be a deluge of abuse waiting to be read in my inbox. The torrential rain outside gave a drumroll as my emails loaded. And there it was, peppered with the characteristic bad spelling and grammatical mistakes, the inevitable message from Carl:

Title: Hi honey.

Message: Well its clear ur avoiding calling me. Fine. have things ur way as usual. I told u to be home within ten weeks and youve got such little respect for me or us that u ignore my resonable request. Sometimes it pisses me off cos ur not always honest u hold back the truth from me. Im even questioning wether i love u or not. u say u want to finish ur contract, well love, I don't know if i can wait til november cos this is getting harder and harder. If u cant compromise then I'll make a time for u. I want u back at heathrow by the end of August. And get it straight i dont know how I'll react when i c u at the airport. Yours, ur probably ex boyfriend.

Melodramatic or what? No holding back with him; away from the glare of the screen, the squall outside summed up my feelings entirely; turmoil. A deep breath helped to calm my adrenaline-flooded veins. Was it worth being with a man whose words stung, not soothed? How would it be to spend the rest of my life with a person whose emotional torrent caused me to cry for ninety percent of the time? His email was filled with so much spite and venom, reading any more would require hospital treatment: an intravenous of serotonin. The evidence spoke for itself; it was clear how Carl felt about me. It finally clicked in my head; the impetus for my journey to Japan had been to escape from him. But what would be the outcome of heart versus head? The naive girl of eighteen when we'd met seven years ago was gone, replaced by a mature woman of twenty-five. What made me so afraid; it wasn't at breaking up with Carl, but at losing more than that. Losing a part of myself in the process, or had that already been lost?

Better to not type a hasty reply; best give it time. Pride filled me and a sense of accomplishment; finally the magma chamber of my subconscious was beginning to open and let lava bubble to the surface. Venting in a poem would help sort through my feelings before writing back. A few more poems was the best medicine: my green travel journal was still half-empty. Nope; half-full, positive mind-set. Writing in the communal space of the kitchen table felt like airing my dirty laundry in public, but then again, what was so sacred or private anyway about me and Carl? Didn't everyone know the skeleton in the closet that was his affair with Shiori? Seven years, all that time, my part in his life had been something to possess and manipulate; sitting there now, in my apartment in Tottori, as nothing more than a void, a cypher. My brain had been a computer that he had programmed and my mouth the speaker for his thoughts; when my mouth opened his words came out. It was a mind-blowing, but depressing reality to comprehend. No thoughts that were my own, no sense of self. Half-empty, not half-full, was more apt.

Poem title: Sticker
When you peeled away
From the wall of my soul
The wallpaper peeled away too
And large chunks of plaster fell
To the floor, crashing into a thousand pieces,
Smashing onto the floor of what was once
My whole, complete self; a blank canvas,
That had been scribbled on,
By someone else.

Was that really what my life came down to? A blank canvas that had been scribbled on by someone else? It wasn't working; it was shit. In a moment of madness, my brain evacuated everything from my head in a hot-blooded stream: my pen ended up smashed against the wall and poetry journal flung across the room. The journal landed face-down, the pages splayed, spine up, pitiful; though not nearly as pathetic as me. Tears flooded my face and yet my hands remained limp, not willing to stem the flow or wipe away the by-product of my catharsis. Not tears:

this was Japan, a Japanese word, a tsunami. Yes, an emotional tsunami. My travel journal taunted me, spine jutting upwards as though it was proudly, arrogantly deriding me. It had been a leaving present from Aaron, Sasha and my other so-called friends back home in London. Were any of them in touch with me now? Not unless my text, or email came first. They'd abandoned me like yesterday's rubbish the minute my feet had stepped on that plane. And as for Carl? Worse than abandoned; he hated me. Maybe he had good reason to. Seemed like self-loathing was my only true emotion these says too.

Such a load of crap, filling my head. Slumped back in my seat, happy to wallow in self-pity like a pig in shit; that was me, all over. That bastard Carl, that controlling bastard, screw him! My chest let loose a pitiful, wretched wail on the world. Jei Pi wasn't home, but even if she were, it wouldn't have helped me to suppress the pain. My battered inner self needed to wail like a banshee, howl like a scolded brat, cry out a bunch of other meaningless similes until the bloody cows came home. Having a tantrum like a ridiculous two year old and letting the storm blow out was better than bottling it up until alcohol inevitably would bring it out publicly later. It didn't matter that Jei Pi and Zoe knew my business, but it would mortify me if Vince or Tomomi or anyone else saw my weak side. Rocking to self-sooth helped until all the sobs had subsided into a few pathetic hiccups. My body was spent. The tears had served their purpose; burying my face in the duvet wiped them away. Time to shed my comfort-cloak to go and get changed. Time to face reality; a trip to the international payphone at Lawson would sort out my tribulations, once and for all.

Jacket on over my pyjamas, trainers on with no socks. Umbrella grabbed, out the door, lock hastily clicked.

Once outside, the wind whipped my hair. Turbulent weather, turbulent heart. This was more than rainy season, this was a typhoon; a bloody big one too, a huge storm. It took all my strength to lean forward against the wind. Wind assaulted my face, water filled my eyes. Wind in my head, water in my heart. What was making me so afraid? What had me feeling too scared to float free on the wind, or be carried off by the water, unsupported? Maybe it was the lingering fear of drifting too far from shore and not being able to feel the safety of the bottom keeping me grounded, of being swept into a whirlpool from which there'd be no escape. Honestly, it made me feel vulnerable, ravaged by rivulets of rainwater streaming down my face. Why did it have to be a choppy ocean? Why couldn't it be a calm pool?

"Damn it, Kim Thatcher, you're in Japan – get over it!"

Work. Men. The inability to decide what was best for me: my wants and needs. Don't reply to Carl right away, let him have squirming time. Worms squirmed, right? But if a worm was used to squirming all its life, would it do any differently now? No, rip the plaster off, have it out with Carl on the phone.

Mad! This was a slow descent to madness. As mad as a bag in a tempest. As mad as a hatter devoid of any hats. Hats had never been my thing. Did it matter? Nothing mattered.

What to do, what to do...? Walk faster, faster, ever onwards. What if we broke up? Head said yes, do it, heart said no, don't risk it. Head full of wind, heart full of water, Yin and yang, upside down, topsy-turvy... what was better, wind or water? Two sides of one coin or apples and oranges?

Crazy!

My umbrella was toast. What a stupid idea to open an umbrella in a typhoon in the first place. The purpose? To seize me and take me away into the heavens? If only.

Water: water on the brain, water heavy in my heart.

The pay phone might as well have been on the other side of the planet. Vulnerable me against the elements, lost in the howling wind. Lost in the midst of a dizzying eddy, plunging downwards. Down, down... people would've called me stupid, stumbling along, arm over my face for protection, blindly fumbling along against rice paddy fences. Turning, spinning, circling into nothingness, the coriolis force sucking me into a plunge pool of despair. Help, cried my heart, help answered my mind. Bloated and drained; a pufferfish in need of rescue, gasping from within a bucket of doom. Bloated and drained; a sluggish circulation system fuelled by junk food and empty desires. The part of me that felt small hated myself. The part of me that felt lost didn't know myself. No direction in my life, only chaos. Chaos theory: out of the frying pan of life and into the fire of Buddhist cremation. Did it give me a sense of control to narrate my life story to myself in the void? No; this was anti-life, this was hell. Black, charred remains of a flame that had kindled and burned out long ago. It had been a fit of self-harm to throw logs onto the burning funeral pyre of my own soul for too long and Carl had pissed the last of the sparks out, bastard that he was. Definition of a blackout: a vast, unfulfilled darkness of the human heart. My heart, broken. The water droplets assaulted my face, pelting me with a stinging attack.

"If only the wind would take me away..."

Arms raised to the blackened skies.

"Take away this pain."

Arms swayed in the wind, flimsy bamboo branches bending at the forces of nature.

"This pain in my heart is killing me."

The walking, talking puppet that was me was dead inside, crumbling from the inside outwards; a long, drawn-out, pitiful decay of my soul, my very essence. Let the elements corrode me, let the wind abrade me, let the water dissolve me. Rivulets streaked down my arms inside my unbuttoned jacket; cold and uncompromising. Water could flow, crash, break rocks. Let it crack me, let it smash me to pieces.

This was too much; an unrequited cry to the winds. The moment had come, the time to stem the flow of hurt.

My fingers worked quickly against the onslaught of rain, numb as they grabbed the payphone receiver. My mind kept its cogs turning; a mechanical motion, free of thought or responsibility. One heroic finger punched in the numbers.

"Hello?" Carl's voice. Slurred. He'd been drinking.

"Carl, it's me."

"Oh, you. Have you come to your senses?"

"Depends what you mean, come to my senses."

Robotic.

"I suppose all that sun you must be getting out there is addling your brains. And by the way, no topless sunbathing, you got me?"

Mechanical.

"You must've been waiting to tell me off for the past two months. For your information, it's rainy season over here. A typhoon is about to blow me away, not that you care."

Cogs turning, grinding.

"Well?"

"Well, what?"

"Did you get my email? I want you back in Heathrow by the end of August, or we're through."

"Then we're through." My response caught me by surprise.

A pause. The wind howled. The rain stung. But the blackness lifted. The pain in my heart diminished, the clouds dissipating.

"You're getting to be an argumentative bitch these days, aren't you?"

His words pelted my skin raw.

"Exactly – we argue too much. Didn't you hear me?"

"What did you say? You don't even know what you're talking about."

"Keep telling that to yourself. Do you need to hear it again? Maybe you'll listen to me this time. We're finished. It's over."

"Fine. Have it your way. It's always gotta be your way or no way. Well, I'm having the final say and you can't do fuck all about it. You can't come home when I want it, so we're over. Thanks for flushing seven years down the toilet for nothing. When you come back to London, don't bother getting in touch. I don't want to see you, or hear from you – or anything about you for that matter. Don't call me or email me – you got that?"

"In other words, we can't even be friends after everything?"

"It's gotta be all or nothing. I want you to know this is all your doing."

"But if we have no contact at all, then we really will be flushing away seven years."

"That's for your guilty conscience then, love. I hope you get all that you deserve."

Click. The bastard hung up.

Dead line. So that was it: click. Seven years, click. Call it a day, no more contact, get on with your life, click. All over, it was final. Carl had set me free. No; it was me who had made the move, me who had set myself free. No compromise; we were both free of each other.

25

附

Typhoon night

"Yo, how's tricks?"

Vince stuck out his hand like a traffic warden, catching me in the midriff with his palm wide, fingers-splayed. A bit too low, and a bit too familiar a gesture for comfort. Bad touch. It made me stop and turn to face him, to look him square in the eye.

"How's tricks nothing. Just meeting Zoe and Ryuji for drinks. What do you want to know for?"

"My mistake, clearly." Vince gave a stupid grin and put his hands up in surrender. "I thought we'd take a moment to catch up. You aren't avoiding me, are you?"

My arms folded across my chest, protecting me. "What makes you say that?"

He sniffed. "That time in the toilet at Club Passion, when we were drunk."

Don't flatter yourself. The words flitted, silent and innocent, through my head, but my tongue stayed put; didn't want to give him the satisfaction of knowing he'd offended me.

"It's just, you don't talk to me in the staffroom anymore," he continued.

Where the hell was the creep going with this? "It's not because of you. Lunch is short as it is, better for me to spend it out for a walk than cooped up in the staffroom."

It was a lie. What was it with men acting sleazy? Carl had been too forward before we had dated, flirting and teasing, saying it was banter. It was always banter when they didn't want their dicks pinned down.

"Well, since you've been *avoiding* the staffroom, you don't know who's hooked up with who." Vince had a devilish smile. Part of me was intrigued, while the other half didn't care. Not that it mattered when Tomomi walked into Bar Zen and sidled up behind Vince. She stretched up onto her tiptoes and kissed the back of his neck. Vince turned and gave her a quick peck on the lips. *Really* romantic. A flick of my hair disguised my surprise, then an eye roll across to the barman, who gave me a smirk of camaraderie at the expense of the soppy couple.

"So, this is a double date and I'm just a tag along? How nice of Zoe to let me know." A wave of indignity hit me.

"No, we heard Zoe telling Jei Pi about how she was planning to meet you and we decided we'd come too," said Tomomi.

Indignation became anger. Pity Zoe and Ryuji couldn't have turned up first – alone – to lend a sympathetic ear for my ex-boyfriend woes. Seven years with Carl was over. Trustworthy friends and a stiff drink would sort me out, not Vince and Tomomi who could be fun, but were also superficial and shallow.

"I'll get the drinks, ladies," said Vince, smooth and slippery as a snake. A 'no thank you, stick it up your arse' was on the tip of my tongue, but Vince cut me off. "I heard you broke up with your boyfriend."

"Who told you that?"

He shrugged. "Word gets around."

Great. Was nobody trustworthy? Wait a minute: the only one who knew was Jei Pi, from a text that morning. Had Jei Pi blabbed to the whole staffroom?

The words on the tip of my tongue metamorphosed. "Gimme a screwdriver. Make it a double."

We sat on a semi-circular sofa under the glow of a soft, orange lamp. Vince sat in the middle, which made me a little uneasy as he was closer to me than Tomomi, but the orange glow helped lull me into a calm state; it was easy to imagine being on a tropical beach at sunset, rather than on a night out in the midst of a typhoon with a turbulent broken heart, no less. Vince's eyes were on me, not Tomomi. He had a look of curious concern on his face, benign, not sexual in any way, which intrigued me. The curious concern part, not the lack of attraction. Besides, Vince liked Japanese women, who didn't know that. Tomomi, bless her little cotton socks, was flavour of the week – for this week at least. He wasn't interested in blondes. That put me off the menu.

Same as Carl, apparently. Pretty Asian girls were his type. A sour thought to add bitter bile to my screwdriver; no thanks.

"You know, it helps to talk."

Everyone said that. Still, he meant well; the corners of my mouth forced themselves upwards. There was no cause to be angry at Vince when he offered words of comfort. He was trying to make amends to our damaged friendship; the effort was appreciated.

"There isn't much to say really. My boyfriend is now my ex, end of story." A swig of my screwdriver to fight the tears.

"Well, no pressure, but I'm here to lend an ear if you need to talk. Or a shoulder to cry on." Vince's voice was soft, soothing.

My gaze drifted to Tomomi. She smiled and nodded. "He's right. You should get it off your chest."

Vince put a surprisingly heavy arm around my shoulder and patted my back. Although it felt stiff, because of our previous tension, it allowed me a chance to rest my head on his shoulder and the consolation became warmer. Human touch, something lacking in my life.

Why couldn't Carl be more like Vince; a man who could listen? Friends always had the qualities to be desired in a boyfriend. Shame the fanciable men didn't care what was on my mind. Carl was a complete scoundrel. He'd treated me like shit. *Stupid. Dumb. Ugly. You'll learn when you grow up...* all common insults that rolled off his tongue smoother than 'I love you' which he used only as a replacement for 'I'm sorry'. What sort of love was that? *Was* it love? What *was* love? Was it more like infatuation, maybe? Maybe it had *never* been love? Did Carl like me only as a trophy girlfriend? No – we wouldn't have lasted seven years on looks and sex alone. Not that we'd had sex that much either. Not for a supposedly loved-up couple at any rate.

Tomomi's phone ringing ruptured the infected bubble of my dour thoughts. "Hey Zoe. Are you on your way?" She whipped the phone to her ear as she stood up, then headed for the door, her hands swinging about as she chatted.

Vince, devoid of distractions, trained his full attention on me, his elbow on the table as he twisted his body to face mine. "I really thought you were gonna leave when your boyfriend went."

Another swig of screwdriver. "It crossed my mind, to be honest. But there are so many more things still on my to-do list out here."

He patted my hand. "I'm glad you stayed. He kept you all to himself for three months, I never thought we'd get a chance to hang out."

My eyebrows shot upwards. "You really wanted to hang out with me that much?"

"All of us at Voyce did." His words were composed, but he spoke quickly, the only indication that he was careful with his intentions.

"Oh, yeah. Of course."

"I thought he was a bit controlling, but I didn't want to say anything to you at the time. Jei Pi didn't have anything good to say about him. Take it you two are getting along better now, you're always over at Passion together?"

If my head could have spun, it would have done a full rotation, he had me psychoanalysed to a T. "Yeah. Seems my first impressions were wrong. She's been like a sister to me through all this." My hands squeezed the screwdriver glass, my fingertips white. "That's me done with blokes – apart from you, of course. You're not like the rest. You're like a, dunno, a brother or something. Shame you'll be leaving soon. September, right?"

Vince squeezed my hand. "We can keep in touch. You can come visit me in Namba. I'm staying with a friend for a couple of months before heading back to Phoenix."

"Yeah, maybe we will. Bet you'll miss Tomomi."

"There's loads of great clubs in Osaka. Now that you're single, we can have lots of fun."

Maybe Vince hadn't heard me; of course he would miss Tomomi. They had flirted for so long and had finally gotten together as a couple. Tomomi walked back in with Zoe, Ryuji and Ryuji's friend Naoki. Vince's eyes lingered on me for a moment, until we both exchanged a smile, then he turned his attention onto his girlfriend. Part of me was happy for them, though another part felt sad. Here was me, a single sad-sack, despite what bluster spewed out of my mouth about having enough of men, while Zoe and Tomomi were happily coupled.

"Another round of drinks, people?" Vince stood up.

"No, you got the last round." My protestations were lost amidst the buzz; another screwdriver was pushed upon me and necked in three gulps.

And another, from Zoe.

Next Ryuji, and Naoki, and Tomomi, and then it was my turn.

"I'll give you a hand, Kim." Naoki accompanied me to the bar. "Ryuji told me you'd split up with your boyfriend, Chris?"

Unbelievable. Might as well have announced it through a bloody loudspeaker. "Carl, not Chris. Listen, not to be rude or anything but Vince had me spilling my guts before you came. So if you don't mind, can we just drink and have fun?"

"I'm up for that." Naoki pressed his lips together; the corners twitched into a smile, but it was clear he felt cold-shouldered. He lowered his head a fraction towards my ear. "Though I'd keep my distance from Vince, if I were you. He's not that nice a guy."

"What do you mean by that?"

Naoki lowered his eyes, confronted by my stare. "He's an egomaniac, that's all. I went into Voyce about a month ago for a demo lesson and he had a session with a young, pretty woman before me. Well, you know, he was all charm with her. Big smile, loads of compliments. When it was my turn, it was a standard lesson, if you follow me. No smiles, no extra mile for me. The man in charge, what's his name again?"

"Ben? Bald head, black beard and glasses?"

Naoki gave a thumbs up. "That's the one. He pulled me aside and apologised."

"It was seriously that bad?"

He shrugged. "Guess so. Ben said Vince is good for sales with women as they love him – women always buy the more expensive contracts when he has them for a demo, though he admitted that men have logged complaints about him."

My face must have registered annoyance, as Naoki leaned back and assumed a more casual manner. "But hey, let's forget that for now. You said you wanted to drink and have fun, not be bogged down by my problems."

"It's no trouble, really. In fact, it surprises me, that's all. Doesn't Vince know you're a friend of Ryuji?"

Naoki nodded. "He met me before at Passion. That doesn't matter though, we all know he's there just for the ladies."

My head was spinning. "Wow, it never occurred to me he could be like that. Everyone knew he was a ladies man, but he was so nice to me just now, about my break-up."

"Well, just watch out, alright? I'd keep a healthy distance from him."

Naoki had met Vince at Club Passion. Club Passion was still on my mind too. "Vince and me – we've had our differences, but we've patched them up. He's a colleague, that's all. Purely platonic. He respects me as a colleague, and to me, he's a friend and that's it."

***

We all sat on my igusa on the living room floor: Jei Pi, Zoe, Tomomi, Ryuji, Naoki, Vince, Ade, Akemi and me.

"Let's get the vodka out." Jei Pi jumped to her feet and made a dash for the kitchenette.

"Wokka?" said Akemi.

"Wha jah say? Wookie! Lessava wookie party." Tears sprang to my eyes and my chest heaved with uncontrollable laughter. This sent me toppling backwards, onto Tomomi's lap.

"Kim, you're drunk. Have some vodka, that'll make you better." Tomomi slurred her words, not much better than me.

"At least my face isn't beetroot. You can't hold your drink."

"Aww-right, stop arguing you two," said Vince. "Are we playing the King game or not."

This time he'd got me listening. "Splain it temmee again."

Vince cut a blank page into nine pieces and wrote 'King' on one. He crumpled them up and put them in a plastic cup. "Whoever draws the one with King written on it dictates the orders and everyone else has to obey. Whoever is King can choose one person, or the whole group. Got it?"

Vince passed the plastic cup around. We each drew a crumpled ball. Zoe had the piece of paper labelled King.

"Mmm, let's see. The King nominates Akemi." She sat on her knees, Japanese style, with a devilish look on her face. "Akemi, you have to say, 'she sells sea shells on the sea shore' five times as fast as you can, without making a mistake. Go!"

"Aww, that's so mean," said Tomomi. Tomomi had a point; whether sober or tipsy, Akemi could barely speak English as it was.

"The King has spoken," said Zoe, sitting back on her haunches.

Poor Akemi. My sympathy only went as far as the booze would allow me, once Akemi made her first attempt. Five goes later and her effort had me rolling on the floor, laughing.

Crumpled balls of paper back in the cup. Jei Pi drew the King paper next. "M-kay, I got this. The King commands that everyone has to neck a plastic cup full of vodka, straight with no mixers, all in one go. Gan gan nomo!"

Jei Pi filled all the cups and everyone toasted and drank: "Gan gan nomo."

Poor Akemi gagged and Zoe winced with her tongue hanging out of her mouth. Lightweights, both of them. Still, the expressions on their faces had the tears streaming down my face. My head spun. This was turning out to be a great evening.

Tomomi drew the King paper next. She clapped her hands together and licked her lips, casting a sheepish look around the group. "Okay, the King chooses Ade. I demand that Ade has to take off his pants and run up and down the street waving them above his head and shouting 'wooo!'"

This made me giggle. "I hope by that you mean trousers, not pants-pants."

"She means American pants, proper pants, oy vey!" Jei Pi rolled her eyes.

Ade pulled a face. "No way man, I back out."

"No backsys!" Tomomi shouted.

Ade gave a wry smile. "Okay, I'll take the dare."

He whipped off his T-shirt and flung it on the floor, then unbuttoned his jeans and pulled them off. Tomomi, Akemi and Jei Pi screamed and whooped. My attention shifted to Vince; he must have felt shit to have his own girlfriend perving over his best mate. In fairness, Ade did look mannequin-perfect as he stood in his tight-fitting jersey shorts and socks: muscular and tanned.

"Hey dude, she didn't say anything about stripping off completely, she only said your pants," Vince protested. So Vince had confirmed my thoughts; he was jealous about Tomomi.

We all piled into my bedroom as Ade stepped outside. Crammed at the window, we watched as he ran a length of the street, whirling his trousers above his head like a lasso and screaming 'woooo' as Tomomi had commanded. Zoe and Tomomi joined me screaming in laughter. My ribcage needed a massage as it hurt so much from all the fun. "He's mental for actually going through with that."

Ade came back inside and caught his breath. "See when it's my turn, baby? I'm getting my revenge on you." He waggled a finger at Tomomi, who grinned stupidly in return.

Sure enough, Ade drew the King paper next. "Alright, baby, here we go." Ade sized her up, looking Tomomi up and down. He turned his gaze to me, his eyes falling briefly on my chest. A jolt of horror seized me; was he going to make Tomomi kiss me? Making an idiot out of myself by kissing Zoe in front of Club Passion was enough of a cringeworthy memory to last a lifetime. Thankfully that wasn't what Ade had in mind; his devious mind was much, much worse.

"The King commands that Tomomi must take off her bra and swap it with Kimberly's."

"Hey, leave me out of your sordid revenge." No way would he make me strip off in front of everyone.

Ade folded his arms. "Are you going to disobey the King?"

"But, Kim has bigger boobs than me," Tomomi whined.

He shrugged. "Not my problem. You should've thought of that before you made me humiliate myself outside."

Tomomi didn't argue. She whipped off her blouse, then turned her back to the room and facing the living room wall, unfastened her black lacy bra. Hadn't she ever learned crafty girl tricks? No such embarrassment for me; all it took for me to un-do my bra was to withdraw my arms inside my sleeves and fumble under the privacy of my top. One arm slipped out from under my top holding the trophy: my blue, satin bra.

"Nah, no way, you girls are cheating," said Ade.

"You never specified that we had to strip off in front of the room, you just said Tomomi had to take off her bra and swap it with mine."

Ade sat back with a dejected expression, knowing he was defeated. Tomomi, covering her bare breasts with one arm, extended the other and handed me her bra. She took mine and turned her back to put it on. Putting on Tomomi's bra under my top was a nightmare: it was only a 32A, compared to my 34C. Straining with my arms behind my back, my fingers managed to stretch the lacy backing enough to fasten the hooks. With the bra safely in place, it was time to whip off my top. My chest bulged over Tomomi's small, tight bra, whereas her chest drowned inside the bigger, looser cups of mine.

"Aww right, can the next King please lay off the stripping, it's getting boring." The words struggled off my tongue, heavy with vodka, though judging by everyone's unspoken nods, they agreed with me.

Naoki drew the King paper next. "All the girls have to kiss the King!"

Jei Pi practically flew off her floor cushion and launched herself at Naoki. He keeled backwards at the impact of her wide-open mouth all over his tightly-pressed lips and politely pried her off, with gentle but firm hands on her shoulders.

"Bet you regret your command now, sucker!" Ade laughed.

Naoki wiped his mouth with the back of his hand, a dazed look on his face that had me chuckling. The next series of kisses brought a smile back to his face: Zoe gave a theatrical bow and kissed his hand, as though he really were regal; Akemi gave a quick peck on his cheek and Tomomi kissed his forehead. Then it was my turn.

"Go on, kiss him," Jei Pi called.

Naoki blushed as my face drew closer to his. He closed his eyes when we were millimetres apart, but instead of a passionate French kiss, that he seemed to be expecting, my lips brushed his in a barely-there peck.

"Aww, no fair. Tease!" Jei Pi shouted.

"What did you want, a peep show? Hentai."

More vodka, more dares. As my head spun ever more, the night rolled on and at some point, the King game was forgotten.

"Right guys and gals, that's me off to bed." Without a further word, Jei Pi stood, staggered to her bedroom and flopped down on her futon. A few seconds later and she was snoring.

Ade got up. "I think I'll head on myself. Akemi, you still wanting a lift home?" Akemi swayed on the spot and didn't answer. Ade smiled. "I'll take that as a yes."

Six remaining, but the party went on.

"Ryuji, I'm pissed. Let's get going," said Zoe.

"But I can't drive like this," he said, red-faced and head lolling.

Zoe crawled towards the sofa, hauled herself up and passed out. Five left. Vince passed around Jei Pi's mostly empty bottle of vodka for everyone to take a sip. Tomomi squeezed herself up onto the sofa and fell asleep, her arm strapped over Zoe. Four remaining.

Naoki struggled to his feet. "Thanks for a lovely evening." He looked at me as he spoke. "I think I'll sleep in my car in your driveway, if that's okay?"

My mouth dropped open, ready to tell him that was fine, but instead of words a string of drool poured out. Damn vodka; incapacitation had come too soon.

Three left: Vince, Ryuji and me.

Ryuji held the bottle up. The last dregs of vodka swished under Ryuji's intoxicated grip. Bottle met lips and he glugged.

"Hey, leave some for us." My hand was steadier than his, snatching the bottle from his drunken fingers.

"Kimberly, not only are you the most beautiful girl in Tottori, but you can drink any man under the table," said Ryuji.

My eyes darted across to Zoe, asleep on the sofa. "What are you saying? Zoe's your girlfriend and she's over there. She'll hear."

He flapped a hand in Zoe's direction, dismissing my complaint. "She's a nice girl, but I'd rather have you. And now you're single."

Ryuji flopped sideways, his head falling into my lap. An elbow nudge was all it took to shove him off. "Oh, so that's how it works? You don't even give me a say? You men are all the same, just out for what you can get. Well, count me out."

The last few sips of vodka were bitter medicine down my gullet. Men. Fucking men. A good night of fun, and drinking, and partying and now a sleazy come-on, as if that would impress me.

Vince reached forward and put his hands under my armpits, pulling me to my feet. "Come on Kimberly, you're getting too wound-up. Let's get you to bed."

26

ა

Blackout

My bedroom ceiling wasn't smooth. There were tiny
bumps all across it, as though it had woodchip under
the surface. Funny that had never occurred to me
before. Or was it my head spinning from all the
booze? What the fuck time was it anyway? Daylight
seeped through my new bamboo blinds. Early hours?

What the hell was going on?

Vince's face appeared, smiling, from between my
legs then sank back down out of sight. Raising my
head to peer along the horizon, my eyes absorbed the
battlefield that was my body: top half-clothed, bottom
half-naked. Vince's greedy mouth opened wide for a
mouthful of my vulva, my blonde pubic hair a
grotesque beard against his tanned, dark-haired head.

The voice that slipped from my mouth was a
feeble, dry-throated squeak. "Wait, what are you
doing?"

My head slumped back onto the pillow, eyes rolled
upwards and all became white.

No sooner than all became white, everything
turned black. Black hair. My hand pushed the heavy
black-haired head off my face. Ryuji. Ryuji rolled
away to my right side, completely asleep as he fell off
my futon and lay face down on my igusa.

But it wasn't me who had knocked Ryuji aside.
Vince appeared above me with a grin fixed on his
face, so wide it crinkled his eyes. His face loomed

closer and his open mouth clamped over mine. My chest constricted as his heavy weight bore down. My face fell under the shadow of his darkness; greasy darkness, black-haired darkness, jeering, leering darkness and pressure. Pressure between my legs. His legs wedging mine ever further apart. His tongue pushing mine further back in my mouth. His uninvited tongue in my mouth and my own salty taste on my tongue. Pressure down below as my legs were pushed apart and my body was buffeted. My head bumped against the wall, rocking one, two, three.

"No. Stop."

Four, five, six. My head rolled to the right. Ryuji lay asleep.

"Ryuji, wake up."

Seven, eight, nine. My head rolled to the left. My top and bra lay by the door. My trousers and pants lay near my chest of drawers. Vince was fully clothed, while my body had been stripped, naked.

"Vince, stop."

Ten, eleven, twelve. Too many times to count.

"Stop."

My hands grappled with his chest, but he was too heavy to push off. Too heavy. Too many times.

"Ryuji, help me."

But Ryuji was out for the count. No one was there to help me. It was just me, and the motion, and the waves of nausea and then my eyes closed and that was all.

27

℃℗

Aftermath

My head throbbed, a dull ache all over. Raising it off the pillow was a tribulation, not least because the bright morning sunlight flooded my face.

After a moment to orientate myself, two things became clear. Firstly, my bedroom door was hanging open. Secondly, my modesty had been rescued by merely bra and pants, should anyone have walked past my bedroom to enter, or exit the apartment. The second thought offered me no comfort whatsoever: everyone who left the party would surely have passed by my door and seen me barely clothed.

One clammy hand plastered itself against my forehead, steadying a wave of nausea, while the other pushed me into a seated pose on my futon. What the hell had happened last night? How had my clothes ended scattered across my room? It wasn't like me to fall asleep in my undies; no matter how drunk, somehow my pyjamas always ended up on – and in the correct way. It wasn't like me to have a complete black-out either. What had happened? My still intoxicated mind struggled to think. We had played the King game. We had passed the vodka bottle around. One by one, everyone had either fallen asleep or left until... Until it was just Vince, Ryuji and me. Then Vince had suggested helping me to bed and. And.

My memory was patchy, but it was coming back to me, filtered, like tiny grains of grit through a sieve. Did Vince have sex with me? A hazy recollection of us kissing, or rather him pressing his big ham-head onto my lips, seemed familiar. My inebriated brain fought simultaneously to restore my short term memory and to sleep at once. An image of Vince performing cunnilingus popped into my mind, and bile rose in my throat. The unpleasant picture of him grinning up at me from further down my body made my legs instinctively clamp together.

A sharp, stinging sensation shot through my left labia as my legs pressed closed. Feeling down there gave no answers; only a mirror would help.

My head pounded on the short walk into the bathroom. A quick check showed that Jei Pi had gone to work and none of our friends remained in the flat. Time for some self-gynaecology. Pants on the floor, foot up on the rim of the sink, makeup mirror wedged to show the view between my legs. My fingertips spread the labia enough to see that all the equipment checked out pink and normal looking. All except – what was that?

Next to the opening of my vagina, there was a small inch-long diamond-shaped split in the skin, about half a centimetre wide. Instinct rather than common sense made me lick my fingers and apply it to the wound. It stung like hell.

"Oh shit." The pain made me wince, made me grit my teeth. A superficial wound, but a cut none the less. That clumsy bastard Vince. What had he done? No time to think about it now. My shift started at eleven. It was quarter past ten.

***

Cycling to work was not an option. My labia minora was swollen. The pain of the cut seared through my groin. Each leg rubbed – one, two, back forth, hurt, sore. Into the staffroom, a perfunctory smile at Akemi on the front desk and Ben marking files at his desk.

"Hey Kim. How's it going?" said Ben. Benign Ben. Jovial Ben. Oblivious Ben.

"Fine, thanks."

And my head swam, and the room spun, then all was white and the world turned sideways.

***

"Kim, he says you need to take off everything below your waist."

My eyes rested on Zoe, comprehending her words as she translated. Somehow, Zoe seemed much more stern and authoritarian than she usually did. She spoke like a medic, as though she were the doctor and not the middle-aged Japanese man in the white coat beside her. A couple of blinks later, and my brain finally processed what she – he – was asking me to do. Skirt off, pants off and up onto the medical bed. My knickers had been up and down more times than a lift in the past twenty-four hours.

The doctor pulled a curtain across my mid-riff, separating my upper and lower halves and hiding him from view. Zoe pulled her chair next to my head and held my hand. It meant a lot: having Zoe there to translate, and for support; Ben being so perceptive that more had happened than simply a drunken party night the previous evening, yet not asking any further questions.

"He's going to look inside you now." Zoe's voice was no longer stern-medic, but soothing-counsellor.

The speculum was cold. My knees wanted to roll together, but willpower kept them apart while he examined me. The ceiling was comprised of grey, foam squares, each around two feet by two feet. Looking at ceilings had happened more than once in the past twenty-four hours too; it also sickened me.

"There's a cut on your cervix. It's bleeding. He says he'll have to prescribe you an anti-coagulant."

"A what?" My throat felt like sand paper.

Zoe spoke to the doctor in Japanese. "It'll stop the blood from clotting. The bleeding should stop in two or three days."

My stomach felt hollow. It had bottomed out. My body had emptied itself of all life, and energy, and existence.

"It'll be okay, Kim." Zoe's words that time, not the doctor's.

"Don't say that." A dry swallow. "That makes things a million times worse."

The doctor spoke again in a monotone to Zoe. "He's going to take some swabs now to check for STDs," she said.

"Great. That'll just be perfect if he's given me gonorrhoea." Another swallow, to supress tears.

More sticks inserted in me, only this time to heal. My body needed cleansing. It had been tarnished. Defiled. "When will the results be in?"

Zoe asked the doctor the question. "He says next week."

After the examination, Zoe led me outside, as my body – and mind – felt numb. The wind whipped my hair off my face. If only it could've whipped off the skin, and sinew, and muscle, and bone too.

"Jei Pi is going to meet Vince after his late shift tonight to have a word with him," said Zoe.

"What's she going to say to him?"

Zoe rubbed my back. "Just to let him know what he's done."

This made me shrug. "Doubt he'll remember, we were all pretty wasted."

She blanched. "Not too wasted that his dick didn't work."

Maybe she was right. Vince had certainly screwed things up between us this time. After how nice he had been too, helping to console me over Carl, better than even Jei Pi, or Zoe had done.

"Vince really made a mess of things. Now there's no way we can be friends."

Zoe's eyebrows shot upwards. "You're kidding, right?"

My eyes locked with hers. "No, really. Everything's complicated now."

"What's complicated, Kim? I'm seriously not following–"

"Sex, if you get my drift. Having sex with a colleague means the friendship has changed. Permanently."

"You seriously want to be friends with Vince after what he did to you?"

"Not friends, no." A sniff, a rub of my nose. "But we're going to have to work together. How can we carry on like normal when, well, you know the saying. Don't dip your pen in the office ink."

Zoe raised both hands. "It wasn't just sex, Kim. Let's call a spade a spade."

Another gust of wind was cool, refreshing on my face. "There's good to be had in everything. In everyone. This is a lovely day. There's no point wasting it. This is a day for some cleansing, you know? Healing."

Zoe wrinkled her brow. "What are you on about?"

"Some reflection, maybe Zen meditation at my favourite spot on Tottori Kaigan."

28

ೞ

Decontamination

Always look towards the sun, then the shadows will fall behind you.

Always look towards the sun, then the shadows will fall behind you.

Always look towards the sun, then the shadows will fall behind you.

Only it wasn't working. First, my stupid shit-for-brains head wouldn't allow me to remember the actual mantra by Walt Whitman. Second, it wasn't possible to achieve a Zen meditative state as my brain was too filled with unwelcome thoughts. Third, physically sitting in a lotus position on the sand was excruciating as it forced my vulva against the ground and the pain was unbearable. My labia might as well have been stung by a million bees. My head had a million bees buzzing around inside it. The way the doctor had talked to Zoe while he was examining me, looked her in the eye and not me, made me feel about as sub-human as a person could get. It was as though my misdemeanour had tainted me, made me into a scarlet-woman, a whore. From lop-sided lotus to loser; my legs rolled forward, knees first and my body followed, curling into a ball on the sand. The pain burst out of me in a torrent of tears, streaming onto the sand. My fists pummelled the sand. Why me? Universe, what had made me deserve so much mistreatment, so much tribulation?

Why me?

This wasn't cleansing, this was self-pity.

No. This wasn't how things were meant to be. The nature of being Zen meant to remove any unwanted intrusions from one's mind and to experience the moment, to live for the here and now. But my recent past carried too much baggage; time to rid myself of it.

Only three things accompanied me on my retreat to this personal sanctuary, my own secret corner of Tottori Kaigan: lined notepaper, a pen and a lighter. Time to write all my demons out of my head.

"Name – Carl." My voice shook, but the wind took hold of it, carrying it away.

"Hurt caused – giving me a broken heart, cheating on me, running me down, using me, taking me for granted." Tears welled, but my confidence grew and my hand moved easily across the page.

"Name – Vince." A deep breath, before continuing.

"Hurt caused – pretending to be my friend while having an ulterior motive, taking advantage of me while drunk, injuring me." A pause after the third point. Wonder how Jei Pi was getting on with Vince, laying it out to him?

Ah, distractions! Achieving a Zen state would forever remain a fantasy if superficial worries were constantly plaguing me.

Both men had wronged me, but obviously it was part of their destiny to do so, trials for them to learn from. The universal order would even out any mishaps during their journeys, whether in this life or the next. As for me, clearly this was a test to strengthen my soul.

Paper would have to suffice for sins: my intention had been to bury Carl's golden watch, but it had escaped me on my hunt, high and low all over the apartment. A subconscious part of my mind must have buried it in my bedroom during the big spring clean after Carl had left Japan. Oh well. Paper was better for a cleanse anyway – burning beat burying.

Another deep breath. Paper in one hand, lighter in the other. Two clicks and one corner was lit. One rotation, anticlockwise, and the flame licked upwards towards the middle of the page. Blowing helped the fire grow, my body leaning forward to allow the wind to burn my burdens away. One spark, thrown upwards on a breeze. One loose blonde strand, dangling too close over my shoulder.

My hair was alight. The fire rushed upwards towards my forehead. My hands slapped wildly, fighting to beat out the flames. This was the worst. This was a message from the universe that it had abandoned me and my plight. My burdens had not been received.

Tears. More damn tears. What was the point? Emotional release? No such luck, far too many stagnant feelings to ever stem the flow. It was time to admit reality. My whole spiritual journey was a fraud. There was no test of my soul. There was nothing for Carl and Vince to learn. They were simply flawed people, who did bad things. No, they were bad people, who hurt people and didn't learn anything from it. They didn't give a shit who they hurt. They didn't live, they existed, simply to take advantage of others and use them.

My fists thumped the sand in my howling, crying fit of rage until every unhelpful thought was burned out of my system, physically and metaphorically. One exploratory hand felt my singed hair. What a mess.

"Hey chica...woah, roomie, are you okay there?"

Jei Pi and Yuri walked across the beach. Jei Pi dropped to her knees in front of me on the sand. Her thumbs wiped tears off my cheeks and when she withdrew her hands, they were black with ash and eyeliner.

"What did you do to yourself?"

"Tried to burn away my sorrows. But it was a mistake." Another pitiful sob rose and my chest heaved. Jei Pi pulled my head onto her shoulder and hugged me.

"I spoke to Vince. We went to Zen for a drink."

A derisive snort escaped me, before any chance of restraint. "Fitting. Not that he could ever be Zen if he tried."

She either didn't hear me, or ignored me, for she went on. "I asked him if he remembered what happened. He said he knew he had slept with you. I told him that's not how you saw it, that it wasn't just sex. I asked him if he knew what you thought it was."

"And what's that?"

"Rape. He raped you, Kim. It wasn't sex. It was rape."

"You said that word to him?"

"I did." Jei Pi rubbed my back. "He sat there quiet for a moment and let that sink in, just so you know."

"But – it wasn't, you know, the 'r' word. That sort of thing happens to women who are dragged into alleyways in the dark by strangers, or prostitutes who get beaten up by their pimps and bruised all over. What Vince did wasn't violent."

Jei Pi's eyes bulged. "Yeah right, as if battering your cervix until it bled and splitting the skin of your labia open isn't violent."

More tears threatened. "Men just seem to take advantage of me, they gravitate to me and they have no respect for me."

"They see you as a possession, something to control. Or if not that, then a commodity. You're better than all of these men – Carl, Vince. You're a trophy girl for them, the ultimate prize. You should really get a good Japanese boyfriend, you know he would treat you right."

An image of Naoki flooded my mind. Quick mental shake-up to drain the image. "It's not the right time for me to be seeing anyone. It's time for me to get to know the real Kimberly. For too long it was me and Carl, Carl and me, like two pathetic halves that couldn't function without the other. My mouth would open and his words would come out. When he didn't have me around, he would shut-down – controlling me was the energy source for his whole nasty existence."

"What you eez burning?" said Yuri, poking her fingers into the ash of my burned paper.

"Nothing really, just trying out a stupid self-help tip from a book that didn't work. It wasn't my plan to set fire to my own hair."

Yuri picked up a fragment of paper and gave it to me. "See this? Shape is look like the Buddha. Eez a good omen. See? Top bit eez look like head and bottom bit eez look like Buddha's round stomach."

The piece of paper didn't look like much to me. Maybe it was like finding a white feather; some superstitious people believed they were signs that an angel was nearby.

"Do you know that here in Japan, mosto people is – how do I say it – burned when dead. Nandatake..."

"Cremated," said Jei Pi.

"Yes, cremated. Mosto people in Japan is Buddhist. After person eez die, body eez get cremated and sometimes pieces of bone does not burn." Yuri tapped the hollow of her own neck. "Bone in throat sometimes eez left and shape eez look like Buddha. Sometimes mosto traditional Japanese families can look in ashes in hope to find Buddha's Bone. It eez say to bring good luck to family."

"The Buddha's Bone?" My eyes fell to the portentous paper fragment in my hand, that only moments before had been nothing.

Yuri smiled. "People eez not know why Buddha's Bone eez not get burn, or why shape looks like Buddha, but we Japanese see it as a sign that our dead family eez reach enlightenment."

Warmth filled me. Had the universe answered my most desperate plea, at my darkest hour? My fingers closed over the paper fragment Buddha in my palm.

CYCLE 3: Rebirth

29

༄

Ode to a blastocyst

Some things got better over time. Take food, for example. Leftovers tasted better the next day, definitely. The anticipation of a holiday only made the countdown better. Admittedly, these were trivial things. Superficial. There was nothing good about my late period, now two weeks overdue. My fear absolutely did not get better with time. I visualised a million of Vince's sperm zooming around inside my uterus like angry bees, assaulting my fallopian tubes. At my gynaecological check, the doctor had explained to Zoe, who had translated to me, that there was no point doing a pregnancy test one day after the matter. It was a case of waiting, fearfully, until my next period was due and seeing if it was late. Only then would the levels of pregnancy hormone, the Human Chorionic Gonadotropin, be high enough to detect on a pregnancy test. Pregnancy. The unopened pregnancy test in my hand didn't help my fear. The long packet could easily have been a tampon in its wrapper. Wishful thinking; no such luck for me. There was no easy way about it; I ripped open the packet and pulled the cap off the test.

After I peed on the absorbent tip, I stuck the cap back on the test. The instruction packet said if a cross appeared, it meant pregnant and if a horizontal line appeared, it meant not pregnant. Thirty seconds passed. A horizontal line began to appear. I didn't even realise I had been holding my breath until I let it out in a huge, happy exhalation. Ten more seconds passed.

But wait; was there a faint vertical line, splicing my perfect horizontal blue line with its unwanted presence? Or was I imagining it?

The full minute had passed. Yes, undeniably there was a cross, although the horizontal blue line was dark and bold, whereas the vertical line cutting through it was a faint pale blue. Could it be that I wasn't pregnant, but it was simply a faulty test, showing up both lines?

To be sure, I took the second pregnancy test out of the box, unwrapped it and peed on it. More urine ended up on my hand than the stick. *Oh my gosh*, the whole ordeal was making me so nervous. Another minute's wait before a reluctant glance at the result panel. No doubt about it, there was a cross as before: strong, bold horizontal line and faint, pale vertical line.

"Oh – My – Gosh. This isn't happening. This is *not* happening."

I rolled my head back against the water tank of the toilet, closed my eyes and cried.

If this was karma, then I must have murdered someone in a former life to have such negative repercussions in my life, and so quickly too: Carl cheating on me and us breaking up; Vince taking advantage of me when I was incapacitated and now, this. As I wallowed in self-pity, hugging myself and sobbing while I sat on the toilet, Jei Pi's cloying voice popped into my head, in her best singsong, let's-see-the-best-in-everything voice: *Look on the bright side, Roomie, at least you don't have any STDs.* She had said that when I was having a dark moment, a self-pitying moment about Vince's violation. What would she say now when I told her I was pregnant?

Why did I always end up feeling so lonely and frightened on my days off? It was as though I couldn't bear to be in my own company for even a few hours, for fear of what might be lurking in my mind, ready to crawl out and devour me. The one thing, the single saving grace from the past few months since Carl had left was that at least I knew I would never let any man treat me so badly again. I deserved better. As a way of enforcing that to myself, I had even managed to quit alcohol. I hadn't touched a drop of vodka in a month since the party at our flat on the night of the typhoon. Not even one drink. Had it been instinct? Had my body subconsciously known I was pregnant? I pondered the thought for a moment and decided, no. No, it was simply because the doctor had told me to wait for my next period to come. Logic dictated that if there was a life inside of me, then the poor little critter deserved to float in the alcohol-free swimming pool of my stomach.

How ironic that I had only just found myself underneath the turmoil from seven wasted years of being one-half of a couple and now I was divided in half again, this time with a soon-to-be-baby. Laughter burst from my chest and my body rocked forward with the ensuing convulsions. My emotions were seriously all over the place.

What about Vince? Now I was inexorably linked to him forever. We had both, inadvertently, become parents to a rapidly growing ball of cells in my womb. How would he take it when I told him? How would I tell him? The thought made my entire body break out in goose-bumps; never mind my physical form, if my soul had hairs, they would all be standing on end.

What sort of dad would he be? Would he want to be a part of his child's life? Would I want to let him be in his child's life? And what then, how would our already complicated relationship transpire as said child grew older. How would my son or daughter feel to know their father was a rapist?

Any trace of laughter, however ironic, vanished in an instant. I wanted to scream. I wanted to smash something hard: crockery, a window. Hearing a satisfying crash would have given me an outlet for my pent up rage at the world. This was more than unfair, the universe had dished out a horrendous punishment for me and all I could do about it was cry, why?

More bad than good had come out of the situation with Vince. Zoe had broken up with Ryuji, though for tangential reasons that thankfully hadn't destroyed our friendship: she blamed him for not saving me from Vince on that night. Ryuji's version of events corresponded with mine: that he had climbed into my bed to sleep, nothing more, and had fallen so deeply into slumber that he hadn't woken even when I had called him for help. Zoe had been less than impressed that he hadn't chosen to fall asleep beside her on the sofa too; she had woken early to find Tomomi strapped across her. Tomomi had broken up with Vince too, and rightly so. But after her initial sympathy towards me, she had become cold and distant at work, around the same time as she had dumped Vince. I felt hurt; how could I not. We had been close friends. She hadn't been a best friend, like Zoe and Jei Pi, but she was part of my inner circle; we were a foursome, a quartet. Now, she blanked me at work and I didn't even dare attempt to see her socially. All my friendly hints had been rebuffed with clipped excuses: I can't, I have to get my car fixed; I have an appointment that day; I'm meeting someone else after work, sorry (but not sorry). She would hate me even more when she found out I was pregnant with his child.

This was not how I saw myself getting pregnant. Not through sexual assault, not in a foreign country, not while I was still so young in my mid-twenties. I had always imagined that when I got pregnant, I'd be married, in my thirties and settled into my career as a Clinical Psychologist in a hospital, or an Education Psychologist in a secondary school. I would have been working at my job long enough to take a comfortable year long stint away on maternity leave that wouldn't affect my ability to go back to work afterwards. My husband and I would have owned our own house by the time I got pregnant, and we would have spent at least 5 years of our marriage getting to know one another and travelling the world together before settling down to be parents. The father of my child would be my soulmate, my best friend, my spiritual twin. That was what I had imagined. Not that I would be a broken down shell of a woman, a single mother, knocked up by a sexual predator.

Another fresh wave of tears assaulted my face. A guttural scream resonated around the small, narrow toilet room. I didn't even know I was capable of such a horrible bovine bellow, not a sound like a lady would make. It was proof that I wasn't a lady. I wasn't even a woman; I was a subhuman abomination; that was why I had been violated. My aura had attracted such subhuman behaviour.

What on earth was I thinking? I slapped my face several times, with both hands in turn, striking both cheeks. Snap out of it, Kimberly. I didn't deserve to be raped and the baby I was carrying deserved better too; at the very least, a mother who could pull herself together.

My tears and angry energy subsided to a few pitiful sobs; a storm that had burnt out, the aftermath of the typhoon that had torn through me, devastating my body. With all negative residue gone, constructive thoughts flooded my mind; maybe I would be able to decide on a practical plan going forward. I was pregnant, that much was true. A tumbling morula was growing in my uterus and in a short few weeks would sprout legs and arms and have a heartbeat of its own. The thought made me shiver, but that was my reality now.

What to do, what to do? A pen: there on the window sill. I snatched it up and grabbed the roll of toilet paper, the nearest thing that would suffice as a writing pad.

Title: Ode to a blastocyst
Oh tumbling morula!
I don't need a
Zona pellucida,
If you catch my drift,
Blasted blastocyst.
You're an enterprising embryo,
But you don't wanna know
How you got there, oh no,
But, granted,
You've implanted,
So we'll stay on a high note,
Baby zygote.

The poem didn't give me any solutions, but it instilled a sense of hope. This baby wasn't a bad thing; I would turn it into something good. With the precious little life growing inside me, I would turn all the bad things from my lack-of-relationship with Vince into positives. Soon-to-be born child and I would forge a loving bond, where Vince and I only had a predator-prey communication. That was all well and good, but the baby wouldn't be here for another nine months. I would be back in England before then; no hope of renewing my visa for another year with a child in tow. In the meantime, maybe I could be proactive another way.

I hadn't seen Vince since that night four weeks ago. Ben had signed me off on sick leave for a week. I had returned to work with dread welling in the pit of my stomach, only to find that Vince had taken all of his annual leave and had gone travelling across Japan; either a cowardly thing to do in running away from me, or repentant, in recognising his actions. Either way, it had left me hanging. Today was the day to resolve it. I had to tell him; we had to work it out. Even if he wasn't fated to be a part of his child's life, it would give me a sense of accomplishment if I could make something good come out of the worst night of my life.

30

❧

Secret admirer

"Vince has transferred to the Namba branch. He started there last week after his vacation days ended."

I stared at Ben and blinked, then blinked again. It was all I could do to comprehend his words. "You mean, he won't be coming back here at all?"

Ben shook his head. "Frankly, I thought you'd be happy considering what happened."

My throat tightened as if a Boa constrictor had coiled itself around me. But no, there was only one predator and he was gone. "I am happy, just surprised. I didn't know you knew what happened. Who told you?"

"Tomomi did. They had a huge fight at reception in front of students, so I had to intervene. He'd been shouting and swearing and you know yourself it wasn't the first time he'd mouthed off loudly. I told him to get lost and not to come back, that I'd sort out his annual leave for him and I'd be putting in for a transfer for him to Osaka."

My head reeled. "I didn't know you could do that."

"Yeah, well, they had an opening at Namba as one of their teachers quit early and I didn't tell them the details about Vince, just that he wanted to transfer." Ben poked his glasses up the bridge of his nose; they had slid down with sweat. "Tomomi was upset after their fight, so I took her for coffee and she told me everything."

My jaw clenched; bloody Tomomi. Insult to injury; she'd given me the cold-shoulder and now had spilled all the beans on my personal business.

Ben's gaze softened as he shifted his focus onto me. "Why didn't you go to the police, Kim?"

I shrugged, but instantly regretted it; such a petty mannerism. "We're both foreigners. I'm sure the Japanese police wouldn't care. They'd have to deal with translators and it would take ages to get to court – Vince would already have left Japan by that point."

"I respectfully disagree, but I understand your reasons why you wouldn't want it to go to court – I'm sure you never want to see him again." His eyes darted behind me and I knew his thoughts were elsewhere. "Listen, Kim. I know it's your day off, but I'm on my lunch break – if you want we could grab a coffee?"

I smiled and nodded. Ben was such a nice man; like a big brother, not a boss. Coffee with Tomomi to talk through her troubles and now me, with both our troubles about Vince.

We took the escalator downstairs. As we passed *Classy Girl* I averted my eyes. Shiori had gone back to being an arch villain in my eyes; if she hadn't slept with Carl, we wouldn't have broken up, which meant I wouldn't have been in a drunken vulnerable state, so then Vince wouldn't have found me an easy target, and I wouldn't be coping with an unwanted pregnancy. Ben led me to a coffee and donut cafe next to Tottori bank. I sat, a numb-lump on my hard plastic chair, while he got us refreshments.

"Kim, I really feel I owe you an apology for something I said." Ben's eyes were sad, behind his glasses. "I gave you really bad advice a few weeks ago."

A few weeks ago? That was a different lifetime, when I had lived in a limbo state, not yet a harsh reality. "You don't need to say sorry for anything. You've been so kind to me."

He continued. "That day you'd had a barbecue with the Yakuza, I told you to stay away from Japanese men in their vans because of the number of rapes that had happened. The thing is, I'm sorry. I set you up to be suspicious of Japanese men and that might have made you put your trust in men like Vince – and look what happened."

I shook my head. "You aren't responsible for what Vince did to me. The only one who made any bad decision was Vince, because he's a bad person."

Ben's furrowed brow relaxed. His taut jaw loosened into a smile. "Thanks. I appreciate that."

I sighed, with relief. "You've reaffirmed my faith that good men exist in this world. I'd started to lose hope after my ex and then Vince. Chiaki is a lucky woman."

Ben turned a bright shade of flamingo pink; from the strip of neck showing below his bushy, black beard to his shiny, bald head. "Speaking of good men, someone has been quite interested in you lately. It's quite sweet really. He pops in from time to time – he bought ten sample lessons and I think he's been hoping that we would schedule one with you, but you were off on sick leave. Since then, he's been coming when he doesn't have work on the weekends and sadly for him that coincides with your days off too."

I took a swig of hot coffee, and winced as it burned my tongue. "Who is he?"

"His name's Naoki Yasuda."

"Ah, Naoki." Ryuji's friend. Hadn't he told me he'd been to a demo lesson at Voyce with Vince, a month ago? "I know Naoki."

"He seems quite smitten by you. He asked after you a couple of times." Ben had a sly grin.

I wasn't sure why, but alarm bells rang in my head; maybe the thought of men generally left me touchy, after what had happened with Vince. "What did you tell him?"

"Just that I'd tell you he was asking. I didn't say anything more than that."

It seemed Ben had added on his second thought as more of an afterthought, really. Could be he'd picked up on my nervousness. Was I nervous? Naoki was cute, sure, for a Japanese guy. Mental shake up; what a thought. I was sounding as racist as Carl, albeit in my own head. No, Naoki was cute, full stop. But he was also shy. If he liked me so much, why didn't he just come right out with it and tell me? There was something about a man who made subtle gestures, quietly gathered information about me without being overt that gave me the creeps; it felt like he was spying on me. Was I being too paranoid?

"Thanks for letting me know." I sighed and finished my coffee. "If he ever does come in for a lesson when I'm on shift, I'd really appreciate if you didn't book him into one of my classes, if you don't mind."

***

I kicked off my shoes in the entranceway of my flat with Jei Pi, as was habit by now, and traipsed into the living room. As much as it had been a lovely chat with Ben over coffee, it hadn't been relaxing. In fact, it had been mentally draining. What I needed most was closure with Vince, only to find out he had transferred to another branch, followed by finding out that I had a secret admirer, or if I wanted to be realistic, a well-intentioned stalker in Naoki. Why couldn't men leave me alone?

Time for some chores. Chores weren't fun, but they at least helped to discipline my mind, or at least distract me from my troubles for a while. Airing my futon on the balcony would help; a few thwacks with the bamboo beater would be cathartic as well as productive. My clothes were still hanging on the line, so I could kill two birds with one stone and bring in the laundry.

I dragged my futon across the living room floor and slid the glass door and mosquito screen back. As I ducked under my work shirts, hanging nearest the door, I noticed gaps on the washing line. The empty spaces forced my memory back to that morning; I had definitely used up all the space on the line and there had been no gaps. Looking down, I saw clothes pegs discarded; further evidence that some items had been removed.

But not just any items. The missing clothes were all pants. All my knickers had been stolen.

"Oh, this is just great! This is just perfect, really what I need right now."

With more aggression than necessary, I hauled my futon over the balcony rail and beat it so hard with the bamboo beater that the loud thuds resonated as an echo, bouncing of the adjacent duplex behind my apartment building. What sort of creepy pervert would steal all my underwear? Had somebody entered the flat itself? But I hadn't noticed anything untoward;

the front door had been locked and nothing inside disturbed. More to the point, I had only been gone for two and a half hours; the time it had taken to call into work and have a coffee with Ben. That meant someone *must* have known I had left. Had someone been watching my flat, watching me hang out the laundry? The pervert must climbed up from the outside and gotten onto the balcony that way. I leaned over the balcony rail and looked down. The flat below Jei Pi and mine had a wooden lattice along the wall for plants to grow. It was bolted onto the bricks and looked sturdy enough for someone to climb. But who? There was a young couple in the flat below us with a toddler girl. They didn't seem likely culprits. Behind us in the adjacent building were an elderly couple who tended persimmons in their field; they didn't seem likely knicker-thieves. Who else would have been watching my flat?

Naoki?

No, surely not? If Vince had still been living in Tottori, I might have suspected that he would do such a twisted thing, but not placid, mild-spoken Naoki. But it wasn't good enough for me to speculate; I had to know. I didn't have Naoki's phone number, but I had Ben's. That was a starting point.

31

ೞ

Dinner date

The large glass walls and high ceilings made the space look more like an art studio than a restaurant. The white furnishings: white wooden chairs and glass tables, with Art Deco paintings added to the impression. Not that I minded; it seemed a very European-inspired eatery and I appreciated that Naoki had thought to take me there. It was very considerate of him, to make an effort with the little things. Carl never made an effort. One of our first dates had been to McDonalds.

Oh gosh, how I wanted to slap myself right on the cheek, and hard. Not only was this *not* a date with Naoki, but Carl was ancient history. He was old news, forgotten, done and dusted. Deep breath.

The waitress brought our food. I looked down at the plate of spaghetti in front of me. It was entirely black.

I looked from my plate to Naoki and back. "What is this?"

He guffawed into his hand. "Sorry, I should've warned you about the colour. Squid ink pasta is always black. But it's so delicious, that's why I recommended it. It's one of those dishes that you have to try if you live in Japan."

I stared at him, looking for a trace of irony in his laugh; but there was none. "You're sure you didn't make me order this as a joke?"

He shook his head, the expression in his brown eyes warm, but serious. "I'd never be that cruel, Kim. Try it, you'll see what I mean. May I?"

He gestured to my dish with his fork. I nodded and watched him twirl the fork in his hand, winding several strands of black spaghetti around the prongs. He lifted it to his mouth, closed his lips and munched, his long eyelashes sweeping shut as he savoured the bite.

"That good, huh?" I took my own fork, wound the spaghetti around it and ate. Naoki wasn't wrong. It was delicious. It looked terrifying, but tasted divine.

"Was I right, or was I right?" He said, a sheepish smile in place as he leaned forward on one elbow, awaiting my verdict.

I grinned. "Oh my gosh, this stuff is to die for!"

Naoki laughed. "You should see your mouth though."

I looked at his mouth as he laughed. His teeth and lips were jet black. "Yours too!"

It broke all the tension of our meeting. I had built up so much about Naoki in my head all afternoon as I had waited for him to come and pick me up for our dinner catch-up: the Voyce lessons he had booked just to get near me, my suspicions about him being the knicker thief; all to have them dissipate over a heavenly horror show plate of black gloop.

"When did you get your hair cut?" Naoki paused before tucking into his own dish of chicken katsu curry with an earnest expression.

I touched the back of my bob. "A few weeks ago."

"I like the bangs. Is that what you call them in England – bangs?"

"That's American English. We say fringe."

My fringe had been cut high, to shear off the singed hair from my accident at the beach, and I wasn't a fan; together with the bobbed haircut, I thought it made me look very *Village of the Damned*. Everyone else loved it though. Jei Pi thought the asymmetrical razor cut was far more modern than my conventional long-blonde-hair look. Zoe thought it emphasised my natural baby-blonde colouring. The only thing I liked about it was that it was symbolic; the past had been cut off and the new look reflected the more mature me.

"Thanks for calling me. To be honest, I've wanted to get your number for ages, but I didn't have the nerve to ask. I'm glad you made the first move. And now here we are, on a dinner date." Naoki puffed out his chest.

"Dinner catch-up." I shifted in my seat; the hard wooden chair was a bit uncomfortable on my bum. "I got your number off Ben. He said you'd been booking lessons at Voyce?"

"Yeah, I had." Naoki averted his eyes, and I saw a red tinge on his ears. "I thought I'd brush up my English a bit."

Time to get straight to the point. "Ben said you usually book your lessons on the weekends. So how come you didn't book any classes today? Did you have other plans earlier?"

He shook his head. "I had to pick up my car. The bumper had been damaged. I saw your colleague there, Adrian."

"Adrian?" A moment to register. "Oh, Ade. Right. What time was that about?"

"Must have been one-ish."

One-ish. Naoki fell quiet as he ate his food. I tucked into my own dish, thinking of the time. One was when I had been at Voyce. So that meant the knicker-thief couldn't have been Naoki. He even had an alibi – Ade had seen him. Relief washed over me, a welcome warm rush of blood breathing life back into my body. I didn't know Naoki well, but at least he wasn't a creepy pervert.

"I'm glad to have this chance to talk, by ourselves. I was a bit worried about you the last time we met, at that party at your apartment," said Naoki.

All the blood that moments before had warmed my body drained; thoughts of that night, night of the typhoon, the worst typhoon of my life, replaced warmth with icy dread. "Oh yeah? How so? What made you so worried about me?"

"You were quite drunk, so I was a little concerned. You remember, I slept in my car that night as I drank a lot too. But sometime in the early hours, I needed to use the bathroom so I came back into your apartment – the door was unlocked, you see."

I stopped eating and stared at the side of Naoki's face as he spoke.

"Well, your bedroom door was lying open and you were spread out, only wearing your underwear. I pulled your door closed, to cover you up. But the only person awake anyway was Vince."

"Vince? Where was he?"

"In your living room. He was fiddling about with the radio and dancing by himself, clicking his fingers along in time to a song. Such a weird guy." Naoki gave another guffaw.

I didn't laugh. There was nothing funny about the new information that Naoki gave me. If Vince was playing with the radio and happily dancing, then that meant he hadn't been very drunk. If he hadn't been very drunk, then that meant he was in control of his actions. If he had been in control of his actions, then that meant he had chosen to have sex with an unconscious, vulnerable woman – me – put her underwear back on her afterwards, and leave her exposed in her wide, open bedroom.

"I hope you don't take this the wrong way, Kim, but take care."

I forced the corners of my mouth upwards. "I don't take it the wrong way, Naoki. Thanks for looking out for me."

We ate the rest of our meal and the rest of our conversation was trivial small-talk that washed over me; the dialogue between us had stopped at Vince dancing in my living room. Vince happily gloating to himself over what he had done. After our dinner had finished, Naoki tried to pay, but I had insisted on us sharing the bill. This was a friendly catch-up, not a romantic date.

We walked outside into the warm, early August evening. Tottori was buzzing with people about to begin their weekend night out; Neon snack bar signs lit up, groups of friends and couples in and out of restaurants and bars. Yet all I wanted to do was go home and curl up on the sofa with comfort food and a DVD alone.

"Thanks for a lovely dinner," said Naoki.

"You too." I leaned forward and hugged him, a platonic hug, no different than how I hugged Ronnie and Aaron back home.

"Do you want to go somewhere else for a drink? I can't have much, as I'm driving, but we could stop somewhere for a quick one?"

I shook my head. "If you don't mind, I think I'd like to head home. I'd like to walk. It's a lovely evening."

Naoki reeled. "Are you sure I can't give you a lift?"

"Thanks, but I think walking will help me to clear my head of a few things."

He seemed to hesitate for a moment, teetering on the balls of his feet, before leaning towards me. Naoki was taller than me, so he bent down, slowly enough to give me time to respond. I knew what he wanted and lifted my chin so my lips met his. It was a soft, sweet kiss, but more than a peck. Naoki really was quite the gentleman.

"Can I see you again?" he said.

"Sure. I'll give you a call. We'll make a date."

Naoki walked away and turned the corner towards his car with a spring in his step. He waved back to me and I saw that he beamed. I stood there on the pavement watching him go. The wind whipped my hair. Party-goers passed me by. I felt nothing.

32

附

Night travails

It was a good decision to walk home. I weaved a path by the Fukuro river for as long as I could, taking backstreets among the wooden houses. A dragonfly skittered by, as large as my palm. Nobody was about, except me and a few *hotaru*, fireflies, which were still hanging around even in early August, darting around bushes, illuminating the darkness six weeks after their main glory season. Tomomi had taken Jei Pi, Zoe and I to view the hotaro in Kyushu park in June and it had been magical, like walking under tiny stars among the trees, though now it was a sad memory. Tomomi and I would probably never be friends again; even worse, our friendship had been damaged by a sleazebag who wasn't worth the heartache.

I turned away from the river onto a main road and walked past a supermarket before a grey van whizzed around the corner of the otherwise deserted road. It slowed as it approached me and pulled up at the next lamppost, mounting the pavement at an awkward angle with the front tyre on the footpath, so that as I caught up to it, I had to veer inwards. The passenger door opened and a man stepped out.

"Hello. Is-you-want-ride-some-place?" he said, in stilted, but comprehensible English.

He was young, no older than early thirties, and wore a black t-shirt and jeans. His hair hung to his jaw and was tucked behind his ears and in the lamppost light, I could make out a stubbly goatee. He didn't look threatening in any way, though the request was odd.

I stopped in front of the van and turned to face him. "No thank you. I'm nearly home."

I walked on. The man got back into his van and it drove on down the street, then turned at the end and disappeared.

At the end of the street, I turned left onto a small bridge. The bridge wasn't familiar. Looking right, I could see the outline of Kyushu mountain, which helped orientate me as it meant Tottori town centre was behind me; it gave me some relief to know I was going vaguely in the right direction.

Out of nowhere, the grey van shot out of a side street and mounted the footpath, causing me to jump back. Unlike before where it had mounted the kerb at an angle, this time it blocked the entire footpath.

The man in the passenger seat didn't get out this time, but he rolled down the window and hung out of it. "You-is walking-long-ways. You-can-get-in-and-we-give-you-ride."

I put both my hands up. "I said no thank you."

The van pulled back and took off, though I noticed the lights weren't on. It took off ahead and as before, disappeared at the end of the street. Was it simply driving ahead, only to lay in wait and ambush me?

I crossed the road, about to cut through an alleyway, but thought twice. Alleyways were where strangers attacked lone women. Got to stick to the main route, even if that meant the van could have easier access to follow me.

At the next turnoff, I was relieved to see over the rooftops the giant bowling pin that was near my district of Akisato. That meant the main dual carriageway was ahead, and if I followed that along it would take me to the Lawson convenience store, which was round the corner from my flat.

The grey van was waiting for me ahead.

It must have been my fight or flight instinct, but the moment I saw it I turned and ran in the opposite direction. How did the driver anticipate that I would try to head towards the dual carriageway? I didn't want to run towards the dark, residential cluster the way my legs were taking me, but what choice did I have?

Screeching tyres sounded behind me. The van must have done a U-turn in the road. As I ran, the driver tooted the horn in a taunting series of pips. My tormentor in the passenger side hung out, rapping his hand on the metal door.

"Woo-eee!" He smacked his lips together, making kissing sounds. "Woo-eee-baby!"

I kept running. "Fuck off! Just fuck off and leave me alone! I'm an English teacher, okay? I'm not a hostess, or a whore. I'm from England, I'll go to the British embassy and report you!"

Without thinking, I changed direction and darted back the way I came towards the dual carriageway. My chest was on fire and my legs throbbed, but I didn't stop running until I saw the bright lights of the main drag. Sure that the van wasn't following me at that moment, I fished my phone out of my pocket. Naoki had been the last number dialled. I clicked to call him. No answer, through to his voicemail. Shit.

"Naoki? If you get this, please pick up. There are some men after me, they're in vans. Please come and get me. I'm just past the Star Bowl, going towards Akisato Lawson. Please come and get me."

Horrible thoughts filled me. Would I die tonight, after being raped in the back of that sordid grey van? Would my body be dumped in the mountains, left to be eaten by bears? Should I phone Mum and leave a message that I loved her and Dad? What about my younger brother, Zac? He would think I was histrionic and my parents would panic. I didn't want to frighten them unnecessarily.

Every car that drew level with me on the dual carriageway made me flinch. I braced myself for the aggressive tooting of a horn, or catcalling, or to have the grey van skid up in front of me. The closer I got to Akisato, the more I relaxed. By the time I rounded the corner behind Lawson towards my flat, the taut muscles in my neck had loosened and my heart rate had slowed.

As I was climbing the steps to my front door at Villa Libido, the grey van rolled around the corner with its lights still off and pulled up in the parking space in front of the duplex.

"Oh my gosh, please fuck off and leave me alone!" My feet flew up the remaining stairs. Luckily I was well practised at opening the lock and it opened without effort. I slammed the door, locked it and barricaded it with Jei Pi's shoe rack in the entranceway. Into my bedroom in the dark; no lights on, better for spying and to give me cover to hide. I peered through the bamboo blinds without disturbing them. The objective was to see what the man in the black t-shirt was up to, not to let him see me. All I could see was the rear of the van.

A rustling sound at my door. "Woo-eee. Hah-low baby. Let me in."

My heart hammered as I crept across my bedroom to peer. The rustling sound was obvious now; a folded slip of paper had been pushed under the door. Now, more than ever was the time to be Zen. I was a statue; not living or breathing, not moving.

Retreating footsteps, thunking on the metal steps. Thud, thud thud. The van door slamming, engine starting. Back to my window. The van disappeared towards the rice paddies further along the street.

Safe for now, I switched the hallway light on and picked up the note. A phone number had been scribbled and three words: I love you. The spidery black letters slanted towards the upper left; signs of a psychopath. Not definitive, but it fit the bill for me, tonight. What kind of creep stalked a lone woman home and harassed her in her own flat?

My phone buzzed in my pocket. Picking it up, I saw the lit screen showed Naoki's name and number.

"Kim? I got your message. Are you okay?"

I gulped air. "Yes, I'm home now Naoki. Where are you?"

"I'm on my way, I'm just past the Star Bowl. I'll be there in about three minutes."

"Oh, thank goodness. I have the door locked. Would you call me when you're outside, I don't want to open it to anyone but you."

A pause on the receiver. "What happened?"

"I'll tell you when you get here."

Three minutes felt an eternity. I stood in the entranceway, clutching my phone. I hated feeling that way, a damsel in distress, in need of a knight to save her. I had only recently discovered the real me buried beneath the ashes of Manny; pure and whole, bright shiny new Kimberly, and now I stood, a shivering wreck in need of a man to come and save her again. There was still much progress to be made on my journey of self-discovery; vulnerability had attracted the grey van to me, sharks to blood, and I would toughen up, take back control of my life.

My phone rang: Naoki.

Door unlocked, a quick glance behind him as he entered; no grey van, permission to relax. Now that Naoki was with me, I put Jei Pi's shoe rack back in its spot.

"Your message said there were men after you?" said Naoki.

I told him everything: the man with black t-shirt and goatee, what he had said, the grey van; all of it — even my stolen underwear. Naoki's expression was neutral as he listened. His brow furrowed briefly as he read the note slipped under my door.

"He was probably the same man who stole your pants," said Naoki.

"I'm guessing so, after everything. Are you able to stay here tonight?"

Naoki's eyebrows shot upwards and his face turned beetroot.

"Sorry — I didn't mean that to sound presumptuous. It's just, I don't feel safe here alone tonight and Jei Pi is staying at her friend Yuri's."

Naoki's eyebrows and lips became a straight line as his stoic expression returned. I would have laughed, had the matter not been so serious.

"Yes, of course Kim. I'm happy to help if you need me."

Naoki helped me drag my futon, blanket and pillow into the living room. I brought my spare blanket and pillow out and set them on the sofa for Naoki. As we both settled down for the night, I became aware of the noisy hum of the air conditioning unit, though was grateful for the white noise. My pulsating thoughts were surely louder than gunfire. No, maybe a tad melodramatic; though my breathing likely gave away the fact that I wasn't sleeping. Naoki's breathing was shallow and quiet; seemed he too lay awake. What a day it had been. I rewound my thoughts to the moment when I had waited for Naoki, phone in hand by the front door. I wasn't a damsel in distress; it wasn't weakness to ask for help when you needed it. Quite the contrary, it was strength.

33

☙

Osaka

The bar was packed. It wasn't a bar either. Not sure why I thought it would be a quieter venue; or at least, somewhere you could hear each other talk. Not an *unreasonable* assumption, since this was where Vince had told me to meet for our first catch-up since the night of the typhoon. I had thought it would be an izakaya, or at worst, a lively sports bar. But the venue we found ourselves elbowing our way through was a hybrid nightclub-bar and a definite cattle-market.

Zoe didn't look impressed, and it was obvious why. The wide dance floor was packed, though not with people dancing. All eyes were turned towards the bar. The majority of customers were young gaijin men in their twenties. At the end of the busy bar, where the counter rounded to meet the wall, a metal pole was fixed. A young, blonde-haired punter was invited by the bar staff to climb up on the counter; two of her male friends helped push her up. She was clearly drunk and after two whirls around the pole, almost fell off the bar, then proceeded to rub herself up and down the pole while the crowd of men whooped and cheered and her friends laughed, mortified. The girl gave a dramatic bow, and clambered down off the bar looking rather red-faced.

"Vince said he'd meet you *here*? At this place?" Zoe wrinkled her nose, her eyes on the girl who was now being patted on the back by her friends.

"Yeah, but he didn't tell me what sort of bar it was," I said.

"It's a strip club," said Zoe, flatly.

"Not quite. But it *is* kind of sleazy." There were no professional dancers. The girls who got up to strut their stuff around the pole were drunken punters from the crowd.

"Do you listen to yourself? You're making excuses for him." She shook her head, her demeanour as angry teacher scolding a pupil. "I told you it wasn't a good idea coming to meet him. You came all the way to Osaka to meet up with him, and look what he does? He disrespects you again."

"I didn't come to Osaka for Vince, I'm not that much of an idiot!" As affronted as I was, it wasn't worth arguing with Zoe over Vince; I'd already lost Tomomi, no point alienating another friend. I had to bite my tongue; she was wrong. Coming to Osaka was more a means of escape from the black t-shirt pervert in grey van, and a chance to clear my head.

We had no time to argue further in any event, as I spotted Vince across the room. He was talking to a beautiful, leggy brunette at the bar, her beautiful leggy friend mingling with his friend. He turned and saw me, and his concentration on her dissipated into the ether as smoke in air; he made a beeline for me, abandoning her to the next hopeful waiting for her attention at the bar.

Vince pulled his arms wide and when he reached me, pulled me into a bear hug. "How's tricks?"

My hands reached up from under his and patted his back. "Fine. Good. Who's the girl?"

The small talk rolled out of my mouth as though I was reading it off a teleprompter. We were here to patch things up, and for me to tell him about the consequences of his non-consensual tryst and here he was chatting up another girl proving how sleazy he was. Not only that but he was acting as though we were the best of friends and that nothing untoward had ever happened between us, never mind the 'r' word.

"She's a Brazilian model. Thought it was a chance to practise my Portuguese."

As if any man would be in such a cattle market to practise his Portuguese. I gave him my best 'I wasn't born yesterday' look and turned to look for Zoe. She was busy chatting to a Japanese man at the bar; both had their phones out.

"Let me grab you a drink. Screwdriver?" said Vince.

My hand jumped to my stomach, though he didn't notice. "Sparkling water, thanks."

Vince blanched. "Not like you to lay off the booze. What's up?"

I shrugged. "Dry August. Bit of a detox, really."

A nine month detox. We got our drinks and made our way to seats at the far side by the toilets. An awkward silence fell. I was wrangling sentence starters in my head, trying to think of the best way to broach the massive gulf between us, when Vince got there first.

"So, about that night." He scratched his head then leaned back in his seat, stretching his arm along the backrest. Trying to feign nonchalance; good. I was happy he was squirming. "Yo, what's Jei Pi's deal, man? She went rough on me."

I bit my tongue from saying 'I bet she did, and good on her'. I needed to hear what he had to say. "Jei Pi wanted you to know how serious it was."

He cast a sheepish glance at me, his head lowered. "Listen Kim, it was a dick move on my part, it wasn't meant to be that way."

I had been watching my drink as he spoke, the tension simmering between us, but the audacity of his puerile pun made me fix him with a piercing glare. Or at least, what I hoped looked like a defiant stare. "You *are* joking, right?"

His expression remained stoic as he watched me. My question hung in the air unanswered. As the seconds ticked by, Vince broke into a goofy grin, crinkling his face. I wanted to punch him, throttle him, pummel his stupid face. But my body remained frozen as he laughed.

"Come on, Kim. I mean, you know me. We're buds." He fist-bumped my clenched fist. "Do you really want me to spell it out?"

"Yes, I do actually. Frankly I think you should after what you did."

He tried to compose himself, but a hint of smile lingered at the edges of his mouth. "Aw-right then, I'm sorry. There, I said it. I'm sorry."

As if that would exonerate him; the remnants of a smile negated his apology and I was sure he knew it. It seemed the whole reason he had said it twice was because he knew it was insincere.

"You injured me, do you know that? I was cut on the outside and inside too. I had to take anti-coagulants because of the damage you did."

Vince tried to look blasé, but couldn't hide his smile. "Girls have said that's happened, you know, size and all."

What an arrogant prick. Here I was, struggling to tell him the literal and metaphorical painful details of how he had ravaged me, and he took it as an opportunity to brag about not only how big he was, but how many conquests he'd had.

I stood up. "I'm not sure why I bothered coming, Zoe was right. This was a waste of time. Men like you don't care — all you think about is what you can get from others. I suppose to you I was another notch on your bedpost. Is that how you get women — you take them when they're unconscious? Is that because the women you like wouldn't give you a second glance when they're sober so you have to take advantage of them when they're pissed out of their heads?"

Vince's face fell. Without his cocky smile, his face looked bland and punchable. "Aw-right, I admit I was a jerk. I was trying to overcompensate. The truth is, you intimidate me."

I sat down again, hard on my seat. "What's that supposed to mean?"

"You always seem so confident, all those times when you were out with Jei Pi and the others, dancing at Club Passion. Men found it hard to approach you, although they wanted to. And you have the hottest body I've seen in real life. I never thought a woman like you would take a second glance at someone like me."

There was a candour to his voice that caught my attention; as much as I wanted to dismiss his words as another ploy to manipulate, his frank manner resonated. That, together with the fact that he had both palms flat on the table, like a suspect coming clean at a police grilling, made me think he was genuine.

"So you waited until I was drunk to make your move?"

He shrugged. "Like I said, it wasn't meant to be that way. I'm not that sort of dude."

My tongue almost tripped on the words I wanted to say: *what, the type who rapes women?* But maybe Vince had suffered enough. Not as much as I had, but enough. I swallowed the words, and my pride, and necked the rest of my sparkling water. "Drink up Vince, let's dance."

I dragged him up onto the dance floor by his hand. He bumbled along behind me, ape-like through the mostly male crowd. I spun on the dance floor, creating a force-field around me; outside my protective sphere, all the men watched me. I pulled Vince into my circle and let him whirl me around. As we danced, I visualised the trauma of typhoon night dissipating into the ether, all the visceral hurt between us vanishing into a ephemeral void. This was good; we were healing the hurt between us. Vince put his hands on my waist and slid them forward, placing them on my stomach. The touch reminded me of what I still had to tell him; though the time wasn't quite right. We had made progress in righting the wrong, but not enough to tell him just yet.

A tap on my back. Zoe. "Kimberly, what the hell are you doing?"

I stopped dancing and spun to face her. "I'm just trying to lighten the mood, it doesn't kill."

The barman cut our chat short as his strong Aussie accent boomed over the microphone. "Okay ladies, who's game for a whirl round the pole next?"

A brunette in a long, denim skirt and red shirt climbed up onto the bar. As she walked, slow and sultry around the pole, she started to unbutton her red shirt with one hand, until only one button remained holding the shirt in place over her breasts. Vince watched her with longing; his tongue might as well have been hanging out of his mouth. Leaning against the pole, she squatted down, her knees splayed wide so that from where I stood, I got a full view of her pink granny knickers. Not sexy, or sultry.

The girl climbed down to applause.

"What are we even doing in this smut bar?" said Zoe, her eyebrows pulled into one, taut line. Zoe pulled me away from Vince. "Come on Kim, we need to talk."

Once we reached the back of the bar, Zoe put her hand in the small of my back and pushed me through the doors towards the toilets.

"Hey, watch it," I said. The door closed behind us, shutting out the loud music from the bar and I heard my ears ringing. I turned to face Zoe and saw her angry, red face.

"Why the hell would you dance with Vince, in this place of all, Kim? You're making a complete ass of yourself." She flung her arms wide in her anger.

"Says who? What's it to you anyway, you're not my mum?"

Zoe grabbed my shoulders and shoved me against the wall. My back hit the hard plaster, knocking the wind out of my chest.

"Oh my gosh, what's your problem?" I gasped.

"You are. What are you doing, flirting with Vince? After all he did and you couldn't keep your hands off each other on the dance floor."

I shook my head. "We were just dancing."

She shoved me again, her face purple. "Get a grip on yourself. Are you drunk?"

I brushed her hands off my shoulders. "Stop pushing me. Of course I'm not drunk, I've been drinking sparkling water."

"I don't know what the fuck your problem is, Kim? I really don't understand you. Jei Pi had to go and talk to that monster for you and I had to take you to the hospital because of what he did to your body. You aren't even friends with Tomomi anymore over this and now, you want Vince to be your boyfriend?"

"You're reading things all wrong," I gasped. "I don't want a relationship with Vince other than friends. I'm trying to make something good out of a bad thing – it's the only way I can forgive him and let go."

"Well it doesn't seem that way to me." Zoe huffed. Her face was contorted, full of hurt.

"I can't understand why that makes you so angry." Tears flowed, uninhibited. "I need healing, don't you understand? But I don't want to lose you too, like Tomomi. You're my best friend Zoe, don't be like that."

I wept, my body heaving with sobs. Zoe breathed heavily. I waited until her breathing steadied.

"There's something else that I haven't told you. I guess maybe I was in denial myself," I said. My hands slid to my stomach and criss-crossed over it. "I haven't told Vince yet, I don't know how to say it."

"Oh my God, Kim." Zoe's hands flew to her face. "You're not, are you? How can you be sure?"

"Because it's nearly three weeks late and I've done two tests."

Vince's voice cut our conversation short. "When were you going to tell me?"

I jumped; I hadn't even noticed him eavesdropping; it was as if he had materialised several feet behind from Zoe.

"I was going to tell you, sort of, at some point tonight." I tucked my hair behind my ears, then pulled it loose to cover my burning cheeks. "I was building up to it, I dunno, it's hard."

"How do you know it's mine?"

My jaw dropped; I had to consciously shut it. My head struggled to allow his acrid words to permeate my brain.

"Can I hit him or will you?" Zoe turned away from me and rounded on Vince, her eyes bulging. "That is wrong on so many levels. You rape her – you violate her and now you imply she's sleeping around? Fuck off Vince."

"I can't believe you said that to me. I'm going to pretend I didn't hear that." I stopped talking as my voice started to crack.

He put his hands up, defensively. "It's not what I meant. Your boyfriend left not so long ago, maybe it's his. I'm just saying, that's all."

I couldn't speak. Maybe there were no words for such a moment. Maybe that was the epitome of Zen; to strip consciousness to its bare essentials. It didn't matter anyway. What did matter? To know that there was no salvaging my non-existent friendship with

Vince? There was no response to his comment as it was clear his mind had already been made up.

Vince stood partially blocking the door back into the main bar. I could have walked past him, side-stepped him and walked on by, left him behind as detritus from my past life. But I couldn't. Instead I strode right towards Vince, looked him in the eye, and brought my right fist up to hit him with a clean jab in his nose. His eyes flickered shut, the impact of my fist registering on his shocked face before the blood spurted out of his left nostril. He caught my fist only too late. I followed my jab with a left cross, striking him again in his nose. Blood spurted over his mouth.

Vince pushed me away, his face contorted like a giant, angry toddler. "If you weren't a woman, I'd kill you for that."

"You wouldn't stand a chance, mate," said Zoe, spitting the last word. She followed me out through the swinging door. I marched to the bar, anger propelling me forward. I wanted a drink, badly, but knew I had to resist for the sake of my child. The angry energy surging in my body probably didn't help the baby either. This was as far removed from Zen as I could get; I certainly wouldn't reach Nirvana anytime soon, or maybe in this lifetime at all after my bout of physical aggression, but it didn't matter. Vengeance felt sweet, and the rush of endorphins a pleasure I'd rather savour than torment of my inner soul for an enlightenment that would likely never come.

"Kim, that was fantastic." Zoe swooped down on me, enveloping me in a sweaty hug. "I never knew you had it in you. Where did you learn to do that?"

"I took a women's self-defence course when I was at Uni," I said, rubbing my stinging knuckles. "Never thought it would come in handy. It didn't help me that night he took advantage of me, cause I was drunk, but it made up for it now."

Zoe's smile fell as she glowered over my shoulder. I knew what that meant before I even turned; Vince was behind me, dabbing his bloodied nose with a tissue.

"Look, can we talk. I meant what I said – it wasn't how I wanted things to go. I'm not angry–" he said.

"*You're* not angry? Hmph, that's rich." I cold-shouldered him, turning back to Zoe.

"Can we go somewhere quieter to talk? Somewhere more chill. I want to straighten things out between us, aww-right? Listen, give me a chance."

I turned to face him; needed to see his expression. He looked earnest, no trace of his normal smug smile anywhere. None in the faint worry lines on his forehead, none hidden among the laughter line creases on either side of his mouth.

"I don't live so far away from here. What do you say we go back to my flat for a proper catch-up, away from the noise?"

I hesitated, formulating a response. "So you can take advantage of me again? I wasn't born yesterday, Vince."

He put his hands up. "No funny business, promise. Yo, you can bring Zoe if you don't trust me."

Zoe, behind me, made a choking sound; half incredulous guffaw, half derisive snort. "You aren't seriously thinking of going with him, are you?"

"It isn't about me anymore, it's about—" My hands fell to my stomach, caressing the small bulge below my belly button. I swallowed.

Zoe shook her head, her face puce. "You're mad. You're seriously crazy. I'm having no part of this." She threw her hands up as she took a couple of steps backwards. "I feel sorry for that baby, I really do."

With that, she was gone. Gone into the crowd, but too soon to say whether our friendship was over as well. There was nothing else I could do; as much as I wanted to go after her, now was the chance to make things right with Vince, for our unborn child's sake.

My head began nodding, before the words had even escaped my mouth. "Okay Vince, I'll come back to your flat. But no funny business, you swear?"

"You have my word." He grinned, his eyes crinkling. "But if I can be honest here, yeah? You taking a swing at me was pretty damn hot."

34

೦ಾ

Grey expanse

I carried the bottle of shower gel and shampoo
tucked in my armpit and a bath towel draped over my
arm as I ascended the steps to the roof of the
apartment building. The communal shower on the
rooftop was coin operated. My lip seemed to have
fashioned itself into a disgusted sneer all of its own
accord; I consciously relaxed the muscles in my face.
But, in all seriousness, this was no way to live. Maybe
it held appeal for some; the price you had to pay to
live in Osaka. I was grateful for my comparatively
spacious apartment in Tottori.

Tennoji, the district where Vince lived, stretched
before me; a grey expanse of concrete apartment
buildings in the grey dawn. Vince was still asleep.
Thank goodness. I needed time to reassess the
previous night's events.

But for now, a wash. I popped several 500yen
coins into the machine. Better too much money than
not enough. I needed a long, hot scrub to wash away
more than bodily fluids. The shampoo was strawberry
scented and packaged in pink. There was no way such
a feminine product belonged to Vince. Yet, why did
he have it in his flat? Yes, I most positively needed a
good scrub.

As I washed, my mind replayed the last twelve
hours like a cinema reel. Vince and I had taken a night
bus to his flat. We had talked long into the early

hours, on the busted sofa in his living room. The frayed Peruvian-patterned woollen throw from his flatmate had provided a welcome ice-breaker, making both of us erupt in laughter, and from there the conversation had flowed. He had offered to call me a taxi back to my hotel, but I didn't want to enrage Zoe any further, and had asked to sleep on the now-held-in-affectionate-esteem busted sofa in Vince's living room.

And then.

But then.

At some point during the night, Vince had come out of his room dragging his duvet and joined me on the sofa. We had snuggled, platonically – at first. With the warmth from his body, bravely cloaked by the darkness of night, and goaded by the incessant ticking of the living room clock, we had become intimate. First kissing, then more.

Ugh, what a mess. Zoe was right; what the hell was I doing? Friends with benefits for the benefit of my baby? No way, no excuse. I scrubbed my hair, digging my nails into my scalp. I hated myself then, hated myself in such a deeply psychological and metaphysical sense that no amount of water or scrubbing would ever make me pure again.

But still, I scrubbed. I raked my nails down my body, scouring every inch of skin until I was foetal pink. Why did I sleep with Vince? Why did I leave myself no choice but to go back downstairs and face the music in his flat?

Each step thundered underfoot as though echoing taunts of doom at me. I hung my head as I walked back inside Vince's flat. There was no sound; my heart danced and my head whirled. Could I sneak out of his flat while he was still asleep and disappear from his life forever? Yes, potentially, though I would never escape my conscience; our baby would always be a reminder of how I had failed us.

The living room was empty. The silence bought me a few more seconds, minutes, hours to process my guilt. Maybe I was suffering from Stockholm syndrome, sleeping with the enemy. Vince wasn't my type. On top of that, he was a deviant, a bully. A rapist. No matter what excuse he made, he had still taken away my dignity while I had been inebriated during the night of the typhoon, and had enjoyed the pain he caused, dancing to the radio after the sordid fact, in celebration.

A creak of a chair in the kitchen. My breath caught in my chest. Please be Vince's flatmate, not Vince. An urge to dump the towel, shampoo and shower gel on the sofa and scurry away overcame me but I fought back; face the music, not flee.

The kitchen door opened and Vince appeared, holding a bowl of cereal. "Wondered where you'd gone to. How's tricks?"

Ugh, how I hated his catchphrase; not only did he overuse it, but there was an element of smugness to the way he said it, like, *I don't actually care how you are, but I'm trying to be cool.*

I cocked my head, intentionally dismissive. "Just had a shower. Nice shampoo. Fruity."

Vince grabbed it from me and tossed it onto the kitchen table. "It was here when I moved in."

Yeah right, Vince, keep telling that to yourself. Aware I was smirking, I sobered my face. Not a time for nagging, or war; such things would only flood my body with cortisol and I didn't want to stress the baby.

"Are you hanging out for a bit or taking off?" Vince spooned more cereal into his mouth, but he slopped milk over his t-shirt and the puppy dog eyes peering over the bowl didn't escape me. Feigning nonchalance, but he was awkward. I was awkward. God, this was so tense.

"Hanging out I guess. If I head over to my hotel this early, Zoe will kill me." The kitchen chair scraped, much too loud as I pulled it back. Kind of summed up my feelings for Vince: one long, shrill noise.

He thudded onto the adjacent chair. "I'm glad you stayed. I'm glad we had a chance to do things properly."

My eyes skidded upwards and locked onto his, but I couldn't vocalise what I wanted to say. Was he genuine? It didn't matter anyway; the sentiment counted. I felt more warmly towards him, dare I say it, even more attracted to him. He wasn't physically handsome, not my type, but showing compassion helped him seem less detrimental. Especially if we were to co-parent our child.

Out of the blue, Vince leaned forward and kissed me. The taste of sugary cornflakes was fresh on his lips. It reminded me of the first time he had imposed a kiss on me, in my bedroom, when my mouth had been full of fish and rice. Guess that was the gist of our association; all of our dalliances tainted by imposition.

Like a lightbulb switching on, everything became clear. Was that the thread attracting an otherwise unattractive man to me? Imposition, control, possessiveness. He reminded me of Carl.

That wasn't a good thing. All this time, throughout the journey of self-exploration that I had been on, had I not learned a thing? When I had broken up with Carl, I thought I had shed that old part of myself that had been dominated by a dysfunctional romantic partner. Yet here I sat, facing Vince, another man that I didn't really like and who acted in an abusive, controlling way towards me.

True, but not entirely accurate. What was different this time? My eyes were on Vince, but I wasn't really seeing him. The difference was in the new self-awareness that had enlightened me during my ten months in Japan. Throughout the seven years with Carl, I had not ever analysed the toxic nature of our dysfunctional relationship. Understanding the limitations of the type of man who attracted me; namely possessive, controlling creeps, was the first step in changing the pattern of relationships I would attract going forward. The grey expanse of my previous romantic relationships would forever be relegated to the past.

"Did you really mean what you said last night – that you're knocked up?"

I screwed up my face. "Not keen on it being put that way, but yes, I'm expecting."

Vince blinked at me several times; an image of cogs turning in his head popped into my mind. "You're not keeping it though, right?"

A response spouted out of my mouth, quicker than my brain could filter it. "And what if I am?"

"Well." Vince scratched behind his ear. "All I'm saying, right, is that if it's mine – if it's mine and you want to keep it, and I don't then-"

"Then what?"

"Then," he raised his eyebrows, raised his palms in defeat. "It's just, we could have fun if it wasn't for that. But something like that would get in the way, and you know, it could be got rid of easily, if it's early enough, you get me?"

"I get you." I stood up. I felt sick to the pit of my stomach. I wasn't against abortion; each woman had her own circumstances, but it was my body and my choice to go ahead with my pregnancy. Not Vince's choice, mine. I'd made a colossal mistake; for crying out loud, I'd made many mistakes, but there was no doubt in my mind anymore about Vince. Nothing good would come from staying in touch. Nothing redeemable about him, or our connection. No future for us. "If you were so sure you didn't want a baby, then maybe you shouldn't have put one in me. I'd better go and see what's up with Zoe. I'll catch you later Vince."

"Yeah." He jerked his head as if to say, *I understand.* "If you change your mind, call me. I'm in Japan for another three weeks."

I managed a taut-lipped smile. "Okay Vince. Well, see you."

35

☙

Water child

"This is going to feel cold."

Zoe's words felt cold indeed, as she focused more on translating the sonographer's instructions than on adding the necessary emotional response. It didn't matter. She was with me, and that meant the world. Especially after what had happened in Osaka; I'd been honest with her about sleeping with Vince, and she was disgusted, though she admitted that I wouldn't have been able to come back to our hotel room in any event. She had spent the night with a Japanese man, Takeshi, who she had picked up in the bar and he'd stayed in our hotel room. I hadn't asked for my share of the hotel money back and Zoe hadn't offered. It was our unspoken agreement to repair our friendship.

The sonographer spread the clear jelly on my stomach and asked me a question, gesturing to my groin.

"He wants to check that you didn't take a piss. You need to have a full bladder," said Zoe.

I nodded. "Hai, toire ni ikanakatta." Was that the right answer? Yes, I didn't go to the toilet... No, I didn't go to the toilet... What would I have answered in English? My brain was confused. I couldn't think straight.

The sonographer held a plastic probe, that somewhat resembled a microphone, in his hand. He pressed it against my stomach. The sensation made me really need to relieve my full bladder. Hopefully the scan would be quick.

"He's going to check for the heartbeat first."

I watched the screen as he moved the probe around. The grainy grey screen was punctuated by a series of black blobs. Or was it the other way round; black blobs on grey? Yes, I didn't go to the toilet, no, I didn't go to the toilet, black on grey, grey on black, yin and yang. Two sides of the same coin. Wasn't that the whole problem in the first place? Two halves, me and Carl, Carl and me, that peeled apart and didn't know what to do once the other had gone. Carl and I, like Siamese twins. Twins? Hopefully not. The thought jolted me back to reality; I was about to see my baby on the screen for the first time.

Any minute now.

A grey kidney bean-shaped blob appeared on the screen to the left side of a black circle.

"There's the head and that's the body. You can see the arm there."

Zoe talked as the sonographer gestured towards the screen. He pressed harder on my tummy. I clenched my toes, fighting the urge to urinate.

"He's still looking for the heartbeat. It could be the position of the foetus as it's still very small and it's leaning towards your back."

Foetus. That was it on the screen, my baby. Our baby; the child a monster had put inside me. It had a human-shaped head and resembled a miniature person, with arms and legs, but it had been spawned by a cold, calculating sociopath.

The sonographer lifted the probe off my stomach and went to the computer beside the screen. He began typing.

"Well? Did he find the heartbeat? Is everything okay?" I raised myself up onto my elbows. Zoe translated my questions into Japanese.

She hung her head and nodded as he spoke. She turned to me to translate, but I already knew.

"I'm so sorry, Kim. There's no heartbeat. The foetus is four and a half centimetres long. He said he's not a doctor, but it looks likely it stopped growing about a week ago. It will probably come out of you over the next few days."

I looked back to the screen, hoping for answers, hoping to see the outline of the baby that hadn't been planned, but that I had come to accept all the same, except the image on screen had gone.

"He'll give you a photo of it," she said.

"Don't say 'it'. That was a person, a little boy or girl." My eyes prickled. I looked upwards, fighting the urge to cry. My hands cupped the gentle curve of my stomach. It had only been twelve weeks; I didn't yet have a bump, but my normally flat stomach had developed a small bulge as I had put on weight.

"If it – sorry, if the baby doesn't come out of you within the next three days, you need to come back. The doctor will give you medicine to help your body remove it."

"You mean an abortion." My voice sounded cold, the words assaulting my own ears as I spoke. "I don't want to abort my own child, I won't abort my baby."

"Kim, the foetus is already dead. If it doesn't come out, it could lead to an infection," said Zoe. She put her warm hand on top of mine. I didn't move; I wanted to die myself. A part of me had already died, the rest could follow.

Four centimetres, what was that anyway? About the size from the tip of my pinky finger to the knuckle. I held my pinky finger up to inspect. This wasn't a microscopic ball of cells. This was a person, a little life that had grown within me.

Guilt swamped me; it was my fault. The baby had heard my internal thoughts floating through my body like poison, saying that it was the spawn of a monster, that his or her dad was a sociopath. The baby must have heard those words and died of a broken heart.

Huge sobs heaved their way out of my body. I buried my face in my hands and cried. Zoe's warm hand massaged my back, rubbing small circles. I wanted to swipe her away; she would disturb my baby inside there, make him or her swish two and fro in the dark bliss of my amniotic fluid. That brought another thought to mind: knocks and bumps. Had I been careful enough? What if I had sat down on a seat too hard and killed my child? Or had I eaten the wrong food? What about that delicious salmon sashimi that I'd eaten for lunch the previous week, before remembering that raw fish was a pregnancy no-no? What if I had poisoned my baby to death with mercury? Or killed it with a bacterial infection? What if. So many what ifs.

***

The rows of stone baby figurines all had smiling faces. Some wore bonnets, others knitted hats, all adorned in bright colours. Some held little plastic windmills, others had flowers laid in front of them or bottles of milk. My eyes travelled over each and every one, not missing a single baby. Every figurine was individual and unique, slight variations in either their height, the plumpness of their cheeks or the carved clothing they wore. One caught my eye; slightly smaller than the others in its row and with a peaceful smile below its button nose and closed eyes. This was the most fitting *Mizuyo Kujo* for me, the *Water Baby* that resonated with my sweet, lost child. I laid a pile of stones in front of it. All those poor lost babies stuck in the limbo land of Sai no Kawara, not alive on earth long enough to have built karma to reach enlightenment, fated to stack enough stones to gain enough to cross the mythical Sanzu River into the afterlife. I had to make sure that my own lost child had enough stones so that his or her stay would be as short as possible in Sai no Kawara. As the last stone rolled out of my palm, the length was about the same size as the area from the tip of my index finger to the knuckle; the same size the baby I had lost would have been. I set it down and tenderly stroked it.

***

The Sea of Japan was calm, the sun low on the horizon. Gentle waves lapped over my feet, sea foam clinging to my ankles. I poked my big toe into the wet sand. How did I feel? Serene? Salubrious? No; too far a stretch. My body had been purged of part of my soul, my own flesh and blood torn from within; this was not a health-giving moment. No, not salubrious. But important to stay grounded in the present, appreciating the here and now.

Was that what it meant to be Zen? The doctor had told me to avoid having baths, or swimming for a few weeks to avoid infection. That made sense, I supposed. I waded further into the water, submerging my thighs, but stopped short of it reaching my groin.

Bright jellyfish floated on the gentle crests. The fading light danced off them. I had to make sure not to be stung. Too many jellyfish lately; a gelatinous mass, white and red, with strings of blood. A perfect red kidney bean in the middle. My palm cupped it as if we were still one being, the same body that for a time had breathed together. My tears fell in the ocean, swallowed by the bigger body of water; they belonged together as I belonged to my pearl. I had made that jellyfish. It had floated happily on the crests and troughs within me, been nurtured by me and now it was time to release it to the wide waters of the world.

I lowered my palm into the water and the red and white strings floated around the kidney-bean baby like frills; a Spanish dancer in the sea. As I closed my eyes I felt the sunset warming my eyelids, sensed the sea stroking my legs. I was truly, irrevocably one with the moment, the real essence of Zen as my hand released my Water Child into the sea.

"Be safe, my sweet Water Baby, until we meet again," I said. Overhead, sea birds serenaded me, an affirmation from my little one that he or she was happy, and safe.

36

ᛒ

Amends, not friends

Sweat poured down my back, making my vest top cling to my back. I pushed on further; there was only a scattering of trees left and then blue sky ahead. Climbing above the tree line was important to me, to prove my level of fitness wasn't atrocious. It didn't help that octogenarians in hiking gear streamed past the three of us: Zoe, Jei Pi and I, making it look like the climb to the summit of Mount Daisen was a walk in the park.

"Do you know what Ade told me? He said Vince was hoping he could have seen you again before he left," said Zoe.

In spite of the torturous mini-goal I had set myself, I stopped walking and turned to study Zoe's face as she pulled up beside me. Really studied her; tried to look beyond the hard exterior to her motive beneath. "Why are you telling me this?"

She shrugged. "No reason. Just that he said nobody was there to see Vince off when he left Osaka. None of his students, or his flat mate or any of the other teachers. Kind of served him right. I thought he was a dick."

I burst out laughing. There was something funny about the way Zoe said 'dick'. "Listen, just ignore me. I'm in a juvenile mood. I think not enough oxygen is getting to my brain."

Zoe stared at me, straight-faced. "At least he's gone now, so you won't be tempted to see him anymore."

I knew what she was getting at: Osaka. All frivolity vanished. I shook my head. "There was no temptation, I made a mistake, that's all. You have no idea what it was like. He did what he did, yes, but it wasn't as simple as that – he got me pregnant. Can you imagine what it feels like to think that you're going to have to stay in touch with your rapist for the benefit of your unborn child?"

Silence fell. Jei Pi caught up panting, her entire face and neck red. The tension between the three of us; Zoe, Jei Pi and I, was like static electricity. Deafening silence; unspoken white noise. Maybe I really was lacking oxygen to my brain, to blurt out my demons to the sky in such a manner.

"Well, *actually* I can." Jei Pi sat down heavily on a boulder. "Not rape, but my ex-boyfriend violently beat me one night when he was drunk. I was eight weeks pregnant at the time, unplanned and what he did sealed my decision to have the thing removed." She shrugged, feigning nonchalance, but her shoulders were taut. "So I dumped him and came to Japan. Shit happens, go figure."

Zoe sniffed. "You never told me that before."

"It never came up," Jei Pi retorted. She stretched her arms upwards, sucking air into her chest.

"I suppose I can't talk myself. I never told you what happened to me." Zoe sat down on a tree stump nearby, leaving me to loom, awkwardly, over the pair of them. "It was kind of like what Vince did to you. I was at a party, when I was a student. I was really drunk and went to lie down in one of the bedrooms and this guy started helping me. We were kissing at first, but then I tried to stop and he held me down. I didn't know what to do afterwards, so we met to try and talk it over and I started seeing the guy." She chewed her lip, her eyes downcast. "I guess I wanted to make it into a normal relationship to prove he wasn't a monster. But he was. A leopard never changes its spots."

I wasn't sure what to do; should I walk across and touch her shoulder, or swoop down and hug her? She looked so small as she sat, curled in a ball with her arms wrapped around her legs, hugging them to her chest. Zoe was normally so tough. Here she was so vulnerable for the first time in the ten months I'd known her. "Is that why you were so hard on me about Osaka?"

She nodded. "I thought you were going to start seeing him properly and I didn't want you to go down the road I'd been down."

The Road Not Taken. Robert Frost's poem popped into my head. Didn't help that when I looked back down the trail we'd chosen, I saw that it lay in shadow compared to the golden sunlight flooding the other trail where the experienced Japanese hikers climbed. After the first few lines of Frost's poem rolled through my mind, I cauterised them. This was a time for reflection, not doubt.

I'd heard that the statistics for domestic abuse and sexual assault were high, like one in five, higher still when it involved romantic relationships; but this was different. To know two other women who had been through different, but as equally traumatising experiences as what I'd suffered put a new perspective on things; ripped the rose-tinted glasses right from my face. But I couldn't apologise for making assumptions about them; couldn't apologise for what they'd encountered. Did it make my own experience any better or worse? I chided myself; it wasn't a competition.

"I wouldn't have started seeing Vince properly, don't worry about that. All that crossed my mind when I decided to meet up with him was that the two of us would forever be linked through the child I thought I was going to have. I had to make peace with him — or at the very least, let him know he would soon be a father." I threw my hands wide, at a loss. "All that's moot now though, isn't it?"

Jei Pi jumped to her feet and stretched. "At least you know you're able to have children. It wasn't even a baby yet anyway, it was only a bunch of cells. You can always have another."

The impact of her words hit me; an invisible elephant crushing me. The elephant in the room. Not anymore; the unspoken had been said and couldn't be undone. If I told her my thoughts, what would she say next? Elephants? *At least you won't become elephantine in size now that you're rid of the burden in your stomach.* No, my own words, my own sadistic mind putting words in Jei Pi's mouth. What she'd said had been bad enough. So-called friends, fair-weather friends. A prattling pack of pachyderms playing with me, playing on my emotions.

"It's not as simple as that Jei Pi. I was attached to that child, to me it wasn't a ball of cells, it was a person."

Jei Pi looked at me as if I was insane. "It would've been worse for the kid if it had lived – imagine growing up to know you were the spawn of a monster."

I wiped sweat off my forehead. "Being alive is better than dead. Whatever Vince did wasn't the baby's fault."

Jei Pi squinted at me. "It never would have lived, period. If they die before twelve weeks, it's because of genetic abnormalities."

She was right, but too blunt for comfort. I turned and sped up the mountain, not caring whether my so-called friends were following. But at the top of Mount Daisen, I was trapped; only one place I could go from there and that was down. The other two caught up to me, panting.

"Roomie, listen. If that sounded blunt, then I'm sorry," said Jei Pi, flapping her hands at me.

Such a non-apology. What would she put her foot in next?

"You're young, and you're gorgeous. All I'm saying is, you could have your pick of men. There's plenty of time for you to find a good guy, get married and have kids – when you're older. What about Naoki? He's a nice guy?"

Zoe grinned. "He's too nice, that's the problem. She wants a bad boy. Someone like her ex. Or Vince."

I glared at her. "As if I would want a man who treats me like shit, I'm not that stupid."

"Well, why not Naoki then?" said Jei Pi, her face earnest.

The problem was, what if Zoe was right. She had a point. Naoki was good-looking and kind. He treated me well. We had been on one dinner date and he had been a gentleman. The complete opposite of Carl, or Vince. "He's not really my type."

"What is your type then?" Jei Pi's voice was thick with sarcasm. "Someone who isn't Japanese?"

I gasped. "Are you calling me racist?"

"Hey, I'm just saying what I see, that's all. You seem to only date Western men, and there are so many Japanese hotties here in Tottori."

I shook my head, maybe a bit too vigorously, a tad too defensively. "It's not the right time for me to be seeing anyone. Right now, I just want to get my head straight. What's so wrong with that?"

"Nothing. But tell me what's wrong with Naoki?"

Zoe rolled her eyes. "Aw, lay off her man. If she says she doesn't like him, then why are you pushing her?"

I was curious to know Jei Pi's deal myself. "I've already told you. He's a nice bloke but he isn't my type."

Jei Pi blanched. "What's your problem Roomie? It's not like he raped you."

Zoe's mouth fell wide. I gawped at Jei Pi myself, not sure of what to say.

"I can't believe you said that. You know what I've been through and we all just talked about some pretty heavy stuff back there. I don't know – callous isn't even the right word."

Jei Pi stared at me, her face as grey and rolling as the waves on the Sea of Japan stretching below Mount Daisen, but she didn't try to apologise. She didn't even *look* apologetic. In the ten months that I had lived with her, I realised I didn't know her at all. Since I had come to Japan, and known the true extent of my loneliness, I had looked for a surrogate family on my spiritual journey; like-minded souls with whom to share both passion and pain, people who could grow with me, to learn from each other. Instead I had found emotional fraud from a bunch of vacuous, self-serving players. Carl. Vince. Now Jei Pi.

Knowledge. How I would have given anything to be ignorant. Ignorance was bliss. The more knowledge I had about people, the less I realised I knew about them. But I had certainly learned more about myself and my boundaries.

Down the mountain I went, gathering speed until I was running. Loose stones rolled underfoot. They made me slide this way, that way, out of control. But it wasn't me out of control; they only made me *feel* like I was.

How strange that running down a mountain in Japan could teach me a moral lesson. Japan had a way of doing that; making every experience a didactic one. Carl, Vince and Jei Pi had no control over my life; I was the one in control. I wouldn't let them govern my feelings. For whatever remained of my journey, the rest would be about me.

37

CB

Loose ends

I swung my suit jacket over my shirt and slipped my arms into each sleeve. The jacket felt oppressive; after my first couple of weeks working at Voyce in Tottori, I had soon learned that the dress code at the rural school was smart casual. Blouses sufficed as long as they covered the shoulders, but suits weren't necessary. But for this lesson, it was essential. I had been selected for a Demo lesson, a sales session to a potential new student.

Tomomi was at reception. My shoulders tensed reflexively as I approached her. We hadn't spoken, other than polite greetings, in three months. Now I needed to talk to her to find out more information about the potential student.

"Ahem." I waited until Tomomi twitched her head a fraction. She didn't turn around, but at least it was an acknowledgement. "Do you have the student's file ready?"

Tomomi spun on her swivel chair. "Erm, Kimberly. How do I say this?"

At first I thought Tomomi was struggling to find the right words, with English being her second language. Her mannerisms soon gave away the game; she couldn't look me in the eye, instead resting her gaze downwards on the student file on her lap.

"What's wrong?" I asked, my eyes on the file. The handwritten name, in English letters, read: Ms S. Hashimoto.

"I just thought you should know I didn't book the lesson for you. Akemi was on shift that day and she wouldn't have known any better. What I mean is, it wasn't done on purpose, kay?" Tomomi stretched her hands upwards, passing the file to me, though she kept her eyes down.

I reached for the file, truly puzzled. What about a Demo lesson to an unknown student should give me cause to be think anything was wrong? My fingers had barely closed around the edges of the file when Tomomi let go. The paperwork fell to the floor.

"Ah! Chotto gomen yo!"

I knew enough Japanese by now to know that Tomomi's apology had been curt. Even, rude. Gomennasai was the polite way to say sorry. Her non apology didn't matter. The passport-sized photo stapled to the application on the floor caught my attention.

Ms S. Hashimoto. S for Shiori.

For a moment, I almost refused point blank to do the lesson. But I was an English teacher, a professional. I would carry on as planned, with only minor adjustments. The lesson I had planned on hobbies and interests was over; I would demonstrate a lesson on how to argue and complain.

"She's here," said Tomomi.

When I clapped eyes on Shiori, I almost did a double take. The last time I had seen her had been at Hamamura onsen, and the time before that at Club Passion, when she had been all over Vince. Instead of the tiny-framed wannabe Goth-punk-slut who had flirted with every available Western man who would look her way, Shiori waddled towards the reception desk, the large mound of her stomach hidden under a shapeless grey pinafore-style dress with a black polo-neck jumper underneath. Her hands were both tucked inside a pocket at the front of the dress right over her belly so that she cradled it protectively. Her cheeks were flushed pink and she had put on a little weight, which suited her as she looked healthy. She was clearly pregnant, at least seven or eight months gone.

"Ah, Hashimoto san, kochira e kudasai." Tomomi swept her hand towards a sales booth desk, ushering Shiori inside. Shiori panted a little as she squeezed her ample frame into the fixed space of the booth and placed a hand on her lower back as she sat down. Tomomi spoke a few more niceties to Shiori in Japanese as I slid into the seat opposite her. Tomomi left before returning with a bottle of water and a glass.

My mind raced, quicker than my heart. Best to stick to the Voyce school script. "Hello, nice to meet you. My name is Kimberly. What's your name?"

"We've already met. I'm Shiori, don't you remember? You were at Hamamura onsen back in—"

"Today, we're going to do a lesson based on making complaints and arguing a point. So let's think, shall we? Has anyone ever done something really *bad* to you, that you have felt the need to argue with them. Maybe they betrayed you in some way?"

"Kimberly, I wanted to say sorry to you."

I ignored her, my chirpy voice an act that spurred me on, made me feel I was performing a character. I was bland, neutral teacher Kimberly, not deceived, bitter ex-girlfriend Kimberly talking to her former boyfriend's lover. "Well, let's imagine then in that case. What would you do if you found out your boyfriend had been seeing another woman behind your back?"

Shiori opened her mouth, then shut it and looked away towards the reception desk, as though for help. I hadn't been able to help myself; I had strayed from the Voyce school Demo lesson script for my own gratification; justice.

"I didn't know Carl had a girlfriend when I started seeing him. He was waiting at the bench outside my shop every day and we got talking."

I dropped the sugary-sweet act. "He was waiting for me to finish work when he was sat on that bench."

She tried to reach across the desk, but I moved my hand away. "I thought you should know that he has been ignoring my calls."

I wanted to smirk, but I kept my face sober. "Why do you think I would care? I'm not in touch with him anymore either."

She reached down and rubbed her heavily pregnant belly. A horrible sickness descended into the pit of my own stomach. She might as well have flaunted her fertility, even though there was no way she could possibly have known I had lost a baby only weeks before. I felt flaccid, barren before her. Especially as I knew what she was going to say, dreading her saying it.

"The thing is, Carl, he... ano ne." Shiori's switch into Japanese, considering her English was so fluent, tore my eyes abruptly away from her stomach to her face. She was nervous. "He's the baby's dad."

I swallowed the rising bile in my gullet. "Have you told him?"

A rim of tears appeared below her eyes. She concealed them from view with her hand as she dabbed them away, but her nodded response was obvious. "He asked me how I knew it was his."

Familiar words; thoughts of Vince asking me the same thing flooded my head until I felt my brain would burst in a tidal wave of anger. My feelings were confirmed; Vince was just like Carl. Zoe was right, I was attracted to bad boys, or worse; abusive creeps.

A backwash of guilt swept anger away. Here I was thinking only of myself, while Shiori sat opposite me suffering Carl's hatefulness in a worse manner than I had. At least I never had to see him again; whereas the poor girl was irretrievably linked to him forever through their child. It was the same as I had thought for Vince and I, except Shiori's child would soon be in the world, whereas my Water Child had been gifted back to the sea.

I sniffed back the sting of tears prickling across the bridge of my nose and assaulting my tear-ducts. "I'm sorry for what you've been through, Shiori, but I don't know what I can do to help you."

She blinked and two streams of tears fell over her pink cheeks. "You can't. I just wanted to tell you I'm sorry I'm the reason you broke up with Carl. If I knew the things I know now nine months ago, I wouldn't be in this mess."

"You did me a favour. In another month, I'll be leaving Japan. At least now, it's not to go back to London and marry Carl." I pressed my thumbs in the corner of each eye, suppressing tears. "What are you going to do? Are you in touch with him?"

She shook her head. "Not exactly. He doesn't want to come back to Tottori. He told me to wait until the baby is born and if it has Japanese eyes, then a Japanese man is clearly the father."

My hand flew to my mouth, all pretence of professional charade gone. "Oh my gosh, what an absolute bastard. Of course the baby will have Japanese eyes, you're the mother. He just wants to get himself off the hook. That's awful. I'm so, so sorry."

It wasn't my fault, but I felt responsible in a metaphysical sense. If it hadn't been for me working in Tottori, then Carl never would have been there and hence he never would have met Shiori. Butterfly effect; small ripples becoming big crises in a stormy ocean. Shiori pregnant and abandoned by Carl, what Vince did to me, then giving an ultimatum to abort the baby.

Such bastards. Hopefully they would both get their karma-comeuppance when the universe had a moment to catch up to their crimes.

Shiori clasped her hands loosely on the table. I reached across and grabbed them, feeling their small warmth within my own. She looked up at me and smiled, a fresh wave of tears streaming down her face. All of my previous resentment towards her was gone. She was suffering as much as I was. Crying wasn't in keeping with the Japanese custom of 'saving face', but who cared. We had wronged each other, both suffered hurt and loss, and now shared a bond. The bond of pain? Probably, but it was something. Better than nothing.

As Shiori leaned forward to wipe her tears away, a golden chain slipped out from inside her grey pinafore. Instead of tucking it back into her clothes, she tugged on it. Out popped a golden watch. Carl's golden watch.

So I hadn't lost it, as I had assumed, after the spring clean in my bedroom following Carl's departure. He had given it to Shiori, before he had left Japan. I clenched my teeth at the realisation: he had rummaged through my private possessions and had taken it back, a supposed token of his love for me, that he had given to his secret lover.

Shiori unfastened the chain at the back of her neck. She let the watch drop into her palm, then extended her hand to me. "When you go back to London, if you ever see Carl again, could you please give him this back. It's something he gave to me."

I let my tense jaw loosen. "I suppose he told you that you were special."

Shiori's eyes widened in innocent understanding. "He gave that to you before too?"

I nodded. I reached for the gold chain, avoiding the watch as though it were a cursed talisman. In a way it was; it had once been an amulet protecting me, but had been instilled with too many lies. Too much evil. I let the watch slide off the chain, then wiped the chain with my hand and put it in my pocket.

"I'll never see that creep again, so I'm gonna toss that watch in the rubbish. But the chain is mine. I bought it. I'm keeping it."

Shiori didn't say anything, but a slow smile spread across her face.

38

 C3

Love hotel

In place of a reception desk at the Waterfall Hotel in Akihabara, there was a brightly lit panel showing a selection of available rooms. Beneath each image was a button to select a room. Jei Pi waggled her finger across the screen and chose a room.

"Are you sure it's alright for all three of us to stay?" I said. Naoki said nothing, though had a bashful look on his face and turned away to hide his crimson face.

"Of course it is," said Jei Pi. "I already told you, I did my research. Love hotels will allow a girl and a guy, or two girls, or two girls and a guy. But not two guys."

"Why not?" I turned to Naoki.

"Don't ask me," he said, shaking his head. "I've only ever stayed in regular hotels or capsule hotels. This kind of experience is new to me."

"Well, worry not. There won't be any kinky business, this is purely for the novelty factor," said Jei Pi matter-of-factly. She turned to Naoki and winked. "Unless you're up for some hanky panky."

"Don't embarrass him," I said to Jei Pi. "You're such a hentai."

"Maybe," she said with an indifferent sniff. "But staying in a love hotel was the only thing left on my bucket-list of things to do before leaving Japan. What a send-off!"

I smiled at Jei Pi. We had patched things up over the last couple of weeks since our heart-to-heart on Mount Daisen. What was the point in staying annoyed anyway? She would soon be gone from Japan and though we might keep in touch on Instagram, it was unlikely I'd ever see her again. The notion didn't sadden me. It didn't cheer me up either. I felt nonplussed about the idea; most gaijin in Japan were ships passing in the night anyway, each on his or her own journey to different destinations.

I smiled to myself; how very Zen my thoughts had become.

"I think we need to pay upfront – works out at a thousand yen each." Jei Pi took the cash from each of us and walked to a panel beside the selection of rooms. There was a small slot at table height that looked like a letterbox. Jei Pi kneeled down and placed her forehead against the slot, looking through the gap.

"Argh!"

The cry of a middle aged female voice behind the panel amused me; I had to walk away to suppress laughter. When I recovered my composure, I returned to Jei Pi's side. She stood, red-faced.

"Sumimasen, er, gomennasai," Jei Pi babbled.

"You scared the shit out of that poor woman. You were supposed to put the money through the slot, not your face," I said, choking back laughter.

"Yeah, well that's obvious now isn't it?" She swiped her ginger fringe aside, still looking flustered. "Oy vey."

We took the lift up to our room. Three thousand yen, about fifteen pounds was cheap for the night, though it was obvious why. The stigma associated with staying in a love hotel was enough to deter most people; they were generally places for adultery or prostitution. Not that *gaijin* cared; love hotels were also cheap places to stay for backpackers and convenient, since they could be rented by the hour or booked for the whole night.

"Wowza, check this out!"

Jei Pi pushed the door wide and I saw a king-sized, heart-shaped bed. Blue satin sheets gave the impression of water and turquoise projected lights on the wall imitated a waterfall. A vending machine near the door was fully stocked with condoms, S&M toys and a variety of outfits: I saw a naughty maid, a fireman and a nurse, among others.

"Look in here," I said. The bathroom had a large, shell-shaped bathtub.

"Do you think we'd all fit in there?" said Jei Pi. She had a wicked grin on her face.

"I'm game if you both are," I said. Naoki had a look of confused horror on his face. "Wearing swimwear, of course, mister modest."

"What?" he said. "Are you making fun of me?"

I gave him a playful slap on the shoulder. "Just a bit."

We dumped our bags at the foot of the bed. Jei Pi ran the bath and poured copious amounts of bubble-bath in it. Naoki got changed in the bathroom, while Jei Pi and I stayed in the main room. Jei Pi wore a black bathing suit. I put on my blue bikini.

"Wow-wee, zowee look at you, sexy," said Jei Pi. "You really should be an advertisement for this love hotel, chica."

When we went in the bathroom, Naoki's eyes rested straight on my chest. He tore them away with the pretence of checking the water in the tub.

"Ladies first," he said, making a sweeping gesture with his palm.

Jei Pi went in first, me second. Naoki was about to get in when he stopped. "I'll be back in a minute."

What on earth could he possibly have forgotten? I barely had time to wrack my brain for ideas when he returned, standing in the doorway. He was wearing a sailor's cap from the sex-toy vending machine and had a six pack of Asahi beer in his hand.

Jei Pi and I screamed with laughter. Naoki certainly was more fun, and less prudish, than I'd at first thought. That was besides the fact that he had a smoking hot body, standing in his swim shorts; taut and athletic, with broad shoulders and a natural-looking six pack.

"I would've wheeled in the karaoke machine, but it wouldn't be a good idea in the bath. Let's leave that until after," he said.

Naoki climbed in and passed the beer around. We splashed, we sang songs, and Jei Pi found a button that projected more waterfall lights and played trickling river sounds. It was the most fun I'd had in ages.

When our bath was over, we dried ourselves off. I noticed a hairdryer on the wall next to the bathroom mirror. The safety sign was in English: *Please do not use for the other purpose other than drying your hair.*

"What do you think the other purpose is?" I said, laughing.

"Sounds kinky," Jei Pi joked.

"Doesn't it make sense?" said Naoki.

"Not really. It should say, 'any' instead of 'the'," I said.

Naoki smiled. "English is such a confusing language."

"But you speak it really well," I said.

"Sort of. I'm thinking of going overseas again to brush up a bit. I went to the States before, I was thinking maybe Australia next." He nudged me gently with his elbow. "Or even London."

Naoki in London. How did that make me feel? What if we got the same flight home together?

And speaking of London. With an unpleasant lurch in my stomach, I saw that the screen of my phone had lit up with an email notification. I walked over and grabbed it from the bed, where I had left it.

"There's an email from Carl," I said. My voice sounded flat in my ears. Jei Pi came over and leaned her head on my shoulder, reading with me.

Title: Hi Manny.

Carl. What the hell did he want? We had broken up, for good, nearly four months previously.

Could it be about Shiori and her pregnancy? Curiosity got the better of me. I clicked it open and read.

Title: Hi Manny. Message: im sure i am the last person you want to hear from. but hear me out. I know we ended on bad terms but ive really missed you and the time we have been apart has made me realise how much i love you. Ive done loads of thinking and it became clear that maybe you would of stayed in London if we had of got married. Ive been thinking about how your contract is nearly over and im sure your making plans to come back to London. Well, if you would let me back into your life, i know i could do better for you this time and be a better boyfriend or if you'll let me, your fiance. Signed off: your ever loving Carl.

"Oh my gosh, can you believe the gall of this bell-end?" I said.

His email was peppered with spelling and grammatical mistakes; if it was in any way important to him, couldn't he have made an effort? I would have laughed out loud, if I weren't so bitter. The only reason that I could think of for why Carl had contacted me was because he was scared about the turn his life had taken in getting Shiori pregnant, and he wanted the safe familiarity of our toxic relationship. It had never occurred to me before that as much as I had been co-dependent on Carl, he had been co-dependent on me. He had dominated me, seemed so in control and manipulative but it was because he was afraid of losing me. That wasn't entirely true either, for it hadn't been *me*, but rather the *idea* of me. Jei Pi had been right when she said he saw me as a commodity or a possession that was his. A comfortable normality for him, but not for me.

"Are you going to reply?" said Jei Pi.

My fingers hovered over the keyboard, ready to chastise him that he should take responsibility for his pregnant lover, but I waited until any spontaneous notions of revenge simmered. The best response was to not respond. Carl was a part of my past, not present or future. There was too much bad blood between us to even continue as friends, never mind rekindle our non-starter romance as man and wife.

"No," I said. Naoki had walked to the far side of the room and was sitting on the dressing table chair, his back to me. I couldn't blame him. Although we weren't a couple – we had only kissed once after

dinner – it must have been awkward for him to hear
me talking about my ex when there was obvious
romantic energy between us: we were slightly more, a
fraction more, than friends.

I closed my emails and shoved my phone in my
overnight bag, with maybe more force than intended.
My thoughts redirected themselves to Naoki. Naoki
wasn't Carl. Carl was abusive and controlling. Naoki
had a gentle demeanour and let me be free. If we
were a couple, he would be good to me. Not only
that, but he was bilingual and had an international
outlook, having lived in the States. He was twenty-
eight, three years older than me, and although he
didn't say it he was looking for a serious romance, not
to get laid.

So why didn't I feel any passion for him? Between
us, there was more of a steady fizzle than any
spectacular firework display. Since our dinner date, he
had given me more than enough hints he wanted to
start dating officially, but I hadn't felt anything more
for him than casual interest, couldn't reciprocate his
feelings other than to return them with polite
pleasantries. When I had told him Jei Pi was leaving
and that I would be taking a week in Tokyo to see her
off before she flew out of Narita, he had joked that
he would love to join us. I had invited him along,
thinking that there was no way he'd accept the offer
and had been surprised when he did.

So here he was, along on our girl's trip. Not that I
was bothered. Really.

Naoki interrupted my thoughts, as though he
could read my mind. "Who's up for some karaoke?"

It was just what I needed; distraction. Naoki had
provided the perfect antidote to a disease that I didn't

want to re-infect myself with: Carl. Even the words in an email from him made me break out in a cold sweat, gave me a histamine reaction that no part of my body was immune to. The past was dead, but not buried enough.

More beers, some vodka and a lot of karaoke. Alcohol had flowed, a medicinal river, back into my life once the baby had gone. The difference this time was that I felt in control of my life. I trusted myself; to drink socially around people who I could be comfortable with and not to get drunk. Karaoke was the injection of fun I needed. When it was my turn to sing – a classic, *I will survive* – I climbed up on the bed to make it a performance, not merely a song. Jei Pi lay at the foot of the bed and Naoki slouched in the dressing room chair, beer in hand.

"Let's make this a real party," said Jei Pi. She grabbed a handful of condoms out of the vending machine and began blowing them up like balloons. Naoki reached into the machine and pulled out a cowboy hat and chaps for himself. He tossed me a sexy police-woman outfit made out of shiny, dark-blue polythene and passed Jei Pi a naughty nurse costume.

Naoki's turn to sing next. He chose Bon Jovi's *Wanted Dead or Alive*, standing up on the dressing room chair for effect. He was a decent singer, even better entertainer. Watching his theatrical performance, I felt an unusual tightness in my chest that I'd never felt before when watching Naoki. He was usually so quiet and composed, a wallflower when we had been out at Club Passion, or at house parties. Granted, that had been when he was *sober*, since he always drove for nights out and so couldn't drink. To see his fun side was another matter.

Maybe there was a spark between us after all.

"Hey lil lady," said Naoki, in an over the top Texan accent. "Wanna grab a bunch of moonshine and head to the nearest rodeo?"

I almost burst out laughing, but if he was playing the cowboy then I had to keep up the act too. I whipped a pair of plastic handcuffs out of a pocket on my police-woman's outfit and clipped them around his wrists. "You're under arrest for drunken disorderly behaviour and propositioning a member of law enforcement."

Jei Pi stepped in between us. "What is going on here, officer? My name is Nurse Ratched and this is a patient of mine at Bedlam hospital. I demand you let him go right now!"

I let myself fall back on the bed, laughing. "This is so ridiculous. I haven't had a lark like this since I don't even remember when."

Naoki dive-bombed the condom balloons and landed on the bed next to me. "Lark? Isn't that a bird?"

"It means messing around," I said.

He gave a sly grin. "Like I'm doing to you right now?"

I rolled on top of him, pinning him in a wrestling move. "You dick. I believed you."

Naoki adopted a newscaster tone. "Dick, a noun, meaning moron. Dicking around, intransitive verb, meaning to playfully lark around." He flashed a teasing grin.

Jei Pi flopped down on the bed next to us. "I'm really gonna miss you guys. You know, you two are really good for each other. I just wish you would both stop wussing out and actually get it on."

Naoki looked at me and we both burst out laughing. "This is hardly the time or place Jei Pi, not unless you want a peep show," I said.

"I didn't mean right this minute!" she protested.

"Then we'll keep you posted," Naoki laughed. When I looked at him, he winked at me.

In the midst of our happy, alcohol haze, sleep beckoned, all three of us with our arms strapped across each other. Nothing of mischief happened, no untoward encounters, just gentle, platonic sleep. Before my mind shut itself off, I realised how happy I was just to share in the company of other humans on my wavelength. Didn't good things come of a solid friendship under it all? I rolled my head to face Naoki and watched his long eyelashes as he slept. He was a good, dependable man with no ulterior motives. How many women would kill for that?

39

⚬

Sayonara and farewell

My breath was laboured as I walked down the aisle;
though whether because the obi fastening my white
silk *shiromuku*, a traditional kimono, was as tight as a
corset, or because Naoki stood watching me from the
altar. Naoki looked dashing in his black silk *hakama*
that perfectly matched his black hair, combed and
slick, a perfect groom-to-be. My hands shook around
the small posy of white roses that I carried and I took
dainty steps in the traditional wooden *geta* on my feet,
as I inched towards the altar where soon the Shinto
priest would perform the ritual purification for us and
offer prayers to the Gods. Today, I truly felt like
Princess Sen, royalty of yesteryear in an Edo period
castle of old. Soon, we would become husband and
wife.

I snapped out of my musings as Naoki handed me
my passport and ticket and I watched our suitcases
slide away on the conveyor belt. My daydreams often
saw me getting ahead of myself. Naoki and I weren't
going to get married – yet. We had only been seeing
each other for two months. But it was a milestone,
nonetheless; we were going back to Southampton for
two weeks for the Christmas break, and he would be
meeting my parents for the first time.

Being back at Kansai airport felt strange, especially
since the last time I had been there was to say
goodbye to Carl. Things were certainly different this

time. When I had arrived one year and one month ago, I had been by myself, didn't speak any Japanese and had been in a relationship with an English bloke. Thirteen months later and I was leaving with my new Japanese boyfriend and spoke some basic conversational Japanese.

Naoki and I had become romantically involved at the start of October; soon after Jei Pi had left, as she predicted. He had invited me out for yakitori and had taken the plunge by asking me directly if he could be my boyfriend. Liking how he had taken charge, I had said yes. In any case, I felt ready to move on with a new relationship after throwing out the dregs that had been my seven year tryst with Carl.

Naoki passed through security and waited for me on the other side of the gate. He pointed at my necklace. "I'm surprised that thing didn't set the metal detector off."

My hand reached up and felt the resin necklace suspended on the golden chain that I had taken back after I disposed of Carl's watch. Inside the resin, I had mounted the charred fragment from my cleansing ritual at Tottori Kaigan; my paper *Buddha's Bone*.

"I suppose the chain must be pure gold and not an alloy then, I guess."

Fitting; my gold chain had been reborn, as I had been reborn. Naoki took my hand and we walked through the duty free shops. My other hand stayed on the Buddha's Bone, rubbing the resin necklace between forefinger and thumb. Maybe it had been a coincidence but the paper fragment had measured four point five centimetres; the exact size of my Water Child when he or she had been gifted back to the Sea of Rebirth. I would wear the necklace forever as a reminder of my baby and of my spiritual journey in Japan.

Outside the passenger lounge windows, I could see fat snowflakes swirling in the winter wind. Would the snow delay our flight? Hopefully not. We would soon be flying south to Malaysia for half a day before carrying on our journey to London Heathrow.

South. Bodies in Japan faced south before they were cremated: one of my students at Voyce Language School, Shinobu, had told me so. I had already died and been cremated myself. In thirteen months I had gone from being Manny, one half of a couple in a co-dependent, dysfunctional relationship to Kimberly Thatcher, a free woman on a mission of self-identity. Know thyself; wasn't that the battle that every human had to face? How ironic that I had a Master's degree as a qualified Clinical Psychologist, yet I hadn't been able to analyse my own fragile psyche for seven years. Seven was a lucky number in Western culture, but meant nothing in Japan. That was the essence of Zen; for me at least. Nothingness. I didn't know who I was, but I knew I was a whole person, and that was a start. Nobody would ever control my destiny ever again. I governed my own fate. Did I love myself? Yes, and I accepted myself flaws and all. That was what made the difference. I didn't know where I was going on my journey, physical or spiritual, but I knew what I needed out of life and what I had to give to others.

Two weeks back home for Christmas, back to Tottori for New Year and then a brand new year in which I could explore the delights of Japan, at my own pace. Maybe I would learn Japanese properly. Maybe I would move in with Naoki. Maybe we would get married. I cut myself off – again. Those things were in a possible future. For now, I had to stay grounded in the present and appreciate each moment. I watched the fat flakes of snow fall outside the window. Each was whole and pristine, unmarred by the world. Pretty much like ashes from a funeral pyre. I was Kimberly, reborn again, into a fresh start. Reborn, a Phoenix rising from the ashes of old, ready to embark on a new, more positive life.

Cheating Carl and pregnant Shiori, predatory Vince and tactless Jei Pi, good-hearted Naoki and misguided Zoe, unfortunate Tomomi and empty-minded me. All of us characters, players in a script that had been written, then scratched out and now left blank intentionally. None of it mattered in the grand scheme of things. Life carried on and none of the bit parts made any difference to the overall fabric of life.

I stopped walking and guffawed.

Naoki let go of my hand and turned, with a quizzical look on his face. "What's wrong?"

"Nothing." I shook my head as if that would help to convince him, as he seemed unconvinced. "My head is just full of shit."

"Anything you'd care to share?"

I slipped my hand back inside his and tugged him, until we both started walking again, idly browsing the shops. "No. Nothing meaningful. Just that, there's no point to anything really, is there?"

Naoki looked pensive, as though I'd hit him with deep, profound thoughts. "Not if you live a narrow existence. Life is what you make it, you create your own point."

"Good point."

"Exactly."

We looked at each other and after a brief hesitation, both laughed.

"You must be thinking I'm mad," I said, somewhat trepidatiously.

He wrinkled his nose. "No, not really. You're as crazy as you need to be to get by in a crazy world."

It was a good answer. I nodded, pondering it. "So, if I wasn't a bit mad, I wouldn't be able to survive in the world. Either that or if the world wasn't as crazy as me, it would have to overcompensate to keep the balance in order?"

"Something like that. But you know, the wind always blows and the water always crashes. The soil always gives new life. Life carries on," said Naoki.

I chuckled. "You're as mad as me. Never thought I'd find someone on my wavelength."

Naoki's expression was one of benign wisdom. "Too many people go through life on one wavelength. But if you're willing to turn the dial, who knows what else you might tune into."

I doubled over laughing, feeling my belly convulse, connecting with every part of my body in the moment. "Like extra-terrestrials."

Turning the dial. Life would never be the same for me again. I was on a different wavelength now, for sure. It was like turning off a country road full of potholes onto the highway of life.

"I'm glad you're in the passenger seat beside me," I said to Naoki, finishing a thought that I hadn't spoken about out loud.

"I'm not even sure if I know what you're thinking, but I guess...I get you?"

"Exactly. You're on my wavelength."

We walked towards the boarding gate. Outside the snow flurries had become a fully-fledged snowstorm. Know thyself. I didn't know me, but if Naoki could give a good guess to the thoughts in the tangled web of my mind, then at least I wouldn't be on the journey alone. Knowing oneself was the ultimate goal for a fulfilling life. Amidst the maelstrom of my mind, a poem popped into my head.

Know Thyself.
There once was a pelagic creature
Who thought that he was a teacher
But out of the demersal depth
A superior being leapt
And ridiculed the fraudulent preacher.

Who the fuck knew what that meant? But it pretty much said it all, nonetheless.

Acknowledgements

Thanks are due to Amy Finlay for her editorial feedback on this story, which helped massively. Thanks also to my wonderful hubby, Joseph Robert, for helping to add polish to the blurb and for all the ongoing support throughout the publishing process. Last, but not least, thanks to little KJ for being such a good baby and sleeping so soundly on my chest while I wrote this book during my maternity leave. Your soothing snores accompanied me as I wrote this and became a rhythm for my writing.

Printed in Great Britain
by Amazon